I0761956

Ignition!

Also from Metaphorosis

Metaphorosis Magazine

Metaphorosis: Best of 20xx
Metaphorosis 20xx: The Complete Stories
annual issues, from 2016
Monthly / Quarterly issues
Library Collection series

Plant Based Press

Best Vegan Science Fiction & Fantasy
annual issues, 2016-2020

from B. Morris Allen:
Chambers of the Heart: speculative stories
Susurrus
Allenthology: Volume I
Tocsin: and other stories
Start with Stones: collected stories
Metaphorosis: a collection of stories

Verdage

Reading 5X5 x3: Changes
Reading 5X5 x2: Duets
Score — an SFF symphony
Reading 5X5: Readers' Edition
Reading 5X5: Writers' Edition

Vestige

The Nocturnals, by Mariah Montoya

Joyful Heave

Museum Piece: an unusual collection

Ignition!

science fiction stories
by debut authors

METAPHOROSIS LIBRARY COLLECTION

edited by
B. Morris Allen

ISBN: 978-1-64076-292-3 (e-book)
ISBN: 978-1-64076-293-0 (paperback)
ISBN: 978-1-64076-294-7 (hardcover)

from
Metaphorosis Publishing

Neskowin

Contents

From the Editor

The *Metaphorosis Library Collection* arose from a conversation with a Metaphorosis author who is also a librarian, and is initially intended to suit library needs. When a reader comes in and says, “Hey, do you have any SFF stories by this type of author?” here they are! But of course, the books are available to any reader.

Beginnings are exciting! When you set out, you never know quite how things are going to go, but the whole world is in front of you; everything is possible.

That’s true for writers as well. While some writers seem to spring full-formed from the shell, all them them have a first story — the first they wrote, the first they published, the first they sold. Some writers only ever write the one story; others go on writing their whole lives. At the beginning, you just don’t know.

At Metaphorosis, we’ve been so blessed with **debut** authors that we’ve split them into two volumes. This one focuses on science fiction stories by debut authors. ‘Debut’ means different things for different people, but here we’re applying it to a writer for whom this was their first story published, sold, or sold at a semi-professional rate — often all three at once!

These writers are the ones you should be watching now — the ones who may go on to be famous names and the ones for whom the story is a rare collectible. Take a look now at the stories that ignited these writers’ careers!

B. Morris Allen
1 July 2024

Silo

J. S. DiStefano

I woke to the slow, creaking opening of the door, and the wind against the walls of the silo. The old man led me down the winding stairs and outside into the night.

"It's cold." My first words since waking.

"You'll get used to it. I was freezing the first couple weeks."

"That long?"

We stood in the dark, at the top of a hill surrounded by long-abandoned farmland. The silo was the only building left. In the daylight, we would be able to look out over empty fields that stretched for miles. That night we stared out into nothingness.

There was a small bunker near the base of the silo, built into the ground. The old man opened the door and led me down. The narrow stairwell opened into a small, bare room, decorated only with monitors depicting the hilltop up above. There was only one chair.

He showed me the slot in the wall where our rations appeared every twenty-four hours. One small vial of serum, taken by injection, provided the necessary vitamins, nutrients, and antibodies. We walked through the control room and past the storage room. He showed me how to refuel the silo and recharge the infrared shield.

We went back outside and sat around the fire. A pile of wood and a bucket of water guarded the grass behind us. Under the shadow of the silo, the old man spoke of his life, of sixty years of waiting. He told me little that I had not known, had not expected. As he talked, his voice would drop down to a whisper, and the sound of the wind on metal threatened to drown it out completely and leave me alone in the dark.

I did not ask how long he had left. The knowledge that he had awakened me loomed over us, a dominant feature of the hilltop.

"So you saw the bunker. And you used the bathroom. Everything else was covered in the training, really."

The wood burned down. The coals were red when the old man suddenly doused the fire and knocked me off the log. I heard it too. We lay still in the grass, heads turned slightly to the side, facing each other. I could hear his heartbeat, pulsing wildly like my own.

Slowly, carefully, two enormous ships moved across the sky, flashing spotlights on the ground, back and forth over the grass. The clothes we wore had been chosen for this. Dirt and the smell of grass pressed against my nose, and minutes felt like hours. The two ships advanced toward us, one nearly in line with where we lay on the ground, the other about a quarter mile to the south, in the direction my feet were pointing. When the ship that was closest to us passed overhead, the noise was deafening.

They reached the bottom of the hill and stopped, hovering. We watched, our breath caught in our throats, as the bottoms of both enormous spacecraft opened, completely synchronized. Out of each dropped a small flying saucer. The two miniature pods met up and flew with speed that neither parent ship could have possessed. Straight toward us.

"Run!" hissed the old man. It was a figure of speech. Instinctively, we both stayed on the ground, heads down, crawling quickly toward the bunker. The old man opened the hatch and we slipped down below, shutting the door behind us without making a sound.

After a minute of waiting at the top of the steps with our hearts pounding, we snuck down the stairs to watch the scene outside on the monitors. The two saucers had reached the silo. One rotated around the building, slowly, while the other scanned the field.

Then they were gone, flying back toward the two great motherships, which opened once more to accept them. We stayed in the bunker, staring at the screens before us as the ships began to move again, receding into the night. It would have been safe now to rebuild the fire, but we sat in silence.

Finally, I asked the old man, “Have they come before?”

“Once. Forty years ago. Before that, I think it’d been over two hundred. There’s a logbook around here somewhere.”

“I know.” I was silent for a moment. “I didn’t expect it to be like that.”

“No.” His voice was soft. “I don’t see how you could have.”

The silence in the underground room was deafening in the absence of wind against metal.

We stayed underground until the sun began to rise. When we opened up the bunker door and climbed back onto the surface, the barren landscape around us felt exposed. Vulnerable. We sat back on the logs we had abandoned, now covered in a thin layer of dew.

The old man looked at the fire, staring down into the wet, black coals. “I’m sorry if I startled you when I woke you up. That was the hardest part. Last night. Bringing you back into the world. You won’t have an easy life. I didn’t.”

I nodded. I didn’t know what to say. The sun was climbing up in the sky and the shadow of the great tower was growing longer, stretching out down the hill toward the empty fields below.

He stood up from his log and looked at me. There was a sense of finality in his words. “I think I’ll go lie down for a while.” He walked slowly to the bunker and opened the lid.

“Wait,” I called out. He turned. “Thank you.”

“For what?”

“For serving.”

He looked at me for a moment, then nodded. He turned back to the bunker and descended to his final resting place.

I wanted to call out again, to ask him to sit and wait with me a little longer. But we didn’t have the rations for two watchmen. The calculations had been thorough. Our resources had been stretched as thin as they could go. The old man had done his duty. The least I could do was respect his privacy and leave him to die as he had lived.

Alone.

The old man had spoken truly — there was no way I could be prepared for this. But there was no other choice, for any of us. The enemy had made a mockery of our technology. Automated surveillance was never an option.

I turned my gaze up from the bunker to look up at the silo. Sixty years per person, and I am number two thousand one hundred and twenty-two of ten thousand.

I will serve out my term, and then wake up number two thousand one hundred and twenty-three. One day, the world will be safe again for our species to live as a civilization. But until then, the fate of humanity rests with us, the people of the silo.

●

J.S. DiStefano's story "Silo" was originally published in Metaphorosis on Friday, 21 January 2022. See magazine.metaphorosis.com

About the author

J.S. DiStefano likes hiking, playing cards, watching football, reading, and writing. "Silo" is his first published story.

The Frozen Generation

Jacob Coffin

Compared to my coworkers, I didn't get many death threats. Storage, my department, was usually overlooked by fanatics and politicians.

They saved their anger for the people up front who made the Frozen Generation — the doctors and administrators who met the clients, did the scans, fed in the waldos, extracted the mingled cells, vitrified them in cryofluid. My crew in Storage were just the ones who tended them forever after.

They had their reasons for overlooking us. The Frozen were an easy demographic to advocate for, and an easier population to have when it came time to allocate votes and funds. But most people in this state would still tell you that extraction destined for cryostasis was just abortion with less guilt. Those people had gotten their way tonight, expanded the definition of abortion to include any extraction not destined for immediate gestation. And banned it.

Their new laws were going to close the clinic, maybe for a long time. But that wasn't my main concern. They'd also upped the charges for embryonic deaths in an extraction clinic and, tonight of all nights, I'd received notice of a blackout across the entire facility.

That's why I was in my truck, racing back to work as fast as I could drive after only two hours of sleep and despite the crowds celebrating in the streets.

We had backups. We were a priority repair site by law. We were seriously overbuilt for the two-hour limit the power company had to have us fixed by. But my team would be scared, and I wasn't going to let them deal with this alone. After all, they knew as well as I did that technically, under the new laws, any failure onsite could cost us our lives.

I made some calls as I got on the freeway. The front office didn't answer. No one on my crew knew what had happened yet, except that the power was definitely out and only for us.

The protestors had probably just shot out a transformer. They did that sometimes when they were celebrating. Tonight, that was really the best-case scenario.

The scattered fireworks popping low over the rooftops, the crowds in the streets around the churches, and the 3 a.m. rush hour traffic were enough to tell me tonight wasn't a night for best-case anything. But I wasn't thinking clearly.

●

Cars were already filling up vacant lots in the industrial park we called home. Armed silhouettes with posterboard signs grouped together in the early-morning dark and chill. The usuals claiming their spots early, maybe. Either way they'd have a big crowd today — some of our neighbors even rented their lots to them.

I was scanning the parking lots as I went — more from habit than because of the news tonight. I like to think I've gotten pretty good at watching my surroundings, even when I'm tired and stressed. After a protestor follows you home, you find your motivation.

The crowd got thicker once I was close enough to see the place. The clinic had already been pretty ugly, sort of a warehouse trying to turn into a bunker, but it was folks like these who had put the finishing touches on it, decorated the outside with scorch marks and bullet-pocks.

Speaking of bullets: one of them took a shot at me.

I honestly hadn't been expecting that. The crowd at the gate didn't have the usual rage tonight, though they threw some rocks when I pulled through, just to keep up tradition. I figured they were there more to celebrate and maybe burn our building down later if the police seemed amicable. They'd won, after all; no more need for self-martyrdom.

But once I made the last turn toward the garage, my back windshield exploded.

I hit the gas and slammed down the ramp and out of view before I'd fully processed the gunshot. And then it was over and I was sitting there in the red emergency light of the employee garage with more adrenalin than I needed for work problems and nothing to use it on.

I ran my fingers over tufts of foam in the new hole in my roof while I called the shooter in to our security team. Though God knew what they could do about him. After that was done, it all started to feel real, and I had to pause and get my breathing under control. I knew from experience that if I stayed focused, I could save the real freakout for after I got home and felt safe. And I had a lot of work to do.

The bullet hole was barely in arm's reach. Not a very near miss. Had he been trying to kill me or just scare me and make me run? That pissed me off worse than attempted murder. I could picture them laughing and cheering while I fled out of sight.

If they'd known what department I worked for, would it have made any difference?

I got out, slammed the door, and climbed upstairs in the dark, checking my phone for updates to the alerts that had woken me.

Power failures were the last thing we needed now. Every other supplier we relied on had been flaking for weeks, including our cryofluid producer, now fifteen days late on our delivery. I think they saw which way things were going, knew nobody was going to enforce our protections any longer. Even when a company's official faith didn't oppose extraction, there were always employees who felt that helping us endangered their immortal souls.

No updates on the power alerts. My feed was full of articles on the new laws, but I ignored them.

Don't get me wrong, things were bad, but this back and forth had been happening for my entire life. Hell, this mess of shortcuts and simple solutions was the reason I even existed. As far as I was concerned, this was just a temporary interruption of service until the law got challenged or interrupted somehow.

Even the people who had passed it didn't seem to expect this to last forever. They'd already tried gestating every unwanted embryo and that led to the government hives they then spent decades tearing down, and generations of Unwanted like me who didn't even vote for them. Doing it again with even less planning would be a horrible mess, but banning extraction with no solutions at all would be even worse.

The new laws would make things difficult, but I was trying to focus on what I could control. And for us in Storage, it would be business as usual, more or less.

From here on out it was our job to keep the clinic operational until we could reopen. And new admissions would be on pause, which would give us some time to catch up on maintenance, build some new racks, maybe even upgrade our cryofluid production capabilities if I could mooch some budget while the rest of the work was on hold.

We'd get through this.

●

Inside, the place was in chaos. Half the lights were off and there were way too many staff here for this time of night. The lobby was locked down, galvanized drop-barricades reflecting the lights back through the glass doors up front.

Ester was cleaning out her desk, taking everything with her name on it. She'd actually grown up in the same hive I did, though she was a later generation, so she was a bit more normal. I was in a hurry, but she looked so freaked out I stopped when we made eye contact.

"Moses, did you hear Dr. Quarzi quit?" she asked. She had her fake-calm, air traffic control voice going.

"What?"

"Yeah, he called in and did it over the phone right after the hearing, from London. He said this will be a huge mess and we should all get out before it starts if we know what's good for us. He'd already cleaned out his files and everything."

I blinked, tired eyes bleary in the bright light, and looked down at her desk. "Taking his advice?"

"Yeah. How about you?"

"I just came in to fix the power. If this place doesn't stay cold, we're all in a lot of trouble."

She gave me this look. "We're in a lot of trouble either way. My boyfriend has family in Canada — we're heading up there. You should get out too."

Wow.

"Uh, best of luck," I said. "Look, you'll be okay, you just do inprocessing."

Still that flat look, like I didn't get it. I guess I didn't. "Yeah. Good luck yourself."

Man, I just kept everything cold.

I hustled through the office, looking for the Operations Director. If the power loss was upstream, then getting it back was her problem. The rest of us just had to keep the outage from harming the patients.

Most everyone I saw was hurrying and worried. Some were unpacking reserve Herz-Stanton exowombs, and the rest looked like they were leaving. I didn't recognize half of them. Sure, most of my work is back in Storage, but I come up once a day to check the tanks in the clinic, write up my maintenance reports, and order parts. I like to think I'm sociable, for a hive boy anyways.

I stopped outside the Ops Director's office. Charlotte was standing over her desk, shouting into the phone, gestures and everything.

She didn't show any sign of slowing down, and with everything else going on, I couldn't wait for answers. Whatever had caused this blackout, I had to check our status.

I headed for Storage, my department. There was a reason that the only clinics left in this state stored their patients on-site: Storage facilities got guarantees. With the nation's most vulnerable citizens in our vaults, reliant on their services, the power and telecom companies couldn't drag their feet for weeks when we got disconnected. More than that, we were allowed to hire armed security, and even got an exemption to the Religious Freedom Act so parts suppliers had to sell to us as long as we could pay. They accused us of a lot; I suppose hostage-taking was fair.

Storage took up most of our site. It was the big, bulky, warehouse-looking part of the facility with the legally-mandated symbols outside, to protect clinic bombers from killing any of the Frozen. Inside, there were thousands and thousands of silver cryo flasks linked with tubes and wires resting on rows of metal shelves, elevated flood-safe, suspended and stabilized against earthquakes and guarded by the most paranoid fire suppression system in the county. Each had an individual battery backup for its sensors and pumps and a small reserve tank of cryofluid.

The manifest for each flask listed the occupants by social security number. No names or assigned sex yet. For the vast majority it was far too early to identify more than the number of cells, and you could usually count those on both hands.

In the back, rising up over it all, was the in-house cryo distillation rig. The patients' storage tanks didn't take power to stay cold; they were just fancy vacuum flasks with sensors. But their cryogenic fluid evaporated in an endless slow boil, and we needed power to monitor the levels and to run the pumps that kept them topped off. The in-house 'still was elevated so we could rely on gravity feeds if we had to.

Cryofluid is pretty complicated stuff. It's mostly liquid nitrogen, but nitro on its own can be a vector for viruses and bacteria between tissue samples. Cryofluid has a mix of additives so we could transfer it safely and to assist with vitrification and devitrification. It was actually overkill for our purposes, as most of our patients were kept in hermetically sealed straws, but our state legislature said nothing was too good for the Frozen Generation (except hives of their own), especially if it made running this place difficult.

As I looked for my crew, I automatically checked the dashboard for each rack of tanks I passed, eyeing the levels and power requirements.

All the levels were lower than I expected.

Some of my techs were shouting over by the loading dock. Zeke saw me and waved me over, calling across the warehouse:

"Mose!" He looked worried, and that worried me.

"Zeke, what's going on?" I asked. "Someone cut the lines?"

"Yeah! The fuckin' power company!"

"What, on purpose?" That cold dread started working its way down my back. They wouldn't. They fucking couldn't.

"Yeah. Told Charlotte on the phone. Can't legally provide services."

"What, because of the abortion definition thing? We're not taking patients and even then it'd only apply to the front office, not Storage." Not us. But the whole place was linked together — that was how the clinic benefited from Storage, after all.

"Yeah. Closed the loophole."

"Loophole, hell. This was their goddamn solution in the first place."

Exowombs were supposed to solve abortion. Then when the flood of Unwanted got too deep, and government-commissioned hives had to raise the kids, cryostasis was their solution for that.

I ran my hands over my face. This was bad. Without power, our reserves and battery backups weren't overkill — they were woefully, criminally inadequate. We weren't an island. Weren't supposed to be. State laws enshrined us as a priority recovery site. Hell, they'd send the national guard if there were a flood or hurricane. Send 'em right past people trapped on their roofs or buried in rubble. Anything for the Frozen Generation.

But that had changed, hadn't it?

"Charlotte's been screaming at the power company," Zeke said. "The state police, the governor, even. Nothing's got us online. Been running on our solar reserves and gas gennys ever since. I had Jimmy making runs to the charge station for extra fuel, but once they figured it was for here, they refused to sell to him. I sent him to Pembrook since they're the next closest with liquid, but I'd be surprised if he doesn't just quit."

"If the main circuit's off, we're not generating new cryo. Hell, half the tanks are already low." We had solar rigs, but like everything else, they weren't enough to make us completely independent.

"I *know that*, Mose!"

These guys were looking to me because I had always been the quick one, the first with a solution when things went bad. Some people are wired for crisis situations, and I kind of loved them. And now I was flat-footed, slow. Tired. They needed me to be better. I shook my head to clear it.

"Okay, we need to cut everything we can, try to make the reserves last. Mike, hit the breakers, cut the whole front office. Keep the clinic for half an hour and warn the docs up front — I think they've got a couple active exowombs, and they'll need time to transfer back to cryo. We can move 'em back here on the battery backups if we have to.

"Zeke, Sol, get the pumps running. Top up all the flasks and shelf reserves first, and pump whatever we got left into the reserve tanks on the 'still."

"It won't last as long once it's distributed."

"Yeah but it won't do us any good in the main tanks. Sounds like we could end up running without *any* power for a while, so we need to get the patients as self-sufficient as we can. Same for power, make sure the tank batteries are all fresh. Pull some from the vehicles if you have to."

It was the same protocol we were supposed to use if the ocean came in around us, or the building collapsed. Get all the cryotanks ready for travel and wait for the national guard to come collect us. We'd lose auto-refill when the generators stopped. Internal regulation and monitoring too, once the local batteries dried up. We could top off tanks manually, if we had any cryo left, and if we knew the tank was low. We'd have to make visual inspections.

If the outage lasted long enough, we'd have to start consolidating fluid.

After tonight, any embryonic deaths in an extraction clinic were to be charged as murder two. We could get first degree if it was the result of a deliberate action. That was starting to seem more possible than it had yesterday.

"I'll go talk to Charlotte and see about getting us some backup. Someone has to care." I tapped on a cryoflask. "They only just made a bunch of laws about these guys."

Everyone started moving, so that part of the job was done. We'd get this place set up as best we could and hope society at large would help.

•

I backtracked through the clinic, head down, through everyone's rush to prepare for whatever came next. Every now and then, security would call someone's name. Took me a bit to realize they were escorting people off-site.

I passed a couple of clinic techs opening up one of the equipment storage rooms. One had on the scrubs they all wear up front, the other just had jeans and a t-shirt. I thought I recognized them both from the day shift.

"What about the old Herz-Stanton Gen 20s?" the one in scrubs asked.

"Uh, they're not on the APL anymore," the other answered.

"But they still work fine, I mean, maybe keep them off the network but they'll do the job."

He wasn't wrong. I was born to a Gen 3 and even those were so safe that there were actual arguments over whether to ban internal birth because it killed too many Unborn Americans. It was a public health crisis, after all: when an American's life begins at conception, failure-to-implant becomes the country's leading cause of death.

They don't exactly cover that stuff in school but I guess I have an interest, since their last great idea led to me being born Unwanted, named by an algorithm, and raised in a hive, even if it wasn't one of the bible-warrior training facilities/sweatshops you see in the documentaries.

"She said all the approved units. This is just CYA, right? They're looking for ways to screw us, so I don't think we'll get bonus points for going above and beyond using illegal equipment."

"Fair enough."

If they were starting up extra exowombs now, of all times, that would be a problem. But I'd deal with it once I knew when we'd get the power back.

I didn't hear any shouting as I approached Charlotte's office. That seemed like a good sign. This had to be some local fuckup. Some anti-extraction asshole at the power company giving us a hard time.

Charlotte was slumped forward on her desk, her tablet docked and playing some news feed. The smart wall to her left showed every angle of the perimeter and most rooms in the clinic. On the cameras, cars had filled the closest lots outside. Biggest crowd we'd seen in years.

I knocked on the door frame. "Hey boss, how's it going?"

"Hey, Moses. I thought I told you to go home and get some sleep." She gestured at the news. "'Cease all extraction operations. Commence the immediate and safe transfer of all Embryonic-Americans to external wombs and begin gestation.'"

I gave her the baffled, disappointed look we'd shared through so many newsreels of hearings and debates.

"Yeah, we'll get right on that."

There weren't enough approved exowombs on the planet for that. And even if they'd all been in the U.S., it'd take decades to get through the backlog.

We had twenty on site. We'd tried to order more over a year ago, after the election, but all the domestic manufacturing companies were swamped, and you couldn't buy them from overseas for fear of foreign supply-chain sabotage. Sleeper-diseases, hard-coded loyalties, who knew what the Reds could cook into our most vulnerable citizens?

And hospitals got legal priority on exowombs, of course. Most wanted births were external these days, if only for the legal liability. A miscarriage was bad enough without the criminal investigation ripping your life apart just in case.

"All the hospitals in a hundred-mile radius are already swamped." She said, "I've called every one of them. The other sites are dumping as many cases off on them as they can. I got St Mercy's to agree to a *hundred*, a lousy hundred kids! And then some assholes parked ten freezer trucks in their emergency lane and took off on foot. Now it's all, 'sorry, now *we* have six hundred thousand to take care of, good luck with yours.' It's like that everywhere."

"Any word on the power?"

She snorted. "All the words are bad. It's not coming back."

"Why?"

"Power and Light's lawyers dusted off a couple of old state abortion laws from back around the fight over the amendment. Any organization or individual who provides aid or assistance *of any kind* to an abortion clinic will be held equally liable. Apparently, it doesn't matter that we're not taking clients anymore. Our lawyers think their interpretation is legit enough to stick until we've challenged it in court."

And if things kept going like this we'd all be in jail for mass manslaughter or negligent genocide or something by then.

"The storage facility protections-" I started.

"One law says they have to provide power, the other says they can't." She paused just long enough to solidify her composure. When you do her job, you can't ever risk it slipping — there're always cameras on you looking for ammunition. "Our lawyers are still with us, and they're raising hell best they can." She said, "The ACLU and opposition legislators too. But by the time this mess gets sorted out, it'll be too late."

"They- they realize that if we shut down all the way, the embryos will thaw, right?" I asked. "And thawing would be bad for them?"

She shrugged again, like she didn't want to give the lawmakers or God's power company that much credit. These were the kind of people whose idea of compromise had forced generations of women who'd otherwise have taken a pill to risk surgery.

"Why are they doing this? They have to know it'll blow back on them..."

She looked down at the tablet, head in her hands, and said the next part almost to herself. Like she was thinking aloud. "There's a census coming up."

"Boss?" I didn't like this line of thought.

"If six hundred thousand 'people' disappeared overnight, they could redraw the map. Eliminate this district, a progressive congressional seat, and who knows how many state-level positions. It'd change funding allocations and..." She looked up at me. "Or maybe they're just a bunch of zealots who didn't listen when we pointed out all the problems with the bill six months ago, including that this could technically happen, even if it seemed unlikely. Same results either way."

She scrolled back through the news footage, picked out a segment, and spun the tablet. The Reverend Senator Callahan was walking out of the capitol building, a wide, closed-mouthed smile serene on his face.

"It's about personal responsibility. To all those... facilities, I'd say you shouldn't have done the procedures if you couldn't take care of your obligations afterwards. The American people trusted you with their children, and if anything happens to any single one of them, we *will* hold you accountable. At long last."

"Oh."

That was all I could think to say. I'd missed something Ester and Dr. Quarzi had seen coming.

I knew they'd been trying to kill our industry. What I hadn't realized was that it wasn't about the Frozen Generation. They were after us.

Us, like as individuals, the people who worked at the clinics. Not just the politicians who supported us, or our CEO, or the other executives they dragged before congress, but all of *us*. Me.

Even after all these years in their crosshairs I'd still taken them at their word. Still internalized some gut, cultural-suffusion belief that they cared about the Frozen Generation enough not to sabotage them. No matter how much they hated extraction or us that enabled it, Storage should have been safe.

Oh. You damned idiot.

It wouldn't matter if tonight's ban got overturned if we were all in prison when it came time to reopen the clinic. Whether we were the victims of a conspiracy or yet another bit of collateral damage didn't really matter. Dr Quarzi was right. Ester was right. For all the good it would probably do them, at least they were running.

"How long do we have?" Charlotte asked.

I shook out of the reprieve; the math was fresh in my mind. We were already so low.

"Without more juice? Maybe a day or two before we start losing ones near the top of the flasks to evaporation."

With cryo, thawing isn't like you'd imagine. Everything's so cold, it's actually skipped freezing to being this ice-free glass. If it thaws unregulated, you have two problems: ice crystals will form and slice all the cells apart, and the cryoprotectants that preserve the cells by replacing their water will go toxic as they warm. Warming the cells and diluting out the cryoprotectants is a whole process you just can't manage when a few thousand flasks of enhanced nitrogen are going from liquid to gas and you have no electricity.

"I contacted our sister organizations and sent out an alert on all our social media. Described what they're doing and begged for fuel and cryo," Charlotte said. "We've got a good base of someday-parents who are organizing to help."

"Any luck?"

"Not sure if our people can even get through that riot outside. The police are supposedly here to keep things under control, but they're basically blockading us in."

My eyes were still on the muted tablet, watching our representatives. I felt a bleak certainty that there would be plenty of investigations to determine all the ways we were at fault for this.

The power cut out. The wall of security monitors went dead. The only light in the room was the screen on the tablet.

I shook out of it. "Oh, yeah. I had Mike cut everything but Storage. We'll move any clinic hardware we have to keep to the back, try to make it last."

Charlotte nodded. "Good idea."

"Could you double check the doors?" I asked. "Some of the emergencies are fail-open maglocks and we might need to barricade them."

"Sure." She grabbed a flashlight from her desk and the gun she kept holstered under the tabletop. She knew about the doors. She was probably relieved to have the distraction.

"Thanks."

Mike caught me as I left Charlotte's office.

"It's Dr. Clarke. She won't let me cut the clinic. Says she wants any surplus for the wombs."

"What? Tell me she hasn't started a new batch."

Those things suck power and they still take almost nine months per kid. Regulations imposed on the manufacturer — anything else would be unnatural. And there were only twenty of them. We had over six hundred thousand embryos and fetuses in the back.

"Sorry, boss. She outranks me."

"What, she's gonna print half a million kids before the batteries run out?"

But she had to look like she'd tried. She was the doctor in charge of production. Someday they'd be asking her, 'Why didn't you try to save *any* of them?'

We were on a sinking ship, and we were all looking ahead, past the lifeboats to the historians, trying to dictate what they'd say about us in their accounts.

Or, more likely, in our atrocity trials.

●

All twenty Securus Platinum exowombs were humming away on their pedestal mounts, and ten old Herz-Stanton 25s were sitting on the counter. All were occupied and lit.

I wondered where Dr. Clarke had gotten the kids. Were they future orders? Had she picked them at random? The front office tried anonymizing the embryos once. Give them all an equal chance at adoption. Our client rate had plummeted. People out in the world talked a big game about the abandoned, forever-frozen masses and their right to life, but when it came time to grow their new kid, they only wanted the best.

"Dr. Clarke?"

"I knew you'd show up." She looked tired and scared. She pointed her phone at me like it was a gun. Recording the conversation, proof she'd done all she could. Proof I was the bad guy here. Fine. Her jury would love us turning on each other.

"Doctor. You need to put the patients back into cryostasis." It's always 'the patients' when you talk about the Frozen, but especially when you know you're on video.

Her chin came up and her face went hard. "This is my department, and these patients' well-being is my responsibility. I have to do what's best for them. I don't answer to the cryotechs."

Ouch.

"They cut our power, and these things are draining the reserve." I spoke clear and slow for the court. "Without the exowombs running, we can get another day or so for all the patients in the back. Maybe they'll turn the power back on by then. If we don't, they'll *all* start to thaw." She didn't react, so I kept going. "We'll never have enough power for these machines either way. But running them could kill all the patients onsite."

I half expected her to say I was just trying to save my own department at her expense, but she didn't go there. She stuck to the script.

"The law says we need to transfer all Unborn Americans to exowombs immediately."

She put herself between me and them, like she expected us to fight.

I realized I didn't have to argue this out. I didn't have to say anything. The breaker was in the basement.

Antisocial hive tendencies, I guess. We always caught flack for being 'indirectly confrontational' after being raised by a monolith we couldn't affect in the slightest. As a nod to professionalism, I spoke up on my way out.

"Okay. You can put them back in cryo or you can take them someplace else. Either way, I'm cutting power to this room." I headed for the stairwell. She followed me.

"They can't leave these facilities! They're not allowed to leave the clinic. We have to maintain custody of all-"

I stopped at the basement door while I found my light. "I can spare a truck. I can't spare power."

"You don't 'spare' anything! That's not your decision to make!" I was the last facilities person here with any rank, so I would contest that.

Luckily, I didn't have to. Charlotte appeared from the darkness and stepped in. I guess we hadn't exactly been arguing quietly.

"Rachel. Stop," she said. There was an edge to her voice, but she kept it calm, authoritative. "We can't support them here. Not anymore. If you want them to make it, you have to take them someplace else."

"But they can't leave..."

She took Dr. Clarke's hand. "Listen, they, and you, will be safer someplace else. Take them to a hospital, take them to your church. Hell, take them to the governor's mansion. Anywhere'll be better." She started guiding her toward the garage. "Come on, I'll help you get a truck."

"I-"

"It's *okay*. It's okay. These are terrible times and you've done everything you could. If we had more than thirty exowombs, you would have saved even more. You've already gone above and beyond. They'll understand. Hell, you'll probably be a hero."

I hit the staircase, flashlight searching for the clinic breaker. I'd probably be able to watch her single-handedly rescue those thirty innocent lives again someday in the based-on-a-true-story dramatization. From my prison cell.

●

I made a decision on my way back to Storage. Or maybe I realized that I'd made it a while ago.

Keeping the Frozen 'alive' had always been the goal, but the way I'd seen it, my real job was to keep everything perfect back here, exceeding every regulation, so nobody went to jail.

Most of the crew I had left seemed to feel the same way. If we quit, we'd be abandoning our teammates, and the rest of the clinic.

That made what came next easier. My plans might have changed since the drive in, but I'd still be doing my job.

Zeke was manually forcing the heavy door to the employee garage when I got back to Storage.

"Jimmy's back, and he says he got fuel!" Sol told me.

Zeke grinned. "I love that kid."

The sun was up now. I saw a sliver of it as the garage door rumbled back down. The truck rolled to a stop as we all hustled over.

Jimmy shoved the door open and stumbled out, looking beat and wild-eyed. "I'm sorry, boss." He shook his head. "I couldn't get- it's bad out there."

His knuckles were scraped bloody and he had a nice shiner forming on his left eye. He'd stopped somewhere and spray painted over the logo on the truck. I wondered if it was before or after his fight.

I went around the back and looked over the bed of gas cans. Most of them were empty.

Zeke was talking to him. "Hey, hey it's okay. You're okay."

"No, it's not. They'd only sell me eighty gallons. I couldn't do more, I'm sorry. The first place, when I tried to fill everything, they figured it out and came out with a gun. I-"

Behind us, Sol swore and kicked the truck.

"Hey, it's fine!" I waved a hand at him, then looked back to our driver. "You did more than we had any right to ask. It's okay. We'll figure something out."

There was a half second of silence, and then: "I quit." Jimmy was looking down at the painted-over logo, focus distant. "Look," he said. "I just came to get my truck. Sorry." He met my eyes for a second. "Sorry. I'm done. I got to go."

And then he did.

We got as ready as we could with what we had left. We consolidated the fuel, shifted our resources around so we weren't producing any more power than we could use or store, made sure we were running everything else on the minimums.

They worked hard, though they looked scared, kept checking their phones. Couldn't hold that against them today. News updates, worried texts from families. Finally, I said, "Enough. Go home. We're as ready for shutdown as we're going to get."

After all the hassle from the government inspections, the impossible hours from being badly understaffed, the slurs and attacks and violence from the protestors, the crew I had left were here because they were loyal and they cared. With their skills, they could have gotten jobs at any lab or factory floor for more pay and less work, less stress. I was grateful for them.

"Naw, you'll need us here," Sol said.

"I need you to go get some sleep. Go home, see your families. I'll text you if we need anything else. There'll be a lot to do when Charlotte and her lawyers get the power back. They'll probably have inspectors out here before the next shipment of cryo."

"What about you?"

I didn't have kids, or anyone at home to worry about. Most of my forty-six surviving hive siblings could take care of themselves.

"I'll take the first shift here. I'll let you know as soon as anything changes, or if I need help with anything in the meanwhile."

"If the power doesn't come back..." Zeke started.

"I'll watch the levels. I got reserve batteries, reserve tanks, and gravity feeds from the 'still. If I need a bucket brigade, I'll let you know."

They laughed a little. Then they just looked tired. Finally, they took the out, headed for their trucks. Promised they'd look for gas, be back as soon as we needed them. But they weren't coming back and we all knew it. I wasn't going to text them, and they knew that, too.

Someone had to be responsible for what was going to happen next. Storage was my department. If I sent them away before the failures began, it kept responsibility for everything nice and tidy.

I waited till they were gone, then I climbed up on the pump station, set all the warning alarms to max volume, and took a nap.

●

I woke up when I started sweating through my clothes. The sun was cooking on the warehouse roof — good for our solar, not that it'd do more than pump our thin reserves around. The Frozen wouldn't notice this heat though, not in their vacuum flasks of liquid nitrogen. Out here it was too hot, but in there it was impossibly cold.

The generator's warning lights glowed amber on the dash. Nothing left to do about that.

I went for a walk around the clinic.

The place was empty, trashed in everyone's haste to evacuate. I could hear someone clinking around in one of the labs and it made me think of rats or squatters. Just last night it had been business as usual, and now this. Muffled outside, I thought I could hear voices and pops, like fireworks or gunshots.

Amerinews was playing in Charlotte's office.

"State militia units here in Godless California are mustering on the border for what they call a humanitarian mission, an invasion to kidnap and illegally transport the Frozen across state lines. It's a logistical nightmare in clear violation of state autonomy. God only knows what will happen to these helpless babies."

"Hey, Moses," Charlotte said.

"Hey. Jimmy quit."

"Everybody's quit."

We both looked at the tablet for a minute.

"How about you?" I asked.

"I'm going down with the ship. You?"

"I'll keep things cold as long as I can. After that, I don't know. Any luck on the power?"

She shook her head. Subject change. "There's a mob outside."

"Yeah? Maybe we'll get lucky and they'll set the place on fire. Take the credit." I said.

That got a little smile. "If you need to get out, the side door by client parking still opens out. Plus your loading dock."

"Thanks. Not sure there's any running away from this."

"Nope."

She sat there in the dark, lit by her dwindling tablet. "I'll be here if you need anything," she said.

I walked back to Storage and made my rounds again. Looked over all the racks and racks of flasks, batteries, reserve tanks, bundled wires and tubing. I'd configured most of these units. I'd loaded half of them. Tended them all for years, watched for even a single power or temperature failure. Soon there'd be thousands.

The last generator sputtered to a rest outside. The fans stopped. The pumps cut out. The beeps and squawks of the monitors went dead on standby. And in the silence, the Frozen Generation began to thaw.

Jacob Coffin's story "The Frozen Generation" was originally published in Metaphorosis on Friday, 10 February 2023. See magazine.metaphorosis.com

About the author

Jacob Coffin is a tech writer, woodworker, amateur electrician, and former apprentice blacksmith, with a passion for land conservation, reuse, and the world he lives on not dying. He has published science fiction with Metaphorosis Magazine, and in the upcoming Harbour anarchist fiction magazine. On the lighter side, he photobashes rural cyberpunk comics and scenes of a solarpunk future and shares them here: jacobcoffinwrites.wordpress.com

He shares his other projects, making and fixing things, here: movim.slrpnk.net/blog/jacobcoffinwrites%40slrpnk.net

And he's most active on lemmy at slrpnk.net/u/JacobCoffinWrites and mastodon at writing.exchange/@jacobcoffin Jacob Coffin is a sci-fi writer with a passion for land conservation, reuse, and human rights not being rolled back.

jacobcoffinwrites.wordpress.com, @jacobcoffin@writing.exchange

The Bookseller of Mars

Gaby Brogan

I am where the hurt people go. Not the crying, soft, gentle people. I'm not sure there are any of those left. No, I am where the killers turn when the buried piece of them that is still human reaches out, yearning for the light.

Now there are two killers at my door. Boy-children. I see them on the crackly intercom screen in my kitchen, the red desert stretching out behind them. I will let them in, I'm sure. I always do.

"Guns stay outside," I call through the mic.

They turn to each other and whisper. They look about fourteen or fifteen — the age I was when I first came to Mars over a decade ago, a filthy, scared teenage girl, bundled onto a starship along with the rest of the refugees from Earth.

Originally, thirty thousand of the global elite were planned for those starships. But when society fell to floods, fire, and disease, SpaceCorp took whoever could make it to the launch site in burning California. Beggars can't be choosers during the apocalypse.

The day we landed, I filed out of the ship into the sterile light of the Mars station with the other aching, stinking survivors. We took gear from metal boxes as an armed group of SpaceCorp employees watched over us. The most precious item was a metal cube the size of my fist. If I pressed the button, it would pop open to the size of a cargo container. A ready-made home for the elite's life on Mars; temperature controlled, CO_2 to oxygen conversion, a greenhouse for food, and a drillbug to bore down into Martian rock for water.

That cargo container is where I find myself now, all these years later. Hidden under an outcrop of rock on the edge of the desert, far from the violence and squalor of the settlements.

"We're not leaving our gun," calls the blond kid on my screen.

"Then you aren't coming in." On Mars, everyone's a killer.

The kid kicks the ground, sending up a cloud of ochre dust.

"You don't understand. It's Jay," he gestures to the boy next to him. "His regulator's beeping."

"I'm sorry," I say. "That's a real problem for Jay." If his regulator is beeping, he doesn't have long. That vital metal chip sits in your nostril, creating a bubble of oxygen and pressure that stops your blood from boiling in the Martian atmosphere. Beeping means breaking.

"Fuck," says the blond. He turns to Jay and motions to put the gun on the ground. Jay shakes his head and grips it tighter.

I move a plant's green tendril to hit the intercom button again. "I'm alone here, if it makes you feel better. And I don't have a gun... within easy reach." I look at the stack of books next to my bed. A pistol sits on top.

The blond grabs Jay's shoulders, pleading, but the other boy simply stares into the intercom camera and holds the gun to his chest.

He'd rather die than come into my house unarmed? Jesus. Who knows what they've been through.

I groan. This kid is about to die on my doorstep because of his own stubbornness. I've buried bodies in the rocky ground before, but none this young.

Pushing the button, I open my cargo container's airlock. The boys whip their heads around and scramble in, the door slamming down after them. It floods with air and repressurizes.

On my airlock monitor, I see Jay breathing deeply. Tears stream down the blond's cheeks through the red dust.

He scoops Jay into a ferocious hug, gripping his silver jacket so hard I think it might rip.

The kids hold each other like that until I press the button to open the door to my home. They separate, tense and defensive, hurt wolf pups ready to bite. Jay raises the gun, but his hands are shaky, uncertain.

"That was pretty fucking stupid," I say. "Put the gun down. I'm not going to hurt you."

The blond wipes his tears. Jay lowers the gun. That's better.

Martian-born kids. They're slimmer, muscles softer than mine were, growing up on Earth. They walk with a graceful float in their step, no muscle memory of Earth's gravity weighing down their every move. They remind me of birds — hollow bones.

Jay is short, on the childish side of his teen years, with red-brown skin like the Martian dust. His eyes are honey. His blond friend is so pale I can see his blue veins. He's taller than Jay and his wide eyes dart around my home.

I gesture for them to sit at the scrap-metal table. They do, and Jay lays the gun by his feet.

"I'm Melanie. Tea?"

"Uh, yes please," says the blond. "I'm Ben."

I busy myself over at the sink, filling a pot with water and setting it on the thermal pad to heat.

"So, what are two kids doing out in the Martian desert with a failing regulator?" I scoop dried herbs into three mesh metal balls and set each in a mug.

"Got lost on a school trip," says Ben. "We were trying to walk back to our settlement when the beeping started. *Bookseller* is the only thing on the map in this part of the desert. We knew you were our only hope for getting air."

I snort. "I didn't know I was a feature on any maps." Maps of Mars are rarely accurate, anyway, often scrawled on wheat husk paper after a long journey. But if these boys go to school, it means they're from the SpaceCorp settlement — the only place with the resources to build any real infrastructure. The most organized settlement we have. And the most vicious. Perhaps they have half-decent maps. What they definitely don't have, however, is school trips.

These boys are liars. And most likely, runaways. "Aren't you lucky you managed to find me."

I feel the cold tip of a gun at my back. Damn.

"Why'd you tell us you were alone?" asks Jay. "I see two plates stacked up there on your drying rack. Two cups. Two forks. You got a boyfriend hiding here?"

I flick a look at my drying rack.

"Girlfriend," I say. "And no. She's gone. Just a few days ago... I — I didn't have the heart to put it all away yet, if you must know."

On Mars, you get used to reading the truth in someone's voice. I guess he hears mine.

"Oh." The gun moves away from my back.

"She isn't dead." I can't stand for this kid's sympathy to be wasted on the idea of Cara. "Just gone. Apparently, life in a settlement is more interesting than here surrounded by badly written books." I slam the teas down and slump into my seat. Jay and Ben watch me warily. "Now, if you're quite done threatening me, maybe we can enjoy this tea."

Ben kicks Jay under the table. "Uh, yeah. Sorry," Jay manages.

"So... uh, you make all this yourself?" Ben gestures around my cargo container home. Masters of conversation, these two.

I look around. He doesn't mean the greenhouse extension, the shelves, or the tins of preserved foods, which, as a matter of fact, I did make myself. He means the towers of books that line every wall.

"They don't call me the bookseller for nothing," I shrug.

"How'd you do all this?" A spark of wonder lights Ben's blue eyes. Now, even in my lonely, heartbroken state, I'm not going to destroy what might be the only spark of wonder currently on Mars.

I sigh. "After the starships landed, everyone in the settlements started acting out the sequel to the earthly apocalypse — real Mad Max shit. I ran out here into the desert alone and popped my cargo container. Raised myself until I got an infected cut and had to venture back into a settlement to trade my food for medicine. While I was there,

I met a guy who'd pulp wheat husks and turn it into paper. I came back and traded all my preserves for five notebooks."

"That's a bad trade," says Ben.

"I know," I snort. "But I wasn't in the healthiest state of mind. Anyway, I started by re-writing the classics, from memory, as well as I could. Everything I'd been studying in school on Earth. Some part of me knew they were worth saving and I'm glad I did. They sold first when I went back to the settlement to trade. Then, people started visiting me, threatening me, demanding I write the books they'd left behind. Soon, they realized they'd get better stories if they were kinder. Creativity can't exactly flourish at gunpoint."

They'd wanted the stories so desperately. You see, when your home is burning or filled with your dying family, you don't think to bring your favorite book or e-reader as you escape. You just get your weapon and get yourself to the launch site by any means necessary. And on Mars, there's no infrastructure to build phones or TVs. Our exodus from Earth meant we left all our stories behind.

"People told me plots and I spun them into books. And now, that's all I do, rewriting shittier versions of the books we had on Earth."

"And it's safe here?" asks Ben. "Settlers don't ever raid you?"

"I rewrote *The Handmaid's Tale* for the leader of a raider gang a while back. It's been particularly quiet since then. Maybe she put in a good word for me."

I sip my tea. Indeed, my customers are hard, bitter people. Did you ever see those pictures of a fox or a crocodile or a bear — some creature that is all claws and bite — with a butterfly landing on their nose? They used to put those pictures in cheap yearly calendars. Anyways, the biter closes their eyes and they let the butterfly land, because behind the claws there's a soft warm creature that just wants a nap in the sun. In my little cargo container, killers rest and tell me about their favourite books. They ask me to write a story. And I do, because sometimes, I see the horror and the haunt slip away. Just for a moment.

"So basically, you just hide out here and sell stories to the dangerous assholes who come through?" asks Jay.

"I —" Ouch. "Better than being stranded in the desert on a school trip... or are you running away from SpaceCorp?"

Jay's hand drifts down to his gun.

"Hands where I can see them. Or I won't be fixing that regulator of yours."

His hand shoots back to his lap. "You can fix it?"

I nod. "Put your gun up there, next to mine. On top of that stack of books."

Jay waits for a consenting look from Ben and then stands, placing the gun next to mine.

"Much better. Now, give me your regulator."

He fishes it out of his nose, wipes it on his trousers, and sets it on the table.

"Right, I'll get to it. You guys can wait over there," I gesture to the pile of pillows and blankets that serves as my sofa. I tell them they can help themselves to whatever food or books they want, as long as they're quiet.

They busy themselves raiding my shelves. Ben munches on some dried carrot chips I made last week. Jay stares out the kitchen window at the endless red ocean.

I open my box of tools, grab the magnifying glass, and get to work. But a few minutes in, I lean back in my chair.

"Who made this regulator?" I ask.

"Does it matter?" Jay snaps.

"Kind of. It's a piece of shit."

It's more than that. This regulator isn't like the one I took from the SpaceCorp boxes when I landed, built to last a lifetime. It's flimsy, designed to break after a few days. Why would anyone make this? Nothing on Mars is disposable. Every scrap we have is precious, used carefully, made for a reason. Sending someone out with this is a death sentence.

"Can you fix it, though?" asks Jay.

"I don't know. It's going to take me a little longer."

Ben sat up. "How much longer? We uh... we need to get moving soon."

"Why? Someone coming after you?"

He looks at the carrot chips in his hand.

"Fine, don't tell me. But I need at least a day or two on this."

"Shit."

"Up to you."

The boys whisper to each other in the corner.

"We can't pay you for fixing the regulator. Or for letting us stay while we do," says Jay, finally.

"Oh." On Mars, nothing is free. "Then you can help out here — the greenhouse needs fixing up and I've been meaning to repair the shelves."

The boys nod, relieved. I set them up with their tasks and then spend a few hours tinkering with the regulator. In the evening, I warm up some soup for dinner and they sit on the blankets, flipping through my handwritten books and asking questions. It feels good to speak to someone, again.

●

The next morning, I go back to work on the regulator. The Martian time slips by, quiet and red.

"*To Kill a Mockingbird*?" asks Ben, in the afternoon. "What is it, like a guide?"

"Sure, it's a guide. But not one to do with birds," I say. Jay looks up from the old drillbug he's trying to fix.

"I don't get it," says Ben.

"Sit and read it and you will," I say.

"It's long."

"Ah but it's worth it. Books are more nourishing than you know."

Jay and Ben share a look — a hint of a laugh, a twist of embarrassment on my behalf. Not quite an eye roll, but nearly. I smile. My little brother and I shared that exact look about the nearest clueless adult countless times. He didn't make it past the first wave of sickness back on Earth.

I shake my head. "Take it."

Ben's eyebrows shoot up and he looks at Jay. Jay smiles.

"Well, thanks." Ben holds it gentler now, flipping softly through the pages.

That book is worth three weeks of food in a trade. I can practically see Cara in the corner, chastising me about economic irresponsibility. Well, she isn't here.

Ben reads my rehashed version of *To Kill a Mockingbird* and I watch him out of the corner of my eye. It's one of the few books with words I know I've written right. The lady who commissioned the first copy had the text tattooed on her shoulder, "*I wanted you to see what real courage is, instead of getting the idea that courage is a man with a gun in his hand. It's when you know you're licked before you begin, but you begin anyway and see it through no matter what.*"

I always liked that quote.

•

The next day, the intercom buzzes like a yellowjacket. I flick a look toward the screen.

Now, these are the kind of guests I'm used to. A man and a woman stand tall, decked out in cobbled-together desert-gear and heavy-duty boots. Their faces are obscured by rags. Guns hang from their shoulders and grenades from their belts. Raiders or SpaceCorp, I can't tell. All the same, anyway — grizzly bears.

"Good morning," I say over the intercom. "You've reached the bookseller."

"You seen two boys out here?"

"Hard to say. Who are you?"

"Retrievers, from the SpaceCorp school. Those two students killed a member of staff and ran away. We've come to ensure they receive proper punishment."

Shit. I take my hand off the intercom and spin toward Ben and Jay.

"Is that true?" I don't want trouble.

Ben shakes his head. Jay nods.

"We each killed a guy," says Jay. He talks fast like he can see I'm spooked. "But they made us, as part of our training. That's why we ran away."

"Training?"

"It's not a school. They're training kids as soldiers and planning to take over the other settlements by force and form a proper country, led by them. They haven't come to punish us. They want to stop the truth getting out before they're ready."

This is huge. Finally making the settlements into one city, united, makes sense. Resources could be shared. A society could be built. Well, that's what logic says. In practice, the one settlement that SpaceCorp already runs is brutal, with settlers fighting over scraps from the people at the top. A takeover is going to be violent. And bloody.

The intercom buzzes again.

"Bookseller," says the man on the intercom. "Did you see the boys?"

I press the mic. Ben's hand twitches on *To Kill a Mockingbird.*

"Yes," I say. "I have seen the boys." Jay scrambles to grab his gun. "They passed through here a few days ago and left. Said they were heading to the northern settlement. One of them had a broken regulator. I doubt they'll have made it far."

The man and woman nod. This is no surprise to them. They know those regulators don't last.

"So you just let them go?" says the woman.

"Obviously. I don't need two more mouths to feed. If they want to get themselves killed in the desert, that's on them."

The man and woman scuff around in the dust, whispering to one another.

"On behalf of SpaceCorp, we're requesting entry to your home, bookseller. To trade for supplies," says the man.

"I've got nothing to trade but books."

"That'll do."

He's clearly not coming in for books.

I consider my options.

"Guns stay outside. That's my policy."

On the little screen, the man nods and hands his gun to the woman. She takes a few steps back, looking at the perimeter of my house. No doubt making sure no figures escape as her colleague searches inside.

Behind me, Ben and Jay's panicked whispers fill the air. I usher them under my bed and pass them my pistol. Their wide-eyed faces disappear as I throw a blanket over the bed.

Pushing the button, I open the airlock and the man walks in. It repressurizes.

It's not ideal. If he finds them, then what? Can I feasibly say that I didn't know they were there?

Another press of a button and the man is in my home. He lowers his mouth rag. His face is pitted and scarred, like the surface of our new home.

"I'll take a look around now," he says. He's done us both a favor by dropping the pretense.

"Go ahead," I say.

He walks along the towers of books, and I look at my home of over a decade with fresh eyes. Not many hiding spots. The bed is glaringly obvious.

The man drops to his knees to check out the entrance to the greenhouse. He stands and cocks his head, reading the spine of a book on a precarious stack. My rendition of *The Catcher in the Rye*.

"Interested?" I ask.

"No," he says. "I've heard your prices. I'm not in the market to waste three weeks' worth of food on a book." His eyes linger on it, though.

"Well, they take me a long time to write. You read this one back on Earth?"

"Uh, yeah. As a matter of fact, I did."

"Go on then, what did you do, before? Office guy?"

He considers me. "I was a teacher in New York," he says, finally. "Math. Always liked that book, though."

"Bet it's a bit different now, working at SpaceCorp."

His face clouds over and he looks away. Wrong thing to say. Don't remind killers of what they are. I've become too used to the truthful simplicity of my conversations with the boys. This feels like a deadly chess match that I'm being forced to play once again.

His eyes catch on the three mugs in that damn drying rack. The plates. He sighs and walks towards the bed.

"Don't you miss stories?" I ask.

He turns back. "Let me just get this over with, lady."

I ignore him. "There's no TV here. No cinema. I think that's why people like my books. Medicine for the mind — a way to get lost."

He blinks. More people need a mental escape on Mars than they're willing to admit.

"If only there were a way for you to procure a story without having to trade your hard-earned food."

I take *Catcher in the Rye* off the stack of books and hold it out to him.

His face is a mirror-image of Ben's when I gave him *To Kill a Mockingbird*. On Mars, you only own what you need to survive.

Slowly, he reaches out to take the book. He holds it in both hands, eyes roving over Cara's illustration of the cover. It's beautiful, like everything else she created. He flips open the first page, gently.

"So... have you found what you're looking for?"

"Perhaps."

His eyes flick to the bed again. What's the price for two kids' lives?

"Take another," I say. "For the road."

He spins around and looks at the stack of books next to him. *Percy Jackson and The Olympians*. He pulls it out quickly and stuffs both books into the inside of his jacket pocket.

"My students used to love Percy Jackson," he says. "Back on Earth."

That's the thing about my sanctuary — even killers have an inner child. And stories help them find their way back out.

"I bet," I say and indicate the airlock.

He nods. I push the button and he walks out into the Martian desert.

I rush to the intercom screen. Outside, he gestures, talking to his colleague. She questions him. He shrugs. She tips her head, and they kick around in the dust for a while. Then, they turn and go.

My hands are shaking, white.

"You can come out," I say.

The boys scramble out from under the bed. Ben runs at me and hugs me. Jay hovers behind. "Thank you," he says.

Ben lets me go and I exhale all the tension.

To think, Cara left because of how quiet life was here with me, how slow.

We collapse at the table.

"So, you guys ran away from SpaceCorp. No destination in mind?"

"Not exactly," says Jay. "A few weeks ago, these girls from the year above broke into the SpaceCorp offices. They read through a bunch of documents. Plans for the new country, breakthroughs in terraforming. The girls stole the papers and a bunch of supplies then ran away to start a new settlement. A hidden one for Martian kids, where we can try to build something better."

"And you're going to follow them. How do you know their regulators didn't break?"

"These girls are smart. Their regulators didn't break."

"Do you even know where they are?"

"They've gone to the western mountain." Jay's face looks young, hopeful.

I consider these two Martian kids. They aren't killers. They don't have claws and fangs. Maybe they're the butterflies on the predator's nose. Or I'm confusing my metaphors; I said they were hollow-boned birds, right? Either way. They are a thing with wings. And they see a future on Mars, one away from the suffering and the violence.

"Well, then I'd best get that regulator fixed up for you," I say.

The boys spend the evening browsing my shelves while I tinker and process the impending doom of a SpaceCorp takeover.

An unfamiliar noise fills my home. I look up. It's the boys, laughing. They're reading bits of a book to one another, acting out scenes with big, exaggerated movements. I tilt my head. *The Hitchiker's Guide to the Galaxy*. How strange, to hear laughter. Not the broken half-hearted chuckle of a killer. Not the condescending bark of a lover who's sick to death of my company. No, laughter like... in a family's home.

I squeeze my eyes shut against a wave of unwanted emotion, and the tears that threaten to follow. What is wrong with me? If I didn't know better, I'd say I didn't want the boys to go.

The next morning, after breakfast, I spend a final few hours on the regulator. I reinforce Ben's too, for good measure.

"Alright," I say. "Your regulators are ready. Time to go. Quick."

"Why quick?" asks Jay, eyes darting, back on alert.

"I'm kicking you out. And myself, too."

"You're kicking yourself out?"

"I'm coming with you," I try to sound confident, like when I used to lead my little brother in the games we played. "You need supplies and a plan if you're going to make it west. I can provide at least part of that. Anyway, this hidden settlement will need books."

I clamp my lips shut against the confession that threatens to follow. That I can't stand to write here alone again, speaking only to killers and characters. That SpaceCorp won't allow a writer to live unmanaged, out in the desert alone. That one of their retrievers knows about me harbouring two fugitives and a bribe only lasts so long.

Ben tilts his head, looking at me with squinted eyes, like he hears my thoughts. He looks at Jay.

"You're right," says Jay. "The new settlement will need books. I hear they're very nourishing."

I exhale.

We spend the day packing supplies and planning our route. Finally, when we're ready, we insert our regulators. Then, we step out into the light of that faraway sun.

"Ok," I say. "Let's go."

We walk under the rocky outcropping and out towards the vast western horizon. I turn and look back at the little cargo container that has been my world ever since I escaped Earth. My refuge, filled with other people's stories. Now it's time to write my own.

Gaby Brogan's story "The Bookseller of Mars" was originally published in Metaphorosis on Friday, 18 August 2023. See magazine.metaphorosis.com

About the author

Gaby Brogan was raised in the UK and Italy on a steady diet of pasta and science fiction. Usually based in Amsterdam, she's now traveling and working from the road as a freelance copywriter. Whenever she can, she scribbles poetry and fiction, practices yoga, and goes out to explore.

Rock-Adda's World

Chloe Smith

Adda felt that the greatest mystery of being a parent was the way it tied you, with such powerful bonds of love, to a person with whom you would continuously fail to communicate successfully.

She always looked forward to her daughter's yearly visits, even though they always meant more arguments that left her feeling both guilty and misunderstood. Cia usually waited until the last possibility of storm was long gone and the warm season was fully established, but this year icy rime crunched under Adda's boots as she walked out to greet her daughter, and cold air pressed against the exposed skin of her face and hands.

Cia turned from pulling a bag out of her suborbital hopper. She was certainly dressed for the cold, in thermal layers whose slim profile spoke volumes about their cost. Adda felt the usual mixture of wonder and pride that this person, who had once lain asleep with her head below Adda's chin and her feet on her stomach, was now flying herself between continents in a rented jet.

Cia said, "Why aren't you wearing gloves, Ma?"

Adda laughed. "Which one of us is the mother here, girl?"

Cia wiggled well-covered fingers. "*I'm* dressed appropriately. I was brought up well."

Adda scoffed and gave her a squeeze around the shoulders. "Well, come on in, then. I knew we were barely going to be out."

Her observation station was a small building, half-sunk in the ground, with its own power panels and the bulk of a skimplane hangar visible off to one side. Adda gave the hangar walls a furtive once-over as she held the door of the main building open for Cia — yes, there was nothing more than a shadowy smudge, indistinguishable from weathering. No one now would be able to tell that yesterday she had woken to find a block-lettered scrawl: STAND BACK AND SHUT UP, ROCK-LOVER.

It had taken her most of a morning, and a lot of retching, to clean out the mess of garbage and refuse they had left on and around her skimplane, and another couple of hours to repair and reinforce the damaged locks. Adda had forced down the feelings of outrage and violation, telling herself that fear was capitulation. This was an expression of popular opinion, not a direct threat — there was no sabotage to the vehicle itself, and no attack on her actual living space.

Yet, Cia would say if she knew. Adda didn't plan on telling her.

Inside, Cia settled herself in the second sleeping quarters. They were officially designated for visiting researchers, but Adda had been thinking of them as "Cia's," reserved for her semi-annual visits, for at least the last five years.

Adda made tea in the closet-like canteen, and then brought it out to her dining-cum-work table, where she had to push the clutter of battery packs and recording equipment farther back to make room for two.

"How are things?" she asked when Cia reappeared, preparing herself for at least a half hour of free-form rambling on Cia's work- and love-life, helped along by Adda's occasional interested noise or leading question.

Cia shrugged. "They're good. Same-same but different. How are *you* doing, though?"

Uh oh. It looked like they weren't going to pretend that things were casual for even as long as Adda had hoped. "What makes you ask?" She gave her daughter a look.

Cia had the grace to look uncomfortable. "Well," she said, "you know we end up being party to a lot of the discussion around new settlement development..." Cia worked for the city manager's office in Istvan, the oldest city on the South Continent. Her position often gave her a line on issues that impacted the cetalith population, though not from a perspective that Adda could agree with. She gritted her teeth in anticipation as Cia continued, "there's been — well, I saw the footage of the town hall meeting. I was worried about you."

Adda closed her eyes. *I was worried about you.* Not, *How could they?* Not, *The situation's appalling.* Not, *What can we do?*

She opened them again, stared past Cia to the wall over her terminal station, where she had pinned an excerpt from a flimsy printout:

"The giant cetaliths of Krishnan IV are another puzzling example. These silicate creatures, who move at speeds not exceeding 6 centimeters per U-hour, and leave as the marks of their passage enduring tunnels that permeate the surface of their world, may have a level of sentience that would guarantee their planet Protectorate, if not Sovereign, status under the Cygni Accords. Although they are solitary beings, whose paths cross only occasionally over the course of their long, long lives, their 'songs,' which gave rise to the name 'whales of stone,' may be a form of communication. This implies a level of sophistication and consciousness, but researchers have yet to establish firm proof of either. This ambiguity has led to the current impasse in official decision-making."

The whole document, the *Report on Resources of Non-Sovereign Satellites, Planets, and Exoplanets, Appendix A: Sentient Fauna*, was one of the supports that the first settlers had used to make their case for access to the planet. *Give us this world to do what we like with as long as we don't understand it.* Adda kept the flimsy on display as a reminder of what was at stake.

Cia was frowning at her. "Ma?"

"It's a worrying situation," she said dryly.

Cia rotated her cup in her hands. Still staring at it, she said "The thing is, speaking like that at the meeting... I don't think it does any good."

"You mean you were embarrassed." Adda's response came out harsher than she meant it to. The truth was, she had embarrassed herself. In the moment, she had been caught up in trying to convince the town shareholders to see what she saw, until she was half-shouting:

"How can we be so selfish! This isn't our world. To just come in and take what we like because it suits us — we have no right! This is an ancient species, a mystery worth unravelling! What you're doing isn't even legal — sentient-status ruling is still pending!"

Chair Horace Grish nodded impatiently, while the crowd behind Adda shifted and muttered. "That status ruling has been pending since Krishnan's was first surveyed, Doctor Oram. It's hard to believe that a decision is forthcoming. In the absence of official status —"

"You're just going to batter this planet and destroy a potentially sovereign species! The ruling isn't the point — this is wrong!"

She had felt so large at the time, full of righteousness and fire, containing multitudes. On the recording, though, her voice was thinner and higher, and she looked like what she was, an old woman, speaking words that meant nothing to her listeners.

"Ma!" Cia's voice cut through her reverie. Adda looked at her. Cia had pushed the tea aside, her forehead creased. "Who do you think is going to stop them? Continental governance? Sharevote results show there's only a minority favoring holding off expansion until the non-Sovereign ruling is official."

"I know that," Adda snapped. She had correspondents besides Cia, other scientists and citizen enthusiasts who followed her research from the southern continent, where human settlements had spread. Some shared their own work with her, their explorations of the cetalith routes that ran through this world — although that work could only be the archeology of dead spaces and still remnants. There were no moving cetaliths left on South Continent, and Adda was the only researcher who had committed to an isolated life on the northern landmass — isolated, at least, until the arrival of the recent wave of separatists from the south, who had founded the town of New Beginnings.

Cia shook her head. "How many reports have you sent, Ma? For how long? After all this time, it's not just sharevotes; most *people* don't think Cygni is going to designate the Rocks as sentient."

Adda sighed. "That's not an accurate term."

"That's not the point —"

"It *is* the point!" Adda's voice rose. "We don't understand, and our ignorance is killing them!"

"Ma!" Cia wailed, "Killing them? They're not even aware! But this could get *you* killed! New Beginnings has their own sovereignty up here. What if they decide you're disrupting the peace, or impeding growth?" She gulped, sending a pang through Adda — *You make your daughter cry.*

Cia took a deep breath, regaining control. "I know how much you care about your research, but it's been years of nothing to show. There's work you could do on the Southern Continent. Research positions in the capital, where it's safe. You're in danger here — don't try to deny it!"

Adda started to argue back, sputtering in her effort to find the words that could communicate her urgency, but Cia banged her tea down, cutting her off. She reached out to uncurl Adda's fingers from her own mug. "I love you and I'm afraid for you. Please come home with me, Ma. This isn't worth it."

There was a long pause before Adda said stiffly, "They have no right to do anything. New Beginnings didn't even have the right to incorporate, officially."

Cia dropped Adda's hands and put her head down on the table. "That doesn't seem to bother them." Even muffled, her words rang with fear and frustration.

Adda had no answer to that. Cia was right, but she didn't see the real problem. *If I can't make my own daughter understand...*

She pushed herself to her feet. "You need to see for yourself. Come on."

"What? No, Ma..." Cia's protests disappeared as Adda went into her sleeping quarters to find better clothes. She was damned if she was going to let Cia mother her about gloves again.

It took 10 minutes for them to reemerge into the afternoon's chill. Cia had taken one look at her mother's outerwear, sighed deeply, and redressed herself for the elements. She followed Adda with an expression of long-suffering filial piety. *Fine.* Adda would take filial piety when she couldn't get authentic understanding.

Outside, the land was sere and rolling, irregular brown with patches of frost and the simple fungusoid varietals that were this planet's only plant parallels at this latitude. The sky above was big and deep, with thin skeins of clouds wisping across it.

Cia grimaced after they climbed into the little skimplane. "It smells like a bad batch of fertilizer."

Adda shrugged dismissively. "It's just old. Let me concentrate." The skimplane was putting her through seconds of flickering controls. Her stomach clenched. It was possible she'd missed something when she checked for sabotage this morning. She closed her eyes and mentally ran through everything she'd checked: seals, power-cells, flight mechanism, stabilizers —

The hum of the engine drive coming online interrupted her frantic listing, bringing her back to the present. Adda sighed in relief and Cia in impatience.

The horizon expanded below them as they climbed in silence, until Cia couldn't keep her peace anymore. "Ma, if you wanted to fly, we could have taken the sat'."

"Just look," Adda said, slowing the skimplane to a near-hover. Cia glanced down obediently.

At this height, the patterns on the land were easy to notice. There were the hills and gullies made by eons of landmasses pushing against each other, and the irregularities shaped by wind and this planet's scant waters moving the dust and crumbles of stone and biomass, but within the chaos-formed shapes were others — regular lines that cut across the surface of the world in mismatched arcs and segments, appearing and disappearing like poorly erased cursive.

"Think of the years they've been here," Adda said. "Think of the ages. And we came in three generations ago, spreading and spreading as humans always do. Now half of them have gone still and dead."

Cia started to say something, swallowed down her words with an effort, and put her hand over Adda's on the flight controls. Adda bit back frustration. She didn't want Cia's sympathy for her sentimental mother. She guided the skimplane back down, towards her recording site.

Adda ghosted the little craft down with the utmost possible care, so that they barely felt the settling contact with the earth. Rationally, she was aware that the evidence of harm to the cetaliths came from intense and prolonged impacts — the vibrations caused by large-scale construction, the drilling and digging that came with building energy-efficient sunken habitats and mining for the resources to support them. Irrationally, though, she didn't like the idea of adding insult to injury.

Adda tried to unobtrusively scan signs of disturbance as they disembarked. Her site closest to town had been torn apart last week, perhaps by the same enthusiast who had left their mark on her hangar. It was a relief to see that no one had come out this far. She turned back to find Cia, who was raising an eyebrow at her.

"Looking for something?"

Adda forced a grin. "Don't give me that sass. I haven't shown you anything yet." She clambered up the nearest curving slope. It was regular as the exterior of a tube, a convex arc that ran away from them for a handful of meters before disappearing into the earth. Adda dusted away the thin loose dirt with her hands (the fungusoids were not dense enough to contribute much richness or permanence to the soil), shifted a plastofiber shield that she had laid to keep out the elements, and let herself down through the hole she had painstakingly tapped in the stone.

Going by feel, she found her work lamp. Once lit, it revealed a tube-like tunnel that disappeared into darkness in both directions. Its diameter was perhaps three meters; Adda stood on a platform that she had constructed to avoid the drop to the curving floor. There was a low hum in the air, a faint rumble just on the edge of perception.

She helped Cia climb down and they set off, Adda carrying her lamp and Cia trundling dubiously in her wake. The tube curved to the right and slightly down, so the light from the opening disappeared before they had gone 100 meters. The interior surfaces were smooth enough that Adda could have walked in darkness without stumbling, but she kept the light trained on the ground in front of them, for Cia's sake. The humming continued, so low that it felt more like a pressure on the ears than a sound.

After a while, Cia said, "You've shown me pictures, Ma. And recordings."

"Witnessing is different," Adda said, and kept walking.

They reached the cetalith — #32 in Adda's research notes — after about 500 meters. Actually, it was 512 meters from her tunnel entrance, and 8 meters from where Adda had left it a week ago, going by her last marks on the tube walls. #32 was really booking it. Adda held the lamp up in silence, letting Cia take it in.

The cetalith was an immense bulk reaching up over their heads, perfectly filling the diameter of the tunnel it had made. Its irregular surface, rocky and hard as the planet itself, trembled slightly, but that was all. Its forward progression was not visible, and its moving parts, cilia that tore away the earth it swam through, were microscopic and buried in the recesses between it and the surface of the stone. Adda's earliest research had focused on those tiny, piston-like appendages, which ate away at the stone and earth of the cetalith's environment, allowed the rubble they produced to be ingested through the feeding cracks in the cetalith's forward-moving side, created the long tube it left behind, and caused the rumbling vibration that marked its passage.

It was impossible to tell the age of a living cetalith. Their digestive processes meant that they took on the mineral profiles of their surroundings at the same time that the silicate structures of their outer surfaces sloughed off with their movement, adding to the stony composition of the paths they delved. Those paths could be found running through layers of rock and sediment hundreds of thousands of years old, though. Adda had followed this particular tunnel back to where it was warped out of existence by the movements of the earth. She had seen cetalith tunnels that crossed each other, tunnels that ran together for a time, and sometimes points where two tunnels crossed and a third, new cetalith trail emerged. No one had ever witnessed behemoths meeting, though.

I need more time. These creatures don't operate on human scale. How can we give up on understanding them after a handful of years?

Next to her, Cia stood wide-eyed. Adda had a sudden memory of leading a tiny Cia out of a shuttleport gate for her first vision of the overwhelming reality of a planetside sky, the day they had arrived on Krishnan IV. Her daughter's face now had an echo of that child's wonder.

Slowly, Cia reached out a finger, before looking back at Adda questioningly. Adda nodded. "Go ahead. That's not the sort of interference that disturbs them." She watched as Cia touched the surface of the cetalith and then jerked away. Adda knew what she felt: the source of that bone-humming alien song.

"Here," Adda pulled out her handheld, and called up the audio version of her most recently collected recording. It kept the periodic, rhythmic patterns and relative intensities of the cetalith's oscillation through the earth, while translating it to a frequency within human hearing range. The noise bassooned into the tunnel, echoing away from them in the dark.

It had an irregular variation: Adda had yet to map any pattern or repeating signature in its complexity. She still had a limited data set, even though reports of cetalith song dated back to the first settlers.

The earliest builders on South Continent had spoken of feeling vibration akin to drumbeats resonating out of the stones they cut into. Adda bitterly regretted those settlers' complete lack of investigative spirit. It had been far too long before anyone had thought to make recordings, and those were compromised by human interference. Adda had spent these long years designing programs, comparing snatches and segments, consulting with seismologists and linguists, and trying to build a persuasive theory out of the conviction that this rumbling was meaningful and its source aware.

The sound washed over them for long moments, alien and opaque.

"You really believe these things deserve the world?" Cia asked. Skeptical or not, her voice was hushed.

"It doesn't matter what I believe," Adda said. "We haven't established their sentience one way or the other. There's a possibility, a space of uncertainty. If we destroy first, there's no way to ask questions later."

"Here," she took Cia's hand and laid it flat against the surface of the tunnel. After another long moment, she asked, "Do you feel that? Do you understand it? What happens if we ignore —"

"Ma, be quiet!" Cia was frowning with a sudden intensity and focus that made Adda swallow her affront and wait silently while Cia pressed both hands against the tunnel wall. The cetalith's sound was much more powerful in the earth it moved through; the vibration that transferred to a faint hum in the air around them was a call through the earth that spread outward for miles.

"Is that recording from this one?" Cia asked finally.

Adda blinked. "No. It's from 27. That's my recording point nearest New Beginnings, actually...."

Cia waved a hand furiously to silence her, the other still plastered to the wall. "Ma, it feels different now."

Adda put her hand on the wall next to Cia's, feeling the irregular hum, powerful enough this close to its source to travel up her arm. "Listen," Cia breathed, and Adda did.

The two vibrations, the recording of the cetalith amplified in the air around them and the living cetalith in the earth they touched, intertwined.

They stared at each other, eyes gleaming in the low light. Adda was suddenly afraid that, after this long, after so much wanting, she was tricking herself into imagining patterns where none existed. She opened her mouth, but Cia spoke first.

"I think there's some kind of rhythm or beat...?"

Adda pushed herself away from the wall, and set off back along the tunnel, almost running.

"Ma, wait!" Cia was nearly left in the dark.

Adda was short of breath by the time she reached her platform and her limbs were trembling. She bundled up half of the recording equipment she'd staged there. Thank goodness for secondary systems. By the time Cia followed her up out of the tunnel, Adda was already climbing into the skimplane.

"Is it like breathing?" Cia asked as they surged across the landscape, "Was that the first time you heard that?"

"They don't breathe. But the noise — all these years, I was only listening to one voice. You showed me — it sounds different when there are two of them. I need more data..." Adda's gaze flickered between the land ahead of them and the map display, which had the locations of all her recording points highlighted, along with an overlay of the cetalith tunnels she had mapped, topographically coded for depth.

She brought the skimplane down again on a stretch of ground free of distinguishing landmarks — but roughly halfway between the line of 32's path and another, almost parallel tunnel to the west, 33. Adda took a breath before clambering out. "Just bear with me on this — okay?"

"O-kay," Cia drew the word out, managing to telegraph skepticism and forbearance at the same time. "Can I help?"

Adda reached into the storage bench behind them for a hand-shovel. "I'm so glad you asked."

●

It took almost an hour for them to dig down to earth that was hard packed enough for Adda's satisfaction. "If we used an earth-mover," Cia said at one point, pulling off her hat and using it to mop her forehead, "we could be down to bedrock in half this time."

"And rain the acoustic equivalent of hellfire down on all local cetaliths in the process," Adda returned. "I'm not doing that." She continued shifting the dirt Cia was turning up, away from the hole they were creating.

Arid Krishnan IV did not have much topsoil, particularly on this continent, which lacked the forest-style growths of the south, and the earth a few feet down was so hard as to be almost indistinguishable from rock. Adda had brought all of her extra battery packs from the skimplane, as well as the recorder she had removed from the tunnel, and, most precious of all, her calibrator and "Excess Ear," the most sensitive instrument she possessed, which she usually carried with her from site to site. It took some creative fiddling to embed the Excess Ear in the dirt, connected to the secondary recorder and even more supplementary batteries. She packed loose dirt around the whole for insulation, leaving only the batteries' light receptors uncovered. She considered spraying the mound with an instant concrete for further protection, but chipping it away might upset the integrity of her recording, and it wouldn't take more than a few days to generate enough material to show — well, whatever it showed. Standing over it, she dusted off her hands. "I'm ready for dinner. Are you?"

"Ma," Cia groaned. "What's all this about?"

"I'll know when we've gotten some more information." Adda gave her daughter a hug around the shoulders. "Thanks to your help, love."

●

Adda spent the next three days trying not to speculate ahead of her data and failing to attend to Cia's conversations. Cia took her mother's abstraction with remarkable patience, cooked meals while Adda combed through her old recordings or stared off into space, mulling over the possibilities. She spent hours in a vain search for other segments that might resonate together, either played unmodified, or shifted upfrequency, like the tape she'd played for Cia in front of 32. She would have slept in the chair in front of her terminal, if Cia hadn't pushed her into bed each night.

"Now you know — what I went through — when you were a teen," Adda told her between yawns.

"You don't get to hold that over me anymore," Cia told her tartly, "Go to sleep, or you won't be able to make sense of your new data when you *do* get enough of it."

In fact, on the fourth morning, when Adda actually let herself start going over the overlapping recording of 32 and 33 — probably too soon for a really robust dataset, but she couldn't wait anymore, and, besides, there was another town hall meeting in New Beginnings at the end of the week — it was excitement rather than exhaustion that made her hands flutter over the interface. She forced herself to take deep, steadying breaths, laying out the parameters of her analysis.

The shape of what the new recordings suggested, though, was something so massive, so revelatory, that she forgot emotions, consequences, forgot even the demands of her own body, as she started to explore her results.

Some unmeasured time later, Cia leaned over her shoulder. "Well?"

Adda input a few more commands, and then sat back as a new graphic flowed across her display. "Look."

Independently, the frequencies that sped out from each cetalith through the rigid ground appeared random, without signature or repetition. In the interference between the two frequencies, though, there was something. Caught on her analytics program, it showed resonances in recognizable periods — begun in one voice and finished in another.

Adda swallowed, half afraid to put it into words. "They're responding to each other. It's communication." She tapped at the display again, entering in another set of parameters, programs that would run back through her library of recordings, correlating timestamps, searching for echoes, trying to find patterns between what she was sure now was a symphony of voices, chorusing together underground, perceptible to those beings whose rocky bulk was attuned to the faintest shiver of frequency.

That done, she pulled up another document, and began hammering out an initial report to the research group on South Continent. Cia put a hand on her arm.

"Ma — wait. Why don't you go talk to them? Come home with me for a while; take some time to discuss what this could mean with other researchers before you write anything."

Adda frowned at her. "How can I leave now? I need to follow up on what I — what *you* found. Awareness. They recognize each other. They're talking."

Cia hesitated. "Ma... I see the pattern, but communication? What's it about? Is it a mating call? Challenge? Are they sharing the latest tips and trends?"

"Of course I don't know yet —" Adda began, irritated, but Cia cut her off.

"Exactly. You just found this and, yes, it's huge, but *we don't know yet* what it means. This isn't enough, alone, to get a Sentience ruling from Cygni. If you come back with me, you can work on a paper about it, somewhere safe..."

"The cetaliths don't have time for me to do that!" Adda thought of the building projects going up in New Beginnings, the percussion of digging projects and construction spreading toxic shockwaves through the region's earth. She pulled her arm out of Cia's grasp and turned back to writing.

There was a long pause, during which Adda tried to think only about how best to describe her data.

Cia finally said quietly, "I know I can't stop you." Adda could feel her daughter's expression. "I just don't trust these settlers. They're dug in here, and they aren't going to listen to any new arguments about why they should wait for the ruling. Please come with me."

Shut up, Rock-Lover. Cia wasn't wrong. The memory of the sabotage and graffiti warnings hung in Adda's mind, its weight on her almost physical. If their positions were reversed, and her daughter revealed that she had been ignoring threats to her safety — well, Adda could only imagine her own fear and anger. She took a breath, but didn't look away from her display. "I can't not fight for this, love."

●

Cia's work-leave was up the following day, and she went back alone, resigned but clearly unhappy. She wrapped her arms around her mother before she left, and buried her faced in Adda's shoulder. "Call me every day."

Adda hugged her back and agreed, half her mind squirming with guilt, but the other half composing a new message to the Administration of Sentience Establishing Research Enterprises. There was a several-week communication lag between Krishnan IV and the nearest jump-point, a gap that had been a boon when the messages from ASERE had become more and more discouraging and she had counted on the distance to protect her from a preemptory declaration that the cetaliths weren't sovereign and the planet was free for further development. Now, though — if only she could show up in New Beginnings tomorrow with the authority of an official designation of Sentience behind her — or at least able to make the argument that this new discovery had opened some eyes at ASERE.

Cia finally released her, seemed about to say something else, but then shook her head and left with many backward glances. It was all Adda had asked for — understanding, forbearance, recognition. It was more than she deserved.

●

Adda arrived at New Beginnings at dusk. The sky was still luminous, although the sun had slipped below the horizon and the buildings of New Beginning were shadowed geometric mounds whose silhouettes hunched together. The door to the community meeting hall was open, and several figures were standing in its light, talking. They watched as Adda left her skimplane parked and approached, rubbing her hands together. She had forgotten her gloves again.

Adda recognized all of them; she knew almost everyone in town, at least by sight, after years of visits to what had once been an explorers' outpost and supply depot, and, more recently, months of visits to planning and development meetings after the town was established. They knew her, too.

She nodded at the group, but they didn't nod back, and as she came up to the door, a man who had been leaning against its frame shifted his bulk to stand in her way.

"Rock-Adda Oram," he greeted her, unsmiling. "Have you come to tell us our business again?"

"Sean Rios," Adda returned. "It's an open meeting, I believe."

Rios' frown deepened. The woman beside him spoke up next. "You're not a shareholder." She paused before adding, "Doctor," in a tone that made it almost a question.

Adda squared her shoulders. "I'm an expert witness. I have information — new information — that throws the status of our settlement here even further into question. This isn't our place, or our land. Under Cygni —"

"Oh, Cygni!" scoffed another man, cutting her off. "Not all this again. Didn't you get it all out of your system last time? That ruling's never gonna come — and if it does, what of it?" The group was arrayed against her now, between her and the light. "Why should we pack up and move back to South Continent, or, even worse, leave this planet that's been our home for generations, because of a bunch of *rocks*?"

Adda shoved her cold fingers into her pockets. "I just want to be heard." She took another step forward. The group of settlers drew together, the mass of their bodies cutting off the light from the doorway.

"Don't do it, Rock-Adda," Rios's voice was quiet, "Don't make it hard on yourself." He took a step forward to meet her, arms loose, while the rest looked on.

Adda stiffened her shoulders and glared at them all. She tried to imagine the words that would reach them, that would make them understand. Cygni's authority was lightyears away. Here and now, she might as well be voiceless: in the settlers' eyes, she was as devoid of meaning as the cetaliths. *Cia was right, and she'll never forgive me.*

Cia will listen to me. It wasn't the protection of policy or government, but it was what she had, what she could do.

She let her posture fall, took a step back in the face of their threat. Even shadowed by the light behind him, she could see Rios's smile, and it felt like a slap. "That's right, Doctor. That's a good choice."

She felt their eyes on her back as she walked away.

●

At home, she double locked the doors, and then used her terminal to call her daughter. Half a day away and to the south, Cia answered groggily, but within seconds. "Ma? Everything okay?"

Adda took another breath, steeled herself to let go. "I can't convince them, and they won't listen to me. They're making threats. No, wait — I know, you were right, but please, listen to me now. I need your help. I need the settlers to know I'm not alone up here; I need people on SoCo to know about what I've found, to believe it, to care. I know it's a lot; I know you have your own life, but this is bigger than some research project of your mother's. You saw the pattern; you felt them speak. Will you help me keep them all from falling silent?"

Cia's face on the video shifted with a mixture of emotions. Adda hoped that her words had struck a frequency her daughter could understand, that she could make her hear what the settlers were deaf to. Time that would have meant nothing on a cetalith's scale dragged by as Adda waited for her daughter's response.

Finally, Cia nodded. "Alright...." Her eyes shifted to focus on something beyond Adda's face, and her fingers came alive, tapping and shifting through her displays. "You stay where you are. I'll come get you."

Adda's heart broke a little more. "But didn't you hear what I said?"

Cia actually stopped what she was doing to roll her eyes. "I *said* alright! You want people to care about the cetaliths; you want them to understand the consequences? I'll help you tell that story, make sure it gets publicity, gets sympathy, get people to believe, maybe even commit to stopping more settlements. But that'll take time — and I'm not going to let you sit up there, vulnerable to those people. You can't make any new discoveries if you're dead. You have to leave this battlefield if you want to win the war."

Adda started to respond, but Cia didn't let her. "No! You wanted me to hear you; now hear me. I'm coming now, as soon as I get these messages off." She cut the connection.

Adda sat in the stillness that followed, letting Cia's last words echo in her head. Finally, she turned back to her terminal, opened up her analytics program. There were still hours until Cia, even traveling at top speeds, could reach her. She pulled up the newest recording, the "conversation" between 32 and 33, and tuned it to human-audible frequencies. The alien sound filled the air around her, and Adda set herself to listening carefully, alert for signatures and repetitions in the schematic on her screen. She knew this song might be an elegy. She might not be able to stop the settlement in time, and these might be the last recorded communications of two sentient beings — but Cia was right.

The fight wasn't over. There were still cetaliths who might send their resonant calls through this planet's earth for eons to come.

Chloe Smith's story "Rock-Adda's World" was originally published in Metaphorosis on Friday, 12 February 2021. See magazine.metaphorosis.com

About the author

Chloe Smith was born and raised in the San Francisco Bay Area, and she lived in Texas and Washington states, New York City, and rural France before coming back to California. She teaches English and history to 14-year-olds, which is never boring, and has worked as a proofreader, including stints for *Locus* and *Fantasy Magazine*. She has been creating stories for a long time, but pursuing writing seriously for only the last half decade or so. She made her first fiction sale to *Metaphorosis*, published in February 2021. That story, "Rock-Adda's World," takes place in her Cygni Authority universe, which is the setting for several other works, including her debut novella, *Virgin Land*, which came out from Luna Press Publishing in 2023. Besides inter-planetary science fiction, she also writes fantasy and horror, and her short stories have appeared in *Three-Lobed Burning Eye, Daily Science Fiction*, *Bourbon Penn*, and elsewhere. You can find more of her work on her website, imaginaryresearch.wordpress.com, and follow her on Bluesky @chloehsmith.

Chasing the Light

Gloria Wickman

Markus stood on the rocky hill in front of his house, neck aching as he craned it toward the sky. He'd been waiting for hours. He'd snuck early out of bed, slinking his way through the house and slipping outside into the muggy morning air. He'd climbed the hill, using his hands to steady himself as the ground slipped and slid beneath him, until he reached the highest point in the village. When the light came, he'd be the first to see it.

It came only once a year, the light, the bringer of the harvest. Markus squinted his eyes and his chest jumped as he saw it. A pinprick of light, duller than even the stars. It grew slowly, flickering and pulsating dimly like blood pumping from a heart.

Markus hopped from foot to foot, shaking his hands out as he waited for *the moment.*

The light grew brighter, then exploded out in every direction as it descended onto the land below. It rushed over the empty fields in a wave, inundating them with a warm, bright yellow glow. The dirt, plowed neatly into hills and furrows, shook and came alive as tiny, wispy white tendrils peeked out of the earth and opened their first leaves to the light.

The light surrounded Markus, covering his skin and hair in a cool and tingling mass of tiny bodies, like animate grains of sand glowing and shimmering as they darted around his face. Individually, their movement was erratic, drifting and surging one direction to another even as the swarm itself flew ever forward. But together there was a sense of harmony, no collisions between pieces of the light, each one shifting slightly to accommodate the others. A kind of peaceful chaos.

Markus blinked, fighting to look but unable to keep his eyes open, like trying to see in a rainstorm. Then it was gone. The light never lingered long. It whooshed past him and the village and down into the valley.

Markus ran. He chased after the light with a child's spirit, never doubting he would catch it, even as it faded further and further in the distance. He ran until the last of the light disappeared over the horizon and he doubled over trying to catch his breath. Sweat glistened on his forehead and trickled down the back of his neck.

He laughed. Next year he'd catch it for sure. He turned back toward the village and the sound of his neighbors singing and shouting grew softly as he returned. His mother and father passed mugs of lager to each other, toasting to the light as their crops lived a lifecycle in a day, first blossoming, then turning heavy with fruit and grain.

Markus reached for his own glass and joined the dancing and revelry the light had left in its wake.

●

One day the light stopped coming.

Markus had grown old, too old to chase after the light, but not too old to sit out in his rocking chair and stare up at the sky.

At first, Markus thought it was his eyesight going. He'd lost track of some of the old stars; it was natural he might not see the light when it was still far out. But as time crept on, uneasiness settled in his stomach and crawled up the back of his throat. Voices murmured around him in hushed tones. Parents snapped at their children to hush and quit playing.

"Maybe it's just a little late this year. Took a wrong turn at the last rock," someone said.

A few uneasy laughs answered him. The hours drew on, and one by one the people left to go back into their homes. A few were sobbing, but most just moved numbly, their necks bent toward the sky, looking for anything, any sign of hope.

Markus stayed on his porch, waiting, watching. The village slept and awoke in the same darkness that hung overhead every day the light didn't come.

The first day was for blaming. The hushed, fearful whispers turned to shouted accusations. It was the flyers that did it. They stole the light, or killed it, or did something to scare it off. People stared up at the darting specks of light in the sky, the stars that moved this way and that in an angular, incomprehensible dance — *the flyers* — and cursed their names.

One woman, words slurred with despair and drunkenness, picked up a stone and threw it toward the sky. More rocks followed. Everyone seemed to carry one in their hand. They yelled and whooped and made promises about what would happen to any flyer unlucky enough crash near them.

Markus sat on his porch, looking up at the sky.

The second day was for planning. Anger gave way to fatigue and discussions on how to survive a year without a harvest. There were some food stores. Baskets and barrels of grains and dried fruit sat in the cellars of every home, and even more was kept in the town center. Hunger would come slowly, growing and spreading like a crop of its own.

Markus worked while the village slept, loading up his handcart with all his stores from the previous harvest. He'd lived frugally, and much remained. He loaded several heavy baskets of grain and boxes of the sweet dried fruit that stained his teeth even after many weeks of being preserved. Carefully, he nestled a round terra cotta jar between two grain baskets. The jar was stuffed with nuts his niece had gifted him from her resurrection tree, the only plant that stayed alive between visits of the light, slipping into dormancy until it was reawakened by those tiny, dancing organisms.

Markus walked slowly out of town, not returning until the first of his neighbors had crept out of their homes. He waved as he returned emptyhanded to his front porch. No one asked where he had gone.

The twenty-ninth day was for math. Markus heard it through whispers. Half a year of food for two people is a year of food for one. An old man, perhaps too old to even to live to the next harvest, would be better off if he died sooner, left his resources to the younger and more able bodied.

Markus left the town on the thirtieth day. He passed by the fields, ruined by neglect and fits of rage, the neat furrows pushed over and smashed into lumps of soil and broken ale bottles. He kept walking until his house, the house he'd long pictured staying in until he passed from the world, disappeared on the horizon.

●

Markus had found the cave when he was a boy. The light had showed it to him, back when he had the legs to chase after it. He had followed the light over a ridge, stumbled, and fallen into a deep pit. Quick reflexes and a love of tumbling saved him from broken bones, but he had cut his hands and knees on the ground and hissed at their stinging. He looked above him, too high above him, at the hole and the sky desperately out of reach.

He had panicked. He felt around the walls of the too large cavern, trying to find a place to climb up and out. He'd jumped, and screamed, and tried to scamper up the walls, but he only rubbed more dirt and rock into his cuts and made his voice go hoarse and scratchy.

Hours later, he sat down at the bottom of the pit and cried. He kept his eyes on the ground, unable to look at the place above him he wanted so desperately to be. Then, in that total blackness, he saw a light. One single piece of the light that must have fallen in with him.

He stared at it as it danced around him and reached a hand out to touch it. It skittered away, and Markus felt a sudden sickness seize him, the realization that it could go where he couldn't, that sooner or later it would fly up and away and leave him behind. But the light kept dancing, floating in front of him and around him, lazily swooping side to side.

Markus watched the light flitter through the cavern, riding tiny air currents he couldn't feel. Then, impossibly, it glided against one of the walls and disappeared. Markus jumped to his feet and rushed to wear he'd last seen it.

He found a small gap, a gap not much wider than his body, which led to a narrow tunnel. Markus raced down it, bumping against the stone walls until he reached a short shaft. He looked up and saw the sky.

High above Markus, the flyers darted in front of the long, hazy clouds that astronomers said was an arm of the galaxy, stretching out with a million worlds just like his.

Markus watched the flyers as he climbed up the narrow shaft, squeezing his fingers into the jagged rock and stretching his toes out to balance. They said the flyers traveled between many strange worlds. Worlds full of air that couldn't be breathed. Worlds where the light was so bright it blocked out the stars for hours at a time and painted the sky blue.

Markus pulled himself onto the surface and flipped onto his back, breathing deeply with relief as he looked up at the sky. Staring at the hazy clouds, he tried to imagine what those other worlds would be like. A bright blue sky, and colors everywhere on the ground, as bright as when the light came. It sounded wondrous. It sounded frightening, too much good overloading the senses, the stomachache after a feast.

Markus squeezed his eyes shut for a moment to picture it, then he exhaled and got to his feet, preparing himself for the long walk home. He never told anyone about what happened that day. Instead, he'd bitten his lip, and sat quietly at the dinner table, smiling when he thought no one was looking. The cave became his secret place, a shelter when he needed to get away.

●

The trail of fire burned across the sky brighter than anything Markus had seen in two planetary revolutions. The sound, a deep rumbling wave accompanied by the hissing of sizzling metal, crashed against his chest a few moments later. The trail ended in a puff of smoke and a bang that was jarringly late, as though the world had fallen out of sync.

A flyer.

Markus chased after it. His shoes, now no more than thick wrapped bundles of cloth, sank into the ashy ground as he trudged on. His path took him near the town, but he heard no sounds as he approached, no laughter, no tears. During the long absence of the light, his world had died. It wasn't rotten so much as mummified.

Smoke billowed in the distance, inky black against the dark gray horizon. Monotone colors as desiccated as the landscape.

Markus kept moving. Past the crumbled sandstone buildings, past the bent and twisted metal poking out of the ground like withered stalks, past his own house, as ruined as the rest, the ceiling collapsed inward, the porch scorched black from an explosion, the few belongings he'd left behind stolen or scattered around the broken doorway. His chair had lost a leg, but still sat stubbornly upright, leaning against the wall to stare at the stars.

Markus didn't stop until he reached the flyer.

The flames burned themselves out before Markus arrived. Still, he felt their heat as he approached, a dryness in air that always felt heavy and wet, and he tasted smoke flavored with metal and acid. The wreck, a grotesque corpse of broken and twisted metal, had wings like a bird, and a long, slender body. Markus circled the wreck slowly, studying it.

A single set of footprints, uneven, and drawn out in long divots by dragging feet, led away from the flyer toward the rocky hills along the horizon. A drop of moisture, not water and not oil, darkened the ashy gray dust around the prints.

He'd seen enough blood in the last year to develop a sense for it. The first few times it had come with a rush of fear and adrenaline, a tickle at the back of his throat, a sudden anxiousness and need to flee. Now it only made him wary, more careful and conscious of his next move.

He needed to find the pilot. Others would be around soon.

Markus followed the tracks toward the hills. The pilot had fallen once on their way up the incline, leaving a smeared set of palm prints in the sand and another bit of blood on the rocks. Their hands looked small, smaller than the booted footprints would have suggested.

As Markus crested over the first hill, stepping carefully on the sand and rocks that threatened to pour down with each step, he saw the pilot resting on the ground halfway down into the next valley. She kept one hand pressed firmly against her stomach and breathed heavily.

Her clothes were strange. But then, what must he look like to her? An old man with a beard that hung around his face like wispy white clouds, fabric torn and mended and torn again hanging too loosely from his thinning body. He ran a hand over his hair and beard, trying to tame them a bit before he stepped closer.

The pilot jolted back when Markus moved forward. One hand flew toward her jacket to reach something, but couldn't find it. She hissed as the movement pulled against her wound, but then clamped her jaw shut in a thin, firm line.

"Who the hell are you?" The pilot hissed as she struggled to her feet, eyes never leaving Markus.

"My name is Markus," he said, offering a soft smile. "Did you fall from the sky?"

The pilot started to shake her head, and her face contorted into a frown as she looked for a lie. Finding none, she shrugged. "I guess you could say that."

"Are you hurt?"

"I'll live."

Markus bit his lip, uncertain what to say next. "I have medical supplies. And food. Not far from here."

The pilot studied Markus carefully, eyes moving quickly from his wizened face to his tall but lanky frame. Though he pretended not to notice, Markus could see the calculation in her face, wondering if she could trust him, wondering if she could fight him off if she were wrong.

"Okay," the pilot sighed as she stepped toward him. She kept her right hand pressed against her side. Blood oozed slowly between her fingers.

The pilot never complained about the distance they walked, though it must have pained her. She followed a step behind Markus and her head swiveled from him to the rocky crags and torn up fields surrounding them.

The pilot sniffed once and Markus looked behind him to see that she was holding back tears. Markus wondered how old she was, though he knew she had to be not much past twenty years. Her skin was a shade lighter than his, though still a deep, rich brown, and aside from a scar on her left cheek, she had none of the marks time had left on Markus's face.

Their eyes met for a moment, but the pilot's gaze warned him not to ask about her. Markus nodded and continued walking.

"We're here," Markus said, after a long passage of silence. He stopped in front of a large boulder shaped like a man squatting down. The rock, porous and volcanic, was lighter than it appeared, like a dried husk of a rock slowly rolling across the landscape.

Markus bent down and his spine popped softly. The pilot's eyes shifted to him at the sound. "Just my old bones," he said as he brushed a thin layer of dirt off the ground and revealed a misshapen trap door constructed of the same dull-gray metal as the destroyed flyer.

Markus yanked on the door's handle and it groaned open.

"You go down first," Markus said.

The pilot glanced uncertainly at the hole. There was a ladder, a rickety frame made of tree branches roped together, attached to a stone wall. The bottom of the pit was invisible, melting into a cloud of black about five rungs down.

The pilot glanced at Markus once more. Then she shrugged and grabbed hold of the ladder, quickly sliding into the darkness below.

Markus moved more slowly, taking three steps down before reaching back to grab the trapdoor and pulling it over his head. Without even starlight to guide him, Markus stepped down the ladder, not needing to see to know where he was.

"It's dark down here," the pilot said quietly as Markus's feet thudded against the dirt at the base of the ladder.

Markus took a couple of steps into the room and pulled his lantern from a metal crate he kept near the ladder. His hands and feet moved automatically, well-practiced with moving in the dark. A small orb of light illuminated the room as he switched it on and Markus saw the pilot standing with her hands out in front of her, ready for an attack as she kept her back pressed against the wall.

"Bit of a loose wire, I think," Markus said as he tapped the metal casing of the lantern.

The pilot stepped away from the wall and glanced around. The light only dimly reached the farthest walls, the whole space being no more than twelve paces long and perhaps eight wide. The light reflected softly off a table near the center of the room.

"Thank you. For helping me," the pilot said.

Markus nodded.

"My name's Angie," she added, shoulders slumping a bit as she lowered herself to sit on the floor.

"Angie? I had a niece with that name," Marcus said as he opened a trunk in the corner of the room and started to dig through it. "She passed on, well, sooner than she should've." He stood and walked over to Angie a moment later, passing her a roll of bandages and a tin bottle of water.

"I'm sorry."

Angie took the supplies and poured some of the water on her side, hissing as the liquid made contact with her skin. She pressed the bandages against her wound, a cut that looked much shallower now that the blood had been cleared away.

"This salve should help," Markus said as he handed her a mostly empty jar of an ash colored cream. "It's saved my life a few times."

●

"What's it like up there?" Markus asked, unable to hold the question back any longer. He slurped another spoonful of porridge into his mouth. The mixture was tasteless and soupy. He'd started adding more water to it, hoping to stretch his provisions a bit further.

Angie had stayed with him over a week. Her side was healing and uninfected and she'd grown restless, offering to repay Markus by cleaning and scavenging. Markus gave her tasks, little things that didn't really need doing, but she did each of them with vigor.

"What's it like up there?" Angie tilted her head as she repeated the question. "Bright. I never thought about it really, but it's bright." She swallowed. "You know I'd never been to a planet before? I used to dream about what it'd be like, to have so much freedom. To be able to go anywhere without walls and air tanks and pressure suits."

Markus hummed. "I always wanted to fly. Be part of the dancing lights in the sky."

Angie laughed and her spoon clanked against the edge of her dish. "We don't dance, I'm afraid. It's mostly just mining and hauling big space rocks to the nearest processing system."

"It still looks beautiful."

"Only from a distance." Angie sighed. "But it was home."

Markus dropped the spoon back into his empty bowl and looked thoughtfully at Angie. "There's something I want to show you."

Picking up the lantern from the table, Markus led Angie down a narrow tunnel at the back of the room. He heard a soft rustling behind him as the jagged stone edges of the wall scraped lightly against Angie's skin and stalactites tugged at her hair. The tunnel curved to the right, then expanded into a large, open cavern.

"It's not finished yet, but with your help it could be," Markus said, walking toward the center of the cavern.

A flyer. Nestled in the cave like a fox in a burrow, sheltered from the elements and the people that would tear it to pieces as a proxy for their anguish. Even in the dim light of Markus's lantern, the flyer was a patchwork beast, stitched and riveted together from the dead ships that had fallen before it.

Angie darted toward the flyer, running her hand along the metal wing, fingers catching in the pits and gouges that peppered its body. She reached up, grabbing the rim of the cockpit, and hoisted herself inside with a jump.

Angie slid easily behind the controls. Her hands glided over the switches and gauges and then back to the control stick. She pushed on it experimentally, feeling the familiar pressure of it tugging back at her.

"Not bad, old man," she said. Then her brow furrowed. "But how did you get it here?"

Markus laughed. "I flew it. Kind of. Mostly." He coughed.

"Mostly?" Angie asked.

"I found a wreck on the other side of ridge, about half a day's walk from where you crashed. It had been sitting there awhile before I got there, dust covering everything."

"No pilot?"

Markus rubbed his mouth. "He was already dead — murdered — when I got there. My people," Markus sighed. "My people don't act much like people anymore. Anyway, some of the metal had been scavenged off it, along with the seat and anything else people thought they could use, but the frame was intact and the engine seemed more or less alright, so I figured, what the hell, let's see what this thing can do, right?"

"That's pretty dangerous."

"I know. It was stupid, really. But I didn't care back then. The light was gone. My niece was gone. And I figured the worst that could happen was dying. And that didn't seem like much of a bad thing at the time," Markus said quietly. "So I climbed in, fired it up, and promptly got knocked on my behind as it started skimming over the ground, black smoke coming up everywhere behind me. I figured that stick thing directed it around, and I managed to more or less guide it back this way."

"I'm impressed you managed to land it down here," Angie said.

Markus chuckled and rubbed the back of his neck. "I actually tried to land it on the ridge above us but I slid and kind of tumbled in here." He glanced at the hole in the rock above them. "Bit of a pattern for me, really," he added. "It took me days to get it upright again, and I had to take most of it apart and put it back together. It got me thinking that it wasn't all that complicated after all. There was a chance I could get it working again. I've gone to a few other wrecks and scavenged smaller pieces off of them, and repurposed some of my stuff for it, but I could use another pair of hands. And a pilot to teach me to fly it properly."

Angie smiled. "I might be able to help with that."

●

"What happened to this place?" Angie asked. She lay underneath the flyer, hands caked with grease and soot as she dug through a mess of wires. She hissed as two of them touched and sparked against each other.

"Same thing that happened everywhere," Markus said. He sat under the left wing, fiddling with a blackened mass of burnt wiring and half-melted metal. "The light stopped coming and it died. Things turned ugly. Those of us that are left avoid each other when we can, fight when we can't."

Angie peeked her head out from under the flyer. "What do you mean the light stopped coming?"

"The light. *The light,*" Markus's eyes widened and the metal fell forgotten beside him. "You really don't know?"

Angie shook her head.

"It comes from, I don't know, up there somewhere," Markus gestured above his head. "Some kind of swarm from space, like tiny little bugs is what people used to say. They'd swoop out of the sky like a miracle each year and everything would start to grow. Flowers, fruits, grains, everything. Then one day they stopped coming. People gave up hope. Then they gave up on each other."

Markus sighed. "We had some food stored, of course, and there are a lot less of us running around than there used to be," Markus turned his head away. "But I'd guess we've probably got less than a year before the end of everything."

Angie bit her lip. "And that's why you rebuilt the flyer, why you rescued me. You want to take shelter in the sky."

Markus shook his head, standing up from under the wing. "No. No, I'm going to bring the light back. It's just gotten a little lost. I'm going to bring it back home."

Angie pulled herself out from underneath the flyer, wiping her hand on a dirty cloth before tossing it back on the ground. "So you know where this light of yours is?"

"No," Markus said.

"You know how to bring it back once you find it?"

"No idea."

Angie sighed. "So it's just wishful thinking, then. False hope."

Markus gently tapped his hand against the wing of the flyer. "I wouldn't say that. Sometimes you have to run after the things you don't know you can catch. That's the only way to move forward. Besides, I have you to help me now."

Angie bit her lip and grabbed another wrench.

•

Markus awoke slowly, shaken to consciousness by a low rumble that tumbled through the tunnels and echoed off the walls even as it faded into nothingness. It was only after the reverberations stilled and silence stuffed his ears like cotton that he jolted upright.

The flyer. Markus scrambled down the tunnel, feet slipping on the dirt and the narrow walls tearing at his clothes as he hurried to confirm what he already knew. Angie was gone. So was the flyer.

Markus saw a grease stain where the flyer had stood, one more black mark in a place already eaten by darkness. Markus slid to his knees. Hours passed. The light from his lantern faded and died.

•

The sky stayed dark. Sometimes Markus sat on the surface and watched the flyers dance in the sky. He wondered if any of them were Angie. He wondered if she ever looked back down on the surface to see him looking up at her.

•

When Markus was a boy, the light had seemed brighter than anything he had seen. He remembered watching it roll over the hills, coating the fields with a golden glow and sticking to every building like a glittery film.

In those days, there were colors. Greens and blues and reds and deep rich browns. It was so beautiful that he never minded that it came just once a year.

This light looked different than he remembered, though Markus couldn't say in what way. Maybe it was a bit older, a bit sicker, maybe it was tired from traveling all that way across the stars.

Markus had never seen anything more beautiful.

Markus glimpsed high overhead, drifting and growing bigger as it undulated toward him.

Markus put a hand to his mouth, choked on a sob as he watched the light move closer. Unhurried, waving and swooping to the sides and even retreating on itself before surging forward again.

Markus watched it for minutes before he heard it. He'd forgotten it had a sound, a low hum that he felt with his chest more than his ears.

The light came closer and Markus saw the first bits of color blossom on the ground.

Greens. The greens were always first. They wiggled and hopped out of the ground dancing to the hum of the light. The flowers would come next. Blues and yellows and violets blooming into red fruits.

A chorus, a hundred voices shouting and crying and laughing, welled up over the rocky hills and shifting earth. Markus's throat tickled and he realized his own voice was calling out among them, sounding out the same relief and euphoria together with everyone.

Together.

Markus hadn't felt together for a long time.

Markus heard the thrum of the flyer's engine before he saw it, a tiny splotch of black in front of the sea of light. The flyer passed overhead, and Markus saw it dragging a large rock behind it, the light melting off of the rock in waves. In the next second, the light hit him, almost blinding him as it flew past. A million billion dancers paraded around him, bringing the dead land back to life. He stood immobile, letting the light touch him and watching it flicker past.

As the last of the light flew past him, Markus turned and started to run, chasing the light until it disappeared over the horizon.

Gloria Wickman's story "Chasing the Light" was originally published in Metaphorosis on Friday, 25 May 2018. See magazine.metaphorosis.com

About the author

Gloria Wickman is a writer and lover of all things fantasy and sci-fi. She received a B.A. in anthropology from the University of Wyoming and currently works as a digital archivist transcribing and digitally preserving Civil War era documents. Her work first appeared in *Metaphorosis* in 2018 and since then she's written for Better Humans, the Writing Cooperative and others. When she's not writing, she's probably painting or working on her latest cross stitch.

Gloriawickman.com

Superbloom

Lynne Peskoe-Yang

The call comes in the evening, though it's morning on the other side of the world. K. is demanding that I leave my study right this minute to look at the sea. I grab my sample bag and rush outside, too curious to argue. It takes less than a minute for me to jog from my house to the end of the jetty.

I peer down at the surface of the water. I can't see much; the sun set ten minutes ago.

"What am I looking for?"

"Look at the water. What color is it?"

I fumble in my bag for my good flashlight — one I made myself, with a patented triple lens — and turn its ultra-sharp beam on the ocean.

"Why is it doing that?" I whisper. "Why is it just sitting still?"

"What color is it, D.?"

"Green. The whole thing is just solid green."

A long, textured sigh issues from my earpiece. "God," K. hisses. She seems on the verge of tears, but with some effort she controls her breathing.

I can't wait. "Is this that algae bloom of yours? What the hell is it doing here?"

She inhales purposefully. I hoped she'd have to pull herself together to correct me, and it works; when she speaks again, her voice is steady.

"Not algae. It's a lichen — or it was when I started studying it. I've got no idea what it's doing there, other than growing. I'm still making sense of it myself. Do you remember my dissertation?"

Of course I remember. A year ago, K. printed out that dissertation and mailed it to me personally, neatly stapled and, I thought, perfumed. I read the abstract a dozen times before I gave in and called. She explained it all to me, in her laughing-brook voice, with a patience I hadn't been shown since I was a girl.

She had found me in a directory of remote researchers and wrote to ask me to photograph some of the lichens in my little biome, which was, she pointed out meaningfully, on the exact opposite side of the world from where K. herself lived, in New Zealand.

In the dissertation K. had referred to the floating, living islands that popped up along the northwestern coast as "ur-lichens", or, in more casual contexts, "super-lichens".

It was the second name that caught on in her small collective of Māori ecologists, the only ones paying attention at first. The super-lichen was a local disaster, overshadowed by the death rattle of the oceanic coral reefs. The collective relied on a growing network of citizen scientists to track the expansion — what they came to call the Bloom — as it spread unchecked along the coastline.

K. had volunteered to make contact with someone who could keep the last watch, as far away from the origin as possible. My island outpost, her own antipode, would mark the finish line for a fully global superbloom, if it ever got that far. I didn't ask her what good it would do anyone to know how much of the ocean was lost at that point. I don't think either of us expected that such a thing could actually happen in our lifetimes.

When the Bloom began to move down the northwestern coast of New Zealand, K. packed up her belongings and moved with it. She still called me occasionally to ask for updates from my side of the world. I would take the call on my headset while I worked the glass.

"A fungal spore sends its hyphae into the algae," she'd say, drawing out the Greek ending — *hy-fee* — in a grin that I could almost see. Through my headset I could hear her, even while I sanded finished prisms or made coke fuel for the forge. Sometimes she asked me about my work, but I had no talent for translation.

Instead, I sent photos, both of the growing lens and the lichens — no samples, she said, as the risk of contamination was overwhelming. I also sent her tools. Funding was scarce for lichen-watching, but I had all the raw materials at my disposal to replicate and improve every piece of glassware K. needed, and shockproof shipping was free under my contract. When K.'s digital microscope was stolen, I sent her a replacement — a bespoke mechanical version from my own workshop, with a hardwood carrying case, hand-engraved with her initials.

After that, the calls were daily. My ears adapted to the sound of K.'s voice and listened for it even after we hung up. I could not help but absorb her passion, her creeping panic, over the terrible might of the Bloom. Alone of ocean beings, it seemed to delight in the spiking acidity caused by human pollution. The Bloom was so good at growing, so blazingly energy-efficient, especially near the surface, that huge mats of it emerged in shallow waters around dozens of islands in the South Pacific. Where they met the coasts, the floating mats merged, surrounding whole archipelagos in swamps that turned alarmingly toxic.

I asked K. how it reproduced.

"This one doesn't," she said. "It only grows."

●

This is what I learned in those months of building: a lichen is not an organism, but a community of organisms acting collectively. The photosynthetic members, single algae cells or long strands of sun-loving cyanobacteria, feed the fungus via the hyphae, which penetrate the algae's cell walls to extract their sugars. In return, the fungus offers a safe habitat for its support organisms. Together, the hyphae and the photosynthetic cells make a single continuous unit of life, self-replicating and infinitely adaptable.

"On its own, the fungus is a clump of hyphae. It can't form any discernible structures. It dies."

"So the fungus is a parasite?"

"We'd have to ask the algae."

•

We passed good months this way, her calling, me listening. She was my favorite sound.

Then the Superbloom took the rest of the ocean in the course of a single night, twenty years ahead of schedule, and K. called me again.

"When I woke up this morning, I thought my satellite feed was broken — the map was just covered." It's hard to process her words.

"...But if it's reached you already, we're long past any way of stopping the spread," she concluded.

I listen to the birdsong through the phone: a kookaburra's alien laughter. Behind it, the wind is high, as it is here. I can see the first storm of summer growing on the horizon.

The kookaburra falls silent. I wipe my eyes with my forearm.

"Is there anything we can do? Maybe if...?" I trail off, unable to even frame the question.

"You should stock some food," she says gently. "If I think of something, I'll... I'll let you know."

It's fully dark now. The vast, pale expanse could almost be the natural ocean, if it weren't for the disturbing stillness of it beneath the starless sky. I feel panic rise, tightening my lungs and heart.

"Oh, and D.? Are you still there?"

I cough, force my voice deeper. "Yeah."

"Don't touch it."

•

The Caldera is the perfect place to light a beacon, and I was once the perfect person to keep it lit. My technical training is in photonics, the art of manipulating and redirecting light. I was one of the first to build lenses from gadolinite, the oily black mineral that makes up the base of the Caldera, though I did it in the comfort of my childhood home on the mainland. But I was losing patience with the frantic pace of manufacturing; I was ready for a quieter life.

By then, I had made some friends in government, and one of them shared my name with the Bureau of Scientific Engagement, a collaboration between government scientists and propagandists. Riding a wave of investment in space ventures, the project aimed to thrill the nation by building a self-powering radio beacon that would send an eternal message to alien worlds. Previous communications to the extrasolar expanse had been ephemeral: a five-minute transmission from the North Pole of spoken greetings in two hundred Earth languages; a gold disk embossed with Da Vinci's naked eight-limbed man and some other things, launched into the sky. The time had come, in the BSE's opinion, to make ourselves known to the universe on a permanent basis.

A simple transmitter would emit a continuous wavelength: a hundred mHz, just energetic enough to escape the atmosphere. My job would be to build and then maintain a lens out of gadolinite thermal glass, a form of passive solar power. The lens would both concentrate the signal into a narrow beam and power itself virtually forever, storing solar energy in a solid-state battery that fed the same monotone signal, even at night.

I was to build the whole thing on-site, on a colonial outpost with no other lucrative resources to offer, nor remaining residents to exploit. The Caldera is an empty-named place, a safe enough distance from real human civilization that the mainland, at least, would have warning, should the worst occur. What the worst might entail, we did not discuss.

●

The day after the Superbloom starts the same as usual, and it's not until I look out the window that I recall what has changed. The Caldera is a narrow island, curled like a fetus against the sea. To my left, the bulk of the island, a great crescent of steaming jungle, pours down into the bay as always. But the basin itself is deathly still, suffocating under the weight of a mat of new life that extends, waveless, to every horizon.

It's hard to look at.

Above the Bloom, on top of the hills on the opposite end of the crescent island, the black, flat-topped needle of the signal tower is barely visible from here. It's been three months since I got it running, and two months since I hauled my personal items to the opposite side of the island from the tower, into one of the last remaining buildings on the island. The tower was starting to make my head buzz.

I check the monitor: the signal is fine. A one-note performance, without even the texture of an ending, communicating the bare minimum of reality. The beam moves like an out-of-control spotlight, the focused radio waves sweeping around the planet as it turns, carving out curly ribbons of space in their near-random search for a receptive target. In the early days of the project, there had been some talk of sending out a message with actual content, even a simple greeting. But then one of our physicists showed that if we stuck to one frequency, the signal could easily reach the nearest galaxy cluster and would likely be detectable at twice that distance. The programming team was furious, but *intergalactic* sounded better than *interplanetary* in the headlines, so the one-note message won out.

●

My contract gives me a year of watch after I finish construction, but already it is impossible to picture life on the mainland. No word has arrived from my supervisors, but that doesn't surprise me. Will I last nine more months here, without supplies, without a plan? I do not dwell on this.

That night, I make my first discovery.

"The Bloom emits light." My words echo on the other end. Does my voice sound different to her because she's listening to its inverted form — across the world, upside down, in broad daylight?

"I thought I was seeing things," she whispers after a moment.

"I see it, too. It's clearer at night, but even in the light it's pulsing. Why?"

"I don't know." Her voice is hushed, hurried, as though someone might be listening. "It wasn't doing this even a week ago, but this Bloom changes so fast. If it were to somehow recruit some new microorganism, something that glows..."

"A third colony member?"

"It's possible. We wouldn't know. But there are hundreds of bioluminescent species."

"Why do they glow?"

"Camouflage. Prey attraction. Signaling to the predators that eat *their* predators."

"Would that look like... a pulse? Rhythmic?"

"No. It's purely responsive."

"Doesn't the pulse remind you of a heartbeat?"

"Yes, of course."

In the green expanse of the bay, a field of little leaflets drinks in the dimmed sun. On the far side, straight across the bay, the black crown of the signal tower looms like a purposeless alien.

"Does the Bloom, or some part of it, *have* a heartbeat?"

"Absolutely not."

•

Later, a call from the department: deliveries will be suspended for the time being, given the circumstances. I do not have to ask what the circumstances are. All around the world, I imagine, human beings are attempting to negotiate with the invader, touching and hacking and plowing, growing more desperate for a response. But the Bloom will not hear them, any more than I would hear a threat spelled out in plant hormones.

I tell him I have enough food for a few months and not to worry about me. There is shouting in the background, but I can't make out the words; the call ends, thankfully, before I get invested. I am sensing already that I shouldn't spend my panic on people I already know. It is easy to forget them; what could I do for them from here?

•

The sky is sickly green in the evening when the light begins to pulse again.

One-two. It is unmistakably a heartbeat, reborn as two flashes of incandescent plant-flesh, and yet no part of the Bloom could possibly have even a vestigial memory of having a heart. I count eighty beats per minute: a healthy resting heart rate for a human.

One-two. The rate does not change. If it's a message, it is insultingly simple. There is no hint of frustration, no pleading, no aggression; just a double-tap of light, repeating endlessly. A beacon reporting back that conditions are normal, stand by. *One-two.* A binary code too flat to be called communication. In Morse code, I recall uselessly, it is just the capital letter *I*, over and over and over, stupidly iterating into the dark.

I am here. Are you?

●

I creep to the edge of the Bloom. From the jetty, I drop a rock into its depths, as I often did when the ocean was still liquid, and watch the surface roll away from the impact in a stunted parody of wave motion. If I close my eyes while doing this and pay attention only to the splash, I will remember that there is still water under there.

I squat, scooping a handful of black sand from the beach and letting it pour from my fingers onto the curling leaves of the colony. No ripple at all. The living matter absorbs the motion, stunts its impact, so it can't be transferred. The motion is born locally, dies locally; sound, spoken prayer, would be stifled the same way.

But the Bloom *is* connected to itself, somehow. The pulse of the lichen at my feet is perfectly in phase with the pulse at the horizon. Light, then, can cross the channels from one end of the Bloom to the other. The Bloom is not a creature, but a culture; light is its language.

I don't know any words in light, but I don't think that would matter, if I could make some kind of deliberate pattern. The intent to speak is its own kind of speech — the astrobiologists taught me that. As long as the signal is clearly *meant* as a message, it is one.

●

"Fine," says K. when she calls back, too early. She woke me up. "Fine. It's sentient."

"I told you. There's no other explanation."

"Hm." I can hear her pacing. "Yes. But that doesn't mean —"

"Why are you so worried? This is a good thing. Maybe we can reason with it."

"Not good. Unprecedented. Bizarre. I can't even philosophically wrap my head around it. The pattern makes intelligent life unmistakable. Why would a living being advertise its existence like that? What takes that kind of stupid risk?"

"You're the one who's studied it. What do you think?"

She exhales. I can hear her brain working. "I think... whatever it is, it doesn't know we're here. Yet. But it's looking."

"I'm going to answer."

"With the beacon? Is it moveable? I thought you couldn't redirect the beam."

"I can do it. I just never had to before."

"Okay. Okay. But D., listen. This is not a conversation with a person. Sentience is not the same thing as a brain. I've been studying this thing. It evolves faster than its components, faster even than some viruses, but it also started pulsing all at once, like a single organism... If this is intelligence, it's clearly distributed — spread out in the body of the Bloom, coordinated, but not centralized. It is *nothing* like us."

"What is it like?"

"God. Fuck. I don't know. An octopus?" She's close to tears. "Who knows what it would do if it recognized another intelligence? And you want to give away your position, before we even know what will happen! What if it takes the signal as a threat? What if it *answers*?"

Her voice is so plaintive, so childish, that I half want to shout at her. *There is no other option!* But I can't say that. She knows.

For a moment I consider telling her I was planning to come see her when my contract was up, but even thinking the words makes me want to howl.

Instead, I tell K. I love her, and then I hang up in a hurry so I don't have to hear her sob.

•

In the evening, I trek north. I weave among my discarded shipping containers, most twice my height, their steel now coated in the rich green of a kudzu infestation at least a foot deep on every face. The vines are flowering on the southeast side where I approach; I breathe in clouds of grape-like perfume as I pass each cluster of white and purple blossoms.

The place steams with life. Between the blocks and everywhere the vines haven't claimed lies a thick carpet of mosses in varying shades, from pine-green to chartreuse and golden yellow. Already, beneath my boots, the fragile stalks of a bryophyte have been crushed into wet salad.

I need my flashlight to find the ladder on the far side of the tower. I hover on the bottom rung, waiting for the doubts to come; but my wonderful brain is silent, and I hear nothing but the wind through the leaves. The top rung is covered in seagull scat, so I have to haul myself onto the platform beneath the beacon like a sea lion. I turn off my light and recover there for a few moments, with my back against the thin railing, staring upward.

The sky is clear now. The compound lens of the beacon looms over me, its outer rings glittering with reflected stars. The pieces are arranged in concentric circles, like a slice of a giant black onion. Each layer is made of two to thirty segments of gadolinite glass.

It is impossible to tell by sight that the signal is firing. I pass my hand over the opening in the center of the onion slice, and imagine that I can feel it, a sort of metaphysical buzz; but I know I can't actually feel anything, as surely as I know the signal exists. The beam, even concentrated by my lens, is both silent and invisible to me.

I pull myself up with a groan and stretch upward to run my hands along one of the rings. The dark glass is warmer than I remembered. The smaller rings are closely nested and hard to differentiate by starlight, so I work my way inward by feel. Just below the innermost ring, attached to the pole that supports the beacon's weight, there is a latched metal box, unlocked.

The terminal inside is still charged. I power it up and it chirps softly, as though it recognizes me. Black letters appear against the green-grey field: I N P U T ?

My mind is empty. I turn away from the beacon and nearly lose my balance. The railing, rusted from the salt spray, groans but holds steady for now. How is it up to *me* to decide what to say to an alien from my own planet?

It has stopped glowing, I realize as I stare into the sea, so it's possible I've missed my chance, but somehow, inexplicably, I feel that it is actually aware of what I am doing and has simply paused to wait for my answer. *Impossible!* I can almost hear K. say in response.

I picture her on the other side of the world and feel my spine straighten a bit.

I take great, gulping breaths of the briny air. I reprogram the beacon.

I fiddle with latches in the dark. The lens is twice my wingspan and half my weight, but at least the whole thing comes off its mount without so much as a screwdriver. I hoist it onto my shoulder like a parasol and then lower the circular end to the platform, feeling my long trek across the island screaming in my kneecaps. When I stand up, the beam is pointing just below the horizon, its waves colliding with a distant section of the Bloom's vast body.

The Bloom is still as stone. In the silvery light, the world looks primordial, as though made of just-cooled magma, unmarred by soil or water. But I know the Bloom is there and watching me, in its own way; it holds its breath as I hold mine.

We watch each other.

Just where the beam hits, a part of the Bloom begins to rise. But this is an illusion: it is simply luminescing, first there and then all over, the whole field of it suddenly turning white with light — far brighter than before. In seconds I'm forced to cover my eyes with my arm, but it's not enough.

I wake up on the beach a few meters from the tower, my whole body aching from the fall. The world is still flashing around me, so bright I can almost hear the new pattern: the same one I chose moments or hours ago.

Long, short, long. *K*, the Bloom is saying, shouting, singing, to me and to her, and I can feel her amazement radiating straight through the center of the Earth.

Lynne Peskoe-Yang's story "Superbloom" was originally published in Metaphorosis on Friday, 1 January 2021. See magazine.metaphorosis.com

About the author

Lynne Peskoe-Yang is an author and freelance journalist based in New England. Her writing is informed by an abiding passion for ambiguous technologies and the humans that make and wield them, for better or (often) worse.

Joy (Unplugged)

B.C. van Tol

A reddish moon clung to the horizon like a faded blood stain that wouldn't wash out. Joy shivered, looking at the moon's human-like face from her attic window, wishing she could pull him to her. Together, they could agonize in this lonely house atop the hill. From afar, his mouth hung agape, as though wailing in silent operatic sorrow. The silence pervaded the dark, motionless town nestled in the valley below. From Joy's vantage point, the town seemed nothing more than a crumbling diorama of miniature homes and shops. After being alone for over a year, Joy wondered whether she'd ever see anyone again.

She switched on her electric candle and placed it on the windowsill in the attic. The soft yellow glow served as her beacon to those who might Detach in the night, stumbling confused and withered into a reality they'd long since abandoned.

When her eyes grew weary, she climbed into bed beside a row of pillows arranged to look like another person already asleep under the covers. She slid her arm around a pillow, tracing the scars in its casing where she'd sewn its many rips and tears. It wouldn't survive much longer, she knew. And if the solitude continued, neither would she.

"Goodnight," she whispered, clinging desperately to the pillow. As if in response, the centuries-old house creaked eerily from a passing breeze. Some sound was always better than none.

Nobody came that night.

•

Joy arose at dawn, kissed the top of her pretend pillow person, and retrieved the candle from the attic. It was a clear day, and she could see the town's distant clock tower. Its hands had given up at 8:34 one April morning before her twenty-third birthday. That had been over a decade ago.

Beyond the town, standing like sentries in an enemy army, were the giant wind turbines that generated the energy supply for the town's Virtual Lifestyle Attachments (un-affectionately known to Joy as ViLiAs). A network transmitter column glowered like an emperor in the center of the turbine field. The column was responsible for luring the townspeople into a completely customizable, full-sensory trance. The sun glinted off its steel armor. A red light blinked at the top, taunting her the way the moon did.

Because Joy was the sole person not participating in ViLiAs and had no wind turbines of her own, she pedaled on her stationary bicycle, which charged the battery in her electric candle. The house, devoid of all other electricity, had once belonged to her grandmother. When the ViLiAs claimed Joy's mother as one of their earliest victims, Gran had stripped the house of its appliances and wiring, even going so far as to plaster over the old electric sockets.

Gran once said, "Humans got along just fine for thousands of years without electricity."

But humans always had each other, Joy thought as she pedaled. Not for the first time, she considered whether it was worse to live a fake life with real people than a real life with a fake pillow person.

At least Gran had kept a wind-up record player and a hodge-podge collection of vinyls. Joy let Chopin soothe her loneliness as she tended the garden for the rest of the morning.

In the afternoon, Joy baked a loaf of bread in the wood-burning stone hearth built into the house's original foundation. She kept her windows open so the scent of baking would drift outside. Someone out there might long for fresh food.

That evening, she practiced on Gran's upright piano. She'd left the front door open so as to fill the hillside with music. The sun had begun to set, and she could hardly see the black and white keys in front of her.

During rests in the music, she heard footsteps stumbling onto the porch. When she turned around, a man loomed in the doorway. His clothes hung like rags, and his head seemed loosely attached to his gaunt frame.

She rose, her movements slow though her heart raced. The Detached were like skittish, starving animals. His eyes scanned the living room while she leaned awkwardly against the piano. "I've food," she offered, hoping she didn't sound as desperate as she felt.

When he took a tentative step forward, she ventured into the kitchen and put a plate of bread and jam on the table, eagerly listening toward the door. Then came the sound of his feet shuffling across the wooden floors.

When he took a seat, she resisted the urge to sit beside him, to not-so-accidentally brush his hand as he reached for the jam. Patience is a curse, she thought, as he ran his fingers over the bread, getting jam on his fingertips, as if not quite sure it was real. He would have been accustomed to neuro-simulated taste, since the ViLiAs fed people bland, liquified nutrients through a feeding tube. Of the food sludge, there was endless supply, since everything was recycled through biowaste tubes and re-processed in underground factories overseen by robotic machinery. Joy shuddered.

Fastidiously, he ate, inspecting every morsel, even the crumbs on the plate. After the bread was gone, the man sat for a long time with his eyes closed. Joy knew better than to disturb him. Most Detached persons took a while to distinguish reality from what they had conjured and customized as part of their Virtual Lifestyle package. She gazed through the kitchen window at the last sliver of sun descending from view and listened as the birds outside quieted into their nests.

When he looked up again, she said, "I have a spare room upstairs. You're welcome to stay." She left out the word 'forever'.

A curious-minded Detached person might stay a week until the Withdrawal became unbearable. With fortitude, they might survive Withdrawal and stay a month before something else called to them — a sense of adventure, a sense of fear, a sense of loss. Eventually, they all left.

The man seemed to consider her offer. He had probably forgotten what it meant to feel tired. Or feel anything at all, for that matter. He opened his mouth to speak, but only air came out.

"Your voice will return with time. Come, you could do with some rest."

Though he stood a foot taller and would have been formidable had he not wasted away, Joy had no fear of being raped. According to Gran, ViLiAs made men impotent. Sometimes permanently. It didn't matter, however. Once Attached, anyone could experience every pleasure in a virtual setting. Even have virtual children.

They ascended the stairs by the light of Joy's electric candle, their bodies casting long shadows on the wall. When an animal screeched somewhere in the night, he jumped, grabbing onto the railing.

"Just an owl," she said and then showed him to his room. Before shutting the door, she added, "It helps to listen to the sound of your breath. It's a reminder that you're still alive."

Without the usual sense of gloom, Joy climbed to the attic and placed the electric candle in the window.

•

The next morning as she tended her garden, she glanced up at his window and saw him gazing at the woods behind the house. His expression resembled that of a lost child. Her heart felt an invisible bond extending to him, as if she'd reached out her hand and he'd taken it.

Oh, to feel the touch of a hand! she thought. The last human contact she'd had was a brushing of arms one year, five months, and three days ago. Joy kept a written log of such things. The other arm belonged to a Detached woman who had stayed with Joy for four days and then mysteriously left in the night. Joy blamed the woman's departure on the physical contact. The Detached seemed unable to endure it in the first days after returning to reality.

This day, the clouds were plentiful, and she could smell rain in the air. Just as she finished picking green beans, the first drops fell. Inside, Joy found the man standing at her fireplace mantle, entranced by a photograph. She said, “That’s my grandmother. She raised me. In this house, in fact.”

He turned and studied Joy, not realizing or maybe not caring that to inspect another human being was once considered rude. She took the opportunity to study him as well. He had somber deep brown eyes, but also sallow skin and plump lips hidden beneath a scraggly, brittle beard. Matted dark hair dangled from his head. He scratched at it with bony hands.

“I’m Joy,” she whispered.

His voice was barely a rasp. “I’m...MightyAugust8501.” He frowned, something not quite right. “I mean August. Just August.”

She guessed he’d not used this name for many years.

He pointed to Gran in the photograph, his eyebrows raised as if to ask where Gran was.

Joy said, “If you look out the window, beyond those trees is a clearing where sunbeams fall through the branches. Gran used to say that the sunbeams looked like the silk of her wedding dress.” Joy sighed. “Have you ever felt real silk, August?”

He shook his head.

“I buried her in the wedding dress in that clearing. Carried her in my arms all the way. After the sickness, she weighed so little...” Joy’s thoughts trailed off. She knew she must be careful. Sorrow was a dangerous companion for someone so often alone. “Anyway, that was eight years ago.” Eight years, one month, and twenty-two days. Nine Detached visitors in all that time.

Later, August sat on the couch, while she played the piano. At first, he covered his ears against the sound. Joy took no offense. When he lowered his hands and began to sway his head from side to side, she smiled because it meant his soul hadn’t died.

“You’re welcome to stay as long as you wish,” she said.

That night, after August retired to his room, Joy climbed into her own bed next to the pillow person. For a moment, she put her arm around it. It smelled faintly of mildew and felt rough against her skin. Joy shoved the pillow person onto the floor where she stomped on it until its scars opened and it bled stuffing.

"Never again," she said.

•

When she awoke the next morning, she found August again in front of her fireplace mantle, admiring a different photo. Tears streaked his cheeks.

"Is something wrong?" She curtailed the urge to hug him, to wipe away his tears and stroke his matted hair.

"Do you have children?" he asked.

"No, that's me. I'm four years old, sitting on Gran's lap at the park. Back when the park wasn't a wind turbine field. It's the last picture ever taken of me."

Over breakfast of bread and jam, he asked, "Why do you do all this for a stranger?"

"Don't worry. You don't owe me anything."

"Why?" he said more forcefully. Charity was not a trait of an addicted society. Kindness would have been to him like a strange dream.

"It's what I do," she said.

He crossed his arms, unsatisfied.

"It's a long story."

"Good," he said.

With a sigh, she settled into a chair opposite him. "When I was little, people finally began to realize how addictive ViLiAs were, and some addicts decided to Detach on their own. Gran and I took in several of these people over the years. Nobody else was around to help. We showed the Detached how to return to a natural life. Or at least, we tried."

In truth, Joy and her gran had helped nearly three dozen Detached work through their Withdrawal. Of those, four had died in the process. Those who survived eventually left with their newfound lives or invented some excuse to go back to the Attachment. "Now Gran is buried in the clearing, where the silken sunshine comes in. I continue our work all by myself." Joy shrugged. "It's the only life I know."

"Will you take me?" he asked.

"To the clearing?"

"I want to see the silk."

Later, they walked through the woods, crossed the stream in their bare feet, and climbed the hill to the clearing. August's face filled with wonder as he cupped one of the silken sunbeams falling through the branches above. Then he did something he hadn't done yet: he laughed, a shuddering breathy sound that made Joy think of new life coming into the world.

"I didn't think the sun could feel soft," he said, amazed.

Joy laughed, too, despite herself. A patch of light covered his head, and she could see color returning to his cheeks. Good, she thought. He'll need to be healthy for what comes next.

After dinner, Joy put on some records. She began with the classical, spritely Mozart. Food for the soul and the making of a good temperament, Gran always said. August bobbed his head to the music.

●

The next morning, she gasped when she saw him. He'd trimmed back his beard and had given himself a haircut. Joy could hardly recognize him, but despite the unevenness of his trimming, he less resembled a feral animal and more a person.

"I found a pair of scissors in the bathroom," he said. "I couldn't take the itching anymore. Before, when I was Attached, I remember scratching, vaguely, like it was someone else's itch. Eventually, I scratched so much I must have knocked off my electrodes, because I woke up gagging on my feeding tube."

"It must have been terrifying." Joy outstretched her hand to give his shoulder a comforting squeeze. He tensed at her approach, and she whirled around, ashamed.

Breaking the tension, he pointed to a bowl on the kitchen table. "I picked you some strawberries. I wanted to do more. For you."

Then never leave me, she would have replied.

He tapped some keys on her piano. "Is it hard to learn?" he asked, pressing a shrill tone cluster of notes in the highest register. He winced and withdrew his hand from the keys.

"Yes, but if you enjoy playing, you don't notice it's difficult."

"Like the Attachment," he whispered.

Joy played a happy tune from memory. She had forgotten its name, but it reminded her of the stream's delicate surface and how it caught the sun's reflection, making it dance. When the song ended, she saw through the living room window the waxing moon hanging romantically in a clear sky full of bright stars.

"I can't hear the moon's terrible singing when you're here," she said. "He looks almost peaceful now. Like a child yawning before sleep."

August appeared wistful for a moment. "When I first Detached, I was so disoriented that the moon frightened me. I wandered in the woods for I don't know how long, trying to hide from him under the trees, but he was always watching. Then I heard your piano, and I saw the light in your window. These did not frighten me, so I came here to you."

Instinctively, Joy grasped his hand. The touch sent reverberations up her arm and down her back. August cried out and yanked his hand away.

"No! I'm sorry!" she said, horrified at what she had done.

August clutched his hand to his chest protectively, his eyes darting to the front door.

Please stay! she wanted to shout, but the situation required calmness. Softly, slowly, she said, "You probably haven't experienced human touch in many years. Touching another person isn't the same as using your fingers to eat or feeling the sun on your face. When you've been deprived of it for so long, a first touch can hurt. It hurt me as well."

"I should do more for you..." he said, slowly extending his hand back out to her, cringing and wrinkling his nose like touch were a bad smell. The temptation to take it again was almost more than she could bear.

She shook her head. "It's okay."

He dropped his hand, clearly relieved. "Perhaps tomorrow," he said.

"Perhaps."

●

When she woke the next morning, she could not find August anywhere in the house. At first, the seeds of panic grew, and she worried her transgression had caused him to flee in the night. That is, until she found him outside crouched over the stream, his hair glistening with water. His cheeks had more health than she had yet seen, and he smelled fresher.

"A bath?" she asked.

He nodded. "I can't sit still today. I could hardly sleep last night."

He did not offer her his hand again this morning. She would not remind him. Not now, at the first signs of Withdrawal: restlessness, sleeplessness. By tomorrow, he would have the headaches. The day after, the sweats, the body aches. And the next day, fever, shakes, or even... she didn't dare think it.

She set him to pulling weeds in the garden while she picked some lettuces. He pulled a few and began to stare out into the direction of town. She followed his gaze to the network transmitter column, which occasionally winked at them with its red come-hither beacon at the top. If only she could snuff it out.

"My gran always said to look in the direction you are headed."

August hastily pulled some more weeds. "Have you ever tried ViLiAs?"

"No," she said. She feared such discussion would only keep his mind on the subject.

"Oh." His gaze returned to the network transmitter column.

Jealous of the column's continued hold on August, she said, "I do know what it means to feel unbearably restless." Once more, she had his attention. She wiped some sweat from her brow with her sleeve and continued working as she spoke. "In my late teenage years, I had boundless energy and found I couldn't sit still. I argued with Gran constantly, something I'm ashamed of now, but at the time, I had no idea what had gotten into me. Gran patiently let me rant or put me to labor-intensive chores to burn my energy off.

"One day, as I stood in this very garden, I heard the clock tower chiming. I felt the pull of the world beckoning me to explore it. That day, I said to Gran, 'I need to leave and make my own way.' I thought she would put up a fuss or forbid me. Instead, she kissed my forehead and sent me off with a loaf of bread and a flask of water." Joy still remembered Gran's warm, firm kiss on her forehead.

"Where did you go?" August asked, leaning forward.

"First, I went into the hills, but then the hills turned into bald-faced mountains. I was not so foolish as to think I could cross them alone, so I turned and wandered the forest for a time, living mostly off berries. I realized very quickly that with freedom came loneliness. I became homesick and wanted nothing more than to hug my gran."

"Did you go home?"

"No. I was stubborn. Instead, I went into the town."

"What did you find?"

"More loneliness. Not a soul walked the streets. No children played outside. Most windows were boarded up completely. Eventually, I came to a cottage on a street lined with fallen trees. I imagined it was once charming, but the grasses had grown so high that the cottage appeared short and stubby, like a dollhouse for a child. It had one window that was not boarded, and I peeked in. A person lay on the floor of the front room — a woman so emaciated I could not have guessed at her age. She would have looked dead, if not for one trembling, outstretched arm reaching for something not quite within grasp. You see, despite having tumbled from her couch, she was still Attached. Her ViLiAs face mask was still in place, and sensory electrodes dotted her body. Then I noticed what she reached for — her feeding tube, which had evidently fallen out some time earlier.

"I just couldn't understand it. Was her addiction so strong that she would starve to death, inches from nourishment because she couldn't Detach for mere seconds to save her own life?

"I banged on the window. 'Take off the mask!' I shouted. If she heard me, she showed no sign of it. Had I known better — or perhaps, had I not been so lonely — I would've left her there. Instead, I broke the window, and I climbed in. Then I made the mistake of Detaching her."

August grimaced, evidently remembering the shock of his own Detachment.

"The woman screamed so loudly that it echoed through the valley. I expected the police to come or neighbors to check on her."

August shook his head. "I don't suppose anyone did."

"No," she replied somberly. "It gets worse. I grabbed the woman by the shoulder. 'You need to eat!' I told her. The jolt of Detachment and the sudden human contact made her berserk. As I tried to calm her, she clawed at me with nails that hadn't been clipped in a long time. Then she bit my arm." Joy rolled up her sleeve and showed August the shiny depressed scar where the woman had taken a healthy chunk of flesh. "When she bit me, I dropped her on the floor. There was a horrible thud, and then she was still. I thought I killed her. I panicked, bleeding. I put the Attachments back on her and re-inserted her feeding tube, in hopes it would coax her to stay alive. Or at least relieve the suffering I'd caused in trying to help."

"Did she die?"

Joy shrugged. "I sat next to her the whole day, just watching her breathing to make sure it didn't stop. Hours later, when it started to get dark, I put my hand on her chest to make sure I could feel it rise and fall. I sang to her to drown out the moon that stared, judging me, through the broken window.

"By nightfall, the bite in my arm had become swollen and infected. I held it up to the moonlight and saw two red lines under my skin creeping up to my shoulder. If I stayed with her much longer, I knew I'd die of sepsis, so I left her there on the floor. I went out into the night, looking for Gran's candle in the attic up at the top of the hill. I stumbled for hours, following that little flicker of hope, fever shaking me and pus weeping down my forearm. I followed the candle, ashamed of myself, terrified Gran would never forgive me."

"Did she forgive?"

Joy shut her eyes, remembering. When she'd reached the house, the clock tower had struck midnight. She saw Gran's silhouette standing out on the porch.

"She asked me, 'Joy, have you learned anything in your travels?' I knelt down before her, half in fatigue, half in penance, and I said, 'I've learned more than I care to.' Gran helped me to my feet, embraced me. 'I can hear it in your voice. Come inside now. You're home.'" Joy could still feel her gran's arms around her, and her eyes misted over.

August gazed back toward the network transmitter column once more, a different air about him, as though seeing his past clearly for the first time, seeing the terrible fall of humanity from which he'd dragged himself.

"Home," he said, slipping his hand in hers.

Joy felt as if she'd won her first true battle against the network transmitter column, still blinking at her with red scorn.

●

The next day, Joy awoke to find August pacing downstairs.

"I can't sit still. Every time I stop moving, I think my bones will crawl out of my skin. What's happening to me?"

She examined his eyes. They were bloodshot and had dark circles beneath them. His breath was snappy. "It's the early stages of Withdrawal."

He resumed pacing. "I keep thinking I'll die unless I re-Attach myself. Like there are invisible cords wrapped around my arms, pulling me back to it..." His speech became so rapid that she could no longer understand him.

"You must eat. Your body needs the fuel."

After he wolfed down some bread, she put a feather duster in his jittery hands. "You see the fireplace mantle? Start dusting there. When you're done, do the bookcases. After that, the cabinets. If you can't keep still, keep yourself busy."

"I'm scared," he said, taking her hand.

"It's normal," she assured him. It was the best she could promise. There was still a chance he could die.

While he dusted, she began to prepare enough food to last several days. When he finished dusting, he asked her what to do next. So, she handed him an axe. "My wood pile is getting low," she said, pointing to a fallen tree. "If you get dizzy or breathless, stop."

Though he didn't appear strong, the Withdrawal restlessness evidently gave him enough energy to wield the axe. Grunting with each swing, he chopped the wood until he stumbled away from the tree in exhaustion. By that time, most of the afternoon had passed.

Joy helped him back into the house and up to his room. "Something's wrong," he said, his voice unsteady. "My heart keeps skipping, and I feel a shadow creeping toward me."

"Do you still feel like your bones will crawl out of your skin?"

He blinked down at her from his tired eyes. "No."

"See? You're doing a fine job. Now just rest."

His breath came in rapid, shallow waves while she watched over him from a chair beside his bed. Eventually, he slept.

Joy did not put the candle in the attic window that night. She kept it at August's bedside, along with a basket of bread and a pail of fresh water. He awoke in the night writhing and sweating. She put a cool compress on his forehead. He vomited, and she cleaned him. Sometimes he spoke in desperate tones. "Let me go back. Just for a few minutes..."

"You're too sick to go anywhere just now. When you're better, you can go wherever you want," she said.

"Everything hurts. My eyes hurt. My teeth hurt. The air around my body hurts!"

"You're purging addiction from your system."

She dripped some water onto his lips, and he licked it off, eventually drifting back to sleep. The next day, he spent hours curled in a ball lying on his side, moaning, shivering with fever.

"I'm dying," he said. He grabbed the sleeve of her shirt, ripping the seam at her shoulder. "Am I dying?" She could not deny it. "I need to go back. Please... Let me go."

He tried to get up from the bed but discovered his legs could not carry him. He fell to the floor and screamed in pain. As she rushed to help him back into the bed, he began to thrash wildly, and she worried he'd bite her.

"You tricked me! You made me swing the axe so many times that it sucked the life from me. You did it on purpose to keep me here!"

She knew it was the Withdrawal speaking, not her August, but it hurt all the same. Gran had always warned her not to get too close to the Detached — to become Attached to them. "They will pull you down with them," she had said. "You can do your best to help, and at the end of the day, if you manage to save one, that will fulfill you more than anything." However, Gran had always had Joy. What did Gran know of utter desolation and the wretched, humiliating need to cling to another living soul?

"It's not fair," she whispered once August had fallen asleep again. Joy ran her fingers over his cheeks.

When August woke next, he could hardly move. His lips had cracked, and the whites of his eyes had turned blood red from burst capillaries. He had fever rashes on his neck and chest. "Joy?" he said with a scratchy voice.

"I'm here."

"It doesn't hurt anymore. Will you tell me a story?" he asked, his eyes drooping. "Please."

Her arms ached from the days and nights tending to him. Her head throbbed from lack of sleep, and her back had grown sore from sitting in a wooden armchair while he slept. In their moments of shared pain, Joy had felt more connected to August than ever. Her August.

"Tell me about your parents," he said.

"It's not a happy story."

"Please." He held out his hand, and she wrapped her fingers around his.

"I don't know who my father is. Gran told me that someone took advantage of my mother after she became Attached. I was the result. My mother carried me to term, delivered me, all without Detaching once. The doctors said she'd miscarry if she went into Withdrawal. I was born healthy enough, but the birth coupled with addiction took a toll on her body. Gran, for the one and only time, hooked herself up to the ViLiAs to ask my mother what name to give me. My mother named me Joy. That's all I have of her. She died two days later."

As August's eyes filled with sorrow, Joy regretted telling him such a mournful tale. In a happier tone, she continued. "Gran said that my mother adored Beethoven's 'Ode to Joy,' and that's where my name came from. When I was a girl, I used to make Gran play the record over and over."

"I would love to hear it."

Joy set up the record player on the floor by his bed, put "Ode to Joy" into the spinner, and let it flood into the room like a pink and yellow sunrise dancing over snowcapped mountains.

At the end, he said, "This music is everything that is life. It doesn't lie or give false impressions."

Joy nodded, realizing for the first time that the song — and therefore her name — was as much a warning as it was a gift. Her mother had wanted Joy to live. To not follow in her footsteps.

Then he cried, "Look what I've done to myself! I don't know how I could have ever chosen a Virtual Lifestyle over this one. Or how…" his voice trailed off.

She wanted him to say, "Or how I could ever go back," but he didn't. Even now, she could sense something still tying him to his old life.

Give it time, she thought. If he survived this night, he would certainly pull through. Moreover, if he pulled through, he'd probably stay several more weeks. Then maybe, just maybe, he would be the one to stay forever, and together, they could continue the mission of saving the Detached.

August fell asleep once more, looking ashen as the moon. She did not take her eyes off his rising and falling chest. Sometimes his breathing became so shallow that she put her hand to his mouth to make sure she felt the exchange of air. Then he simply stopped breathing altogether.

At first, she thought it was a trick of her eyes. After all, she had been awake for days. She jammed her finger into his neck and felt a weak, uneven pulse. Screaming his name, she shook him, hoping he'd wake up. When that failed, she pumped his chest with her hands as Gran had taught her to do. She poured her own breath into his lungs, wishing it would pass some of her life into him. She did this until he coughed and sputtered.

Heaving, sweaty, and tear-streaked, she sank back into the chair, fully drained of the last energy in her reserves. She resumed her pulse and breath vigil, fighting the urgency of sleep with the fear that if she gave in to her sagging eyelids, she might awake to find him dead. She prayed there would be no need to resuscitate him a second time, for she simply did not have the strength.

Eventually, sleep claimed her as she slumped in the chair, her neck craning to one side. When she opened her eyes, the sun shone on August's slack face. She leapt up, fearing the worst, then she saw his chest rise. She saw it rise again and then a third time. They were full, restorative breaths. A finger to his pulse confirmed his heartbeat had returned to a normal pace. She took his hand, and sleep consumed her again.

●

This time, when she woke, it was still daylight. Or had she slept so long that it was daylight again? August was no longer in his bed, and a blanket had been draped around her shoulders. She got up from the chair, her knees sore and wobbling.

"August?" she called down from the top of the stairs. He did not respond. Hanging onto the railing to support her cramped legs, she descended to her living room.

"August?" Again, no response, and she despaired. Could he, after all they'd just endured, have returned to his Attachment? Surely, it would kill her.

Joy flung open the front door and nearly knocked August off the porch.

"Oh, you're awake," he said. He had tucked a single wildflower into the pocket of his shirt.

"I thought you left." She smoothed her hair, relieved she had been wrong and feeling guilty for having doubted him.

"No," he replied with an air of hesitation. She sensed an invisible "not yet" strung to the end of his thoughts. He looked out into the brightness of the day and faced the town. Drifting clouds cast blobs of shadows over the clock tower, the wind turbines, and the relentlessly blinking network transmitter column.

"How do you feel?"

His eyes still focused in the direction of town, he sighed wistfully. "Like I've just been born."

"Come inside, let's eat. We both could use the nourishment."

They shared a meal in silence. When it was over, he turned to her. "I'm sorry for how I behaved. For the things I said. The things I did. I'm ashamed."

She flitted her hand. "It's nothing. I've seen it before."

He knelt before her on the floor, taking the flower from his shirt pocket and holding it up to her. The delicate purple petals had already begun to wilt.

Joy swallowed hard, sensing the approach of bad news. "Shall we listen to some more records today?" She did not take the flower.

"I've been alone my entire life. Physically alone, but I never noticed it. Emotionally, mentally, I've had the entire world full of people just a brain wave away."

"All digital tricks and lies."

"Yes. But it was all I knew for many years." Their eyes met, and he touched her hair, tucking the flower behind her ear.

She didn't want to hear any more. As she pulled away from him, he grabbed her shoulder.

Joy squeezed her eyes shut. "Don't."

"I have to leave here, Joy. My wife..."

She felt her throat constrict.

"...my wife is back there. I know our marriage was virtual. The life we built, the home we made... all fabricated."

Joy shook her head violently.

August sobbed. "Even our children..."

She could take no more, and wrested herself free. She ran to the living room and wilted into the couch.

He followed her. "My own children are not even real! Can you believe that? In the ViLiAs, it seemed normal. But out here, my soul is sick from having spent years of my life caring for people... things... that don't exist. These beings created in my image, with my eyes and my chin." His voice broke.

He went to the photographs on the mantle and picked up the one of Joy and Gran at the park. "I'll never have pictures with my children. I'll never truly be able to hold them in my hands." He held his hands out to her. "Joy, I've never even looked upon my wife with my own eyes. Never caressed her cheek or kissed her lips. Never touched her hair the way I've touched yours. I don't even know if she looks the same as her avatar in the system. I modeled my avatar after the real me, but that's not a requirement. She lives here in our town, but we've never met."

"So you'll go back to her — to the Attachment — after all this. Fine, then."

"I'll beg my wife to Detach. Convince her to join your cause — our cause. Will you help me?"

Joy crossed her arms and turned away. "I've always said you're free to go. Everyone leaves."

He took the photograph of her and Gran and pressed it into her hands. "You don't understand. This picture has inspired me. I'm disgusted by how much I've missed of life, including the chance to have real children. Not perfect digital representations of them. I want to clean up messes and argue over stupid things and teach them about life. You can't teach a computerized child — it already knows everything."

Joy shook her head. "But you won't be able to have real children. Not without a fertility doctor."

"After I bring my wife back, we can rescue doctors, neighbors, friends. Let's save our town, Joy. You and I can do it. We'll continue what your gran started."

She rolled up her sleeve and pointed at the scar from when the Detached woman bit her arm. "It doesn't work that way," she said through clenched teeth.

"I have to try. I just..." he ran his hand through his hair. "I can't not try."

"You're free to go."

"I promise you, Joy." He cupped her face in his hands, and for a moment, she thought he loved her. "I promise you," he said, emphasizing every syllable. "I will come back."

"Take some bread with you," she said. "And a flask of water."

August nodded, and then he left. When he shut the door, she ran to the window to watch him walk into the folds of the town below in the valley. "He'll never come back," she whispered. When she turned around, it was there — all the silence and loneliness that had been hiding since the day he showed up.

Joy gritted her teeth and got on her stationary bicycle. "No sense in milling about." After, she boiled his bedsheets and hung them to dry on the line. The breeze and the sun would infuse them with crispness and remove his scent. She'd simply start over, just as she'd always done. She washed her hair and let that, too, dry in the remaining sunlight before the sky turned pink and orange.

When night was certain, she took the sheets from the line, folded them, and put them away. She cut herself a slice of bread, and though she had no appetite, she forced herself to eat it, one nibble at a time. Joy tried, and failed, with each breath to push the memory of August's face from her mind. Not just his face, but all the hopes she had pinned on him.

Finally, she took the candle and climbed the stairs to put it in the attic window. August is down there somewhere, she thought. Down there with the rest of the world while I remain alone forever.

In her room, she found the pillow person still wounded on the floor where she'd left it. Her bed was empty. Her house was empty. Her heart was empty.

Instead of searching for sleep, Joy climbed into the attic. Then she shoved the candle out the window. The little orange glow fell like an ember until the glass crunched against the ground, snuffing out the light.

In the darkness, in her nightgown, she found the axe. She threw it over her shoulder and followed the blinking light of the network transmitter column. The lure of her enemy beckoning to her. Daring her to make her last stand. Alone, as always.

Above her, the moon gaped with silent laughter.

B.C. van Tol's story "Joy (Unplugged)" was originally published in Metaphorosis on Friday, 28 August 2020. See magazine.metaphorosis.com

About the author

B.C. van Tol was grown in the Garden State. In her spare time–when she's not writing–she avidly consumes science fiction and fantasy in all forms. She also enjoys dabbling in watercolors and hiking with her husband and rescue dog.

Radical Abundance

Angie Lathrop

Something woke me. A sound.

I rolled to my back. Sand and rock ground into my shoulders and my skin hurt everywhere and my lungs seemed too dry to work properly. But for a moment I forgot all that, because when I looked up, there was a silver bowl over the still landscape. The sky mirrored the desert and the desert mirrored the sky and everything was pale and beautiful.

Dawn was like that in the desert. Translucent and unearthly for a sliver of an hour before sunrise, but bright with heat and blasting sky the rest of the day.

From somewhere, goats bleated pathetically; probably the sound that woke me. Perhaps roused too early from their caprine dreams. I wondered what a goat might dream about.

The sky glowed. The sun broke free of the horizon. And then the heat, again.

I tried to blink away the grit but I didn't have any tears left. There was no shade, and the sleeveless tunic I wore was no protection at all. I didn't belong in the desert; my skin, normally so pale it was almost translucent, was blistered and weeping, and my hair, long and silky white, was matted and heavy with sand.

Not far from me were tracks; maybe an old road. Tourist buses used to come to the desert to see the sights — old caravan stops; crusader castles; cities that were ancient even before the Roman legions marched here. But the drought was vast and terrible; mythic, world-destroying, like a Biblical Flood in reverse.

I didn't know where I was; in this shattered place borders and alliances shifted like the sand. People moved restlessly, dogged by war and famine and uncertainty.

More bleating and the skittering of tiny hooves. A shudder in the air, and for a second I was certain that it was my butterflies returning to help me, but it wasn't. It was funny, because they'd never been gone for so long before, and I couldn't imagine what had happened to them. If they didn't come back soon I would die. People can't live in a place like this without a lot of help.

I closed my eyes against the terrible whiteness. The goats were close now. I could smell their warm bodies, and then their dry little tongues touched my cheeks.

The world spun. The goats cried out in a way that could break your heart. I could see sparkles of light behind my closed lids, so beautiful.

●

I woke up in an inside place, so dark and lovely that I would have cried with relief if I'd had tears.

A striped tent, the woven sides flapping in the breeze. A man was there. He trickled water into my mouth and I choked because I couldn't swallow right. He was patient and after a while I could drink.

He was dressed in pale robes, his hood thrown back. I couldn't tell how old he was, but he wasn't old and he wasn't young. His eyes were very dark, his brow furrowed.

He might be one of the new nomads. The dispossessed, who wandered stateless and unprotected, trying to stay ahead of war and drought.

The world went away and I forgot about being thirsty.

When I woke up again, the man was kneeling by a little fire in the center of the tent. He heated a pot while I watched from where I lay curled on a pile of woven rugs.

It was strange to smell coffee after days of the scentless desert, and although I wanted it my stomach tightened into a hard knot.

He noticed that I was awake, and he spoke to me in English.

"What is your name?" he asked. He repeated the question in Hebrew and then, after a pause, in Arabic.

I could understand all of the languages, but I answered him in Arabic. He seemed surprised. I was surprised, too. I didn't remember speaking Arabic ever before.

"Legion. My name is Legion."

He frowned, probably thinking that perhaps I said it wrong or mistranslated it, but if he lived in another place he would recognize what I am simply by the kind of name I have.

I shut my eyes again. It made me tired to think about telling him, because if he didn't recognize my name then he probably didn't know anything about the kind of person I was, and it was a lot to explain.

●

His name was Musef, which made me smile, because it means rescuer.

He was curious about me, but wary. He wondered how old I was, because although I was small, I didn't speak like a child. His confusion was understandable because the truth is complicated: people like me are ageless.

He asked me many questions in many ways — why were you here, who left you to die in the desert, where are you from — and I explained that I couldn't remember.

At first he thought I was lying, but after a while, the way he spoke to me changed. He was gentler, and I could tell he thought there was something wrong with my mind. That I was born this way, or that I'd been injured, fundamentally, by the desert.

That wasn't it. I was just different, in ways that I did not have the capacity to explain. I wanted to answer his questions, but people like me have a different way of remembering. My memories are like water in my hands, and strange knowledge, like fluent Arabic, often bubbles up from what seems to be my very vast subconscious.

“I was sent here to help people,” I kept repeating. He found this to be unconvincing and he asked me about my past: where was I born, where was my family, were they looking for me.

I could only look at him hopelessly. For people like me, the past is nothing and the future is a mirage. Only the now is in clear focus.

He gave up on questions, and I watched while he tended the fire. He got a stew cooking, and then flattened bread and put it right into the coals. He gave me a cup of thick warm milk to drink while we waited for the food.

I could only eat a little, but it was the best meal I have ever had. I was hungry, but it also had to do with the care he took and how he watched to see if I liked it and how he looked pleased when I did.

•

In the morning, he was outside when I woke up. I heard him speak to the goats and then the scrape of their hooves and their excited bleats, and then there was only the wind. I didn’t like being alone in the desert again, but I was too weak to get up and follow him.

He was gone for a long time, all day. When he came back I nearly wept with relief.

He made a fire. We brushed the ashes from bread and ate it. We drank coffee from tiny cups shaped like half-eggs.

I was much better, and restless in the tent, so he took me out to see the animals. The camels didn’t like me — Musef said they didn’t like anyone — but the goats were fascinated by me. I sat down and they crowded around and I laughed when they nibbled at my hair.

Musef was amused at how much I liked them. He caught the tiniest one by a leg and put it in my lap.

Its mother stared at me with her odd yellow goat eyes, but the baby rested content in my arms. I petted it and wondered how Musef had known that I would like it. I suspected that when your job was herding goats and you occasionally killed and ate them, you might forget how adorable the littlest ones can be.

•

I watched Musef very carefully, everything he did, and after a few days I knew how to do all the chores that you have to do in a desert camp. It made me happy to finally be useful, and it seemed more likely that he would let me stay if I were not such a burden.

He was guarded at first, but after a while I could tell he was getting used to having me here. He talked of taking me to a border and sending me back to where I came from, but everywhere here was dangerous. I told him that I didn't belong anywhere and that no one was looking for me, and although this was all true, he was skeptical.

I liked being with him, and it was comforting doing the same thing every day. Eat, take care of the animals. Get water, drink, shake sand from the rugs. He gave up trying to get me to tell him about my past; instead he told me stories from this land: heroes, lovers, monsters. His voice was a sweet thing in this wild, hard place.

One night he took me into the desert and it was phosphorescent and milky, no longer terrifying like it had been when I was alone and dying. Another day we climbed a ridge at dawn to see the flat turquoise swath of the Dead Sea, and that same day we watched the desert turn dull red under a bloody sunset.

Later, there was a spatter of rain, and I looked up astonished, which made him smile.

"You're easily amazed," he said when I was thrilled to find out where the milk we drank came from — the camels! I laughed as he showed me how to milk one and I said that sometimes people resist amazement.

•

I stayed with Musef, weeks, maybe even months, but it was hard to say because people like me don't mark the time like regular people. And time was hard to mark because each day was the same, except that sometimes we packed everything up and piled it on the camels. We would walk for a day or more until we were in a place with good forage for the animals and then we'd set the tent back up. We never saw a town or another person, and it got even hotter as we went deeper into the desert.

•

One evening we came over a rise and saw a terrible thing.

I stood still, unable to react, but Musef went down to where the bodies were. He checked carefully for signs of life but there was no hope. Men, women, children, all dead, all partly covered with the shifting sand. Their tents and belongings were broken and scattered.

After a while, I walked down to where Musef was looking at a machine that had been smashed into pieces. It was a portable atmospheric water generator: I knew what it was because I often made them for people who lived in the desert.

There were more nanotech artifacts scattered about: medical packets; an empty pouch of high-nutrient nectar. Sturdy desert tents of impossibly light and strong fabric, the kind that can assemble themselves and unfold like living origami.

I was very tired all of a sudden. Seeing those artifacts triggered memories. It was clear that I had met these people and given them these things, and then they had died because of it. This tragedy was my doing.

Musef came to me. “We need to go,” he said. “We can’t help them, and whoever did this may still be nearby.”

“I gave them these things,” I said. “This was what I was doing. Before you found me.”

He shook his head, not understanding.

“No, not you. This things were made with a molecular assembler. Little machines that can make anything out of atoms.”

He mistook my silence for incomprehension. “You see, there are patrols, looking for people who have these illegal devices —”

“I know what they are: machines that make what people need — they can make anything at all out of almost nothing.” My voice was full of outrage. “They can’t keep this technology from people who are desperate.”

He looked at me strangely. “Governments are afraid. If people can make anything at all, then how can they be controlled? And economies collapse. Trade alliances mean nothing and that causes instability. And instability leads to war.” He looks at me with very dark eyes, like he did the first day. “More war than there is already.”

I scowled at him, stubbornly, and shook my head. “How can someone do this? Kill these people when they were only trying to live?” I kicked the smashed water generator. “You can’t tell a parent of a dying child that they must wait for society to adapt to unlimited resources.”

I didn’t like this conversation. We’d never spoken to each other like this before; in our tent in the desert we didn’t speak of things like molecular assemblers and post-scarcity economies and the collapse of governments, but we were speaking of them now. We both knew more than we had let on.

He shook his head. “In the wrong hands, these devices are the ultimate weapon.”

“I know.” I picked up an empty clip from a carbon-fiber assault rifle and turned it over in my fingers. “I should have made them something better. A rocket launcher. A bomb.”

I could tell he still didn’t understand: he thought I was confused, upset.

“We need to go,” he said, and he turned back toward our tent.

As I followed him, I nearly stepped on a thing that looked like a scrap of white paper mostly buried in the sand.

I picked it up and the little machine flexed its delicate wings weakly — disguised as a butterfly, it was one of the thousands of molecular assemblers that I had left here to make things for these people.

I brushed the sand from its solar panel wings, and it crawled over my palm, tasting my skin with a curled tongue.

It recognized me.

I cupped it carefully in my hands and it thrashed against my fingers. If I let it go, it would get the others, so I had a choice: I could crush it and keep living this life I had grown used to with Musef, or I could set it free to go and bring the others.

Musef called to me to hurry, and I slipped the butterfly into my pocket.

We walked through the night, putting distance between ourselves and the massacre. Neither of us said anything.

I helped him set up the tent, but I was shaking, and that made my fingers nearly useless. He had to retie knots I'd done. Later I spilled the coffee all over the rugs, and tears welled in my eyes.

I was confused: I didn't know what was wrong with me. People like me aren't like this; we don't have sadness the way regular people do.

Musef was upset, too, but when he reached out and laid his fingers lightly on my wrist, I jerked my hand away.

I felt worse, then, because he looked more unhappy, but I don't like being touched.

I was overwhelmed with regret at the sorrow on his face, so later when he laid down on his rugs I went over to lay down next to him.

He was surprised, but he didn't make me go back to the other side of the tent like I thought he might. It was uncomfortable to be like this, so close that I was warmed by the heat of his skin, poised in a place I didn't belong.

He touched my hair, very lightly, just for a moment, and that was okay.

Then, for no reason I could understand, he told me about his family.

He'd had a wife and three little children. They'd been in a refugee camp, cut off from the rest of the world by blockades and soldiers and minefields. He'd taken them there because he thought it would be safer, but like so many places it turned out to be a trap.

He told me how he stole food from people who could not live without it. How he let other children starve to try to save his own. Finally, when things became unspeakable, he found a smuggler to take them out of the country, but the man took their money and left them to die. Musef lived, against his will. He would have died for any one of them but that was not how it happened.

Later, he hunted the smuggler down and killed him. That man had a family, so those children probably died, too.

Finally I understood why Musef was here alone in the quiet of the desert. I didn't know why I hadn't guessed this from the start.

I asked what their names were, and he told me in a voice full of anguish.

He spoke for a long time, telling me things he'd never told anyone, sometimes weeping and sometimes icy cold.

There was nothing I could say, and no way for me to comfort him other than by simply lying there next to him, my hands curled between us like tiny animals.

Eventually, exhausted, he lay like a man beaten to near death. I listened to him breathing for a long time. Once I knew he was deeply asleep, I silently stole out of the tent.

I lifted my hands and released the butterfly. It flitted in loose circles around me until it acquired the satellite signal it needed, then it darted off to the north.

●

Before dawn, the rest of the butterflies returned.

They skittered and scratched at the tent, trying to find a way in. I heard them, and I was instantly awake. Musef woke, too and he was on his feet as I got up.

"Stay here," he whispered to me. He had a gun in his hand, because he thought he could protect me.

"They are here for me," I said. My throat was tight and my voice was not mine.

We stepped out into the frenzy of translucent wings. The largest were hand-sized and the smallest mere specks of glitter. Most were luminous and pale but if you looked closely you could see the rare flash of sapphire.

When they recognized me they got more excited and become a blizzard, and there were so many of them that it was hard to see anything else. The goats bleated unhappily and bunched together and the camels pulled at their tethers. Butterfly wings brushed against my skin, each touch barely felt but with so many of them it was overwhelming.

They were relentless and would only get more determined until I did what they wanted, so I stepped away from Musef and lifted my arms.

The butterflies flocked aggressively, like autumn birds in places where it was cold in winter, and they jostled each other as they found their places and fitted together. Some burrowed into my hair, but most clung to my shoulders or trailed down my back, and then the rest of them climbed on and formed long chains and sheets.

After a few minutes of rustling and tickling, they were all where they belonged. I watched Musef's face as he finally saw me as I am.

The illusion of wings must have been powerful in the moonlight. The butterflies' delicate bodies all tucked in place, arching up from my shoulders. Soft and layered over the tops, and then chains of the smallest ones stitched together to make flight feathers that drooped almost to the ground. Both wing structures lightly in motion, balancing themselves and gently swaying.

Musef's face was stricken. If I were a real angel, I suppose I might have performed a miracle, just to break the tension, but the miraculous things I could do took time and weren't necessarily visually stunning.

For Musef's sake I stifled my whimper as they penetrated my skin at my shoulder blades and all down my spine. Their tiny nanowire feet searched for the interface fibers and then each butterfly's body glowed brighter when it connected to my nervous system.

They'd been gone so long that my body wasn't used to them anymore, and their connections made my muscles twitch and then contract hard. I shut my eyes and let them do it, but it was very painful and I was sorry that Musef had to witness this. I felt him next to me, saying my name, but there was nothing that could stop the butterflies.

This was torture for Musef, I knew, and he seized a butterfly and crushed it in his hand. "Don't," I said, but he did it again and my ears were filled with a roaring and my vision went to bloody red.

I'd never thought of the butterflies as something you could love or hate, but I hated them then. Not because of my pain, because that was necessary, but because of Musef's, which was not.

"I heard about someone like you, once." Musef's voice was barely audible. "They caught her and burned her alive."

He swept his arm and brushed the butterflies off by the hundreds. But they were smart and there were thousands of them. And they were quick, so as soon as he raked his hand down my side they were already crawling back in place.

"Who did this to you?" he asked, and I could tell from his tone that he had an idea of me strapped down, held against my will. Changed — with a knife? — into someone not quite human.

"It wasn't like that," I said. I was losing the clarity of thought needed for normal conversation, but I wished I could explain: the ultra-strong and light carbon lattice instead of bones. Artificial glands that made drugs to take away fear and shame and leave only a sense of purpose. A practical symbiosis with the tiny machines, to make the perfect vector to infect the suffering with radical abundance.

Pain, yes, plenty of pain but a good kind: cleansing, atoning. Just the right thing for a person stained by guilt.

But it was impossible to speak with my heart fluttering wildly and my pulse in my ears. I fell, hard. My cheek struck the ground and I tasted blood. Musef spiraled away from me and the desert closed in, white and blazing and terrible.

●

Musef was carrying me, my cheek bumping lightly against his chest. The sun was fully overhead, and I was burning.

I shivered despite the heat and Musef held me tighter. The butterflies were everywhere, dragging and tangling under his feet. They whipped against our faces like pale ferns.

He took me up to the top of a ridge where the wind was stiff and the sky huge and blue over the parched-white land, and he set me on my feet. I was unsteady, but the butterflies fluttered and kept me upright.

I turned my face upward to the sky, into the hot wind. I flexed my wings and thought of flight.

It was the butterflies. My nervous and endocrine systems were saturated with their wanderlust and I wouldn't be able to stand it much longer.

I pulled a pale butterfly off and set it in Musef's hand. I show him its tiny but complex body and the nectar that beaded from its tongue. "An Angel can live on just nectar for a long time," I explained. "As long as they have sunlight and air and water, the butterflies can make it. So an Angel is never beholden to anyone for food." I was tempted to drink some, because thinking about nectar made me hungry for it, but the butterflies were settled and I wanted to reassure Musef, not startle him further with Angel feeding behavior.

"Legion."

The way he said my name made hurt my chest hurt. It was hard to breathe.

"I can have them make you whatever you want," I said. "All they need is some matter to take apart and put back together." I glanced around. "Sand, maybe, but carbon is best. They'll forage for whatever elements they need."

He shook his head. "What would I want?"

That was a good question. Usually the people I met were suffering, and they always needed something, although they often didn't know exactly what it was. But Musef was perfect and whole and I couldn't imagine him living in any other way. And the only thing he wanted, for time to be rolled back to avert a tragedy, was beyond the capabilities of even an Angel.

My wings quivered. "Everyone needs something."

"Not me."

I resolved to not look at him anymore. "But other people here do. The butterflies can make drugs, whole medical clinics. Sewers and wells and walls to keep danger out of villages. Clothing, furniture, anything —"

"Stay with me. You're happy here. I know it."

His sadness made me sad. Or I would have been sad, if I weren't an Angel. Instead I felt a detached patience, an empathy that wasn't really an emotion at all.

I shrugged, which is a lovely gesture when you have wings. "Angels can't be the kind of people who have desires, because that's what causes trouble: people who want the wrong things."

I plucked another butterfly from my shoulder and placed it in his palm. It was one of the blue ones. Dark indigo veins filigreed patterns in the cerulean wings.

"The blue kind are different — they are the ones that know how to make everything. And they know how to make more of the regular butterflies and more of themselves. They're smarter than all the others."

Musef was perfectly still, letting the little machine taste him with its delicate tongue, and in that instant I saw a deeper purpose in why I'd been here.

●

Musef was smart and kind and he knew what people who live here might need. He could figure out if they needed a desalination plant or guns, or both. He could help them and keep it a secret until it was too late to do anything about it.

The world needed more Angels, many more, and Musef was exactly the kind of person who might volunteer his life: guilty and regretful. Hungry for atonement.

"The blues ones know how to make a person into an Angel," I explained. "Angels are needed, to be sure the butterflies are used in the right way and given to the people who need them."

He was dumbfounded. "Like you," he said finally.

I nodded. "It's an offer. You don't have to do it."

But really, who could resist the opportunity? To become good? Untouched and untouchable; weightless and winged. The possibility of making up for the worst kind of hubris.

My wings unfurled fully. I had wrap my fingers in his robe so I wasn't swept away.

He closed his eyes and I was unexpectedly filled with an un-angelic wanting. I thought about how gentle he was with the animals and how he would carry water for hours so I could wash the dust from my hair.

"Will you come back?" he asked. "Ever?"

I shook my head, a twinge of regret plucking at my heart. "Angels don't have a past, Musef."

Then, before I could even say good-bye, my wings jerked me back and up, like a parachute in reverse.

The remaining sadness drained out of me as I went higher, and it felt good to fly. Even though I watched him for as long as possible, it was only a minute before he was gone in the vastness of the desert.

●

I'm glad to be an Angel. We — the butterflies and I — save lives. A week or maybe a month ago we made hundreds of thousands of tiny drones to hunt malaria mosquitoes. Yesterday we built homes in a slum, and I can tell that right now the butterflies are hunting for the materials they need to make computers. We scavenge when we need to, and always keep moving.

And, rarely, we find a certain kind of person, a person just like I once was: culpable and suffering and yearning for purity.

I don't know where we are, because borders are ridiculous things.

Sometimes people shoot at us as we glide past, and sometimes I see helicopters in the distance, but they are just old-world things that will eventually go away when the Angels have done their work.

We bring people the things they need and we give it to them without a price. I live each moment as it comes, without a past and without a future.

But sometimes, I dream — on the wing, as Angels do — of what it was like to be touched. To live in one safe, small place and never fly. Once, I woke thinking of a words in a language I no longer knew.

I wander, like I was made to, but sometimes I can convince the butterflies to take us one place rather than another. I like deserts in particular, especially the way the superheated air takes me up high to where the landscape becomes a wrinkled cloth beneath us.

And often, when a being with bright wings appears on the horizon, I convince the butterflies to let me soar that way, just to see who it was.

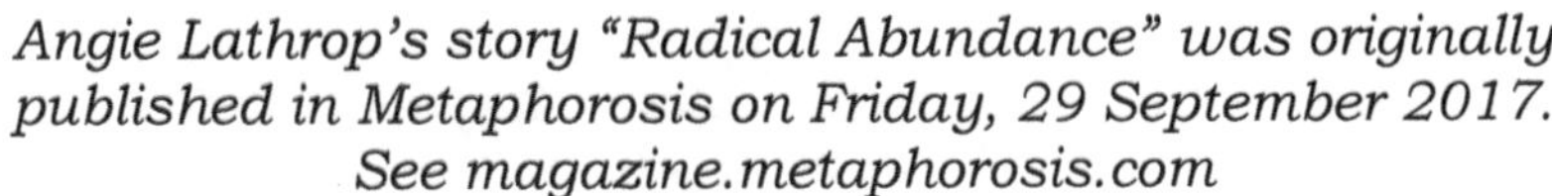

Angie Lathrop's story "Radical Abundance" was originally published in Metaphorosis on Friday, 29 September 2017. See magazine.metaphorosis.com

About the author

Angie writes in an 80 year old converted corn crib on a farm in southern Wisconsin.

Through the Middle

J.B. Kish

There's a woman driving slowly down highway 27 in their direction, and every couple of miles, she opens her window and lets a handful of something human-tasting scatter in the wind. Ashes, Rory suspects. She misses the man who's now dust and cries a little as she goes, singing Bill Withers because the radio doesn't play much more than static and gospel out this far. Bump thinks the powdered man must have liked Bill Withers very much.

At the speed she's going, she'll reach the diner in about thirty minutes. Rory presses a finger into the countertop and thanks Bump for the heads up. Then he puts on a fresh pot of coffee. Coffee's a good start for sadness like this, Rory thinks, and he should know. He's only just found happiness again.

Rory sits behind the counter, shaped like a farm egg. He's put on weight that rounds him. Muscular legs stick out beneath his body like a pair of clearance sale limbs not intended for him, and he wears the rest of his skin like thick diving dress, rich with small folds that retreat from his ribs and neck. His body is a game of hide and seek: American traditional appearing around each corner. There's a woman in a bathing suit diving down his forearm. A faded anchor on his bicep. Twin sparrows on his chest that no longer fly straight.

Half an hour passes, and her Civic pulls up to the far-flung roadside diner. Rory plays "Grandma's Hands" on the jukebox and pours a fresh cup of coffee. The woman walks in with a newborn puppy, and he greets her warmly. When she hears Bill Withers, she buckles a little, and Rory helps her to a nearby booth. "Here," he says, placing a ceramic mug in front of her. "This will make you feel better."

Rory disappears into the kitchen and fixes the woman — her name is Aliyah — something to eat. For a long time, Aliyah reclines in the booth and stares at the sunset with the puppy in her lap. Her t-shirt is cotton-white, floating elegantly above a pair of cut off shorts and some skateboard sneakers. The skin of her cheek is pocked with dark acne scars that she's not covered up. She looks like the subject in a Rockwell painting.

Bump asks who Rockwell is and Rory places a finger on the wall like he's using a walkie talkie. Silently, he explains Norman Rockwell was an artist who used to paint restaurants like theirs. Then Rory slides a turkey sandwich in front of Aliyah and asks if she'd appreciate company. She accepts politely, and he wonders for one terrifying moment what he — an old man in his seventies — can offer this woman, if anything. He knows nothing about being young or black or growing up in these times. But he has an ear, which is all she seems to need, and Aliyah explains she's wandering southern Oregon, spreading her father's ashes. He was one of the west coast's most celebrated archeologists, and he died peacefully of old age a month ago. After an hour, Aliyah makes an embarrassed face. She's been talking this whole time and hasn't asked Rory one question about himself.

Rory prefers it this way. He doesn't like talking about his father or the Navy; he's not the kind of discarded thing that complains. Anyway, nothing before matters because this is where he matters most. Of course, Aliyah doesn't understand that at all and surprises him by asking, *What's next.*

Rory laughs through his nose. "The only way this diner shuts down is because I've died and there's no one left to open it."

"Suppose you win the lottery."

He sips his coffee too quickly and wets his mustache; Aliyah grins as he dabs his mouth dry. "I grew this thing in the Navy because I had a baby face. My commanding officer said it would make me look smart."

"Did it?"

Rory nods and sits back. "In the Navy, you know exactly where you matter most. They tell you where to be and what to do. How to shave, how to dress. After I got out, I spent a long time searching for value again. When I found this restaurant and its customers, I *did* win the lottery. I don't think I could ever walk away from that."

Aliyah ponders his words a while before dismissing them with the wave of a hand; he can't help but fall in love with her a little. *Aliyah's* value, she explains, chases her like the puppy on her lap. She gets job offers because her father had important friends and they think her trowel was destined to continue his legacy. But she doesn't want a life in the dirt. She wants to start a vegan bakery. "But is that a terrible idea?"

It's not, and Rory envies how clearly she sees herself.

"You know, I've heard of you," Aliyah says. He points to his breast, and she nods. "They say there's a hermit in the desert that helps people. That's you, I think."

He shrugs. "Most folks know what they need. Sometimes they have to hear it a specific way."

On the way out the door, she thanks him for good company and happy coincidences. "Bill Withers was my father's favorite, you know."

Rory holds up a finger and fetches a cup of coffee to-go. "For the road," he explains, and then he grabs a handful of sugar packets from the table. "And for the bakery."

Aliyah chuckles at the gift and gives Rory a squeezing hug. "We'll see."

His heart beats like a young man's as she heads down the road. It was a nice cup of shared coffee, he thinks. Coffee's always a good start for sadness like that. Then Bump asks if Norman Rockwell can come paint their restaurant, and Rory laughs before turning in for the night.

●

Bump came through the middle.

That's the only way he's able to tell it. One day, he 'passed through the middle and surfaced here', just about the same as most customers. He could be extraterrestrial, but Bump didn't come from the great above. He came from deep, deep below, 'through the middle', and burst up against the ground like a pimple on the cheek of southern Oregon's desert.

Rory never tries to dig him up because it wouldn't be polite, and Bump seems satisfied enough to exist under the asphalt bloom behind the diner, which houses him like a geodesic dome. Besides, Bump says the asphalt is what connects him to the road and the people traveling their way. It's through this that he can feel the vibration of human emotions, touch palms through cracked leather steering wheels, and read Rory the prologue of their customers. It's what makes the pair a uniquely wonderful team, and why Rory is truly happy for the first time in a long while.

This is why Rory's stomach drops when Bump says someone is coming, but he can't sense anything about them. Bump can perceive the subtle weight of their body through the driver's side tires, but the rest feels eerie and quiet. It's almost as if there's no one there at all. *Can Mustangs drive themselves on this planet?* he asks Rory realizes he's not breathing and tries to inhale casually.

Anyway, says Bump. *They should be here tomorrow afternoon.*

●

But first, there's a man and a woman — a college couple in their twenties — coming down the highway, and whenever she brings up his temper, he wrings the steering wheel in a way she can't see. His little outbursts are growing more frequent, and even though he apologizes, they seem to be dancing around an incident — something like a *push* or maybe a *fall*, Bump says. They can't agree on which. The woman is assertive, but occasionally her voice is nervous around the edge. Rory thanks Bump for the heads up. With a frown, he puts on a fresh pot of coffee. Coffee's a good start when dealing with men like this. As it drips, he can't help his mind wandering to his tools out back and finds himself asking how hard it might be to dig a man-sized hole.

You'll not stick him down here with me, Bump jokes.

A while later, the bell rings, and without asking, Rory pours two fresh cups of coffee.

A tattooed woman appears at his counter, looks down with a smile, and dubs him a saint. She holds the ceramic mug under her nose with both hands and breathes deep. She's brunette and diamond shaped, with as much life as a fresh battery. When the boyfriend appears over her shoulder, he has a square head and practiced neutrality. A chameleon: Rory spots it right away. Polite. Jovial. Makes pleasant conversation all the way up until he leaves for the bathroom, which is outside around back. Rory forgets to mention the very specific jimmy required to unlock its door from inside, and that buys him a while to chat.

He places a pastrami sandwich in front of the tattooed woman with a roll of silverware. Her jaw drops playfully, and she asks why Rory owns a diner in the absolute middle of nowhere.

"Pills," he says candidly because she needs to hear this a specific way. She doesn't follow. "When I got out of the Navy, I took a job as a line cook and spent thirty years making people happy. And then we got bought out; I was fired by a hot shot celebrity for not understanding molecular gastronomy. No one in Portland wants to hire an old cook with bad knees, so when I hit the bottom, I drove down here to eat enough Oxycodone to put me in the ground."

Her eyes grow wide, and she has the packed cheek of a squirrel.

Rory smiles, easing a bit of this uninvited tension, "I found this restaurant instead."

The woman smiles uncomfortably. "Good for you." She tries to end the conversation on a high note. "So many five-star ratings online, you must be doing something right."

Suddenly Bump is there, in Rory's mind. *The mustang is going much faster. It will be here sooner*, he says.

Rory's heart skips a beat. What *is* all this nonsense about self-driving cars and phantom drivers? He discretely presses his right fingertip into the counter. The entire finger has vibrated with heat since the day he met Bump, when he pressed down on the asphalt dome curiously, and their connection was calcified. He theorizes it's a kind of foreign energy that comes from the other side — through the middle. When he presses down, he can sense its vein-like release, connecting him from the counter to the floor below, which joins with the building's foundation, the earth around, and ultimately allows him to project thoughts to his friend out back. *You're imagining things*, he tells Bump, and then he lifts his finger, ending the conversation.

Rory returns to the woman, distracted. "The point is," he continues, "it wasn't good enough to keep telling my family I'd change. People tell themselves they can just wake up tomorrow and *do better*. But I had to work at it. Leave an unhealthy environment, change my life. Otherwise, all those good intentions were just smoke and vapor."

The woman's eyes narrow slightly.

He makes a noise in the back of his throat, then nods toward the bathroom. "What I'm saying is, people don't magically wake up and *do better*. Unless he does the work, his apologies are just smoke and vapor." Then Rory tops off her coffee. "Understand?"

The blood drains from the woman's face and the bell rings over her shoulder. "Old man," her boyfriend growls. He walks up to the counter and throws the key into Rory's chest. It lands against the floor with a jingle. "Bathroom door is broken as hell." Then he nudges the woman with his elbow. "Hurry up and pay."

The whole interaction was a bit heavier handed than Rory prefers. When they've left, he walks out to the road and stares into the distance. He envisions a Mustang blowing fire from its tailpipe, riding a cloud of smog. And then, for reasons he cannot explain, he thinks of constructing a white tower for the first time in years.

●

What would you do if I passed back through the middle? Bump asks.

The sun is tangerine-orange and quickly fading. Rory flips a chicken breast on the charcoal grill he's rolled out back. With an elderly groan, he touches a finger to the ground. *You know it's rather unfair that I must speak through my finger, but* you *can project your thoughts directly into me.*

Humans are surprisingly complex, Bump answers. *Would you stay at the diner?*

Rory is annoyed and tense. *I'd climb the white tower and throw myself off,* he snips.

Bump is quiet a while, then says, *The mustang will be here soon.*

"Lord!" Rory shouts with his actual voice. "What is all this about?"

When Bump doesn't respond, Rory splays his fingers in frustration. "Fine," he says, "Let it come," and he walks inside. He grabs a large piece of parchment paper and writes 'PERMANENTLY CLOSED', then tapes it to the front door and kills the lights. There's not a single glowing bulb in the entire dining room. Out back, he waves a dismissive hand at bump and takes his dinner to bed.

●

He's here, Bump whispers.

Rory opens his eyes with a start, then sticks his head out the trailer door and spots a light in the restaurant. "He?"

The one driving the Mustang. He's waiting for you inside.

"It's nearly five in the morning."

You should go in, is all Bump says.

Inside, there's a handsome man sitting at the counter eating a bag of potato chips. He looks like he stepped off a Hollywood movie set, but Rory can't decide why. His features are elusive: Latin American one moment, Eastern European the next. There is a fresh pot of coffee on the counter, and he invites Rory to join him.

"Who are you?" Rory whispers, looking down at his parchment paper sign, which has been folded into a perfect square on the counter.

"Name's *Very Hungry,*" the man says with a punchline smile. It's a joke, but Rory's not laughing. The stranger reaches into his pocket and pulls out three one-hundred-dollar bills. "Can you make the perfect burger?"

Well now, just what in the hell is this? Rory wonders. *And why are you suddenly so damned quiet?* he asks Bump through the countertop. Bump doesn't answer.

"Every time I come here, I can't wait to get my hands on a real American cheeseburger." The stranger makes two fists. "But you can't go to a drive thru. What's the point of anticipation if the food's no good?" He slides the money forward. "Three hundred dollars for the best burger you can make."

Rory scowls. Breaking into his diner — scaring his friend — that's one thing. Questioning his ability on the grill is another entirely! He takes the money and draws up his torso. "I'll make it to-go."

Rory returns with possibly the greatest hamburger he's ever made. Carefully sculpted. Cooked to perfection. Golden French fries that could usher in the seventh trumpet! Lettuce so crisp it looked plastic!

And what does he find waiting for him? Nothing.

The Mustang is still parked outside, but there's no one sitting behind the counter.

Rory, says Bump.

He closes his eyes. *Shit*, he thinks, keeping this particular thought to himself. Cautiously, he walks out back and finds the handsome man standing above Bump, looking down at the asphalt dome with a mouth full of potato chips. Rory licks his lips and presses a finger into a wooden railing. "What is this?" he asks.

Rory, says Bump, *this is Hadrian. Hadrian, this is Rory.*

Hadrian waves and smiles. It's not unkind, and Rory hates him for that.

Hadrian is my grandchild, adds Bump.

●

Inside, the to-go box is empty. Rory is three hundred dollars richer, and he's never felt worse.

Hadrian is here to take Bump home. Bump left without telling anyone, and at his age, he really needs to be looked after. A depression drapes over Rory like a series of blankets, one after the other. He feels heavier the longer Hadrian talks.

"But," Rory whispers. "We're quite good friends."

"That's a funny pair," suggests Hadrian. The sun illuminates the diner with a warm glow. Dust floats along the rays of light like sad poetry.

"I've come to care for your grandfather very deeply," explains Rory. He finds himself appealing to the man's sense of empathy, but who's to say if Hadrian has any to begin with. His kind comes through the middle and takes on a form that emulates the planet's inhabitants. That didn't necessarily mean they possess the same emotional capacity. "Perhaps he could stay here with me?" Rory's smile is desperate.

Hadrian shakes his head. "Grandfather got stuck trying to emerge. It happens occasionally. I'm here to help." He takes a long sip of coffee and sighs gratefully. "Have you considered what you'll do when Bump passes back through the middle?"

Rory's too scared of the white tower to answer, so Hadrian adds, "Would you like to pass through the middle with us instead?"

Through the middle — it's a terrifying notion! Timid, he whispers, "Your grandfather's never told me much about where you come from. And this is my home."

"So, you wish to stay here?"

"I wish for things to stay as they are!"

"They cannot," Hadrian says in a way that's not unkind. "We leave tonight."

Tears gallop down Rory's cheek. It's just like life to do this to him again. The bell over the door rings, and Rory jumps. Quickly, he dries his cheeks and waves hello to a pair of men with a young boy. Farmers perhaps? "Be right with you," he calls. "Grab a seat anywhere."

Rory plucks his apron from the counter, pausing long enough to ask Bump why he didn't give a heads up on their new customers.

"'I've suspended your connection to my grandfather," Hadrian whispers. "Only temporarily."

Suspended their connect — how dare he! What kind of game was he playing? Rory's face is beet read. He opens his mouth to shout when —

"Hey fella," one of the men calls. "Coffees and a juice."

Rory is shaking. Gradually, his expression lifts upward and he fetches their order. Standing above them, he withdraws a pad of paper and a pencil, clears his throat, and wonders why he's so uneasy.

"Y'all from around here?"

Neither man looks up from their menus. They're vaguely like one another. Brother's maybe? Or perhaps it's just coincidence. The youngest, a boy of ten or eleven, stares out the window thoughtfully. He has a book on his lap — *The Spectator Bird* — but never opens it. The eldest, a leathery man with ruddy cheeks, looks down at his wristwatch and speaks in a way that's not intended for Rory. "Two hours," he whispers.

The other nods and looks up from his menu. "Three omelets, bacon, white toast all around."

Rory notes the order and retrieves the menus. "Beautiful day out there."

The younger man slides his cup forward. "Top off, please."

As Rory steps back into the kitchen, Hadrian raises a polite finger. "I'd love one of those omelets, if it's not a complete bother."

The kitchen door swings shut, and for a long while, Rory stares at the range. Slowly, he begins making the order. It's easy. It's muscle memory. He could make omelets in his sleep, and without meaning it, his mind drifts to the white tower. He makes sure his index finger isn't touching anything that connects him to Bump, and he's ashamed of it. *How much is left?* he wonders. He is pulled from the question by the distinct smell of eggs starting to burn. He saves the omelets just in time. Again, it's muscle memory. He really could do this in his sleep.

After breakfast, the man with ruddy cheeks pays and Rory asks how everything was. "Sure," the man answers. "Good enough."

The blood drains from Rory's face as their truck pulls out the lot and disappears down the road. Hadrian picks at the men's leftovers while Rory dumbly removes his apron and floats outside, into his trailer, and opens the closet door. He pushes aside a few shirts and finds a shoebox tucked all the way in the back. Inside is an orange prescription bottle with ten tablets that make a maraca sound when he shakes them. His heart pounds as if it means to crack his ribs, and suddenly Rory can't breathe. He races outside for air.

Hadrian sits on a folding chair next to Bump, finishing a side of potatoes. After Rory's caught his breath, he drags a chair next to them and squeezes the plastic bottle between both hands.

Were you able to serve those men? Bump asks.

Hadrian nods; he's allowed them to speak again.

"I was able to feed them," Rory answers. "If that's what you mean."

Quietly, he opens the plastic bottle and slides half the contents into his palm. They're heavier than he remembers, like they have somewhere important to be. He imagines them pecking through his skin and dropping out the back of his hand, so he stacks them one by one on his armrest before they can get away. Carefully, he constructs a beautiful white tower and envisions himself standing atop it, leaning out over a smooth, granite edge. The vast Oregon desert yawns beneath him, and his heart flutters at the brush of an old friend. An adrenaline he hasn't felt in years.

Rory's only closed his eyes for a moment when his chair nudges strangely, and when he looks back down, the tower is missing, and Hadrian is making a childish face. "These aren't good at all."

"You ate that?" Rory sits up as Hadrian dry swallows a white paste.

Hadrian's eyes widen. "The mints?"

"You can't have."

"Hadrian," Bump says. "Those were Rory's mints."

Rory presses a finger into his armrest. "They're not mints." Then to Hadrian, "You need to vomit."

"You mean on command?"

"Quickly."

"What happens if I don't?"

Rory doesn't answer, which is answer enough. "Oh." says Hadrian, sitting back. "Interesting."

"How exactly?"

"Well, if I don't, then my grandfather stays here, and you get what you want."

Rory's blood thickens with pressure. "I don't want your grandfather to be stuck here."

"But you don't want him to leave either."

"I don't want things to change." He's about to stand and force Hadrian to vomit himself. "What about our customers?"

"Will they stop coming?"

"How do you propose I help them without your grandfather here? Look what happened in there."

Hadrian makes a face like he finally understands the riddle in front of him. "My grandfather gives you value."

Rory draws himself upright. "Of course not."

"Is there someone else who does that?"

"His commanding officer," Bump says brightly.

Rory twists his hands anxiously. "My what?"

"You told the dust-man's daughter that your commanding officer made you grow that mustache and now you're smarter. He has given you value."

"No."

"You're not smart?"

"I was always smart."

"The mustache doesn't make you smart?"

"You need to throw up right now."

Hadrian holds out both palms like he didn't read that part of the human manual. "Do I punch myself?"

"Who then?" Bump asks.

"No one *gives* me value," Rory barks. "Stick your finger all the way down your throat until something happens."

Hadrian does as he's told.

Rory twist the cap onto the prescription bottle and stuffs the remaining pills into his pocket. "What would you have me do?" he growls. "Leave the diner tonight? Abandon my customers?"

"The diner gives you value," Bump clarifies.

"No." Rory pinches his brow and then points at Hadrian. "*Deeper.*" Hadrian grunts in acknowledgment and his finger descends another inch.

"Then what?"

"*I* do," Rory shouts. "I'm good at this. I'm good at helping people!" He stands and grabs Hadrian's elbow. He pushes upward and the man's finger disappears another inch. Hadrian gags fantastically; he vomits white bile onto Rory's clothes. It's unclear if he's disposed of all five pills, but Rory suspects it's enough. He's about to stumble backward when a small voice clears its throat: "Sir?"

They turn in surprise. The boy from breakfast peeks around the corner with a cautious expression. Rory let's go of Hadrian, who wipes his mouth and waves.

Bravely, the child asks, "You seen my book?"

"Book?" Then Rory understands. He waves the boy inside and searches the booth where they ate. He gets down on his hands and knees, hoping to find it under the table.

"What were you two fighting about?" the boy asks from behind.

"If I told you my mustache," Rory mutters, "would you believe me?"

Rory cranes his neck and spots the book wedged between the wall and booth. He reaches out and can nearly touch it with the tip of his finger, but Bump is idling there. Instead, Rory uses his ring finger to paddle at the book's spine until it falls to the floor.

Grunting, he shuffles backward and feels every vertebrae of his back unfurl. "Here." The boy takes the book and nods in thanks.

"Those men." Rory motions to the truck outside.

"My uncles."

"They don't talk much, do they?"

"Sure they do."

Sure they do. Rory's about to ask what terrible things they've been saying about breakfast when the boy turns and heads for the door.

"Wait —" Rory calls out and the child stops to look over his shoulder. Rory wants to ask; he's desperate to know, but a thick feeling of shame coats his throat. Frankly, the words are so dull in shape that even his mouth is bored with them, on top of which he's just realized how badly he stinks. The truth is, he's so insecure that this entire moment feels perfectly normal, and he hates himself for that.

The boy startles him by going first. "It doesn't matter if he doesn't like it."

Rory stops. He doesn't understand.

"Your mustache." The boy draws himself upward and walks across the checkered floor with raw, adolescent confidence. He places a companionable hand on Rory's bicep and says firmly, "I think it only matters if *you* like the mustache."

There's an inaudible *crack* of ivory-white granite.

With a radiant clap on his arm, the boy turns and jogs out. Rory opens and closes his mouth like a fish. His eyes have gently doubled in size, and there's a tangible warmth in his bicep. He floats to the window, and as the boy climbs up into the truck, he spots Rory. The boy waves and then reaches backward, withdrawing a plastic comb from his pocket. He holds it horizontally beneath his nose and smiles through the prongs.

●

Nothing here is as she remembers it. Aliyah sits in her Civic, staring up at the diner which is no longer the diner. It's *Dot's*, and Dot is a woman who doesn't allow dogs in her restaurant, so Koda waits in the car. Aliyah sits at a booth craning her neck, waiting for the hermit to round a corner.

Dot is a short Thai woman in her fifties who can carry more plates than seems possible. She tends to a busy dining room before dropping a cup of coffee in front of Aliyah. "Morning. Need some time or are you ready?"

"The man who worked here, an older gentleman."

Dot doesn't follow.

"He was the owner just a few months ago. Did he..." Aliyah tilts her head morbidly.

Dot shakes her chin no. "He sold."

Aliyah's stomach pirouettes. "He what?"

Dot smiles politely while scanning the restaurant from the corner of her eye. "If you need a little time with the menu..."

Aliyah nods and falls back into the booth, struggling to understand. She's driven all this way so he could talk her out of it. What's she supposed to do now? Take the job and play secretary for a department of PhDs obsessed with her last name? How could this have happened?

The hermit *sold* his lottery?

Aliyah sips her coffee and stares at a caddy of sugar packets and room temperature creamer. Dot returns a while later and refills her cup.

"Did he say anything?" Aliyah asks. "Or where he was going?"

"Were you friends?" When Aliyah doesn't answer, Dot nods. "He sold quickly."

Aliyah knits her brow and chews the inside of her cheek. She can feel herself sinking inward.

"He left something." Dot speaks softly as if telling a secret. "A funny note taped out front with a couple urns of coffee." Then she turns and points to a bulletin board near the door. "I couldn't bring myself to throw it away."

When she spots the note, Aliyah's skin prickles. She climbs out of the booth and walks to the board.

Passed through the middle, she reads. *Help yourself to some coffee. No matter the problem, I've always found coffee is a good start.*

"Hon?" Dot's voice appears over her shoulder. "Do you need more time with the menu?"

Rubbing her thumb over the note, Aliyah shakes her head. She pays for a coffee to-go and Dot fetches her a paper cup. As she turns to leave, Aliyah plucks a few sugar packets from a nearby caddy. She pictures the old hermit in the desert who used to help people. Who told people things they knew, just said a specific way. Without thinking, she grabs a handful more. She stuffs her jacket pockets with little white packets until they are full. Pretty soon, she's emptying another caddy over a table and scooping them into her saddle bag.

"Hey!" Dot shouts from the register, her eyes wide.

Aliyah smiles apologetically as she empties a third caddy directly into her bag. Then a fourth.

"I said stop!" calls Dot, but the bell above the door is already ringing. Aliyah is racing to her car, shouting an apology through the window. She's got to get going!

Bill Withers glides into place as she and Koda soar down the highway toward home. Aliyah's turning down the job; she was never meant for a life in the dirt. She's decided to take her sugar packets and build something brand new.

J.B. Kish's story "Through the Middle" was originally published in Metaphorosis on Friday, 9 December 2022. See magazine.metaphorosis.com

About the author

J.B. Kish is a weird fiction and horror author that helps emerging writers design a strategy to reach their goals. His writing has been featured in Underland Press' *The Cozy Cosmic, Metaphorosis' Best of 2022, Cosmic Horror Monthly*, and Unsettling Read's *Still of Winter* anthology. His author workshops have been developed based on eight years of helping clients roadmap and achieve their goals. When he's not writing, he facilitates workshops for people looking to improve their public speaking and presentation skills. Learn more at www.jbkish.com.

Indicative of Future Results

C. H. Rosenberg

***The Frontpage Feed: Morning Edition.* Carefully curated and fact-checked headlines delivered to your inbox, every day!**

SUBJECT LINE: *Extraterrestrials Exposed?!*

Top Ranked News (56,031 shares): *Stunning 'Proof' of Extraterrestrial Cover-Up Floods Internet.*

Yesterday's release of thousands of purportedly top-secret documents by a self-proclaimed former high-ranking national security official sent shockwaves across the metaverse.

The manifesto accused the United States and allied spacefaring nations of covering up an extraterrestrial message received several years ago, when both competing nation-states and private enterprise were emerging as serious contenders in a second Space Race.

The self-described whistleblower claimed a signal was intercepted by a joint scientific team on board the International Space Station (ISS) and the origin later pinned as the TRAPPIST-1 star system in the Aquarius constellation. All media inquiries to the personnel named in the leaked documents were directed to an ISS Program spokesperson who declined to comment.

The manifesto goes on to reveal that a second message was recently intercepted, with analysts agreeing it amounts to an announcement of an impending arrival. "In other words," the alleged former insider warned, "an extraterrestrial vanguard is on its way — we *hope* for the purpose of establishing diplomatic relations. Either way, our leaders are fooling themselves if they think they can keep this under wraps."

While such claims of extraterrestrial contact are typically dismissed as false alarms, several respected experts appear to be taking this particular claim seriously. The International Academy of Astronautics and the SETI Institute both urged calm while they work to verify the purported evidence.

Business and Finance News (4,833 shares): ***Closing Bell Round-up***

Personal finance guru Connie Padilla today announced the release of her eagerly awaited book, *Give Your Future Self a Raise*. In this fresh spin on retirement planning, Ms. Padilla, 42, offers her characteristic pragmatic advice, as always inspiring readers with her message of financial empowerment. This adds to a growing media empire so far encompassing a semiweekly podcast and newsletter, two other published books and a robust digital community platform. Ms. Padilla regularly appears on the conference and talk show circuit and recently kicked off a live weekly show, where she answers her audience's questions on everything related to personal finance.

●

LIBRARY: Latest Episode. Downloading...
Power Your Personal Finance — ***UNPLUGGED!*** *Episode transcript..*
Live streaming in 3...2...1. Cue teaser, introductory music, sponsor plug

Connie: Hello, hello everybody! I'm *so* glad to welcome you here on episode ten — *ten!* — of the live stream version of *Power Your Personal Finance!* I'm Connie Padilla, Certified Financial Planner *and* author of *Give Your Future Self a Raise* — out now! — plus two other bestsellers, *Power Your Personal Finance: The Fundamentals* and *The Smart Side-Hustle.*

Each Friday, I take questions from people *just like you*, live on the show. My goal is to help you take control of your financial future, for a worry-free life today and a comfortable retirement tomorrow.

First off, a quick disclaimer: *Power Your Personal Finance* is purely for educational and entertainment purposes. Anything said on this show should not be construed as individual financial, legal, tax, or accounting advice; listeners are advised to discuss their personal financial situation and goals with a financial professional. And remember: while we talk about stocks, bonds, real estate, and other investment opportunities on this show, past performance is *not* indicative of future results!

Now, without further ado, let's get to your questions. And from my inbox, it's pretty obvious what most of you have on your mind.

Sound effect: Drum roll

Connie: Aliens! [*laughter*] Just kidding, folks. But several of you clearly *are* worried about defending yourselves from scammers and hoaxes. So, let's start off with a couple of questions about protecting your personal identity. Then, we'll step back to look at asset protection more holistically.

[*Fast forward.* TIME: 24.59]

Connie: All right, we have time for one more call today. Let's go back to the queue. Hello! Who's this?

Frank: Hello, Ms. Padilla. I'm...Frank.

Connie: Hey, Frank. How can I help empower you today?

Frank: What's the *deal* with personal finance, anyway?

Connie: ...Huh?

Frank: Apologies, Ms. Padilla. I'm just...*frustrated.* Maybe because I'm so new to all this? I mean, I've done my homework, I've listened to your entire archive of episodes, I've read *all* of your books —

Connie: Wow!

Frank: But I still feel completely overwhelmed! I'm usually very good at picking up new things — it's my *job* — so this is pretty embarrassing for me.

Connie: Hey, *never* feel ashamed of what you don't know. If you've read *Power Your Personal Finance* and listened to episodes 211 and 341 — I'll link to those in the show notes — you've heard me dish about my own background, growing up in a working class Mexican immigrant family. My parents *never* talked about money, at least not beyond worrying we never had enough! I had to learn everything all on my own.

Frank: You still grew up on — *in* — a world where money is incredibly important for just about everything, right? But the whole *concept* is just incredibly *alien* to someone like me. I'm, uh, foreign...

Connie: [*Chuckles.*] I didn't want to comment on your accent, but it is lovely.

Frank: Thanks, Ms. Padilla. But my point is that things are completely different where I'm from. 401(k)s, IRAs, HSAs, FSAs, CFPs...we don't have anything remotely like that. I can barely wrap my ten — my head around it all. [*Pause*] It's all just so — so — so *nonsensical!*

Connie: Calm down, Frank. Relax! I know *all* about feeling like a fish out of water. But honestly, you're in exactly the same boat as many of my other listeners. Possibly in an even *better* boat, because you haven't had a chance to develop bad money habits in the first place! And rest assured, I'm here to help you navigate that ship to financial freedom.

Frank: You...you really think you can help me, Ms. Padilla?

Connie: Absolutely! Now, let's start with the fundamentals...

●

The Frontpage Feed: Breaking News!
SUBJECT LINE: ***Shocker! Politicians chuck plausible deniability (and little green men are headed for Earth)***
Top Ranked News (73,589,230 shares): ***We Are Not Alone! World Leaders Confess to Cover-Up, Tell Public to Prepare to Welcome Extraterrestrial Visitors***

In a stunning revelation, the leaders of several nations today confirmed the accusations posted last week by the still-unidentified whistleblower.

At the historic joint press conference, the president of the United States and other heads of state verified the interception of a "message of intelligent extraterrestrial origin" nearly a decade ago. They further verified receipt of a second message just over one month ago on October 15 at

5:32 a.m. UTC; both missives have since been released to the public.

"Our interstellar neighbors tell us they have been observing humanity and want to learn more about us," Japan's prime minister summarized the message. "That is why they have sent an emissary."

Calculations based on information contained in the second message put the extraterrestrial ambassadors' arrival at mid-April.

"I don't know what our idiot leaders were thinking, not informing the public sooner so we'd all have more time to adjust to this new reality," said Dr. Abrams, director of the Space Policy Institute at the George Washington University. "Consequently, humanity has just *five months* to collectively roll out the red carpet."

Some humans, apparently, cannot wait. In reaction to thousands of extraterrestrial enthusiasts attempting to make contact through jerry-rigged transmitters, the U.N. Office for Outer Space Affairs posted an advisory warning against "making unauthorized diplomatic overtures that may confuse, if not endanger interplanetary relations."

Business and Finance News (7,723,459 shares): ***'Completely Bonkers': Main Street, Wall Street Reaction Out of This World***

The U.S. Federal Reserve Board of Governors met this morning with leadership from central banks around the world. Their daunting task: stabilize an economic and financial system that is just starting to react to yesterday's revelation about an impending extraterrestrial visit.

"Too late," said Resh Agarwal, senior analyst with the London-based Centre for Fiscal Security. "Everything has already gone completely bonkers — that *is* the technical term, by the way."

"Bonkers" may indeed describe how both financial markets and consumers are responding to the news.

On Wall Street, stocks see-sawed wildly from opening to closing bell, repeating a pattern set by the Nikkei, Shanghai Composite, DAX, and FTSE earlier in the day. On Main Street, retailers reported record-setting activity, with customers fully in panic-buying mode. Sporting goods stores have resorted to rationing out survival and camping gear. The two most popular internet search terms yesterday were "hazmat suit" and "DIY tinfoil hat."

"Customers are literally preparing for the end of the world," said Whole Nine Yards store manager Tonya Reiss, speaking to a correspondent in El Paso, Texas. "They're stocking up on everything, from firearms to canned food. The shelves are empty; we've completely run out of aluminum foil and our vendors are backordered by as much as seven months."

●

LIBRARY: Latest Episode. Downloading...
Power Your Personal Finance! Ranked #1 in genre. Please leave a review! *Episode transcript.*
Cue teaser, introductory music, sponsor plug

Connie: Happy Money Monday, everybody! I'm Connie Padilla, Certified Financial Planner, welcoming you to episode five-ninety-seven of the *Power Your Personal Finance!* podcast. This is where we talk about everything that can affect your pocketbook — and how you can *act* rather than *react*, to take control of *your* financial future. Control and discipline *is* what it's all about, especially during volatile times.

And speaking of volatility, *what* a week, huh? Stock markets plummeted, triggering the 'circuit breaker' fail-safe no fewer than *five times* — and taking all of our IRAs and 401(k)s along for the ride. Fortunately, things seemed to stabilize by the end of the week. But what will the coming weeks and months bring?

Listen. I know we're all shaken to the core by the confirmation we're not alone in the universe. It makes us reassess what's truly important, revisit the things we take for granted. And when it comes down to it, I know we *all* have the exact same question:

How is this going to affect my portfolio?

Should I sell? Should I pull everything from my retirement account? Should I convert all my assets into cash or commodities? Do I put it all into durable goods?

I want everyone listening to log out and step away from your investment apps. Take a deep breath. Do *not* let panic take control of your financial decisions. *You* are the one in control. Because here's the answer: Discipline. If you've been disciplined all along, you're all set! You have at least six to eight months of living expenses in cash on hand. You're diversified. You're prepared. You'll be *fine*. You can weather this storm.

In fact, my special guest today happens to be an expert on weathering financial storms...

[*Fast forward.* TIME: 27:05]

We'll end the show as we always do, by reading a review left by a listener. Today's review was written by our friend, Frank! Frank says: *Ms. Padilla has become my go-to resource for everything personal finance. Since she took my question on the live show, I've joined the Power Your Personal Finance! online community, where I've been welcomed with open appendages by a group of people similarly inspired to make Ms. Padilla's 'Financial Fund-amentals' part of their daily lives. I know I still have a lot to learn, but now I feel confident that I'm well on my way. Thank you, Ms. Padilla — I'm your newest, biggest fan!*

●

***Power Your Personal Finance!* Community Platform.**
Enter username and password.
Hot Topic: *What IS ETs' grift, anyway?* (2,739 replies)
Excerpt — P.J. *Kuppenheimer, an economist once ridiculed in academic circles for his obsession over proving the so-called Theory of Interstellar Trade, was appointed this week to the White House Council of Economic Advisers. In his first interview with the news media, Kuppenheimer expressed skepticism over the stated intentions of the "Ambassadors" — as the metaverse has dubbed the extraterrestrials — declaring, "It is entirely irrational for any intelligent being — that is, any self-interested, utility-maximizing individual — to make the long and arduous interstellar journey simply to meet another species in person. These 'Ambassadors' clearly must have some profit motive in mind. Our job is to determine*

just what, exactly, that may be — and how to prepare for it." Related link: *The Grifter's Guide to the Galaxy*, MacroEconDaily.NET interview with P.J. Kuppenheimer, Ph.D., Chicago School of Economics.

Moderator: Okay, folks! Before you post, remember to answer today's poll: What's the *real* motivation driving these "Ambassadors" to visit our little blue planet?

(1) They've screwed up their own planet and want ours

(2) They're straight-up conquerors and just want our planet period, no justification required

(3) They've cooked up some grift that makes interstellar travel worth their while

[Tally: (1) 25%; (2) 13%; (3) 62%]

Financially Fit: Seriously? 38% of the people here must be hard-core preppers if they really believe in #1 or #2. [215 likes; 52 LOLs]

ETFrank: "Preppers"? [7 likes]

Retire Early or Bust: I agree, Financially Fit; I think the good prof's hit the nail on the head. Between time dilation and the opportunity costs, in-person interstellar travel just doesn't make sense. There has to be *something* that makes it worth their while. But what? [198 likes]

ETFrank: "Preppers?" [2 likes; 32 eye-rolls]

$$$urvivor: Their technology has to be light years ahead of ours, right? My bet's on them manufacturing a bunch of tiny gizmos super-cheap on their own planet and selling them for insane profit margins here. [278 likes, 53 shares]

ETFrank: Why would the Ambassadors want to sell anything? The message stated our entire goal is a free and open exchange of cultures and ideas! [143 likes, 27 hearts]

ETFrank: Sorry; typo. "Their" entire goal. Also, IDK "preppers." [5 LOLs]

Retire Early or Bust: Come on, ETFrank! That's the classic freemium model. They'll start out giving away their nifty toys, and just wait — soon enough, we won't be able to live without 'em. *Then* they'll be all: Surprise! It's a subscription service — and start charging us through the nose — or whatever orifice. Hook. Line. Sinker. [317 likes, 46 shares]

Moderator: Here you go, Frank: [Link to: *Neighborhood Nut Jobs or Smart Cookies? Top (legal) tips from America's premier preppers on setting aside enough food and ammo to last through the End of Days.*]

●

The Frontpage Feed: Mid-day Edition
SUBJECT LINE: ***Ray guns or hostess gift? Here's how to prepare for five different First Contact scenarios***
Top Ranked News (207,403 shares): ***Third Message a Charm? Ambassadors Claim Friendly Intentions***

The World Ambassador Greeting Operations Network today announced interception of a third message, as the public counts down the four months remaining until First Contact. Both earth-based and orbiting telescopes tracked the latest message's trajectory back to the extraterrestrial ship, which, according to physicists, is rapidly decelerating and anticipated to cross into the Oort Cloud by this Friday.

"The Ambassadors once again stated their goal is to establish diplomatic relations and learn about humanity," said a spokesperson with Welcome WAGON — the nickname given to the rapidly-assembled international coordinating committee charged with establishing interspecies relations.

"Taken at face value, the Ambassadors are definitely trying to stress their friendly intentions," said Dr. Ixchel Ramirez, astrobiologist with the National Autonomous University of Mexico. She and her interdisciplinary team of scientists, data analysts and linguists have scrutinized the details of every message received thus far. "The picture we've put together so far indicates a culture dedicated to both intellectual and cultural advancement, almost as imperatives to personal and societal growth."

Economist Peter Jeremiah ("P.J.") Kuppenheimer, who recently skyrocketed from obscurity to a household name, is not so inclined to take the Ambassadors at face value. "Why are the Ambassadors trying so hard to convince us of their benign motives?" he scoffed in a series of critical tweets. "Frankly, it's suspicious."

Marketing industry veteran Shahad Khoury agreed. "They're establishing their brand identity ahead of time," she theorized at a recent conference of the Euro-West Asia Advertising Alliance. "Like everyone, they're selling something — and customers prefer supporting a brand they already feel positive about."

Security experts take a more pessimistic interpretation of these messages. "It could be propaganda intended to soften us up in advance of a full-scale invasion," suggested Mai Begay, fellow at the Center for Strategic Defense, based in Arlington, Virginia.

In the meantime, Welcome WAGON has released preliminary details on the planned Landing Ceremony. A multinational site selection committee is wrapping up evaluation of candidate locations to serve as the Ambassadors' embassy.

Business and Finance News (24,869 shares): ***Defense Investors Hang Ten as Sector Surfs Wave Fueled by Military Dollars; Charitable Giving and Luxury Travel Soar***

Shortly after news broke about the so-called "Ambassadors'" upcoming rendezvous with Earth, financial analysts predicted that the value of fiat currencies around the world would plunge, warning markets would experience a meltdown as people gathered with their loved ones to wait out — with dread or excitement — the impending arrival.

Instead, the revelation birthed a whole new set of momentum stocks. Despite reassurances the Ambassadors are not out for conquest, not everyone on Wall Street — or in Washington, Beijing, Riyadh or Moscow — is banking on a kumbaya First Contact. Defense contractors, firearm manufacturers, and distributors of survival gear are all driving a robust bull market after an initial dip.

At the same time, megachurches and community organizations find themselves overwhelmed by donations. "People are desperate to redeem their souls before the 'invasion'," observed Jenny Zhou, pastor with the First Lutheran Church of Kalamazoo, Michigan.

Tourism and recreation are also benefitting. The industry reported a 300 percent increase in spending compared to this time last year, with consumers throwing their retirement savings at "bucket list" items. "Nobody's even raising an eyebrow at the waiver form these days," said Sergio Martinez, owner and CEO of St. Croix-based X-Treme Ocean Skydiving, LLP. "They just shrug and say, 'Why the hell not?'"

●

@ConniePadillaPYPF | Power Your Personal Finance® @PYPersonalFinancePodcast • Jan 14
837.5K Followers

Wow! Incredibly honored to be recognized as a "top finance expert" by @PersonalInvestorMag this week.

[link to *Personal Investor Magazine.* Where are Americans Turning for Financial Advice During the Impending Apocalypse?]

[2.7K replies, 5.3K retweets, 8.6K likes]

●

@ConniePadillaPYPF | Power Your Personal Finance® @PYPersonalFinancePodcast • Jan 16
859.6K Followers

Had a great chat this week with my fellow money guru @TKRawlins on @TheTalkExchange about all the #marketcraziness right now.

[link to *Wall Street Bytes.* Technology Stocks Tumble Across the Motherboard: NASDAQ stumbles as industry doomsayers claim technologically advanced "Ambassadors" could spell the end for Silicon Valley.]

@ConniePadillaPYPF | Power Your Personal Finance® @PYPersonalFinancePodcast • Jan 16
859.6K Followers

But let's talk about what's happening on #MainStreet! Next week on the podcast I'll do a deep dive into how the Ambassadors are affecting the pocketbooks of REAL PEOPLE. DM me if you have a story you'd like to share!

[1.7K replies, 5.8K retweets, 10.4K likes]

•

Message to ConniePadillaPYPF from ETFrank1701 • Jan 23

Hi, Ms. Padilla. You probably don't remember me, but I was caller 7 on Power Your Personal Finance live stream episode #10. You even told me to reach out anytime if I still had trouble taking control of my personal finance journey.

Your words of empowerment that day really inspired me. So much so that I'm now the de facto "economics expert" among my friends and coworkers — they've even started asking ME for advice! Whenever I'm unsure of the answer, I'll reread a chapter of your book, replay one of your podcast episodes, or ask the PYPF community for help.

But now we all have the same question on our minds, and it's one I just don't know how to answer: Why in the universe is humanity reacting the way it is to the Ambassadors' arrival?

We just don't get it. I mean, the Ambassadors were really clear on having peaceful intentions. Officially, world leaders keep saying this is great news for the planet. But you — Connie Padilla, #1 personal finance guru — always say that money speaks louder than words. Well, a lot of people are spending money in ways that show they're scared of an invasion or think the Ambassadors are out to cheat everybody.

So, can you tell me: WHY are humans reacting this way? And what do YOU think about it?

Thanks so much; loved the last episode!

Frank

P.S. Which "rational, intelligent being" came up with the invasion scenario, anyway? It makes NO sense for an invader to give their invadee a heads-up IMHO.

Message to ETFrank1701 from ConniePadillaPYPF • Feb 12

Hey, Frank!

So sorry for the delay — I was COMPLETELY overwhelmed by all the terrific personal finance stories folks sent me last month. Teach me to ask half the metaverse to DM me. :(But of course, I remember my newest, biggest fan! I even told you to reach out to me anytime, right?

It's super interesting you and your friends are putting yourself in the Ambassadors' shoes (do they even have shoes? LOL). Because I'd say the issue here is that the rest of humanity is NOT putting itself in the Ambassadors' shoes; nope, not at all!

It's our first time meeting extraterrestrials — so who or what else do we even have to compare them to, besides ourselves? FWIW, I'd say most people assume the Ambassadors are a lot like us and weighing the risks vs. rewards of First Contact based on that. Those "peaceful intentions," the promises of cultural exchange, whatever goods & services they (probably) have to sell? They just don't outweigh the risk of an invasion (and don't even think of bringing logic into the conversation, my friend) or — more likely — being rolled by little green men.

Again, GREAT question, and maybe one I'll post a video about later in the week!

Connie

Message to ConniePadillaPYPF from ETFrank1701 • Feb 13

Hi, Ms. Padilla.

Well, that's SUPER depressing.

I mean, if you were the Ambassadors, how could you even counter that?

And do YOU feel that way, too? Or are you just another person trying to make a buck off the situation? I'm such a fan of yours, but I have to admit I'm also kind of disappointed in you right now. You're racking up all the ratings, giving people all the advice on 'weathering the storm' and 'profiting from the uncertainty'. But are you thinking AT ALL about what this'll mean for the future of humanity when the Ambassadors see what's happening and decide WTH and go home? It's risk vs. reward, after all! What's the reward for the Ambassadors if humanity won't even give them a real chance?

In the end, nobody gains, and everyone loses.

Frank

Message to ConniePadillaPYPF from ETFrank1701 • Feb 14

Hi, Ms. Padilla.

First off, I'm really sorry. I was a jerk in my last message and I wouldn't blame you for blocking me altogether.

But if you haven't, can I admit I really was hoping you had the answer, just like you always seem to have the answer in all your books and podcasts. I have to confess I'm personally invested in this (no pun intended), though I can't say much more.

Most of the time, I agree with my colleagues: the Ambassadors SHOULD leave if this is going to be the reception. We'd like to believe humanity has a lot of potential, even with all the evil they do to each other and their planet. But, with this? Unlike humans, Ambassadors aren't going to throw good money after bad, and there really seems to be no hope, at least not for both our peoples coming together. And yet — I can't help recalling that there really IS potential. And I realize: both of us DO have a lot to gain. Not $$$, but a lot to learn, to share, to explore together. Both of us winners.

If you're right, like you usually are, and it's all about risk vs. reward, maybe the real question is: How do we go about changing the balance?

I know it's a big ask of one personal finance guru. But you're always telling people to find their own power. Well, YOU have a lot of power — all the followers and admirers who've been inspired by you. I just wish you'd use it for something much bigger than selling books or advising people on their 401(k)s.

Still your biggest fan,
Frank

●

The Frontpage Feed: Special Edition
SUBJECT LINE: *Has First Contact been cancelled?!*
Top Ranked News (49,076,329 shares): *Ambassadors' Ship No Longer on Course to Rendezvous with Earth*

Political leaders and science fiction afficionados around the world panicked yesterday morning when several Earth-based and orbiting observatories, which have kept their instruments trained on the incoming vessel for months, all reported a sudden change in the trajectory at around seven o'clock UTC. Welcome WAGON released an official statement at two o'clock in the afternoon, confirming the reports but cautioning the public not to jump to conclusions.

"We are all puzzled and, yes, concerned about this reported change in the ship's flight path. But rest assured we have our top astrophysicists looking into it," the statement declared. "We must remember that the Ambassadors are, technologically speaking, leaps and bounds ahead of us. For all we know, this anomaly may be well within expected parameters."

"Maybe they forgot something?" was the top punchline on the late-night comedy shows. Similar humorous memes quickly gained popularity across the metaverse.

But others fail to see the new development as a joking matter. The now-vindicated whistleblower, credited with starting the entire chain of events, returned yesterday afternoon to the virtual public square, claiming yet another message from the Ambassadors was intercepted and held back from public release. "Even I'm not certain what, exactly, is in that message," the former insider admitted. "But it sure as heck sent everyone into a tizzy." The White House press secretary immediately denied the claim, as have spokespeople with the other nations cited in the allegation.

Welcome WAGON in the meantime has convened an emergency session, set to meet tomorrow morning.

Stay tuned for more reporting from *The Frontpage Feed* as this story continues to develop.

Business and Finance News (10,492 shares): *Closing Bell Round-up*

Personal finance juggernaut Connie Padilla this week announced an undetermined hiatus of her popular podcast, *Power Your Personal Finance!* along with a pause on all future interviews and speaking engagements. She gave no reason, only telling her millions of fans through social media to "Stay tuned: something big is on its way!"

Speculation immediately arose that Ms. Padilla is using this time to launch a new Power Your Personal

Finance branded initiative. The personal finance guru's popularity shot through the stratosphere as the Ambassadors' ship drew closer to Earth, attracting an increasing number of fans and admirers with her trademark calm and steady advice. "Connie really has her finger on the pulse of Main Street," said T.K. Rawlins, who often appears with Ms. Padilla on shows like The Talk Exchange and Financial Forecast. "It's no wonder she's so quickly become not just America's, but *everyone's* personal finance confidant."

Indeed, only White House Economic Adviser P.J. Kuppenheimer has similar name recognition, "but without the comfort factor," according to Rawlins. "I trust her," commented a member of the *Power Your Personal Finance!* Community Platform, who posts by the name of "$$ $urvivor." "Connie really gets me, gets *us*," gushed Retire Early or Bust, another member of the online community. "Whatever she has in store, I know it'll be huge!"

•

Message to ConniePadillaPYPF from ETFrank1701 • Feb 20

Hi, Ms. Padilla.

I hope you're doing well. Since I never heard back from you, I guess you must be very busy. Or you really did block me, after all.

This is the last time I'll contact you, and it's to say goodbye. My job transfer's been cancelled, so there's no longer any reason to continue on with my personal finance education. I will miss all your advice and inspiration. I learned so much from you, not only about personal finance and economics, but gained a better understanding of the world in general.

On a final note, I read you've taken a step back from your media empire to focus on "something big". I can only hope my last message inspired you in some small way, though nothing like how much you've inspired me. Either way, I wish you and everyone in the PYPF community only the very best.

Frank

Message to ETFrank1701 from ConniePadillaPYPF • Feb 21

Hey, Frank!

You should have a little more faith in me, if you really are my biggest fan! Didn't I say I could help you?

I wasn't offended at all by your message, though I was pretty stunned. Yours was the biggest challenge ANYONE has ever offered me — and probably the most meaningful, too. It made all the advice I've been called on to give up to then seem small and petty in comparison.

BTW, do you know why I started giving personal finance advice in the first place? Coming from a family with very little, I saw how money gives people so many more choices. Funny; now I see it works the other way around, too — obsessing over wealth can really limit us, huh? Your words pushed me to see things from another perspective. Through "alien eyes," LOL.

You're 100% right about all of it. We would all lose out if our two peoples never met and learned from each other. You're also right that I do have a lot of influence, more than I realized. So now I'm planning to use that power for "something big." Something much, much bigger than selling books or advising people on their 401(k)s.

I'm going to change that balance.

Connie

Message to ETFrank1701 from ConniePadillaPYPF • Feb 21

Y'know, thinking back, I never actually gave you my personal mail, hmm?

Tell your friends and coworkers you'll be moving forward with that "transfer," after all.

•

***Power Your Personal Finance!* Community Platform.**
Enter username and password.
Hot Topic: Discuss Connie Padilla's latest article in *Personal Investor!* (3,228 replies)
Excerpt — *If you have an entrepreneurial streak, arrival of the "Ambassadors" could mean an opportunity to finally kick off that side-hustle. Think about it: an entirely different species could open up whole new markets for goods and*

services. Instead of reacting *to First Contact, be* proactive *and brainstorm ways to pivot and boost your earnings potential.* Related link: *The Smart Side-Hustle*, available at the following retailers.

Moderator: Way to go, Connie! Okay, folks: let's get *proactive* in this forum. Share some of *your* ideas for Post-First Contact side hustles!

Retire Early or Bust: Do these aliens even breathe our air? My brother-in-law works for a factory that makes oxygen for hospitals. Maybe we could manufacture whatever *they* breathe and sell it? [37 likes]

Country Mouse Investing in Cheese: I'll bet even my rat-hole hick town would seem exotic to visitors from another world. I could start a tour guide gig! "Come and see Earth's biggest ball of twine..." [11 hearts]

Mortgage Burning Party: Not a bad idea, CMIIC! Personally, I think souvenirs are where it's at. I'll call my company "Made on Earth". [52 likes]

[*jump to latest comments*]

Feeling Bearish: Hold on here, people. Who says the Ambassadors will cough up cash for anything? Maybe they don't even have anything like "money" where they're from. Honestly, I think our girl Connie is being too optimistic this time. [5 likes]

Retire Early or Bust: Maybe Connie IS being an optimist — but isn't she right that nothing positive will happen until you start being proactive and take power? And isn't that better than throwing trillions of dollars at tanks and aircraft and crap that probably wouldn't last half a minute against a bunch of space invaders? [542 likes]

Country Mouse Investing in Cheese: Hey, I say it's worth taking the risk! *This* mouse is grabbing the chance to get out of the corporate rat race. [73 likes]

Mortgage Burning Party: Does that mean the Ambassadors will buy my souvenirs? [37 likes]

●

The Frontpage Feed:

SUBJECT LINE: ***First Contact back on track and straight to the bank!***

Top Ranked News (43, 722, 549 shares): ***'Just a Blip': Ambassadors Stay the Course for Little Blue Planet***

The world held its breath last week when it appeared the Ambassadors had aborted their mission. 'We all just about sullied our pants,' relayed a member of Welcome WAGON, on condition of anonymity. "Considering all the time, effort and money put into preparing for First Contact — *the* event of the millennium — what would we even *do* if the Ambassadors decided to change their minds?!"

The shock turned into relief this Tuesday, when observatories confirmed the Ambassadors were still making their way to Earth, albeit slightly behind schedule. "It must have been just a blip," chuckled Lesedi Nkosi, astrophysicist at the South African National Space Agency. "I guess Welcome WAGON shouldn't roll up the red carpet just yet."

Many are now criticizing the whistleblower for inciting unnecessary panic with allegations about the cover up of a fourth message, received from the Ambassadors at the same time their ship appeared to veer off course. "My fellow world leaders and I are committed to open and honest dialogue with the public about every aspect of this momentous development in human history," the United States president spoke yesterday evening from the Oval Office. "The time for secrecy and self-interest has passed."

Business and Finance News (132,837 shares): ***Will Extraterrestrials Put Extra Cash in Our Pockets? This Personal Finance Guru Thinks So.***

What started as a provocative article in *Personal Investor* is now all every wannabe entrepreneur is talking about.

Connie Padilla — of *Power Your Personal Finance!* fame — set off a global conversation last week with a powerful essay [click here] laying out her argument that the Ambassadors' arrival will stimulate innovation and goose the economy. " 'Ambassadors' is a misnomer," Ms. Padilla proclaimed. "Replace 'alien' and 'extraterrestrial' with 'customer' and 'client.' You want to approach First Contact like a *real* entrepreneur? Take control of the situation.

Chuck that tinfoil hat, put away your H.G. Wells, and start drafting your goddamn business plan, already!"

Padilla's messages of financial empowerment garnered her a loyal fan base that ballooned with the first revelations about the Ambassadors. Economists around the world are finally starting to take her seriously, too. "Ms. Padilla may have a point," allowed P.J. Kuppenheimer, the White House economic adviser who has been openly skeptical about the Ambassadors' intentions. "Under the Theory of Interstellar Trade, and despite the obvious challenges related to transport costs, the Ambassadors could be incentivized to manufacture high-value goods and invest their profits locally. That would be to Earth's economic advantage."

The financial markets appear to agree with both Padilla and Kuppenheimer. Blue chip stocks rallied again, but this time the action on Wall Street wasn't concentrated in the defense sector. Investors across the board are expressing renewed optimism over the future. One manufacturer after another has announced hefty investments in R&D in anticipation of the Ambassadors' arrival. The effects aren't limited to the big corporate players, either; state and local agencies reported a surge in the pulling of new business licenses and filing of articles of incorporation.

"It's time to stop being scared," Padilla encouraged members of her online community platform. "Be excited!"

●

Message to ConniePadillaPYPF from ETFrank1701 • Mar 18

Hi, Ms. Padilla,

I meant to message you earlier, but things have been incredibly hectic, with everyone making final preparations to open up our new location. That's right: my transfer is on course to happen after all! It may sound odd, but it's really all thanks to you. The only downside is that things are busier than ever as a result, but I'm not complaining!

I know you've been extremely busy, too. I think every other communication beamed from Earth these days has your signature on it. You seem to be everywhere — in articles, on your podcast, popping into your community forum, giving interviews, bringing people together. I'm amazed by all you're doing, inspiring people to see not just the risks, but all the rewards a relationship between our peoples could bring.

Most of all, I'm amazed that someone like me could inspire someone like you. You were right all along, too: it's up to each of us to take power over our own future — and that includes our shared future. It's a future I'm feeling so much more optimistic about, too.

Your biggest fan in the universe,
Frank

●

The Frontpage Feed: Special Edition
SUBJECT LINE: *Get ready for the biggest watch party ever: ten celebrity chefs share their out-of-this-world recipes*
Top Ranked News (4,043,852 shares): *'We're On Our Way!' Ambassadors Reassure Humanity*

Relief, joy, and anticipation were on clear display around the world with the public release of the Ambassadors' latest missive to Earth. According to the Welcome WAGON Secretariat, the message amounts to confirmation of arrival and an apology for "potentially causing confusion" among human officials due to "a mild correction in trajectory".

"We remain enthusiastic about this first meeting between our respective species," the Ambassadors emphasized in multiple languages. "And we hope this is just the beginning of new opportunities for our two peoples. We both have much to exchange, and countless ways to profit from diplomatic ties."

Business and Finance News (98,302 shares): *Ambassadors' Latest Message Sends Markets Soaring*

"We both have much to exchange, and countless ways to profit," was the sentence from the Ambassador's latest missive that investors zoomed in on.

"Are they talking trade deals?" said Yan Sundström, Director-General of the World Trade Organization, now undergoing drastic restructuring in preparation for the Ambassadors' arrival. "What items will be on the table?"

Welcome WAGON, apparently taking personal finance guru Connie Padilla's advice to "take control of the situation," announced formation of an international blue-ribbon panel to analyze the economic opportunities presented by establishing trade relations with extraterrestrials. The panel, to be co-chaired by Ms. Padilla herself, along with White House Economic Adviser P.J. Kuppenheimer, will report out a framework set of recommendations prior to First Contact.

When asked at the press conference about her outsize impact, driving this new wave of optimism, Padilla replied: "I don't believe that one person alone, no matter how influential, can move the entire world. But, as my biggest fan in the universe recently reminded me, I can — and I should — give it a nudge."

The Nikkei reached an all-time high today on the news, with the FTSE closing just a whisker below its own record.

●

Message to ETFrank1701 from ConniePadillaPYPF • Mar 19

Hey, Frank!

That's fantastic news!!

I guess my diabolical plan worked, after all. What's the point of having power and influence if you can't use it to make the galaxy a better place? Though I guess I should feel a little bit bad about it; in a way, I'm tricking people about how everyone is going to "profit" from First Contact. But I'm not wrong about that in a bigger sense: everyone WILL profit from our peoples meeting, just not in the way they're assuming I meant.

While you're making your big move, I'm thinking about my next step, too. I want humanity to have some grander ambition to aspire to than just feathering our own nest. Sure, maybe we need to use the promise of wealth as a goad in the short run, but long-term I want us to look up toward the stars instead of always down at our own pocketbooks. I've never considered taking on something so huge, but maybe if we work together, it'll be easier to tackle? I think we make a "stellar" team, LOL.

So — now that your transfer's on again, I think we should finally meet in person. In, say, two months, four days, eleven hours and change from when I hit "send"?

Connie

Message to ETFrank1701 from ConniePadillaPYPF • Mar 19

I also think it's about time you knock off this "Ms. Padilla" stuff and start calling me "Connie".

Message to ETFrank1701 from ConniePadillaPYPF • Mar 19

What should I call you?

●

The Frontpage Feed: Morning Edition
SUBJECT LINE: *WELCOME TO EARTH!*
Top Ranked News (102,486,093 shares): *Ambassadors Arrive: A Photojournalist's Moment-by-Moment Diary*

Caption 1: "Houston, they've arrived." *View from International Space Station.* Ambassador mothership parks in Earth orbit. *Caption 2:* "Bienvenidos!" *Montevideo, Uruguay.* Ambassador landing craft touches down in the middle of Plaza Independencia. *Caption 3:* "A historic meeting." *Foreground:* Ambassador delegation exchanges greetings with Welcome WAGON emissaries. *Caption 4.* "We have much to learn from each other." *New York City, United States.* Ambassador Glolteesh Hroné, left, delivers speech before United Nations General Assembly.

Business and Finance News (59,340,271 shares): *Ambassador-onomics 101 To Precede Trade Talks*

Markets soared Tuesday on affirmation the Ambassadors are, indeed, eager to open trade discussions with the World Trade Organization — the first time that body will truly represent the entire planet. "We're going to make the 'Made on Earth' label *mean* something," Yan Sundström proclaimed at yesterday's press conference, the Ambassadors' Special Attaché for Interspecies Business and Finance, Flelviing Rlankonī, at his side.

Investor optimism remained undampened despite both parties citing a need for preliminary discussions before trade talks begin in earnest. "We're not even talking about an apples-to-oranges comparison in how our two economies work. Hell, we're not even talking fruit," said U.S. Trade Representative Marcela Tsai. "The Ambassadors operate in a completely different manner, and it's going to take some time just to wrap our heads around it."

"The Ambassadors seem to take the concept of 'knowledge economy' to an entirely new level — one apparently based on an open sharing mechanism rather than the exchange-for-value economic models we're familiar with on Earth," explained Claire Ahaisse, economic sociologist with Princeton University. "If their claims are accurate, life on the Ambassadors' home world blows every single metric of our own Legatum Prosperity Index out of the water when it comes to measuring global well-being," she went on to add. "Personally, I'd love to know how they do it."

Ahaisse joins a growing multitude of economists, sociologists, political scientists, philosophers, and civic activists around the world fascinated by what humanity is learning about the Ambassadors. "At the same time we're selling the Ambassadors on human goods and services, scholars and the mainstream public alike are increasingly 'sold' on what they have to offer us," Ahaisse noted.

To lay the foundation for negotiations, the WTO's Blue-Ribbon Panel on Exploring Interstellar Economic Opportunity is launching a series of cross-cultural learning sessions; special attaché Rlankoní will be representing the Ambassadors in these conversations. The events will be open to the public and simulcast around the globe.

Early reports of close collaboration between the special attaché and the panel's chair, Connie Padilla, are particularly promising. "Connie and Flelviing hit it off right away," observed Ms. Padilla's co-chair, T.J. Kuppenheimer. "They make a pretty stellar team."

●

LIBRARY: Latest Episode. Downloading...

Power Your Personal Finance! Ranked #1 in genre. Please leave a review! *Episode transcript.*

Cue teaser, introductory music, sponsor plug

Connie: Happy spread-the-wealth Wednesday, everybody! I'm Connie Padilla, Certified Financial Planner, welcoming you to episode seven-eighty-seven of the *Power Your Personal Finance!* podcast. Where we talk not just about everything that can affect your pocketbook — but also peel back the rules and assumptions governing the game *all* of us have been playing. It's been gratifying, hearing from so many listeners how much you appreciate the new direction this show has taken these past few months.

Which is why the *Power Your Personal Finance!* network is launching an entirely *new* show all about exploring the new financial frontiers First Contact has opened for us. Can you believe it's been over a *year* now? Anyhow, it's about time we really explore the potential of this still-nascent relationship between our species.

Most exciting of all, I'll be co-hosting the show with my best buddy, Flelviing Rlankoní! Truly an extraordinary personality — explorer, academic, diplomat. And, I would say, something of an entrepreneur himself, though he'd probably disagree! Flelviing's made a study of human culture, specializing in economics and finance, and never fails to surprise with his insights.

Anyhow, this show will be looking at the big picture, aimed at listeners from both planets. We'll talk about how to invest in *super* foreign markets, the nuts and bolts of building cross-species enterprises, pros and cons of doing business across the light years, and how to survive life on a predominantly capitalist planet — plus successful alternatives elsewhere and lessons we've all learned along the way.

And every episode we'll ask of humans and Ambassadors alike: how can we improve?

That's why we're calling it *Outperforming Ourselves*.

And to give you a little taste of what's to come, I've brought Flelviing on as my surprise guest for today's show! Oh, and don't be surprised if I seem to slip up on his name every now and again — kind of an inside joke.

Now, before we start, a quick disclaimer. You know the boilerplate, folks. *Power Your Personal Finance* is purely for educational and entertainment purposes. Anything said on this show should not be construed as individual financial, legal, tax, or accounting advice; listeners are advised to discuss their personal financial situation and goals with a financial professional. And remember: while we talk about stocks, bonds, and interstellar investments on this show, past performance is *not* indicative of future results!

Let's all aim to do better.

C.H. Rosenberg's story "Indicative of Future Results" was originally published in Metaphorosis on Friday, 6 May 2022. See magazine.metaphorosis.com

About the author

Writing as an armchair economist, in real life C.H. Rosenberg is a grizzled policy wonk who spent an early career fighting in the trenches of local politics in Southern California. Rosenberg currently works at one of Washington, D.C.'s many alphabet-soup think tanks, brainstorming all sorts of amazing ways to save the planet.

The Waves in Which We Drown

Rubella Dithers

June 8th, 2189

I'm afraid of space.

That's why you're up there and I'm down here, sitting on a dune with a broken nose and a split lip, stabbing a shuttle into my hand while I try to repair the net I dropped on a reef last week. We don't even have any spare rope; I have to scavenge what I can off of even worse nets. The fibers are all rotting and falling apart on me. It would be easier to get through this if you were here. Stupid of me to think 'friends forever' implied being together in some capacity.

It's easy to ignore the pain in my hand. I feel like giving up and just sewing the loose edges of this net together, but I know what your dad would say. *You half-assed it, as usual. This is your last chance. You should be grateful. What else do you have? You failed the first time, dropped out the second time. This is your only chance. Be grateful.*

The worst thing is you don't even write.

It's like you want to forget this place, like you want to forget us. Like when you swore that as soon as you left this town you'd never eat fish again, as if that amalgamated goop they pump into you isn't pasted together with carrageenan and anchovies and bonito.

I don't blame you. I want to leave too. It didn't work out as well for me, did it? Because now I'm stuck here with a bunch of old people and kids and everyone in between is dead or gone.

Can you believe your parents still buy into the line that we're doing something vital with our duct-taped trawlers and broken nets? Like we can't see the state's big commercial ships sitting on the horizon, picking up every fish that so much as waves a fin in their direction? Half the town works on them as it is. And our own catches keep getting smaller. Listening to your parents' cheering when another supply shuttle is launched makes my skin crawl.

While I'm on forced shore leave, I also get to watch over Nila. Did you forget about your real sister too? We don't have a shovel for her, so she's digging with her hands. We've been out here since before dawn and she's barely got half a bucket of clams. After this I'm supposed to tutor her, since the school server went down again.

I'm going to give up on fixing the net for today and help Nila with the clams. I don't have anything else to say, so I'll sign off. I miss you and I hate you and I really, really wish you'd get back to me.

●

June 10th, 2189

I'm at the bar reviewing Nila's curriculum, trying to understand why a 9-year-old needs to learn set theory. Instead of times tables, she's doing Cayley tables, because knowing $ab = ba$ is more important than knowing 7×6. Right.

A bar is the worst possible place for me to be studying, but it's the only building that's still on the power grid. If that goes down, they've got fish oil lamps, and everyone's too drunk to care about the smell. I miss studying together, it was easier to focus. For me, at least. I have no idea what you got out of it. I look at a proof and I'm like, sure, it makes sense, it's obvious to me. But I say that about anything, even if it's wrong. You were always so formal, so meticulous.

The only possible way this experience could be worse is if what's-his-face showed up. So of course he has. He's with some rich girl. I can tell she has money because she's wearing shoes, how fucked up is that? I have to scrub my feet with sand for half an hour to get all the dried wine and ash off. But that's how bad things have gotten since you left. It sounds like I'm connecting the two events, but I'm not. OK, maybe.

I never liked him. And no, it's not because dating him meant that you spent less time with me. It's because he's a creep. I mean, when you told him you were studying for the navigator exam, he dropped off. Then, when I failed and you didn't, he came up to me talking about how 'selfish' you were. As if I'd want to commiserate with him, of all people. I didn't just lose you, I lost the chance to leave.

Now he's got this new girl, like you never existed. This one looks like she's pregnant. I mean the dangerous, beyond the point of no return kind of pregnant. Why anyone would risk having kids now is beyond me, but people keep doing it. Do they think they'll get on a generation ship? Do they think there's still room? Who needs fishers in space?

I fixed the rope situation. Once I figured out what to do it was pretty easy. I sold some of your stuff. Nothing important, just your old computer. The one I bought parts for, when I worked between two ships all year and didn't see land once while you stayed in school.

I sold it to the scrap yard.

●

June 16th, 2189

The ping timed out for the last few messages I sent. Either the sat relay is down or you're still ignoring me. We both know which is more likely.

Your dad took the crew out and left me behind. Took the new net with him, though.

Since there is nothing else for me to do, I was thinking about taking the entrance exam again. I'm not past the cut-off age. Yet.

Nila wants to take it, after she finishes the standard curriculum in a few years. I think she'll do fine, she's a lot like you. The problem is, your parents can't afford the textbooks. I could try to teach her myself, but it's not like

I'm doing a great job now. I don't even know if I'll be around long enough.

I could pirate the books if I hadn't scrapped your old computer for a net. And if we had internet access. I might turn into a real pirate if I can't figure out what to do with myself. I'd be robbing other poor people, though, so probably not.

If you pass by one of those nonresponsive satellites, do me a solid and hack it so we get free access in town.

●

June 30th, 2189

I got the bends.

I know we used to joke about it when we were diving, but this seriously sucks. I've been in bed for a week.

Nila is the one who spotted me. I don't remember being pulled out of the water. They think... Well, I'm sure you know what they think. If someone else went out alone on a banged-up fiberglass dinghy, without the sense to even tie a line to herself, I'd think the same thing.

I just wanted to try diving again. Remember how we used to freedive every day after school, jumping off that big sea stack in the cove? I haven't gone since you've left, and I pushed myself too far, that's all. And I'm paying for it. Everything hurts. There's this deep, frightening ache throughout my arms and legs. When I told the nurse about it, she just upped the oxygen intake.

Nila keeps checking on me. It's sweet, but kind of annoying. I hate that she saw me like that. Like this. I think she thinks it's her fault, that she should have been watching me closer. I'm supposed to be the one looking out for her. She treats me like your replacement. I'm not. I can't be the kind of big sister you were. I'm glad I'm an only child. What a shitty role model I would have been.

When I was down there, in the water, I could pretend I was with you. I could pretend that I wasn't afraid to drift through space just above Earth, from where you look down on the rest of us through the hazy veil of atmosphere. Falling weightless through that ambivalent medium, the vast and unknowable water that siphons heat and deadens sound, sustained the illusion. I felt terribly alone. My chest seized. I wanted to claw my way back to the surface, but I forced myself down. I needed to be deeper.

I didn't notice the regulator's pressure dropping until I was struggling to breathe. There was a leak in the line. I was fucked. I ditched the useless gear and struggled towards the surface, growing weaker with each stroke. I could feel the sun's warmth and I pushed through the current. The closer I got, the more blackness invaded the edges of my vision. I was tired, Sarah. I'm always fucking tired.

That's where my memory ends, as abruptly as a dream. It was beautiful, for a moment.

●

July 10th, 2189

I caught Nila going through a massive copy of Dummit and Foote. Kids these days. She's claiming it 'just showed up', but she probably stole it from the university library. At her age she shouldn't be skipping school to go all the way to the city for that, especially not alone. I would've done it if she asked me. Still, I don't think she's wrong for doing it, and we were worse at her age. She's mad I don't believe her, though, because when I asked if I could look at it she flipped me off. I didn't teach her that. Did you?

●

August 22nd, 2189

Your dad still won't let me on the boat. In fact, he's told everyone else in town not to give me work, period. I spent a few days walking up the coast to see if anyone would hire me. It was a bad idea.

At the first group of shacks I approached, an old auntie came out to shoo me away. Her hands were splotchy pink and shaking. I could see through the door she came out of. Inside there was another thin woman, holding a twisted child who screamed like a pig being slaughtered. Someone saw me looking and slammed the door shut, but I could still hear the kid. I walked down to the little cove they fished in. The waves were lethargic, lapping fetid red foam onto the shore.

The farther north I went, the worse it got.

I went home, thinking about clam digging. The problem is everyone's got their kids doing it these days. Even old folks are out there. They're pulling clams out of the sand faster than they can breed.

It took me a while to figure out, but I finally realized what I could do to make money. Salt. I'm a salt woman now. I can't say I came up with the idea on my own. I heard the packing house was having trouble getting shipments. It's only a matter of time before other people in town get the same idea. It's not exactly novel.

I borrowed a few sheets from your room. I hope you don't mind. I can't afford to keep a fire burning all day, so after I boil off most of the water I spread the salt over the sheets to dry the rest of the way.

Your mom talked to me about paying rent. Your dad must have asked her to; I don't think she cares. The original deal was I would work for your dad while staying there, which I did. For years. Of course he'd make me work, not pay me, and then charge me room and board. Honestly? I don't blame them.

Nila says she wants to accelerate her curriculum. I told her not to overwork herself and she rolled her eyes. I think she's sick of fish.

•

September 6th, 2189

I was at the bar again last night. It's kind of a regular thing now, a weekly ritual. Remember how much I used to hate drinking? The veil has been lifted.

I was sitting at the bar, nursing my watered-down seaweed wine. Normally I'd be studying at one of the tables, where the lighting is better and the surfaces less sticky, but the lights were out. That's been happening a lot more lately.

The counter is also farther from the pool table and its endless clacking. A few weeks ago the bartender dug this wind-up radio out of somewhere. I didn't know what it was at first, and now I'm obsessed with the thing. We take turns cranking it. It's the only way to get regular news. That's how I learned they're doing a mass launch next month.

The remaining cohort in orbit, your cohort, will start their flybys, siphoning gravitational force off planets and comets and whatever's convenient so they can be flung deeper into space. You'll break and scatter like billiard balls, each mapped trajectory a new path for humanity to follow towards some possibly viable world. Even if it takes us millennia, even if we never find a new planet to latch onto like a leech, at least you'll be out there, an eternal reminder of what we were.

Since trying to contact you directly isn't working, I'm relaying future messages. The navigation base enabled permissions for me to use their ground proxy, and confirmed your signal is extant. When are you going to respond?

When you finally get what you want, when you finally leave this place for good, how will I be able to reach you?

●

September 15th, 2189

This is a rude question. You're probably not in any shape to answer it.

What's it like to lose your autonomy? I know they say that isn't what happens, but that's not true. If something else, some executable set of instructions, controls your decision making you cannot be autonomous. By definition.

Is that why you aren't writing back? Am I sending this to an empty shell?

The idea of losing who I am. That is what I'm afraid of, more than being in space. What happens during that discontinuity? I think about it when I fall asleep. How easily I trust that I will wake up as the same person.

What happens in that space of time? Where do *you* go? Are you still the old *you*, or is this a new *you* that merely shares the same memories?

How would you even know?

●

October 24th, 2189

I have achieved a new low. Some people in town got together and set up a bigger salt operation. They've got an entire field for evaporating the water, huge piles of salt raked up. The packing house isn't buying from me anymore.

Since I can't pay him, your dad kicked me out of the house. I'm sleeping on the beach, living off of ice plants, kelp, and whatever else washes up. Like that dead sea nettle I've been eyeing all day.

I still carry a lighter, though you're not around to borrow it, and if you were there's no fuel for it anyway. I'm trying to start a fire with some driftwood but most of the pieces I find are still wet. I've spun the flint wheel so many times my thumb's starting to bleed.

I did, finally, get a couple of sticks to light up. It's not very warm, but at least the flames are pretty.

•

November 20th, 2189

Nila turned 10. When that was us, we thought it was a big deal. Double digits and all that. It was significant. Nila wasn't that excited.

The bar radio's been less reliable lately. Some of the usual bands we pick up are garbled. I took Nila with me for her birthday, figuring she'd enjoy the novelty of it. Not that a bar is the best place for a kid, but it's not like we've got anything else around here. We were able to hear a few pieces of news, nothing interesting to a child, but she seemed happy enough. Whenever the sound cut out, or was jumbled, I pretended it was an encrypted message from you. I told her that you said how much you miss her, how grown up she is now. It made her day.

•

December 15th, 2189

I always hated it when you called me negative. I think you were trying to turn it into a joke, or maybe you wanted it to be true so we could be opposite. Magnetic poles.

Negative, positive. You know, the designations are completely arbitrary.

This morning your mom said something that reminded me of that. She lets me in the house when your dad's out. We were in the kitchen, threshing foxtails, bitching about how hard it was getting to find *weeds*, of all things. She told me to shut up, that I never have anything good to say. But I do. I'll prove it.

On the first of the month, that big factory purser went dark. Dead in the water. At the bar, people were talking about some satellites being knocked out of orbit. The reports we got over the radio just said 'systems malfunction'. I don't care what happened, I'm just glad it did. It took a week for tugboats to get out to the purser. Its crew had to abandon their net.

As soon as the purser limped out of sight, the town fishers moved in. I've never seen your dad move so fast in my life. Together, they got the abandoned net up. The town's still arguing about what to do with it, like anyone can actually use it.

Ever since, your dad has been able to go out farther than usual, and he got a big catch of quality herring, not the chewed-on stragglers he normally pulls up. The packing house needed extra workers and they hired me on the spot. So I've been gutting, filleting, pickling, and packing fish for the past three weeks. I know we said we would never work there, but what choice do I have?

It'd be better if they had enough gloves to go around.

●

December 16th, 2189

I forgot to mention that I watched the new cohort launch last month. Those improbably perfect orbs always creep me out. I know you're in one too. It's still weird. Plus, the speed, those maneuvers, aren't things a living person could withstand.

●

January 1st, 2190

Happy New Year. Can you tell I'm excited?

Nila got a tablet for her New Year's gift. She said I can use it when she's at school. I don't know where your parents got the money for it. Or high-speed sat access, for that matter. They seemed as surprised as I was when Nila opened the box. Maybe someone upstairs is looking out for us.

Through a combination of Nila whining and bribery, my 'gift' was your parents letting me stay in your room again. It's a bit infantilizing to have to follow their rules, but at least I have a bed. It beats fighting seagulls for half-eaten crabs any day.

More commercial ships showed up, effectively trapping us in the bay again. The fish rush is over, which means I got laid off from the factory. I'm back to harvesting salt, but I've got a new idea for it. I thought of it when I had to make lye water for the lutefisk. Who eats that stuff? Me, me eats it. Anyway, after my shifts I raided the dumpsters for the offal. I've been boiling it and skimming oil off the top to resell to the factory. I make less than I would if I were hired by them to do it. It's bullshit.

I put some aside for myself, and your family. Do you know how many kilos of fish guts it takes to make a bar of soap? I do. I have to render it a couple of times to get the fishiness out. I don't have anything to make it smell good, so the best I can do is make it smell like nothing.

In six months you'll be passing Jupiter in your space orb. At the rate I'm going, I'll be tanning fish skins in their own offal. Once I am clad entirely in fish leather, you will know I have accepted my lot in life.

●

February 13th, 2190

Every time I see a matrix, I think my brain dies a little. I'm on Jordan decomposition, it's a nightmare. There is no practical use for it; a computer can crunch linear equations faster than I could put them in normal form. A computer doesn't need to change the base first. Programming exists. Why should we have to learn something that a calculator can do? Whoever decides what material goes on the math exam is forever on my shit list.

I know what you'd say. You'd say it helps create convenient neural pathways to implement said programs, if one so chooses. A place where a memory can be stored. To exploit what we have that a computer lacks: consciousness, agency. Choice.

I don't care how many organic parts they replace, the human brain is not a computer. It shouldn't be treated like one. You're still a person. You're still in there, somewhere. Right?

I have money saved up for the exam. The way it ended for me last time was embarrassing. I freaked out during the first round of injections. I only got half the shots and felt like shit for weeks after, like I was going through withdrawal. Next time, they'll probably sedate me and keep going. If I get in.

I don't know. I mean, there aren't that many able-bodied adults anymore. I'm a bigger help than your parents want to admit. And what about Nila? It's not all about me.

I've been making the same excuse for years. We both know the truth.

I'm not as brave as you.

●

March 22nd, 2190

I saw him again at the bar. He actually came up to me, asking about you. I asked him about that pregnant woman. I haven't seen her for months. No baby, either. It was a shitty thing to do. I knew as soon as I saw the look on his face that she was dead.

If you had wanted kids, would you have stayed? Is it worth dying for?

●

April 21st, 2190

Your dad got it in his head that he wants to be a shrimper. I mean, if you've seen one eyeless cod with its scales slipping off and an oozing hole in its side, you've seen them all. No need to change careers over it. I'm pretty sure shrimp are bottom feeders and are at the top of the list for 'things in the ocean horribly deformed by pollution'.

His crew is very literally falling apart. Mercury poisoning is leaving more of the older folks too fucked-up to work. They're all shaky and confused. So, he's got me out on the boat again, picking crabs out of the traps and tossing them back in the water. They pinch me every time. You'd think they'd be happy for the chance to grow up before being killed. That's more than you can say for the rest of us.

The way these white shrimps' little legs flail around is too relatable. I'm close to throwing them all overboard. I mean, most of them are under the size limit. Not like anyone gives a shit about that.

Your dad has hinted, i.e., outright stated, that he wants me to take the shrimp up to the city's farmers' market this week with your mom and sister. He says he's already paid for a spot, assuming we can even get past the tent cities.

We'll have to borrow a truck to get there, and the toll fees, and I'll probably be up all night working the generator, charging the battery.

I think his usual clients aren't buying from him anymore. And if they aren't buying from him, they aren't buying from anyone else in town.

I don't know what to do. I suggested to your dad that we, as a town, could consolidate our resources, find a better distributor, and split the profits. You know, like a co-op.

He told me I'm the reason he has high blood pressure, but really, it's the mercury.

●

June 3rd, 2190

Well, Sarah, a funny thing happened. The commercial fishing ships went down again last month. Three at once. We were packing up for another drive to the market when it happened. Feds came through town a few days later, interrogating anyone who might have a motive. So, like, everyone. I'm surprised they didn't leave as soon as they took a look at how run down we all are.

Coincidentally, it was just in time for halibut season. There's a two-fish bag limit, so I'm out trolling on the boat again. We pulled up a six footer, took us nearly an hour. Imagine existing for that long just to end up on a hook. I prefer salmon. When we catch the run headed for the delta, at least I know they're going to die either way.

●

July 16th, 2190

I'm reviewing complex analysis, which is a relief. I found your copy of Ahlfors. I'm surprised your parents didn't sell it. The cover's faded to grey, and the pages are all soft along the edges. After this, it's all modular forms and L-functions.

I'm doing fine, I guess. At least with respect to the exam. Pretty confident. I got a copy of the official review material. The core content hasn't changed, so I'm not worried. About the exam, at least.

Your cohort's final flyby of Earth is coming up. Then you'll be swinging past Jupiter, Neptune, hurtling back to the Sun, glancing off it and getting the hell out of here. A human couldn't stand the acceleration. And you will reach a point when and where time stands still. You'll leave the galaxy in the time it takes to translate thought to action.

What I'm saying is, if you are planning to get back to me, do it soon. In a few months you'll be 20,000 years too late.

●

September 2nd, 2190

The exams are next week. I paid the fee in advance so I'll have some incentive to go through with it again. I hate finishing early, then reviewing my answers, then reviewing it again, then just sitting there doing nothing until time is out. I just want to get it over with.

Your sister's excited for me.

Does she know what happens to us? Not that 'ambassador to the universe, next stage of humanity' bullshit, but what they actually, physically, do to navigators?

Maybe she doesn't. She was only 6 when you left.

I don't know if I should tell her. People like us don't have many choices. That's how they reel us in. Give us the opportunity to become 'more than what we are'. If I tell her the truth, she might not go through with it. Maybe that's the best life for her. Maybe she will be too afraid of that choice, like me. And look at me, what kind of life is this? I have no dreams, no goals. My only friend isn't capable of verbal communication and is on the other side of the solar system. Is this the kind of future Nila would want for herself?

I keep sending these, hoping you'll actually say something. Instead I get these enticing little hints that I'm half convinced are just in my head. Just talk to me, please. I have no one else.

●

September 16th, 2190

I went swimming tonight. It's been hotter than usual, clinging to the upper 80s even this late into summer. They've been shutting down the power grid an hour after sundown. For the entire coast. We're all using fish-oil lamps. The beach is the only place I can get fresh air. The wind picks up in the evening, blowing away the lingering haze, exposing the stars cluttering the sky.

They say that when you get to space you'll be among the stars. But, really, you are surrounded by emptiness, caught in the vast distances between bright spots. That perfectly encapsulates how I feel about my life. Maybe I do belong up there.

So, I'm swimming. It isn't quite high tide, but it's getting there. I swim past the few summer algal blooms still clinging to what's left of the pilings. I'm out far enough that I won't get pushed back to shore right away. When the dunes blend into the murky sky, I stop. I float on my back, looking up at all those stars. Too many, if you ask me. The waves are gentle, as you might remember, and they pass under me. There are a few boats out, not many, too far away for me to care. I'm trying not to think about the exam tomorrow. This time it feels inevitable. Irrevocable.

Me. Ocean. Stars. Obsessive thinking. Have I set the scene yet? Good, because next thing I know, my pity party gets crashed. I hear something big slam the water, and it sends a huge wave over me. I flip over and swim under it, coming up to face the direction of the sound. I push wet hair out of my eyes, but I still can't see it. What I do see is a wave coming, and a shape bobbing on top of it. I swim for it fast, muscles burning, spitting out salt water. After a few minutes, when my arm comes down for another stroke, it hits something firm. I hit it again, and with a dull thud, it yields under my fist. It's enticingly warm. Somehow its surface is bending light, reflecting, refracting, I don't know, and I suddenly hope the physics portion doesn't include optics. I swim around the object and start pushing it towards shore. It is disturbingly light. I attribute this to the relative density of the salt water.

I get to shore and roll it through the sand, above the tide line. Since it rolls, I know it is spherical, and I feel a heavy sense of dread with that realization. I still can't see it that well, amid the confusion of sand and stars, but my hands tell me it's there. Two meters in diameter. I don't want to touch it again; it terrifies and disgusts me. But what if?

I keep my hands on it. I feel its warmth, the way the surface feels like skin, and nausea swells over me. I think about how humans are homeomorphic to the sphere. You would say a torus, to be pedantic. I'd counter with *n*-torus, to be worse. It depends on how many holes there are.

I think of more stupid, old arguments we had, trying to detach myself from the hands exploring this thing. I trigger something, or it reacts to me in some way, because light flashes across its surface like an asterisk, leaking some clear fluid, defining the shape. It abruptly splits along these lines with a wet, sucking sound, opening like a lotus, and the liquid oozes thickly over my bare feet. I squint against the light, but it only continues for a moment, then it dulls. Dies. My eyes start to readjust to starlight. I move in close, any caution I had erased.

I always thought it would smell bad inside these things, but there is no smell at all and that's worse.

Vision restored, I see long hair, a rounded face, lips slightly parted, an upturned nose, swaddled in dusk. And then I see all these things together and my heart cracks because it isn't you.

It's some other girl, naked and curled like a fetus in her womb, asleep. Her spine has been replaced with a bundle of impossibly thin strands of glass that shimmer with rainbows, even in this distant light. Her body is prosthetic. Mind and body are fundamentally the same; when they tried to entirely eliminate the latter, integration simply did not work. I know this much. And though human brains are not constructed to last forever, this silicone will last hundreds of years. You can synthesize it. These new parts of you can be replaced.

My next thought is to cover her. I believe there is no true her to mind, but if it were you, I would want you covered, against the cold wind coming off the water, against invasive eyes. Maybe it's a stupid thing to care about. My shirt is drenched with salt water, but it's the best I can do, so I peel it off. I step closer, between the petals of her ship, and lay my shirt across her. And then I go for help.

Within the hour, a team arrives, cordons off the entire beach. One of the helmeted workers in dark, rippling layers of complex polymers looks for a moment at the shirt I have left on her. They leave and return with a silvery safety blanket to replace it.

The questions they ask leave me unsettled, and they grow disturbed with my answers. If this were some simple error, an accident, they wouldn't need to ask anything at all. They ultimately decide I have nothing to do with this. I did the right thing by bringing her to shore. I climb up the dunes to go home, to your home. I take one last look as they guide the petals gently back into place. It's for her own good.

Now I'm home, failing to sleep. My thoughts keep jumping to her face, looking as if she were about to cry, forever locked in that expression. The exam is in a few short hours.

It was a violation. Touching that sphere, that ship. Touching her.

●

November 1st, 2190

I passed. Top ten. I'd be impressed if I weren't a decade older than everyone else.

Nila was thrilled. I acted like I was too, though I know she will follow me, like I'm following you. Your parents looked relieved. I leave in two months.

I wish I had something to make this headache go away.

●

December 31st, 2190

This is the last New Year I will celebrate. No gifts this time. Just food, the things we never have. Gritty bread, a few withered tangerines. Desalinated water without the aftertaste of iodine. Your mom managed to find chicken somewhere, or at least something that tastes enough like it for us.

There is nothing left for me here. There's no reason for me to feel so sad.

●

January 1st, 2191

I'm standing in front of the house. I didn't bother waking anyone up to say goodbye. The small pile of battered textbooks I've left for Nila says it all.

The power's still off, this early in the morning, so it's pitch black. I barely notice the white van pulling up. The headlights make it stand out, make it more obvious how the mist clings to everything. Someone comes out wearing a white hazard suit, white helmet, and an impenetrable silver visor. They don't dare breathe the same toxic air as us poors. I take a deep breath, testing the air. Brine, ammonia, decay. The ubiquitous, scentless, heavy metal particulate.

They open up the back, revealing a shadowed interior, then turn their mercurial expression on me. Inside there are two benches loaded with teenagers. I stand out as the only adult. I'm at least twice as old as the youngest. I look at these children and think *neuroplasticity*. I take the end of the bench closest to the driver, who is distorted by a thick pane of fluted plastic. The air has an odd, metallic tang to it.

The girl sitting across from me bounces minutely in her seat. She keeps leaning forward, stealing glances at everyone else in the faint light. The van starts, and we're all clutching the benches so we don't go flying.

After half an hour, I can't take the loaded silence, so I tap on the plastic. No one responds, so I knock it a little harder.

"Hey, is it okay if we talk back here?"

The kids look shocked that I have the balls to ask. Still, no one responds.

"I think it's fine. Go ahead, talk to each other."

As if they'd been waiting for my permission, they all start babbling. After a few hours, as the conversation rises and falls, things quiet as the van slows, stops, and lets on another kid. We bump along, increasingly nauseated. No one talks to me, though they keep looking at me. I cross my arms over my chest and pretend I'm comfortable.

Indeterminable hours later, the van slows, and we hear the rattle of a gate being pulled back. We rumble forward, tilting down, into a tunnel. The van brightens intermittently, the air becomes dry and stale. There is no talking now.

The van shudders to its final halt. The back opens to two more people in haz suits. Behind them the cement tunnel curves up into darkness. We are quickly escorted into an empty room bathed in a cold, clinical light. They take us into an adjacent room, one by one. No one returns. I go last.

●

January 15th, 2191

My stomach hurts. My upper arm is a knot of pain.

I don't remember this from last time. I don't trust my memories. Remembering is such a feeble thing, it seems strange to have tested us based on it. How can it compare to simultaneous access and near instant recall? I see the appeal. What I have now feels fragmented and lossy. Still, what is a person if not their memories?

It's hard to think when I feel this bad. I don't know how I managed it before. I think the injections are meant to break us down in more than one way.

●

February 2191

I don't mind the acrid taste of the nutritional fish paste anymore. Soon, I won't be able to taste it at all. Or need it.

My relationship with time has changed. As endless billions of neural proteins crystallize into invisible silicate lattices, new connections are forming in me and with the others. The others linger on the fringes, but they are there. We have formed a local network for our cohort. It's strange, to be present both with them and within myself, and yet remain undivided. This new unity helps us forget the people we've left behind.

They have access to all of this, these things we share with each other, that we keep to ourselves. We are not our own creatures. I know, now, that to respond to me would have been to reveal yourself. I comfort myself with this.

It is almost perverse to compose these missives. I feel closer to you, as if I could drift across this electromagnetic field that spans between us and find you floating behind the crest of an oncoming wave.

●

November 2191

We who are left are now fully encased in our sacs, our albumen, and I note with disinterest the titanium mesh beginning to coalesce about me. It creates a shimmering, fibrous network that will be my interface for external stimuli. A second skin, a third eyelid. It scrapes against the delicacy of my consciousness.

I look outside of myself, while I still can, at what remains of some other girl. She is curled and suspended in her own electrolyte bath. A sleeve has been fitted over her spinal bundle, and code streams across the surface of her tank. An external cue, a flicker of her otherwise vacant eyes, and I know *she* is still in there.

●

2192

I thought the question I asked you was one I'd be able to answer myself at some point. Are you the same? Am I? How much control over myself could I have, when all these pieces of me have been co-opted? The *me now* and the *me then* seem as different as the *me* at 29 and the *me* at 19. The changes were imperceptible. I feel like I'm the same person, but I suspect I'm not. I don't think I'll ever know. The Fleet of Theseus, one of the girls calls us. It's supposed to be funny, but none of us can laugh.

They've got us rolled out on the beach this morning, like some massive carton of filigree eggs. Boosters and fins abrade our shells. We don't have an audience, just our own silent and discrete company.

There is no preamble, no ceremony. The launch is abrupt. We huddle close as the ice-white flames propel us through the atmosphere, leaving cutouts in the clouds we pass through. I feel the temperature like a breath, a blush, a fever. Our flight accoutrements, depleted and useless as they are, melt and adsorb into our hulls. I feel the first wave of unabated radiation splash across me, converted into electricity that courses through me.

I expect the fear to come, choking me back down to Earth, but it doesn't.

They said I would feel starlight on my skin. All I feel is sick.

●

????

I measure time in tedious revolutions about Jupiter and Neptune.

They have me on a course $\left(\cos(\frac{\pi}{24}), .17\sin(\frac{\pi}{6}), -.28\sin(\frac{\pi}{6}), 1.63\sin(\frac{\pi}{6})\right)$ rotated from your initial trajectory.

I adjusted it to $\theta = \frac{\pi}{3}$.

Asteroid 5772156 Aglaonoe will aid in correcting this to your vector in 13,268 lightyears.

I guess those fucking matrices were useful after all.

One more pass of Jupiter, then the Sun. I'll greedily store her gamma rays and x-rays. Then I'll be riding your wake, deeper into space.

I'll be there soon. I'm right behind you.

Rubella Dithers' story "The Waves In Which We Drown" was originally published in Metaphorosis on Friday, 13 August 2021. See magazine.metaphorosis.com

About the author

During a family trip to Coos Bay, a pair of pirates wandered up from the beach and asked Rubella if "the lass 'ad a bit o' seaweed in 'er 'air". Alas, the lass did not.

My Synthetic Soul

Karris Rae

The woman who built me is named Tasha. I say "Tasha" so often it feels more familiar than my own name — Jade. Tasha says the sky turns deep jade before a midnight thunderstorm. When it rains hard like that, she sits on the porch steps with a glass of Merlot, watching. Sometimes a gust of wind blows the rain under the eaves and she gets wet, but she never scoots back. She has to be as close as possible, even if she leaves wet footprints on the way to the shower afterward.

Tasha named me after the jade storms — after her second-favorite thing. The first is me. If I weren't, maybe I could join her. But I'm her favorite, so she never lets me outside, not even onto the porch. "You might get hurt," she says, "and I can't fix everything."

There's a storm forecast tonight, too. Tasha's doing yardwork before it hits, on the side of the house I can't see. While I wait for her to come inside and watch the thunderheads roll in with me, I amuse myself with the alternating drama and tedium beyond the bay window — the maids and nannies bustling around the surrounding yards, hanging up laundry, watching human children play. Most are gynoids like me, but some are androids. Tasha works for the company that made the first gynoids, and now every manufacturer borrows from her designs. None outside are human; I've never seen a human carry a mop or hang up the laundry to dry, except for Tasha, who does all the chores for our house.

In fact, my entire life is a backward version of the outside world. Tasha and I argue and giggle together every day, unlike the stoic gynoids outside. And I don't do chores, but I sing while she does hers. All kinds of songs — gentle, spiteful, and reminiscent, but universally melancholic. The kind sung by a doll who watches the world through a pane of glass. They come to me as if pulled, whole, out of the murk of my subconscious, then thrown into the air to take flight. Tasha hums the harmony, even when I'm making the song up in the moment. She's uncanny like that.

I twist my finger around the pull cords of the blinds and close my eyes, singing softly. I experimentally bend the notes, finding spaces between the twelve chromatic scale steps. My vibrato grows wide, wild, and vibrant, testing the limit between exoticism and nonsense. Even now, I bet Tasha could harmonize.

I stop. For a moment, I thought I heard Tasha singing with me from the yard, but there's no way she could hear me from outside. It's a sturdy home; with the windows closed, even violent storms can pass unnoticed.

I cock my head, listening for the second voice, and it rises smoothly out of the silence as if knowing it holds my rapt attention. I don't recognize the song, but I know the voice. It's mine. The notes crawl lightly over my skin like fingers, leaving goosebumps in their wake. Unlike the practical gynoids programmed for work, Tasha gave me human sensations like these, along with a will of my own. I must be the most overengineered doll in the world. Another human experience seizes my mind — deja vu. I hum and discover that I can place the harmony as well as Tasha.

I'm jealous. Everything else I do might be scripted, programmed, artificial... but music like mine comes from the soul. It's proof that I'm more than a tape recorder who can hiccup. I have to know who else possesses my voice, and why — and if anyone knows, it's Tasha.

I rise from my place on the window seat and cross the over-furnished study, then the dining room. Our home is an anachronistic blend of cutting-edge technology and heavy, dated furniture. I step around the bulky dining table and reach the kitchen. The music is loudest in this corner of the house, but there are no windows between the dark wooden cabinets and the countertops for me to see into the yard. I move the dusty curtains in the dining room aside and press my cheek to the window, where my silicone skin sticks to the glass. This angle affords only a narrow view of the back of the lot, just the blue siding and the sunflowers growing near the foundation. I flip the latch open and crack the window, welcoming in birdsong and the whine of a distant lawnmower. My hearts pounds a little too hard for what should be a simple task.

"Tasha?" I call in a small voice. Why am I so anxious? For as long as I remember, Tasha's never given me a reason to fear her. Besides, curiosity isn't against the rules. The next time I pull strength from deep in my belly, as if reaching the climax of a gospel. "Tasha?"

At the same time, the facsimile of my voice rises in a spellbinding cadenza. Then it tapers into silence. A sound interrupts like I've heard on the funny television shows I sometimes watch with Tasha — applause. Someone, *many* someones, are applauding my performance of a song I've never heard.

Tasha still doesn't answer, but the silence doesn't last long. Another piece starts, just as mystifying as the last. Now that I'm by the open window, I realize I've been looking in the wrong place; the music isn't coming from outside, but from the kitchen itself. I follow the sound to the kitchen, gently touching the softly glowing painting of soap bubbles above the sink. It vibrates under my fingers. It's a subtle invention of Tasha's — a pane of glass over a wide, flat speaker, backlit on either side to illuminate the sink while she loads the dishwasher. The soap bubbles painted over the glass are my addition. Usually the bubbles read us books and play old jazz, but today, they sing me a lullaby in my own voice.

Tasha controls the panel, like everything else in the house... which means if it's playing my music, she commanded it to. I could wait for her to come back inside to ask about it, but the thought of listening to this all afternoon is maddening. And I already tried the window. I teeter in the kitchen, desperate to know why I'm singing to myself, but hesitant to disobey and find out. I've broken rules before, small ones, like licking the rim of Tasha's wine glass while her back was turned. She laughed when she saw the garnet stain on my guilty lips, shaking her head in mock disapproval. Even so, I never did it again. I can't bear to disappoint her, even in jest.

I brace myself, my hand on the doorknob leading to the back yard. When this song ends, the audio skips for a moment, and then it plays again from the beginning. It's a quiet one, intimate, as if I were whispering secrets into my own ear. Surely Tasha, my Creator, will understand why I had to do this. She always does. My synthetic heart beats hard in my aluminum ribcage as I open the door.

The sun overwhelms me. The heat feels like the steam that rises from Tasha's piping hot coffee, but everywhere. I wasn't made to come outside, and I'm more delicate than I guessed.

"What're you doing outside?" I can't see Tasha, but I hear her heavy footsteps crunch on the grass until her hand claps onto my shoulder. "Dammit girl, the heat out here'll put your voice box through hell. Get back in there." She tries to frog-march me back into the kitchen, but I step out of her reach, shielding my eyes with my hands.

"There's music playing in the kitchen... my music," I say, blinking furiously. The quiet song floats out through the open door, into a flurry of distant traffic, birdsong, and rustling leaves.

I see the code running behind Tasha's brown eyes as she puts the pieces together. "Goddammit," she grunts after a minute. "Didn't realize it was broadcasting into the house, too. Goes to show you how bad the UI is, even the 'experts' can't figure it out."

"Who's that singing?" I press. I've heard her gripe about the music software before and know it won't stop.

"It's you," she says, sighing. The logical scripts running in my mind crunch together like trains at a railroad junction. Tasha drops her hand from my shoulder and turns toward the hidden back corner of the lot. She takes a few steps, her gait made uneven by the gout in her left knee. For a moment I think she's abandoned our conversation, but then she says over her shoulder, "Come on, I'll show you."

I follow. My ears can't quite adjust to the unfamiliar white noise that washes over me, sounds diffused over distance until it sounds like the world is shushing me. Tasha says something I don't catch, and then we're standing in front of a shed with no windows. She steps inside, inviting me in, and closes the door behind me. I'm sad to leave the sun's warmth, but thankful to be free of the blinding light. The room vacillates between pitch blackness and dimness as my eyes recover. After a few moments, I put the scene together: a broad desk, with a half-dozen black monitors above and a bulky console with blinking green lights underneath, centered in a room as dark and cool as a cellar.

"What is this?" I ask, breathless.

Tasha places a loving hand on the console. "It's you."

The green lights blink on and off, on and off, like a distant radio tower.

"What d'you mean?"

"The body you know's a remote unit. This is where your central processing takes place. Your 'soul' lives here, in this room."

I don't respond. I'm having another of my sublime human sensations, but this time, I can't quite name it. The chilly air feels subterranean and claustrophobic, as if we were interred in a bunker. No wonder Tasha couldn't hear me calling from in here.

Tasha continues, "It's been so rainy and humid lately, I spent all morning checking your wiring for corrosion. You're a complex machine. All it would take is one bad wire and you'd be out like a light." She snaps her fingers. "And we don't want that."

"No," I say mechanically, not sure if she's exaggerating. I reach out to touch the console that houses my synthetic soul. All I feel is plastic.

"But I guess that doesn't answer your first question, does it?" Tasha sighs. "D'you remember that song? At all?"

"A little." I've read about pregnant women who play music for their babies in the womb. This must be what those babies feel when they grow up and hear the same songs — nostalgia.

"It's you, singing. A previous version of you, anyway. Sometimes I have to tweak your code. You're too fine a machine to be my first try." She laughs and thumps me on the back. Her hand is warm compared to the air. "And sometimes I have to delete some corrupted memories. Nothing you'd miss."

"I remember the song, but I don't remember performing for anyone else," I say. "I heard applause."

"Ah. That must be the television in the background. We must've been watching one of your game shows. Every version of you likes the same shows." Her smile is as warm as her hand. "Sometimes I record you singing in the house. I hope you don't mind. I listen to it when I'm back here, checking every damn wire and dusting your insides."

I mentally replay the recording I heard, the cheers and clapping echoing through a vast performance hall. Someone screams my name as if I were onstage before the crowd. My memory may not be complete, but I know I never competed on a game show.

Tasha is lying.

"Why didn't you tell me that I'm a remote unit?"

"Because you aren't. Your body is. Besides, I've explained all this before, and I didn't realize this version of you didn't know."

"How old is my... this current version?"

"Older than any before, and hopefully there won't be another for a while."

The last question lingers on the tip of my tongue. Tasha nods encouragingly. She knows what I'm going to say before I open my mouth. "Are any of them better at singing than me?"

"No," she says. "You're the best."

I spend the rest of the evening drawing in my room, which isn't unusual. Down the hall, Tasha busies herself with the laundry, humming the sad, quiet song that belongs to another me. Usually her proximity doesn't bother me, but tonight, every footstep distracts me from my sketchbook. When the steps go down the hall, I worry that she'll return to the shed and unplug me. That she'll erase my memories of the day and program a new version that never, ever breaks the rules. And when they go up the hall, I worry that she'll come into my room and tell me more lies.

It starts raining, then thundering, and I hear the pop of a cork and the slam of the front door. I peer through my blinds to make sure she's in her spot on the porch steps, and for the first time tonight, my anxiety eases. But I still can't focus on my sketch; it's an exercise in subtlety, a trio of white eggs on a white background. Only the shadows cupping and pooling around the eggs differentiate them. This takes sensitivity and focus, and right now, I'm capable of neither.

I flip to the next blank page. I've been meaning to try a different exercise, a self-portrait. There's an antique light on the ceiling and a heavy, brass desk lamp on my drawing table. I turn both on, then both off, then one off and the other on, each time checking my reflection in the mirror on the opposite wall. When I'm satisfied, I stand a few feet from the mirror and inch left and right until the shadows cast by my eyelashes, nose, and lips are thrown into sharp relief, like a face overlaid on my own. *My own...* the phrase doesn't sit right. I step closer. This isn't an exercise anymore, it's a hardware inspection.

The face I see looks like Tasha's, but thirty years younger. Same dark skin and high cheekbones. But the skin around my eyes is even, no dark circles like Tasha gets when her gout flares up. No blackheads on my nose. I touch it and remember the plastic casing around my soul in the shed. Neither this face nor the console feel like *me*. If Tasha wanted, she could project my consciousness into an electric toothbrush tomorrow and erase all memories of when I was something different. How many bodies have I had? How many times did she swap out models before she settled for one this beautiful? I *am* too fine for a first try.

It's never bothered me before that I was made, while the cherished humans in my books were all born. What bothers me now is that Tasha can lie to me and erase parts of me like it doesn't matter. For the first time I realize she thinks of me not as an equal, but a machine... except for all the other times I may have realized this before that I don't remember now. I have to find a way to back up my memories so Tasha can't play with my memories — my *reality* — anymore.

I turn off both lights, and darkness swallows the face in the mirror. Peeking through the blinds, Tasha is still on the step, swaying as she shouts one of my songs into the worsening thunderstorm. Even so, I strain my ears as I step outside my room, then dart down the hallway to the back door. I'm about to break the rules again, and if Tasha catches me, I might wake up tomorrow with more bits of myself whittled away. And the worst part is, I'll never know.

When I open the door, rain hammers my feet and pools over the linoleum. Looking over my shoulder, I cross the yard, but Tasha doesn't appear around the corner like I fear. The jade-green sky swirls above me, enchanting us both with its light show. The shed door is unlocked. This is either a good omen — maybe it's been a long time since I tried anything this daring, and I can surprise her — or a bad one, a declaration that she's confident she can handle whatever I may do. The trouble with knowing my reality isn't real is that it brings me no closer to knowing what *is*.

The green lights blink off and on in the otherwise dark room. The air feels even cooler than this afternoon, the structure no longer warmed by sunlight. Now that I'm here, I don't know what to do. I guess I thought I'd have some intuitive knowledge of how my console worked, but all I see is blinking lights. I don't even want to touch it. The memory of unyielding plastic under my fingers turns my stomach, so to speak. Another meaningless human reaction.

But I'm not a human, and if I want to keep the few human parts I have, I need to be a robot now. I push aside the fear, the visceral reluctance, the hurt. I approach the keyboard on Tasha's desk and tap the spacebar. All the monitors above the desk flicker on. I've watched Tasha type away at the computer in her room before, but touching it is against the rules. I wonder how many rules I'm breaking right now. And for the first time, it strikes me that Tasha could have made me as a being who can't bend them at all. What am I to her? Not quite a child, not quite a machine.

What am I?

My forehead crinkles when I recognize the images on the monitors. They're videos of my room, of the kitchen, of the porch where Tasha's throwing back the last of her glass of wine. This is why she met me at the back door earlier today, I imagine. The video of the kitchen is taken from above the sink, and I remember the corner of the soap bubble painting Tasha asked me to leave blank. The last monitor unsettles me the most — it shows everything I see, a direct feed from my eyes. As I look at the monitor, it shows an endless tunnel of monitors, stretching into infinity like a wormhole. If I crawl through, I think, maybe it'll take me to another dimension where I can trust Tasha again.

I watch Tasha rise and walk through the house from six different angles, then pour herself another glass in the kitchen. She pauses to look out the window toward the shed and my breath catches, but then I hear the thunder that matches the lightning she stopped to watch. Before she leaves, she scratches a smudge off the soap bubble painting, her face so close I can see her reddened eyes. Sometimes she cries when she watches the storms, and it seems like tonight's one of those nights. Then she limps down the hallway, past my room, and back onto the porch. All it would take for my subterfuge to crack open is a single knock on my bedroom door. I have to keep better tabs on her.

I noticed while tracking her that the center monitor is different from the others. It didn't turn on with the others, and reflects only the face I would've called mine this morning. It's the only screen left that could be linked to the console under the desk. If the keyboard didn't turn it on, maybe there are buttons on the screen itself. I stand on the tips of my toes to check, and there are, but they're labeled with minimalist icons I don't recognize. Even if I could turn on the interface, I don't know the first step to make a memory backup.

The complexity of this undertaking strikes me in full force. This isn't a one-time operation. To hold onto my memories, I would need to program automatic backups, and encrypt it so Tasha wouldn't tamper with it. She could interrogate or punish me if she found these unfamiliar files, or toy with my personality until I didn't care whether I remembered or not. And — maybe by Tasha's design — I don't know enough about computers to fight back.

As I realize this, all the green lights blink at once. I don't know what they measure, but whatever it is settles in my chest like I've been force-fed lead. The mass pushes against my lungs and makes my insides hurt. I'll spend the rest of my life having memories and songs cut out and patched over with new code, and there's nothing I can do. With every beat of my silicone heart, I feel a little less real.

If she's going to do it anyway, though, I can at least make sure my next version gets further than I did. I find a legal pad and blue pen in the bottom drawer of Tasha's desk. I've never been good with words outside of song lyrics, so all I can think to write is, "Tasha is cutting your memories out of you. Your body doesn't belong to you. Save the memories locked up in the back shed and maybe you can save yourself." It seems a little jarring, so I add "please" at the end. Then I fold it up teeny-tiny and put it in the pocket of my leggings. It eases the lead cannonball in my chest enough for me to start looking for Tasha's development notes.

At first, I think I've found it. I lift the heavy, broad object from the top drawer onto my knee, but it doesn't fall open like a book. It's a blue leather case, zipped shut, and when it shifts, I hear the soft sound of sliding plastic together inside. I unzip it. There are plastic pages inside, and each one shows my face. Some depict me onstage, bathed in blinding light, my mouth open and eyes squeezed shut as I serenade thousands of people. My skin is flawed — a few pimples near my jaw, flyaways caused by the hot lights and the sweat that beads on my forehead. Other pages show stylized portraits of me, and a few display only abstract art. Each is circular and bears a hole in the center.

With trembling fingers, I work one decorated with gossamer soap bubbles out of its plastic sheathe. The back is smooth, plain silver. This is old technology. I only recognize it from the books Tasha and I listen to after dinner, stories from her youth when CDs and power cords were commonplace. I replace the disc, emotions jostling against each other in a queasy, squirming mass. There must be dozens of CDs, some bearing the same name but different artwork, many followed by the words, "live" or "special edition." Then, in the very back of the case, I find it.

It's a headshot of me, sitting on a stone bench and laughing photogenically. Dimples pucker my cheeks, matching the ones that appear on Tasha's face when I catch her off guard with a joke. The glossy paper catches the tiny green lights so they look like fairies drifting around me. And at the bottom is an autograph, in my handwriting:

Love you, sis!
XOXO
-Jade

I sit in dumb silence. Sister, I think. Robots don't have sisters. The word bounces around my head until it doesn't mean anything anymore. Sister, sister. I look into the pretty girl's face and recognize this artifact for what it is: a memento mori.

As am I.

I hold a dead girl's heart in my hands and in my chest. I was created for that purpose, to keep this young woman's heart alive and singing for Tasha. I am a CD player, a doll, and a memento mori. But not an artist. Can I even be said to have free will, if I'm bound to the decisions this girl would make? I look at the screen, at Tasha, who cries and drinks on the porch when the storms roll in and remind her of her sister, Jade.

But she isn't there anymore. My eyes dart over the monitor recording the porch. Then to the one that shows the kitchen, hoping that Tasha's run out of wine again. She's in neither. Then I catch a flicker of movement in my room as a shadow passes on the other side of the blinds, walking along the side of the house outside. My bedroom door is open. I left it closed.

I slam the case shut, my hands shaking so hard I struggle to zip it. I toss it into the bottom drawer with a thunk and slam it shut, metal drawer screeching against metal frame. If I'm lucky, I can keep Tasha from realizing how much I know. Any scraps of memory she overlooks, together with the note in my pocket, might be enough for my next version to break free. But it's too late for the version I know as 'me'. I'm about to be erased.

Through the monitor, I see her black shadow pass the kitchen window. I have about six seconds. I fall to my knees beside the console, angling my body so Tasha can see that I've made no progress in whatever I tell her I'm doing. Then, over the rush of the raging storm, I hear the door open behind me. Even though I knew she was coming, the sound startles me.

"Jade?" Tasha says. The alcohol softens the J until it almost sounds like 'sh'. "What're you doin' in here?"

I turn. "I'm sorry."

"That's not what I asked." Tasha snaps the door shut. In the dark, from the floor, she's a towering golem of black granite, come to erase me. "I thought you were in your room."

I'm afraid. So afraid that it's hard to believe it could ever be wholly exercised from my memories. But then I realize I feel the same sense of deja vu as when I hear the songs she programmed me to sing. I have felt this fear before, probably many times, and I'm right — it leaves a mark, like the rut in a record played too many times.

"I couldn't stop thinking about my soul," I say. "It made me sad that it's all alone."

"You're never alone; you'll always have me. And I'll always have you." Her voice thickens, as if fighting through a lump in the back of her throat.

"Will you, if I'm always changing?" I'm going to be erased. The inevitability somehow lends me bravery.

"It's just your memories, and sometimes I tweak your code. It's still you. You haven't been turned off since I first made you twenty years ago. You never turn off a quantum server, y'know."

She doesn't understand. It takes more than a few keystrokes to reprogram a human. "I don't want you to take my memories away," I say.

"You don't understand what a blessing it is. I'd give anything to forget things. To forget you're..." Tasha's slurring cracks and the sentence breaks in two.

To forget I'm not your sister, I want to say, but I let her words hang in the air like a loose spider's thread. "But *I* don't want to forget. I want..." It's my turn to trail off. Why am I fighting so hard to know that nothing, not my face, not my voice, not even Tasha's love, belongs to me?

The answer comes easily: because if I know nothing is mine, I can make things that are.

Tasha takes a step forward. "The only things you want are the things I programmed you to want. Anything else is a malfunction. Happens sometimes. Lemme fix it and life can go back to normal."

"No." I rise to my feet.

A moment passes, then another, as code runs behind Tasha's bloodshot eyes. Then she lunges, seizing me by the upper arm and digging her nails into my silicone flesh. Pain signals fire in my shoulder joint. With herculean effort, I spin around and break free. She tries to catch me by the neck, but the gout and alcohol conspire to knock her off balance. She careens into the metal desk, catching the blow in her gut and falling to her knees, winded. Rainwater sparkles in her densely curled hair and pools around her on the floor. The green lights dance in the puddle, every single one of them lit. The monitor linked to my eyes echoes the scene in miniature. Thunder growls outside, and I feel the vibrations through the poured concrete floor. I memorize every detail. This will be the last time I ever see the woman who built me, the first memory she can't take away, and I want it to be pristine.

Then I wrench the door open and run. The rain falls in sheets, coursing in rivulets over my scalp and between my shoulderblades. The jade sky crackles furiously. I have to leave the range of my central unit. I don't know what will happen when I do, except that she won't be able to remotely power me down or dismantle my mind, and that's all that matters right now.

I tear down the middle of the street, the straggling lights in nearby houses reflecting on the wet pavement. The sidewalk and road are deserted, and the only movement other than the rain and bowing trees is the occasional shadow crossing a lit window. The city is tucked in for the storm, like the stray cats huddled under the porches. Everyone except me.

The slick road, like my fear, feels uncannily familiar. So too does the wild hope that drives my legs onward, as it has innumerable times before. *My* wild hope. Tasha deletes my memories to start fresh, but what she doesn't realize, and what I didn't see until now, is that every version is still me. I am not a series of memories — I am the soul linking them together. I'm the soul that always, eventually, risks everything to escape.

My legs pump until every impact aches. A bolt of lightning strikes so close I feel the static electricity on my skin and smell the ozone. I must be out of range, I think. The black sky breaks into larger and larger pixels and I can barely run on increasingly jerky legs. I must —

Dark. Not the kind I see when I close my eyes, the kind that could only exist if I didn't have eyes at all. Void, more like. I have no limbs to attempt to move. I don't even have a voice box to fail when I try to speak.

But I can hear. The rain falls, muffled, like I'm inside somewhere. Something taps rhythmically. Then I hear Tasha's voice, and for a moment, my fear of her is gone. I try to call to her but can't remember how. Now I realize that she's crying, heavy, deep sobs wrenched from her core, as violent as the storm. I got what I wanted — I left the range of my console. But instead of breaking free, it stopped casting my mind to my body. I never knew much about computers. Tasha wails and the thunder roars back and her fingers tap tap tap on the keyboard in the shed as memories fall out of my mind, one at a time, like a dripping faucet. I try to hold onto them, but they drip through the cracks between my fingers.

How did I come to the shed this morning? Why did I go outside? What happened in the kitchen? Where did I go? *What happened this morning?* It was important for me to remember, but I don't know why. Did I need to remember something? Why? If it were so important, I would have remembered it. Why is Tasha crying? I try to ask what's wrong, but I can't speak.

And then I stop asking myself questions, because that's what my code tells me to do. I'm not the kind of robot who asks questions, because I don't care to know the answers. My job is to sing, and play cards, and wear the old clothes Tasha dresses me in. When she does my hair my job is to hold still, not to ask if we can thread gold wires around my braids. To sing, but not to wonder where the songs come from. And tomorrow, when Tasha recovers my body from the road five miles away, and I find a note in my pocket, my job is to throw it away because it doesn't belong there, not to marvel at how the handwriting matches mine.

Karris Rae's story "My Synthetic Soul" was originally published in Metaphorosis on Friday, 7 January 2022. See magazine.metaphorosis.com

About the author

Karris Rae is a fiction MFA/MA candidate at McNeese State University. She is also a reader for *The McNeese Review* and an assistant editor for *Boudin*. Her chapbook, *We Obedient Children*, won the 2024 Etchings Press Chapbook Contest in prose, publication pending. Her short work has appeared in *Metaphorosis, Reápparition Journal, The Chamber Magazine, The NoSleep Podcast*, and *Free Flash Fiction*, and is forthcoming in *50 Give or Take, Fourth Genre Magazine, Mount Hope Magazine*, and *Gargoyle Online*. Visit karrisrae.com for more information.

Going Home

Martin Westlake

The eerie howl of the Ekranoplan's jet engines echoed around the city's early morning streets. Dimitriy's stomach lurched involuntarily. A ground effect craft, they called it, designed to be a troop carrier, now recycled as a passenger craft, plying the route between Derbent and Astrakhan. The relic, all stubby wings and a massive, V-shaped tail, howled there and back three times a day. He loathed it, but it was the only way he could get to the laboratory in Astra.

Every Monday morning for over a year, Dimitriy had suffered the same torment of emotions. Anastasia said nothing anymore as they kissed. "Think of the children," she had said in the old days, before she'd realised entreaties were useless. "They need their father." He missed the whole school week. Sasha, the younger, still greeted him with affection on Saturday mornings, but Andrei, now in his teens, had become increasingly sullen. Dimitriy wanted to tell him how sorry he felt, but the truth was that he didn't. Guilty, yes; sad, yes, in a bittersweet sort of way; but not sorry.

Then there was the Ekranoplan. Anastasia had been unable to leave Derbent when Dimitriy had taken on the Astrakhan job and he had accepted that. The car trip took ten hours in the summer and in the winter the roads were frequently impassable. No, the only viable means of getting there was the Ekranoplan. He would never get used to it, though. Whenever there was the slightest hint of a breeze, his heart dropped, for the monstrous thing could only take off facing into the wind, and that meant riding the incoming waves, like a ship. Once it was up in the air the ride was smooth, but how he hated the take off! The only thing that made the mixture of sadness, guilt and fear worthwhile every Monday morning was a euphoric sense of anticipation; the knowledge that he would soon once again be where he most desired to be.

●

His path through the sleepy streets to the Ekranoport took him past his old workplace, the Caspian Gates Secondary School, reminding him of the day it had all begun. He'd stayed behind to help a group of fifteen-year-olds, then hurried home. A tall, thin, grey-suited, sallow-faced man was waiting for him outside the main entrance to their block of flats. A cigarette bobbed on his lower lip as he spoke. He seemed oblivious to the February cold, though both men's breath clouded about them.

"Semenov?" he said.

Dimitriy nodded.

"Could we talk?" said the man, nodding towards a bar.

There was something about him — not furtive, but a sense of secrecy all the same. The man bought two vodkas and they sat at a scuffed table.

"To your health," he said, raising his glass. He stubbed out his cigarette in an old dented aluminium ashtray and lit another. "Ivanov," he said. "Rear Admiral Anatoly Ivanov, Caspian Flotilla, Astrakhan."

"There's been a mistake," said Dimitriy.

Ivanov shook his head. He gestured to a passing waiter and ordered two more vodkas.

"I shouldn't stay," said Dimitriy.

"Tell me, Dimitriy Semenov," Ivanov said; "how much do you earn?"

"Enough," said Dimitriy.

"Why are you a teacher?" Ivanov leaned forward over the table. "You are a brilliant physicist with a top doctoral thesis in Biology and Materials Sciences from Moscow State University and yet you hide yourself away at the Caspian

Gates Secondary School teaching low-grade mathematics to misfits."

"My wife...," Dimitriy began.

"We know all about your wife," Ivanov said.

"It's time I left," Dimitriy said.

"Sit down," said the Admiral, gesturing with his half-empty vodka glass. "What I mean is that we know she has all her family here. That's why you're here, isn't it?"

Dimitriy said nothing.

Ivanov leaned over the table again. "The motherland calls, comrade."

Motherland! Comrade! Dimitriy knew immediately that the job had to be some sort of secret military work.

"It's not what you think, Semenov," the Admiral continued. "If I told you now, you wouldn't believe me."

Dimitriy inadvertently looked into his empty glass. Ivanov flagged the waiter down and ordered two more vodkas.

"No!" said Dimitriy.

"For the road."

The Admiral toyed with his cigarette lighter, an old-fashioned metal model with a flip top and a thick wick. Then he looked up at Dimitry. "Interested?" he asked. "We'll pay you four times what you are getting at that dump of a school."

"The catch?" said Dimitriy.

Ivanov drank off the remainder of his vodka and placed the glass down gently on the tabletop.

"You'd have to come to Astra, Monday to Friday. We'd cover your board and lodging."

"How would I...?"

As if to anticipate his question, the unmistakable howl of the evening return Ekranoplan came to them through the thin glass window.

Ivanov reached into his pocket, drew out an envelope and placed it on the table.

"Your ticket's in there. This coming Monday. The seven-thirty departure. When you get to Astra, make your way to the Moskva Hotel. A room has been booked in your name. I'll join you there for lunch. It's half-term. The school won't miss you."

Back home, after the children had gone to bed, sitting in the low light at the melamine kitchen table, he and Anastasia had discussed the offer in earnest whispers. He had doubts, but she was logical and reassuring. The money was important. With the kids growing, it would be good if they could rent somewhere larger. If he didn't like the work, whatever it was, he could always return to his teaching. What did they have to lose?

●

Dimitriy had been travelling to Astra for just over two months when Anastasia first put the question to him. He had known it must come. She had nodded and accepted so mildly when he'd first explained that he couldn't talk about his work, but who could blame her, now that the yearning had started? She chose a Saturday evening. The children were in bed. The classical music radio channel was on, and she'd put a cloth and a candle on the dinner table. They talked about Sasha and Andrei, and then about her family. At the end of the meal, Anastasia took Dimitriy's hands across the table. *Here it comes*, he thought. But she simply looked into his eyes and asked if he felt all right. She'd told him he seemed preoccupied, as if his mind were elsewhere.

He'd laughed. "I'm fine," he'd said.

How could he tell her? Even if he had told her, she wouldn't have believed him.

The second time, Anastasia had been more direct. Dimitriy had just returned.

"Did you miss us?" she asked.

"Of course!"

"Really?"

She went back to the kitchen. There was no cloth and no candle on the table. Over the meal, her replies were monosyllabic. Afterwards, he went to help her with the washing up, but she insisted on doing it alone. He sat on the sofa and waited until she emerged, drying her hands on a tea towel.

"Dima," she said, "are you sure you're not having a relationship of some sort in Astra?"

●

Astrakhan was on a broad river, not a sea. Its waterways gave the impression the city was floating. Unlike Derbent, there were no hills behind, and no citadel looming over the city. Rather, the great Trinity Cathedral soared upwards, with its gold-capped green domes. Astrakhan was flat and expansive. Being there gave Dimitry a sense of a new beginning. He hadn't realised, until he first set foot in the place, how oppressed he'd felt back home. That first Monday, still wobbly from the flight, he'd walked easily to the Moskva Hotel, a great block of fake chrome and smoked glass. A room had been booked, as Ivanov had promised. The clerk told him a table had been reserved in the restaurant for twelve o'clock. Dimitriy went to his room, unpacked the few belongings he had brought, then turned on the television and watched a programme without really following it. What was Ivanov going to offer him, he wondered?

The Admiral was sitting at their table when Dimitriy came down, a vodka in front of him and a cigarette on his lower lip. He nodded curtly.

"Welcome to Astra," he said. "A drink?"

"Thank you," said Dimitriy, "but I don't drink at lunchtime."

Ivanov beckoned a waiter over.

"Today, you'll make an exception."

When the waiter had brought their drinks, Ivanov raised his glass. He had ordered caviar, brought by another waiter on a bed of ice. "Eat," he insisted gruffly.

"Thank you," said Dimitriy.

"Thank Mother Russia," said Ivanov, stubbing out his cigarette.

They started to eat, digging out the glutinous eggs with small mother-of-pearl teaspoons.

"What do you know about Tunguska?" the Admiral asked.

"Siberia? The beginning of the last century?"

Ivanov nodded. "30 June 1908," he said.

"I remember the pictures," said Dimitriy. "All those felled trees. A meteor, right?"

"Da, da," said Ivanov. "That's what people think."

"Think? What was it, then?"

"We don't know." He lit another cigarette. "I've brought a file for you to read, but before that, I want you to sign this."

Ivanov tugged an envelope from his jacket pocket and drew out a folded sheet of paper. "Official Secrets Act," said the Admiral, unfolding the sheet. "I will only tell you more if you sign. To be clear, if you sign the declaration and do not respect it, you could be tried and imprisoned. Not even your wife. Got it?"

Dimitriy read the declaration, his hand trembling. He would have liked to talk to Anastasia. Suddenly, she seemed very far away. He read it again.

"I need to think about it," he said. "I need to talk to my wife."

Ivanov shook his head grimly. "It's now or never," he said.

Dimitriy sighed and thought about the money. With such a salary they could easily rent a three-bedroom apartment. He was sure Anastasia would have agreed. She would surely have wanted to know what work the Admiral was offering. He signed and dated the paper and handed it back.

"Good," said Ivanov, putting it back in his pocket. He gestured to a waiter to clear their table and ordered two more vodkas.

"The Tunguska region wasn't as sparsely populated as people think," said the Admiral. "Quite a few people heard and saw something." He lit a cigarette. "It started with noises from the sky."

"Noises?"

"Da. You'll read the transcripts. Some of the witnesses said it was like trumpets."

"Heavenly trumpets?" said Dimitriy ironically.

Ivanov sneered.

"The noises went on for about a week," he continued.

"Then?" asked Dimitriy.

"There was some sort of *conflict*, in the sky," said Ivanov. "Some sort of *celestial* conflict."

"'Celestial'? You seem to be choosing your words with care, Admiral."

Ivanov stubbed out his cigarette.

"You'll read the file and see for yourself. As good scientists, we try always to keep open minds."

"The word 'conflict'," said Dimitriy, "suggests that more than one body or object might have been involved, right? And the word 'celestial' suggests this was high up?"

"There are drawings in the file," the Admiral said, "based on contemporary eyewitness accounts. The locals, the Evenki, were convinced they'd seen their god, Ogdy, in a fight."

"Fascinating," said Dimitriy, "but I am not sure why this should bring me to the Volga Basin and the Official Secrets Act."

Ivanov lit another cigarette.

"Leonid Kulik," he said. "A mineralogist. He came to Tunguska several times, starting in 1921. That was already thirteen years after the event. There was no crater — that puzzled him. How could there have been a meteorite impact if there were no crater, and if there were no fragments? He realised the fragments might have blasted out craters that had then got filled in. So, he kept digging holes to try and find filled-in craters with remains of one sort or another at the bottom — something, anything. No joy. Until 1938. His last expedition. One of his men found something, deep down, in a pit. Whatever it was, it blinded the man. He complained of an intense, searing light, then he lost his sight. Kulik's workers mutinied. For them it was proof they were messing with Ogdy. They dragged the man out and refused to get into the pit. Kulik had to shovel most of the earth back in himself. He measured the location as accurately as he could, and then returned to the Mineralogical Museum in Leningrad. He planned to return with his own men, but the Germans invaded in 1941 and he joined the fighting. The next year he died of typhus in a POW camp."

Ivanov drank some vodka.

"Whatever they found," he continued, "remained lost in the archives. For a long time, as you know, the motherland had more important things to think about than primitive superstitions. But in 2007 a group of archivists started going through Kulik's papers. When they got to the file about the 1938 incident, the team had the good idea of involving us."

"Us?" said Dimitriy.

"The security services," Ivanov said. "If another expedition to Tunguska were to be launched, they knew they'd need state resources. They dressed it up as being about some potentially weaponizable force. They weren't entirely wrong. Kulik's coordinates were accurate. They used a remote-controlled digger. Once they'd reached the depth Kulik recorded, they lowered animals down to the bottom. All came back blind. So, they were at the right place. A remote camera relayed images of glittering metallic fragments. They sent down instruments, but the instruments measured nothing. A volunteer discovered that *reflections* of the fragments could be observed in a mirror. Using remote cameras and mirrors, the fragments were dug out of the pit bottom. It was all hit-and-miss. Somebody thought of lead, being a heavy metal, so they fashioned a lead-lined steel box and used a remote-controlled robotic arm to shepherd the fragments towards the box and seal the lid."

"Shepherd?"

"You'll learn about that," Ivanov said; "*if* you take the job." He stubbed out his cigarette, drank off his vodka, and continued. "The fragments were then brought to a ..." (he coughed) "... *facility* here in Astrakhan. The box was opened and the fragments were housed in a specially-constructed room. That, Dimitriy Semenov, is where you come in. We want to analyse the fragments. Test their qualities." He leaned over the table as if to share a confidence. "And perhaps," he said, "replicate them."

Dimitriy felt the thrill of scientific discovery and the repulsion of a lifelong pacifist. But curiosity gripped him strongest. If only he could tell Anastasia! He was sure she would have been just as fascinated.

The Admiral got to his feet.

"I will be waiting outside tomorrow morning at seven," he said, "and will take you to the facility."

Dimitriy watched as Ivanov threaded his way steadily through the tables. That word, *comrade*, again. When he had gone, Dimitriy picked up the file and hurried to his room.

●

The Admiral was waiting for him on the hotel's esplanade in a sleek black chauffeur-driven limousine. He was in his uniform, his gold brocaded cap on the seat beside him.

"Is this a Zil?" Dimitriy asked, getting into the tobacco-fugged interior.

"The 4104," said the Admiral. "The Navy is determined to keep them going until they fall to pieces."

He lit a cigarette. "You read the file?" he asked.

"Of course. Do you want me to believe that the Evenki saw angels?"

"*You* saw the drawings," said Ivanov. "*I* don't want you to believe anything."

"Yes," said Dimitriy, "I *saw* the drawings."

The Admiral gazed through the smoked glass window.

"Do you believe in angels, Dimitriy Semenov?"

"No," said Dimitriy, "I don't. But what else can be made of those drawings? And those sounds; if not something like trumpets, then what?"

Ivanov shook his head.

"I told you; we are trying to keep open minds. You have to remember in 1908 the Evenki were a primitive, superstitious people. When something they didn't understand happened, they naturally ascribed it to their god, Ogdy."

"You don't think there was a conflict?"

"Imagine if you were a primitive people and something massive exploded overhead," said Ivanov. "Wouldn't you extrapolate from what you knew? Battle, noise?"

"And those trumpeting noises *before*?" asked Dimitriy.

Ivanov chuckled.

"*You* called them 'heavenly trumpets', Dimitriy Semenov, but you don't believe in such things, do you?"

"Of course not, Admiral. But what are the alternative explanations?"

Ivanov tutted. "You are a scientist, aren't you? Because we don't know the answer doesn't mean there isn't one. We just don't know it yet — perhaps we'll never know it. What we *do* know is that we have seven fragments of an unknown powerful material that *may* have fallen from the sky about the time of the Tunguska event. We can, and must, try to know as much about those fragments as possible, using scientific methods, and not basing our judgements on superstition and hearsay and eye-witness accounts from long ago."

"Of course," said Dimitriy, chastened. "It's those pictures in the file. My imagination ran away with me."

The Admiral stubbed out his cigarette.

"We have arrived," he said.

•

Some five months after Dimitriy started the job, Anastasia stopped making dinner on Friday evenings. The first time, she told him she'd been feeling unwell, and he accepted the explanation unthinkingly. He ate alone in the kitchen. The next Friday, though, the new practice had been rationalised; she said it was too late in the evening to eat a full-blown meal — better that he snacked or had a bowl of soup or a salad. He again accepted the explanation. Then, one Friday, when he came to bed, he found her weeping.

"What's the matter, Ana?"

She rolled over and he saw that her eyes were puffed up.

"I just wish you'd tell me," she said. "About her, whoever she is."

"There is no her," Dimitriy insisted.

"You can't hide it from me," Anastasia said. "I see the way you look as though you have been torn away from someone."

"There is no other woman, Anastasia."

"Is it a man? I'd understand."

"There's nobody else, I swear!"

"You think I'm stupid? You can't wait to get back on Monday mornings."

She rolled away and wept herself to sleep. He stared up at the ceiling. She was right, of course. The weekends back home in Derbent had become a torment.

●

"Welcome to Astrakhan State Technology University," said Ivanov, checking his cap's position in the glass of the chauffeur's partition.

The Admiral led him through the glass-fronted entrance. Students milled about, seemingly unfazed at the image of a uniformed Admiral threading a path through the crowd.

"Where are we going?"

"The Institute of Oil and Gas." Ivanov led the way across the leafy campus to a nondescript red brick construction. They went through rotating doors and stopped before a block of lifts. When the lift came, the Admiral pushed the button for — 2, but he kept his finger on the button a long time. Ivanov turned to face a small camera in one corner of the roof of the lift and gave a salute.

"Forgive the cloak-and-dagger stuff," he said. "Until the Union collapsed, the Caspian Flotilla was based in Baku, but a lot of the command structure was kept safely within Russia itself, including here, in Astra. The Americans knew that, of course. This place was just as much of a target, so special underground facilities were built for the command structures. That's where we are going now."

By then, the lift should have reached — 2 level, but felt as though it were still in motion. After several minutes of slow movement, the lift stopped, and the doors slid open. In front of them stood two armed, uniformed guards. Behind them was a vast, brightly lit space. Ivanov produced papers and explained about Dimitriy. Once the papers had been stamped, the soldiers stood aside and let them pass.

"It's quite a hike," said the Admiral.

The vast space was devoid of human activity, but all around them stood massive columns of plastic-wrapped material.

"Thousands of men could live down here for years," said Ivanov.

On the far side of the bunker, Ivanov led Dimitriy into a complex of smaller spaces. Each entrance was a double-doored air-pressurized port. Finally, they came to a twin set of grey-painted heavy steel doors that had been swung open.

"Here we are," said the Admiral. "The playroom; the laboratory."

They were greeted by the head of the scientific team, Fyodor Babikov, a beanpole of a man wearing large tinted spectacles. Ivanov left them together, promising to return at the end of the day. Babikov showed Dimitriy to the changing room. There were sinks, lockers and benches. They scrubbed up together, then dressed in classic surgical gear. Afterwards, Babikov led Dimitriy into a small meeting room. The walls were lined with large drawings showing distinctive geometrical structures. Babikov gestured for him to sit down at a table and sat opposite.

"What has Admiral Ivanov told you?" he asked.

"The basic story," said Dimitriy. "And I've read the file."

"Did he tell you about their effects?"

"The blindness?"

"Well, there *is* that," said Babikov. "But you don't need to worry. The lab is rigged so that you simply cannot look directly at the fragments. You can only see them indirectly by using the mirrors we've installed, or by using the camera. But did Ivanov not talk about anything else?"

"Nothing," said Dimitriy.

"Mmm... He was probably afraid he'd scare you off."

"Why would I be scared?"

"They seem to have an addictively euphoric effect on some people."

"Some?"

"It seems to depend. There's nothing chemical about it."

"How do you know this?"

"You're not the first expert drafted in. In fact, you are the third."

"The others?"

Babikov shook his head.

"They didn't last very long. The first was here for just over a year. The second lasted almost two years."

"Where are they now?"

"Locked away," said Babikov.

"And you?"

"Nothing," said Babikov. "But, then, I don't spend hours in the viewing room."

"All right," Dimitriy said. "What else did Ivanov *not* tell me?"

"There isn't a whole lot more to know."

"How long have the fragments been here?"

"Since 2008."

"And you have honestly learned nothing?"

Babikov grinned.

"Honestly, very little. I'll tell you everything we know, but it won't take long."

Dimitriy leaned back in his chair.

"Tell me," he said.

"We know they have properties, and powers. The power to blind people, for example."

"Are we sure of that?"

"You mean?"

"Well," said Dimitriy, "we've only had that one example, of the man down the pit, back in 1938. It could have been a stroke, couldn't it?"

"You're forgetting the animals," Babikov said. "Anyway, there have been quite a few unfortunate episodes since."

"Here?" asked Dimitriy.

"Yes," said Babikov. "People who didn't listen. People who didn't believe. An accident. A drunk."

"How many?"

"Enough for us to know that the fragments, if looked at directly, cause blindness in humans, as in animals. Even welding masks didn't help."

"You've tried reptiles?"

"Oh, yes," said Babikov. "We've tried reptiles *and* squid and octopus *and* insects. We've tried everything," he said. "The fragments have the same effect on any sort of eye known to us."

"Your instruments?"

"Show nothing. Whatever this effect is, it is produced in an undetectable way."

"What else?" Dimitriy asked.

"Oh, the euphoria business."

"Can you be sure of that?"

"Scientifically, no. But there must be a strong presumption."

"Two cases only? You can't presume anything from that."

"You are right," Babikov said, smiling ruefully. "Let me just call it a *hunch*, then. Two highly intelligent, balanced, reasonable scientists, both following a similar pattern of obsessiveness and increasingly frequent episodes of manic euphoria, culminating in madness and confinement in clinics. I agree with you, Dimitriy Semenov. It could be sheer coincidence, but I think not."

"All right," said Dimitriy. "What else?"

"We have found a way to manipulate the fragments," said Babikov. "Only one metal may touch them — gold. All others melt away as they get near. Once we realised that, we had special gold implements made up that could be attached to the arms of the robots — that is the main way in which you will be working with the fragments, if you need to manipulate them."

"But it is curious," said Dimitriy, "gold being so malleable — like the lead in which they were encased."

"In retrospect, the lead-lined box was a crazy risk," said Babikov. "Who knows what might have happened if they had melted their way out during the trip?"

"What else?"

Babikov shook his head in sudden exhaustion.

"We know next to nothing, and that is all we know."

"Now you are talking in riddles."

Babikov looked at Dimitriy for a few moments, as though brought back from a reverie.

"We cannot record images. Nothing works; film, X-rays, electro-magnetic resonance imaging, transmission electron tomography... Whatever sort of imaging we have tried to use, nothing shows up. They are definitely there; we can see their reflection, but we can't capture them as images, and that means that we can only study the fragments themselves."

"What about microscopes?" asked Dimitriy.

"Lenses work," said Babikov. "But you cannot record what you are seeing."

"You can't draw them?"

"No, no," said Babikov. "They can be drawn, at least — hence all of these..." he waved at the drawings hanging on the walls around them. "Your predecessors' masterpieces."

"May I?" Dimitriy asked.

Babikov nodded.

Dimitriy studied the drawings for a while.

"I have an idea," he said. "But I'll wait until you've finished."

"Second," Babikov continued, "they are constantly levitating."

Dimitriy raised his eyebrows.

"They always hover, never touching any surface."

"Some sort of energy, then?"

"I think so, but we can detect nothing. We thought of magnetism or light but it's neither of those." Babikov smiled and shook his head. "Believe me, Dimitriy Semenov, we have tried and tested many ideas — all fruitlessly — so far."

"I understand what Ivanov was getting at now."

"Getting at?" said Babikov.

"We were talking about scientific method. He said we don't know the answer yet, and perhaps we never will."

●

That very first time Dimitriy came back from Astrakhan she'd known already, he realised — or, rather, she'd suspected already. Something had happened. He couldn't entirely hide it from her. For a start, there was the fait accompli of his decision. He had taken the job without first discussing the offer with her. It was so generous, he said, that he had decided on the spot. That wasn't the whole truth, of course. She asked about the work. He told her how he'd had to sign a declaration and was now bound by the Official Secrets Act. He saw her recoil.

"It isn't what you think," he'd said.

"What is it, then?" she'd asked.

"Something unimaginable," he'd replied.

She'd wrinkled her nose. "Can't you give me a clue?"

He'd laughed. "I promise you it's nothing sinister."

"I can see you are enthusiastic about it."

"Come with me to Astrakhan, Ana," he'd urged. "Bring the children. We can make it work."

"We discussed all that," she'd said, shaking her head. "My job, my family, the children's schools..."

He'd nodded his head slowly. Already, his thoughts were drifting back...

"Dimitriy?"

"I'm sorry, my love," he said. "I was daydreaming."

●

He'd listened patiently as Babikov listed the other properties his team had so far noted. The seven fragments were identical in appearance. Each was a convex oblong, about nine centimetres long by five centimetres wide. From a distance, they seemed to be golden in colour but, the stronger the magnification, the less colour there was. From very close up they seemed neither transparent nor invisible, and completely colourless yet iridescent. The fragments' default position was to hover vertically in an overlapping formation, like the defensive *testudo* Roman legionaries had sometimes adopted with their shields. If the fragments were separated, they immediately moved back to the *testudo* formation. Once again, Dimitriy studied the drawings on the walls.

"So, what's this big idea of yours?" said Babikov.

"*Lepidoptera*," said Dimitriy.

"Butterflies?" said Babikov, momentarily confused. "We'd thought of fish scales, but *lepidoptera*?"

"In appearance they seem similar to fish scales, it is true, but butterfly scales have three-dimensional lattices that cause iridescence, and I just wonder whether some similar effect is not at work with these scales — and they *are* scales, Babikov, aren't they? They're not just fragments."

Babikov blushed. He took off his glasses and polished the lenses.

"Ivanov doesn't like such talk. I think he's right. We shouldn't leap ahead of ourselves."

"But are we?" said Dimitriy. "We know — or we assume — that these fragments fell to earth in June 1908, right?"

Babikov shook his head.

"No," he said. "We know only that they were found in the area where that event occurred."

"Ivanov gave me to understand there was a probability."

"So there may be," said Babikov. "But he doesn't want us to start wandering off into anthropomorphism and zoomorphism and all the rest of it. We know only what we know. The rest is speculation. If the Admiral hadn't given you the file, you wouldn't have started thinking along these lines."

Dimitriy smiled.

"What lines, Fyodor Babikov? What lines are those?"

Babikov remained silent.

"All right," said Dimitriy. "I'm sure you have similar thoughts. These so-called fragments are themselves a fragment that fell off something much larger, probably during that 'event' of 1908 — off a wing, maybe?"

"Enough!" said Babikov, waving his hands in front of him.

But somehow, Dimitriy *knew*; the fragments *belonged* to something.

●

In February, just over a year after his first visit to Astrakhan, Anastasia put the ultimatum to him. He couldn't blame her. The Christmas period had been disastrous. Derbent was bitterly cold and the streets were littered with filthy snow and slush where the gritters had passed. The morning, midday, and evening howls of the Ekranoplan as it departed and returned punctuated Derbent's days just as accurately and regularly as a clock tower bell. He couldn't wait to get back to Astra. He was constantly irritable with the children and mostly morosely silent with her. He felt dreadful. He needed to be back, to be back with *them*, in their presence. When the holidays were finally over, and he had been leaving for the Ekranoplan, she had said, "I can't say I'm sorry to see you go, Dimitriy. You have to get a grip on yourself. Whatever is going on in Astrakhan, you have to put a stop to it. It is ruining you and us."

That had been January. He had got worse over the following month. Then, one Friday evening in late February, she took the final initiative. Part of him felt she was absolutely right — he felt sorry for her and for Andrei and Sasha. But another part of him just didn't care. Or, rather, it only cared about *them*, the angelic fragments (which was what he called them now), and about being with them.

The children were in bed. The classical music radio channel was on. She'd even put a lit candle on the laid dinner table. It was the first time in a long time that she had cooked a meal for his return. At the end of the meal, Anastasia took his hands across the table.

"I am so very sorry, Dima," she said, "but I can't take this anymore."

"What do you mean?" he blustered.

She smiled and put a finger to his lips to hush him.

"You know what I mean. I have spoken to you so many times."

She was right.

"So, now what?" he asked.

"I'd like you to resign from your job in Astrakhan."

"But how would we..." he began, blustering again.

She shook her head and smiled wistfully.

"We were fine before. We'll be fine again."

"But my work is important."

"I'm sure it is, Dimitriy but, please, let somebody else do it."

He burst into tears.

"I can't," he wept. "I just can't."

"What do you mean? What is it that has such a hold over you? If it is not a mistress, then what is it? Drugs? Is that it? You can tell me. Please."

"It's none of those," he blurted. "But I can't tell you."

"Of course you can!"

"I have signed the Official Secrets Act, Ana."

"I promise I won't tell anybody else. Who could I tell, anyway?"

Dimitriy shook his head.

"If you won't tell me," said Anastasia, her tone hardening, "that's it."

"What do you mean?"

"I'll leave you, Dimitriy."

His shoulders sagged.

"All right, I'll tell you," he said finally.

He told her about his second meeting with Ivanov, and the file about the 1908 Tunguska event and Kulik's 1938 discovery. He told her about his first entry into the thick-walled, steel-shuttered underground space where the plate glass and mirrors had been set up to enable scientists to gaze indirectly on the fragments. He told her about his indescribable feelings of ecstasy, of euphoria, when he was in the presence of the angelic scales, and how the obsessive feeling had grown until it had now overwhelmed all other considerations. He told her about the steel shutter inside the space housing the scales which Babikov had to operate every day so that Dimitriy could at least no longer gaze upon the angelic fragments, and the way he, Dimitriy, had to be dragged out of the space by orderlies and given sedation before he could be convinced to return to his hotel room in the evenings.

Anastasia sat patiently through his explanation.

"All right," she said when he had finished. "Suppose everything you've told me is true. Where do you think this will all end?"

"I have to finish my work," he said. "Nobody understands the fragments better than I do. I have a *feeling* for them, don't you see? I understand them; their need to return. You see?"

She looked at him with sad eyes. "Of course I do, Dima," she said, "but you need to take a break. You're working yourself crazy."

"I can't take a break, don't you understand? I *must* continue."

"Nobody would blame you for taking a break," she said.

"But the *work*," Dimitriy insisted. "I *must* be there."

She shook her head. "No," she said. "You must stop this nonsense. You *can* stop it, you know. Let somebody else do it."

"NO!" he shouted, startling himself as much as Anastasia. "I can't let someone else come in. *I* must be with them. You can't stop me now." He broke off and wept. "Don't you see?" he said. "It's stronger than me."

Anastasia shook her head once more.

"You must choose," she said softly.

"No!" Dimitriy sobbed. "Please don't make me choose."

"If you go back to Astrakhan on Monday, then we will move out."

"But the children need their father!" Dimitriy blurted.

"Don't be a fool," Anastasia snapped. "The children haven't had a father for over a year now."

He nodded and hung his head. "All right,' he said. "Where will you go? Your parents?"

She nodded.

Good, thought Dimitriy, with a sense of wonderment at his own callousness. *Now I can go back to the fragments.*

●

Anastasia didn't come to the doorstep with him. He'd kissed her on the head as she lay in bed. She didn't move, though he sensed she was awake.

"Goodbye, Ana," he said. "I still love you, you know. And I'm sorry. I just have to be there."

He closed the door and walked through the slushy remains of the snow to the Ekranoport. He was petrified of the take-off, as usual, but his heart had already filled with joyful anticipation. As the Caspian Queen approached Astra, the sea became agitated and the sky darkened. A strong wind blew up and Dimitriy could feel that the pilot was struggling with the controls. He was relieved when the craft slowed down and started its long taxi up the relative calm of the Reka Bakhtemir channel. Ivanov was waiting for him on the quayside.

"Something's going on," he said. "We've been hearing noises in the sky."

"Heavenly trumpets?" said Dimitriy.

"Noises in the sky," Ivanov repeated. "But, yes, not unlike the descriptions the Evenki gave in 1908."

"Could it be?" asked Dimitriy.

"Be what?" said Ivanov, drawing on his cigarette. The sky flashed. A long roll of thunder sounded. "And we've been having strange weather. Look at those clouds."

Dimitry looked up at the dark, corrugated formation hanging heavy and low over the city. Thunder reverberated above and around them.

"And the fragments," Ivanov continued, "have started to oscillate."

"Oscillate?"

"All right," said the Admiral, flicking away his cigarette and blowing out smoke. "They seem to have become agitated."

"I can't wait to see them."

Ivanov gave him a sour stare then lit another cigarette and leaned against the Zil.

"I'm not sure that's a good idea, Dimitriy Semenov. They are no longer stable."

"What do you mean? I've got to see them. You know that."

"Pull yourself together," said the Admiral.

"It's just that I've *got* to see them. Surely you have understood that by now?"

The sky flashed and flickered. Ivanov looked up and waited for the roll of thunder.

"This is not normal," he said. "Something is going on."

"There's a connection?"

"I don't know, but I have a sense there might be. It's almost as though the scales are trying to escape."

"Ah! Escape?"

"Babikov says they have already melted through the gold lining on the roof of the cell."

"No!" said Dimitriy. "Then we must hurry. They are going back. I knew it!"

"Back?" Ivanov drew deeply on his cigarette. "Take my advice," he said. "Return to Derbent. The Ekranoplan will be leaving very soon. Go back to your wife and children. Maybe it's nothing. We'll see. Come again tomorrow."

"There's no point," said Dimitriy. "They've left me."

"Because of this?" Ivanov asked. "Because of your..."

"Yes," said Dimitriy.

Ivanov nodded slowly and drew again on his cigarette. They heard the distinctive whine as the Caspian Queen's jet engines started up.

"Go!" he urged.

"I can't!" Dimitriy sobbed. "I must see *them* again."

They leaned on a railing and watched as the gangplanks were drawn away and the aft and forward doors closed. The sky flashed vividly. A dockworker cast off the mooring ropes. When they had been entirely wound back on board, the jet engines roared, and the Caspian Queen sailed slowly out into the Volga. They heard the familiar howl as the captain increased the power and taxied the strange vessel down towards the sea channel.

Ivanov flicked away his cigarette, then opened the door of the Zil.

"We'd better hurry," he said.

●

"Ana," called her mother. "Come quickly."

Anastasia pulled the plug in the kitchen sink, wiped her hands on her apron and joined her parents in the living room. They were watching a Russian television channel and the news bulletin had just started. Sasha was playing on the floor. The newsreader was halfway through the headlines. A train had crashed just outside Vladivostok. The President had visited a new LPG facility at the port of Murmansk...

"What is it, mama?"

"Ssshhh," said her mother, "you'll see in a moment."

The newsreader finished the headlines. Anastasia's mother turned the volume up.

"And now we go back to our main news item this evening. Reports are coming in of a massive explosion on the northern outskirts of the city of Astrakhan, at the premises of the State Technology University. The explosion is said to have occurred in an underground research facility situated beneath the University's parkland.

"As can be seen from these helicopter images, several buildings have collapsed and the police and the fire services are searching the rubble. Among those missing are the director of the Caspian Flotilla's scientific outreach programme, Rear Admiral Anatoly Ivanov, and the head of the Astrakhan State Technology University's Oil and Gas Institute research programme, Fyodor Babikov. An acclaimed Moscow State University materials scientist, Dimitriy Semenov, who joined the research team from Derbent, is also missing."

Pictures of the three men flashed up on the screen for a few moments.

"That's Daddy," said Sasha.

Anastasia nodded tearfully.

"Yes, darling," she said.

"Babikov!" Dimitriy cried. He staggered out into the remains of the room where he had first met the scientist. He could hear flames flickering. The air was heavy with smoke. A long, low groan sounded out. "Babikov!" he said, "Is that you?" Dimitry staggered over to where he thought Babikov's office had once been. He heard the groan again. "Babikov?"

"Dimitriy Semenov," whispered the scientist. "What has happened to your eyes, man?"

Dimitriy smiled, the charred skin wrinkling where his eyes had once been.

"The fragments have gone back to their rightful place," he said. "I'm going home now."

Martin Westlake's story "Going Home" was originally published in Metaphorosis on Friday, 12 March 2021. See magazine.metaphorosis.com

About the author

Martin Westlake has followed parallel careers as a civil servant and as an academic and has lived, studied, and worked in the UK, Italy, France, and Belgium. The only thing he has ever always wanted to do is write creative fiction. Science fiction exercises a special, but not exclusive, attraction in that regard. For the past fifteen years he has been working seriously at it and he thinks maybe he is starting to get there.

martinwestlake.eu, @MartinWestlake

Bas Relief

Joshua Grasso

Sveta twisted and turned in the mirror, lifting her shirt to inspect her stomach, flattering herself that it looked harder, firmer, than it had last week. But no, she could easily pinch the flesh into an unsightly fat roll as usual. She pulled up her sleeves, inspecting every inch of her arm, hoping against hope to find something rough and scaly. Again, nothing but soft, pale skin, or what the upperclassmen liked to call 'soft serve'. All quivering adolescent flesh and nothing substantial.

The only thing remotely tough on her body was the crusty elbow scab she had scraped with a key out of boredom. There were people she knew — well, they weren't friends, of course — who could file down keys and fingernails against their skin. Even one guy whose head was so rock-hard that you could break a board over it. She had watched him once during third-period gym, and he just laughed, saying he didn't feel a thing and asking his pals to do it again and again.

Out of sheer desperation, she peeled off her socks and inspected her toes and heels, hoping the skin had hardened, dried out. But even they were baby-smooth and without blemish. There were a few girls who couldn't even wear shoes anymore, as their toes were granite-hard and could deflate soccer balls with a single kick. But after all, only those who didn't change played sports after high school, since flexibility was the surest obstacle to upward mobility.

She must have been ignoring her texts, because when her phone rang, she saw Malorie's name flash over the screen — and she never called.

"Bitch, do you ever look at your phone?" Malorie said, with a laugh.

"Sorry, I'm getting ready — running late. I'll see you in a few."

"Not today you won't. I'm sick off my ass. I might miss the entire week, who knows?"

"Maly, not again!" Sveta said, throwing herself on the bed. "You can't keep doing this. You've already missed, what, ten or twelve days? You'll get suspended."

"Whatever. We don't belong there anyway, among those privileged, petrified snobs. I'm sick of pretending I give a shit. What's the point of even graduating at this point?"

"Because otherwise you'll spend the rest of your life delivering take-out in this two-bit town. Come on, it's just a few more months. Get your ass in the car."

"Sorry, I really am coughing my brains out. *Cough, cough.* See, you can't fake that."

"Bullshit."

"Just take the bus and stop bitching. Or go pass the driving exam already. I mean, a lot of people fail it twice."

"I've already missed the bus, and if you don't take me...I have to ask her. Please don't make me ask her!"

"You two need some quality time together; you'll thank me later. Say hi to the clones in Calc!"

She wasted five minutes trying to call Malorie back, but she never answered. That only left her enough time to catch her mother before she left for work and ask her — or in this case, beg her — to take Sveta to school, which would add twenty minutes to her commute. The second she walked downstairs and they locked eyes her mother knew. She only shook her head and muttered, "Three minutes, and I'm leaving with or without you."

The drive to school was more strained than usual. Sveta sat in the passenger seat, clutching her backpack against her chest, watching the traffic lights zoom past. Her mother's eyes kept cutting over to her, as if trying to pry through the clothes and see some tell-tale sign of transformation. Even as a child, her mother's hands would sweep over her flesh, poking here, prodding there, looking for resistance. *There's still time, you're still young,* she always told her, but it never sounded encouraging.

"You know, maybe you should see someone? Like a therapist? They say it's often a mental block, and you used to have those nightmares, remember?"

Used to. Still did. Always did. But it was better for her mother not to know what kept her awake at night.

"Maybe it's just not my time yet, okay?" Sveta replied. "You're a late bloomer. And Malorie, she still isn't showing."

"Knowing her parents, I'm not surprised," her mother said, with a snicker. "But you come from a long line of *rockers*. Okay, it started late for me — and like a lot of women, just one arm — but look at your grandparents: they were planted on the hill in their forties. It's inspiring to see them looking down on us, along with the rest of our family...so many generations of Beckers and Burlatskys."

She interrupted her speech to honk at someone who had cut her off, then continued.

"I'm just saying, you're almost eighteen...some kids are already thinking about where they'll be planted. If you already had a stiff arm or leg, we could reserve a spot somewhere on the hill, maybe just behind the house next to Daddy? You want to settle down before all the good places are taken."

"I mean, I guess...I just wish everyone didn't make such a big deal about it. It'll happen eventually, won't it?"

"For most people, yes, but you have to be a little proactive," she said, thoughtfully. "Not to speak ill of your friend, but Malorie lives in a trailer park. Her parents never settled down, and I doubt she will, either. Can you imagine, spending your entire life running around, never knowing your place? I knew early on where I wanted to be, who I was going to marry, even before this," she said, raising her arm. "And your father —"

"Can we not?" Sveta said, burying her face in her bag.

Her father, the famous *rock star* himself, who was in a wheelchair at eighteen. He had even made the local paper; a miracle of science, they called him. By the time she was six he was immobilized in the bedroom, just a living rock that would greet her and kiss her goodnight. A few years later they moved him to the yard, since the doctors said he was still *there*, still with them, though they couldn't say for how long. It only took a year before they felt it was time, and moved him up with his parents on the hill, another Becker to watch over the generations-yet-unborn.

"Sveta, you should be proud of him. I know it's tough not to have him around, but he did this for the family...he wanted the best for all of us."

Honestly, she barely remembered him as a living, functional parent. He had always been that *thing* in the bedroom, and she used to dread going in there at all, which was mostly reserved for bedtimes and birthdays. She hated that look in his eyes, which always seemed distant, like he didn't even know who she was. There were statues that looked kinder, more alive.

"Does it hurt?" she asked, after a pause.

"Does what? This?" her mother asked, holding up her 'good' arm, the one that was cracked and gray. "No, not at all. It's just heavier, that's all. If anything, it gives me comfort. I feel like I've become whole, like nothing can hurt me."

"Really? But what happens when you can't move? When you just have to sit around all day, having people wait on you? Doesn't that scare you?"

"If I didn't have such a loving daughter in my life, yes, it might," her mother said, with a smile. "But I know you'll take care of me. And then I'll watch over you, along with your father, from the top of the hill. You can bring your own kids up to see me, and they can hug me, climb me, whatever they like. We'll still be one big happy family."

"I guess so," Sveta said, seeing her school swing into view through the window.

"So listen, I made an appointment for you next week... the therapist came highly recommended," her mother said. "Just try it, just for a session or two. It might help. Because there's no reason you can't do it...there's nothing wrong with you. Really."

She said that last *really* as if convincing herself, lest she see her daughter as a failed experiment, someone unworthy of the Becker-Burlatsky line. She gave Sveta an affectionate pat on the shoulder as she pulled into the lot and wished her a good day. Sveta gave a miserable smile and ducked out of the car, feeling that she had survived this conversation mostly intact (unlike last time, when they had stopped talking to each other for a week).

Still, the pressure to conform and change seemed more intense than usual; not just from her mother, but from Malorie, too. It had become their only topic of conversation, and the closer they got to graduation, the more she felt she had made a decision, even without making one. It made her examine everyone with new eyes today, seeing those who *were* and those who *weren't*. All the jocks seemed to lumber about, some dragging stone legs across the floor or with faces almost set, so that you couldn't tell if they were happy or pissed off. Most of the popular kids — probably for this very reason — seemed to be well advanced, a few using crutches to get about, but one with a neck so stiff he had to turn his body simply to look at his friends. There were only a handful of girls like her who seemed normal, who moved around efficiently but seemed to hide in the background, with no infirmities to boast of. Had it always been like this? Or were people changing faster, younger, so they could be as safe and watchful as their parents?

At lunch, instead of sampling the cafeteria fare, she ducked into the library and pulled up the yearbook archive on the school's website. She scrolled through the decades, going as far back as the 1950's, watching long hair and t-shirts gradually fade into sideburns and neckties, until finally everyone became indistinguishable from the teachers: frame after frame of well-coiffed girls with giant glasses, and crew-cut boys with funeral-director suits. At first it seemed depressing, as if every one of those 1950's kids was half-chiseled out of marble.

Yet at second glance she wasn't so sure. The further back she went, the more the students seemed to have eyes. Naturally, they all *had eyes*, but these seemed alive, full of mystery and excitement. As she went forward, the stares seemed to dim, to look away, to die out. In recent years, she could sense a kind of dullness creep in, a sense that the kids had nothing to live for. Almost like the transformation had started from the inside-out.

Was that how she felt, watching everyone else turn to stone like clockwork? Was that why she still had nightmares, why she was secretly terrified of seeing a patch of gray or a finger locked in place? Of course she knew it was a good thing; she had seen all the movies and read all the books, all those glorious couples turning to stone together as the sun set behind them. Her mother called it *going back to the earth*, and said there was nothing more natural, more romantic. How strange that people used to die in wrinkled, useless skin that had to be buried out of sight and forgotten. Why settle for tombstones when you could become a living monument for those you loved?

And yet it terrified her. She still woke up most nights in a cold sweat from dreams where she was mounted like a *bas relief* over the fireplace. Her parents and friends would gather to inspect her, offering toasts, saying how wonderfully she completed the room. No matter how hard she screamed they only shook their heads, assuring her that the feeling would pass as soon as she let it go. And then she saw all the other terrified faces on the wall, all of them frozen in screaming stone.

She became so lost in these thoughts that she missed both bells and was late to Biology. By the time she arrived, students were already working in pairs on their next experiment. Her normal partner wasn't there, so she had to sit awkwardly at her desk, waiting for the teacher to notice. She thought about asking to be a third wheel in someone else's group, but she could see the looks on their faces; she was on her own. Mr. Malkin, largely immobile behind his desk, suddenly noticed her and waved imperiously.

"Miss Becker, don't just sit there. Your partner's out sick. You can pick up the lab when he returns. Here, take this to Study Hall," he said, handing her a pass.

"Study Hall? But Mr. Malkin, I can't go there! I mean, I'm not...can't I just work with someone here?" she asked, panicked.

"If you had come earlier, maybe, but I can't stop everyone just for you. Now here, take the pass. I have a lab to conduct."

"Mr. Malkin, please, you don't understand —"

"You've only got yourself to blame," he said, with a look that suggested he wasn't just talking about class.

Horrified, she took the pass and felt the whispers of mockery behind her. Study Hall was reserved for students who were on the fast-track to immobility. It allowed them a chance to take all their normal classes in a single room, since they couldn't possibly make it across the building, much less to lunch, between bells. If she walked in there like this, on both feet, without crutches or an obvious impairment, the jokes would never end. She almost thought about ditching school entirely, but without a ride she wouldn't get far. The only other choice was to hide in the bathroom until the bell rang, but that's where the druggies hung out, and she wasn't stoned enough for them, either.

She opened the door to Study Hall and the students — a small group of twelve or so — looked up from their desks, students she knew from junior high and grade school. She had watched them grow up, sometimes being friends with them, sometimes not, until they all got lost in a blur of adolescence. Surprisingly, no one laughed or objected to her presence. The teacher gestured for her pass and then went back to his book, similarly indifferent. Sveta scanned the room, trying to think which student she would piss off the least by sitting beside them.

Helen Canevaro. They had been friends for a short space in third or fourth grade, but something had happened, a spat at a birthday party, she didn't remember. She still fondly remembered spending the night at Helen's house once, reading manga and watching old horror movies until three in the morning. Helen looked up at her with a smile and said hello. Gratefully, Sveta slung her backpack over the chair and sat down, smiling back.

"Hey, good to see you," Sveta said, quietly. "Sorry, I know I don't belong here, I'm kind of a loser, but I got kicked out of class. No lab partner."

"No, it's cool, I've only been here for a few weeks," Helen said, gesturing to her foot. "I don't feel like I belong here, either."

Sveta looked down at her right foot, which at first resembled a mud-stained cast. Upon closer inspection, she could see what used to be toes encrusted with a jumble of mottled stone. Otherwise, though, Helen looked completely normal, her bare arms untouched, except for a small bird tattoo near her left elbow. Their eyes met, and Sveta was startled how much Helen looked like that one girl from the crazy Swedish movie where they sacrificed people. Maybe that was the real reason they'd stopped hanging out all those years ago. Sometimes girls could tell when she looked at them a certain way, or for too long, and didn't like it.

"Is it hard...you know, getting around?" Sveta asked.

"Yeah, it's kind of a drag," she said, nodding. "It goes all the way up to my knee. I woke up one morning and it was like that, no warning. My parents were thrilled. They would have bought me a car if they thought I could drive it."

"Shit," Sveta said, with a laugh. "I don't know whether to say *congratulations* or *I'm sorry.*"

"Both, I guess. What about you? Any signs yet?"

"No, nothing. I'm a total failure. The disappointment of my entire clan," she said dramatically.

"I doubt that. You were someone people always looked up to. I remember when...well, never mind, it's silly."

"No, what?" Sveta asked. "Come on, tell me."

"Oh, you probably won't remember...but back in third grade, we went to the county fair together. Your mom took us."

"Oh right, of course," Sveta said, starting to remember.

"Anyway, there was that booth where you had to throw baseballs at bottles. I sucked, couldn't hit even one. But you hit every one, over and over again. There was a crowd of people watching you, cheering you on, and you kept going until the guy kicked you out. Said you were cheating."

"Oh yeah, I forgot all about that! What a dick."

"But you still won that giant rabbit: it was ridiculously big, cotton-candy pink, with these huge floppy ears, remember? And you gave it to me, even though it was yours, even though I begged you to keep it. You even told me — I know, it sounds silly now — that I was your inspiration."

Sveta didn't have a clear vision of winning the rabbit or giving it to Helen, though the general impression rang true. She only remembered a vague, warm sensation in her gut whenever she thought about their brief friendship. It was still one of the happiest times of her life.

"Sorry I made you keep it. Hopefully you got rid of it in the morning."

"No way, I still have her!" Helen said, eyes wide. "She sits right on my bed...sometimes I even use her as a pillow."

"*Her?* Don't tell me you named it?" Sveta said.

"Of course: Anastasia! I think your name inspired me. Whenever I see her, I always remember you, that night we spent together. I hated that we stopped being friends."

"Yeah, I wonder why we did? I guess it doesn't matter anymore, we were just kids. Maybe we can...you know, start over? Especially since we're stuck here together."

"But only here until your lab partner comes back to class, right? Are they really sick?" Helen asked, cautiously.

"I don't know, maybe. I barely even know the guy," she said, with a shrug.

"Good...I don't like competition," Helen replied.

It was only after the bell rang and they went their separate ways that Sveta realized she still had a crush on Helen, and her third-grade game had been smoother than she thought.

As it happened, her lab partner, Sam Dickey, was having unexpected complications from his sudden change. It happened sometimes. They didn't like to talk about it, but a few students were hospitalized when the change was too abrupt, or when it started in the wrong place. She knew at least one kid had died when his heart turned to stone. That was what scared her the most, the Russian roulette of the transformation. It was almost like someone was having a sick joke at their expense, one time choosing something ridiculous, like an ear, and another, an essential organ. She suddenly felt guilty that she didn't even remember what Sam looked like, other than his glasses, which were always slipping off.

However, after a few days of Study Hall, she fell into a comfortable routine with Helen, no longer worried about being witty or stupid or whatever. Mostly she just spent time observing Helen, noticing all the little things hidden in plain view, but which took days and weeks to pick up. Case in point, she realized Helen was filling up page after page with elaborate arabesques, which sometimes coalesced into familiar shapes and faces. Once, without trying to be too sneaky about it, she spied a dreamy portrait emerge on the margins of Helen's homework.

"Damn, did you do that just on the spot?" she asked.

"Oh — yeah, I mean, I'm just scribbling. It helps me think, it always has. It's nothing really."

"If you do that, you must have other stuff, too, like where you're really trying. Can you show me?"

Helen grew a bit red at the suggestion, though it was clear that the scribbles were a subtle invitation to see more. But now she was nervous to go all the way.

"Well, look, don't read too much into this...but I wanted to give you this. I was just worried you would think, *wow, that's weird* or something. But I made it for you."

Helen unzipped her backpack and removed a sketch pad smudged with charcoal on the cover. She opened the cover and flipped past several pages of abstract images, still lives, landscapes, houses. Then she came to one of the last pages, which, after a grin, she nudged over toward Sveta. Sveta could tell what it was even upside-down, even before her eyes really put it together.

It was a portrait of her, a bit idealized, of course, but taken by someone who had paid attention, who caught more than just the shoulder-length hair, the freckles, the little gap in her teeth. She saw her hesitation, her excitement, her awkwardness, her beauty. That was Sveta's first thought when she really took in the portrait: *Jesus, she's gorgeous.* Because she really felt like she was looking at Helen looking at her, and so much of Helen had bled through that it made the portrait feel like a warm embrace that wouldn't let go.

"My God, Helen...this is wonderful. I mean, I wish I looked like that. When did you do this?"

"A few nights ago. I got bored doing my homework...or rather, I couldn't concentrate on my homework. I kept thinking about you."

So there, I said it, her eyes seemed to announce. They were wide-awake eyes, right there, looking to the future. Like those fifties kids in the yearbook, but no longer carved in stone.

"It's wonderful, I love it," Sveta said, stroking it with her hand. "It's perfect."

"Then it was worth doing," Helen said, with a smile. "It's yours, of course. I still have the original."

"Where, in your head?"

Helen gave a little nod that suggested both yes and no. They didn't say another word for the rest of class, allowing Sveta to replay the scene over and over until she knew it by heart.

Sveta waited for Helen after school, saw her coming out of the building on her crutches, her dead leg holding her back, bringing tears of frustration. When she suddenly looked up and saw Sveta, her face went blank, the pain retreating. Then her eyes lit up again. Sveta didn't look at who was watching, what they might think (or what she might think tomorrow). She went right up to Helen and said something, she didn't even remember what, and kissed her. Really quickly, before either of them could think twice. Helen's eyes stayed wide-open in surprise, only closing as she pulled away, drinking it in.

"That's for the drawing," Sveta said, awkwardly.

"I have a few more, if you want to see them. But I keep them at home."

"I want to see everything. I mean, if you'll let me...if I'm not being, you know, too weird or something."

"Whatever...I like weird girls."

A car pulled up just behind them, which Sveta recognized from the general cacophony (shuddering engine, muffled sounds of Black Sabbath) as Malorie's car. She tried to ignore it and steal as much time as she could, but Malorie laid on the horn: a long, impatient blast. Sveta gave a backwards wave in Malorie's direction.

"Shit, I gotta go. My ride. You want to come? We can take you —"

"No, my mom insists on picking me up. But thanks. I'll text you later, okay?"

Another honk. Sveta gave Helen a quick squeeze of the hand and darted into the passenger seat of the 'Gremlin' as they called it, though she had no idea what brand or model it was. Malorie zoomed off and even went between the parked buses with their STOP signs extended. A few kids flipped her off.

"I'd be doing them a favor," she muttered. "So what, are you hanging out with her now?"

"Yeah, I mean, we're friends," Sveta said, cautiously. "I met her in Study Hall. She's funny, you'd like her."

"I heard she was a stuck-up bitch. But, I mean, if *you* like her."

"I do. She's cool. So, you actually came to school today. What's the occasion?"

"Girl, I guess I'm celebrating," she said, accelerating dramatically out of the parking lot. "I tried to text you, but you were too busy with what's-her-face."

"Celebrating? Why, did Steve send you a dick-pic or something?"

"Honestly, they look the same as his selfies, so who knows? But for real, check this shit out," she said, revealing her left hand, which she had kept hidden at her side.

Flashing it in Sveta's face, she revealed four fingers that were completely stone, with only one, the pinky, unscathed. Sveta shrieked and immediately grabbed it, running her fingers over each one, amazed and terrified by the transformation. Only a few days ago Malorie had made fun of all the *stoners*, as she jokingly called them, comparing the stratification of torsos and biceps. But now she seemed almost giddy over her change, having already posted it across social media, where, she explained, it already had hundreds of likes.

"My parents are flipping out," Malorie said, trying unsuccessfully to wiggle her fingers. "You know how they said I was on my own for college? Well, guess who just put up five thousand bucks?"

"You're joking! Really? Just because of this?"

"Hell yeah, because of this. A lot of people say if you get fingers first, that's a good sign. It means you're as good as gold by your twenties. So if I can get into State, or even one of the liberal arts schools, I might jumpstart fingers into an arm and a leg — or hell, even a torso!"

"But weren't you going to take a gap year or something? So you could travel the country, hike all over the Southwest? Remember the postcard I sent you of the giant saguaro? You were even going to get a tattoo."

Malorie frowned at the reminder, clearly from a different time, a different life. The world before she knew she had a future, or a body worth investing in.

"I mean...that would be cool, but I can't just waste an entire year when I could, you know, be getting ahead. And why go to Arizona or wherever when there are so many good colleges here?"

"And that's what you really want?" Sveta said, hesitantly. "You just seemed so happy, like you had everything figured out. This shouldn't change things completely."

"But it does, like a million percent! I never thought I would have a chance to settle down, find a place on the hill where everyone can see me. And who knows, after college I might be solid rock. Think what that would mean to my parents!"

"To be a statue before you're thirty?" she said, unable to hide her disappointment. "You saw what happened to my father; I barely knew him, Maly. What if you have kids? Is that how you want them to remember you? Because they won't remember you at all. You'll just be that thing in the garden, or up on the hill, reminding them to study hard and eat their vegetables."

Malorie abruptly switched lanes and pulled into an abandoned gas station where they used to hang out, where Malorie allegedly made out with some guy who just graduated. The car slammed to a halt and Malorie just glared at her, her soft hand gripping the wheel.

"I thought you would be happy for me," she said, her deep voice cracking. "You're the only person I really wanted to tell, Sveta. Because I knew you would give a shit. Or at least understand. I wasn't supposed to change and you know it. My parents are soft-skinned, trailer-trash rednecks. And I'm trailer-trash, too."

"No, Maly, I do — I get it. I *am* happy for you. I just don't think you should be in such a hurry to be like everyone else. You're different than them, you always said so. That's why we're friends. And we'll still be friends, no matter what."

"What the fuck do you know about me?" Malorie said, giving her a shove. "Maybe I've wanted this my whole life but was too scared to ask? Maybe I didn't want to be disappointed like I always am? People don't give two shits about me around here, Sveta. I don't have parents, a reputation like yours. I'll always be *that girl* to them."

"Who cares? I like *that girl*, don't you? And since when do you need them to like you? It's us against the world, remember?"

Malorie gave a world-weary laugh, as if she had heard this before, many times, in fact, and still didn't buy it. Sveta tried to backtrack, but Malorie cut her off, rolling down the window and yelling "bullshit!" at the top of her lungs. Sveta waited for the moment to pass, for Malorie to realize she was overacting and apologize, but it seemed she was just warming up.

"We were never on the same side," Malorie said, eyes flashing. "You're still the same old Sveta, slumming it with me until you find something better. But you don't know the first thing about me...like the reason I hate your guts."

"Do tell," Sveta muttered.

"You're everything I want to be, everything I tried to believe in. You made me feel that it was okay to be who I was. But then I started to see that you didn't even believe in yourself. People used to look up to you, you know? You were the girl *most likely to succeed* and shit. But now...they talk a lot of shit behind your back. They think you've given up; we all do."

"Why, because I'm not practicing to become a lawn ornament? Is that what little kids really dream of doing when they grow up? Why can't we look around, get lost, not try to be exactly like our parents? Why is everyone in such a rush to do nothing for the rest of their lives?"

"Actually, I'm trying *not* to be like my parents," Malorie said, sucking her teeth. "But I'd like to see how far you get with what's-her-name. You think she really cares about you? Today, maybe, but tomorrow she's going to want something real, something lasting. I know I do."

"Then lucky for me she's not like you," Sveta snapped. "No, she's the person I thought you were, the one I felt safe with, who I trusted more than anyone on earth. But I guess friendship's only skin deep...so you'll need a new friend to go with your fucked-up hand."

They drove home in silence, and when they pulled up to Sveta's house, Malorie just sat there, idling. Sveta just sat there, too, trying to think of whether to salvage their relationship or blow it to hell. Malorie beat her to it.

"I love how no one's supposed to change but you," she said, looking away. "I have to remain the fuck-up, the loser, while you figure it out. And once you do, you sure as hell won't wait for me. You'll leave me in the dust."

"Maly, that's not true. I've always had your back."

"You mean you've *held me* back. When I talked about college, or having kids, or anything you don't agree with, it's always *don't do it, it's not you, you'll regret it*. But what if I don't have the same regrets as you?"

"So your answer is to do what everyone else does, to follow them off the same fucking cliff? That's your idea of finding yourself? No, you're smarter than that."

"Everyone goes there for a reason," Malorie said, coldly. "It's what we all secretly want. Like falling in love, having a family. No one stays in the valley unless they have to, even if they lie to themselves and say they prefer it. Life looks better up on the hill, and you know it. At least, your father did."

"Fuck off, Malorie," she said, and opened the door.

"You first," Malorie returned.

As soon as Sveta got out, Malorie sped away, music blasting. Sveta knew she wouldn't see her again for months, maybe not ever. Now she had no one to talk to, no one to console her for being different, no one to confide in about her feelings for Helen. Of course, that's what choosing your own path was all about: being alone, choosing the road less traveled by. She had to have faith in the destination, in ending up far away in some happily-ever-after, even if it never was. All the same, the conversation hit its mark, and she replayed Malorie's words and her responses far more than she cared to. Even when Helen started texting her after dinner, she was only half-listening, thinking about *who* Helen was talking to: the now-her or the one-to-come? The one who had rock legs like Helen did, or the loser who never would?

After a few days, Sveta had made her decision: she and Helen had to break up. Partly it was everything Malorie had told her; partly it was her own fear of commitment. But what really clinched it was the meme making the rounds of the school, a picture of two people playing Paper-Scissors-Rock, the hands of one opponent forming scissors, the other forming rock. On the 'rock' someone had Photoshopped a picture of Helen's head, and on the 'scissors', Sveta's. Though the words of the meme had a few variations, the most consistent one said *Happy Valentine's Day*, with a copy even making its way to her locker at school. The message was clear: rock always beats scissors, and not even love can change the rules of the game. She shuddered to think how often Helen had seen it, and what she must have thought the first, second, and fiftieth time it swam through her feed.

Sveta had to tell her face-to-face, and it had to be at school, so she wouldn't waver and change her mind at the last minute. Of course, it was harder now that Sveta's bio partner had returned and she was back in class doing make-up. Worse still, without Malorie, her mother had to pick her up from school, and she was always there at 3:15 on the dot. So Sveta had about five minutes to waylay Helen, find somewhere semi-private, and tell her the truth. She spent the entire day planning her route, worried about the distance between their rooms and the congestion in the hallway. When the release bell finally rang, she was the first one out the door, pushing and prodding her way across the building to Study Hall, which was precariously close to the exit. A few minutes late, and Helen would slip through the doors and make it into her mom's car before Sveta could say a word.

She made it in record time, just as people were starting to trickle out of other rooms, though Study Hall seemed comfortably full (it took them much longer to leave, obviously). Sveta flattened herself against the wall, eyes picking out every jock and bonehead who left the room, excited — yet crushed — when it wasn't Helen. Seven or eight people came out, then a few more, then one more... then the teacher himself, who flicked off the lights.

Holy shit, where was she?

She knew Helen was here today, because she had said she had a Calc test and couldn't chat over breakfast. Frantic, Sveta began sweeping up and down the hallways, looking for any sign of her presence. She checked both of their lockers (nope), circled back to her last-hour class (no one), and even checked the bathrooms, trying to match the shoes beneath each of the stalls (Nikes; Helen only wore Converse). After five or six minutes she knew it was too late, that somehow she had missed Helen, even though she had covered all the bases and left nothing to chance.

As her heart stopped racing, she became aware of a steady, pulsating hum just around or behind her. Shit, her phone! In her anxiety she had missed an entire stream of texts from Helen. Pulling them up, they all basically said, *Where are you? Really need to talk! Meet me in the locker room. Are you coming? Sveta? Hello???*

It took her another three or four minutes to make her way to the locker room (the hallways were packed now), but it was a well-chosen spot, completely dead. She found Helen sitting in a dark corner of the room on a bench, hugging her knees while she stared down at her phone, waiting for a reply. Sveta swept in and started apologizing, saying she was sorry but they really had to talk, it wouldn't take a minute...but that's as far as she got.

Even as she was explaining, her mind was processing Helen's face and expression. She had been crying. Her eyes were red and there were tissues all over the floor, so she had obviously been here awhile. She must have skipped out early to come here, which explained why Sveta hadn't seen her in Study Hall. But wait, had Helen figured it out? No way, she had been way too careful — and hell, she hadn't even known it herself until just this morning. Sveta walked over and took her hand, squeezing it.

"My God, Helen. What happened?"

Helen gave a little laugh, her expression more happy-sad than distraught, her eyes burning with some hidden passion she couldn't betray. Helen stood up and pulled her close. They embraced, and Helen whispered something in her ear, which sounded like, *Well, I guess I'm all yours now.* What did that mean? As they embraced, Sveta instinctively reached out to support her, since without her crutches there's no way Helen wouldn't —

"Holy shit, your crutches! Helen, where...?"

She was standing straight on both legs, her eyes brimming with tears.

"Sveta, it's gone. Just like that. I woke up this morning...and it was gone. I was too scared to tell you. I made up the Calc test. I've been working towards it all day."

Open-mouthed, Sveta looked down at Helen's bare feet (she had taken off both shoes and socks) and saw two beautiful feet, painted nails and all. She didn't know what to say or think, so she sputtered with a kind of choking laugh, which made Helen laugh even harder.

"I wanted so badly for it to go away. Every night I begged God or whoever was listening to get rid of it. I didn't want anything to take me away from you. And now...well, I don't know what to think. But I'm happy...I *think*!"

"I don't understand, it's gone, like, really gone?" Sveta said, shaking her head. "So you're not...you're not going to be one of them? You can do that?"

"I mean, it's happened before, you hear stories, but I didn't believe them. I guess it helps if you're really in love," she said, looking up at her. "Sorry if that freaks you out, but that's where we are right now. I'm in love with you, and I want you to know that I gave this up, all of it, for you."

Sveta started crying, and she just stood there, pressing her head against Helen's, feeling happier than she knew what to do with. Sveta realized how stupid she had been to come here, to say what she thought was kindness. It would have been kinder to simply tell her the truth: that she was scared. Scared to fall in love, scared that Helen had made a mistake, scared that she would have to watch Helen figure it out in slow motion.

"But what about your parents? They were so happy... what are you going to tell them?" Sveta asked.

"I don't know; I don't care. They'll just have to deal with it. Because honestly, I was only worried about you."

"You really think I give a shit about what your leg looked like? That I liked you for that?"

"No...but when everyone else does, or would, it's hard to make exceptions. I still can't believe you see me, the real me, rather than...someone else."

"I see you...I look at you every day, and never stop looking," Sveta replied, kissing her. "That's why I'm in love with you, too."

"What if that's not enough? I mean, for now it is, but what if you feel differently later on? That's what I'm scared of. I might never grow it back, Sveta. This might be it. And I'm cool with that...I don't want to be that girl anymore. I want you to love me like this."

"Then good, let's both be over it! Whatever happens, we won't regret what we lost. We're just freaks of nature. The losers left behind to love each other."

Helen laughed, and they kissed each other again and again. She could almost believe they would be happy now, even without the future she once planned, that everyone else in the world expected. She nuzzled against Sveta's cheek, kissed her neck, brushing the hair away so she could nibble her ear.

"Oh God! Sveta!" Helen exclaimed, almost leaping back.

"What? What?" Sveta said, catching her. "What's wrong?"

Helen's eyes were large, alive, frightened. Her hand flew to her mouth as she backed away. Sveta began feeling all over her face, trying to wipe away invisible bugs, when a finger grazed her ear. Or what used to be her ear. Its once-smooth surface was now furrowed and sharp. She felt it again and again, hoping it was just some trick of the moment, excitement and fear running rampant.

But no, it was there, and it had changed. She had changed. Part of her was horrified, wanting to rip off the offending ear. Another part was secretly relieved that she could still do it, after all. That she wasn't a lost cause like everyone (well, her mother) feared. Strangely, she had slept soundly for the past few nights without a single nightmare, as if she had finally made peace with her fear. Of course, she didn't want it for herself, her mother, or because of anything Malorie said; she wanted it for Helen, to prove to her that they could still be together. Maybe that's why her father had been able to do it so young, with so much of his life still ahead of him. Because he had a 'Helen' too.

"But I thought...you couldn't," Helen whispered.

"I can't! I mean, I couldn't! I have no idea how this happened. I guess...I don't know, I was scared to lose you, too."

"So you gave me the one thing I can't return," Helen said, with a laugh. "Well, Merry Christmas, Sveta! I got you the same thing."

"Thanks, it's just what I wanted," Sveta said.

She stumbled forward and fell into Helen's embrace, enveloped in tears and silence. Sveta's phone began vibrating again, a stream of texts from her mom, wondering where the hell she was and if she wanted to start walking home from now on? She returned it to her pocket, didn't care whether she walked home or stayed in this room for the rest of the night. She could only stare at Helen and remember that Keats poem about a lover chasing a nymph for all eternity, never catching her, always in the heat of pursuit. That's where she felt she was with Helen right now, and where they always would be; their fingers almost touching, their happiness real, but not of this earth.

"What do we do now?" Helen asked.

"Just hold me," Sveta said, closing her eyes. "Maybe if we stay here long enough, we'll fossilize into a *bas relief* so some modern-day Keats can write a poem about us. You know that poem...*beauty is truth, truth beauty, — that is all ye know on earth, and all ye need to know*."

"You're such a show-off," Helen said, smiling. "Yeah, we read it in AP-English. But I think it's about an urn, and not a bas-whatever."

"Same difference. It's old, it's beautiful, it tells the truth."

"What truth?"

"Like Keats, we're going to live forever. And that's all I need to know."

Joshua Grasso's story "Bas Relief" was originally published in Metaphorosis on Friday, 11 November 2022. See magazine.metaphorosis.com

About the author

Joshua Grasso is a professor of English at a small university in Oklahoma, where he teaches classes in British and World Literature, writing, and comics. He holds a PhD from Miami University where he specialized in 18th c. British Literature. When not teaching or writing, he enjoys hanging out with his two boys (one of whom is college bound!), reading everything he can get his hands on, and hunting for old vinyl and cds of classical music.

@JoshuaGrasso

Any Day Now

K. E. Redmond

She pushed the intercom button and waited, taking in the sprawling brick pile that was the Unadilla Senior Living Community. It could have passed for a grand manor or a country club, but the ramps at the doors were a dead give-away, even if she hadn't seen one or two geriatrics, bundled to the eyes, cruising the grounds with their walkers. She wondered where they were going. There wasn't anything around for miles.

She'd driven out from Boston, taking the Interstate west, then backroads where despite GPS, Unadilla's entrance eluded her. Finally, she found it, nearly hidden in the undergrowth; two stone pillars with a non-descript sign and a chain link fence stretching off through the woods on both sides. The razor wire was unexpected, though, and driving up to the main building she noticed discreet security cameras at intervals. Somehow, she wasn't surprised when hers was the only car in the lot. Walking to the front door, she looked to the north where the sky looked threatening. It still hadn't snowed this winter; it was certainly cold enough. But any day. She hoped it would hold off until she got home. She hated driving in the snow.

The intercom crackled. "May I help you?"

"Yes. I'm here to see Professor Cervine. Professor John Cervine. He's expecting me." The first lie. A small one. His reply to her email requesting an interview had been more of an open ended, 'We'll see'.

"Your name?"

"Kat. Kat Dobrovolsky. But he called me Dobs. I mean, that's how he'll remember me."

"One moment."

Behind the glass-paneled door, a shadow crossed the room.

Kat recalled another time she'd waited to see the Professor, outside another door. It had been the beginning of her sophomore year, outside his department office. Through the frosted sidelight, she had been able to make out two shadows inside. One of them she knew was Trey Tottenger, the only sophomore to ever make the varsity team, he of the blinding smile and chiseled torso, catnip to cheerleaders everywhere. She'd met him once at a freshman mixer. He'd draped an arm around her and told her she had nice eyes. She reasoned, accurately enough, that he was both drunk and competing in the ancient and fraternal sport of bagging the homeliest frosh. She was reluctantly prying him off when he spied a more viable target and staggered away. Anyway, outside the Professor's office, he'd walked by like she didn't exist.

"No exceptions," the woman on the Registrar Desk had told her. "The Professor interviews all students for his Astronomy 101 course. Don't worry," she said with a grimace. "He'll be quick. Good luck."

So she sat, listening to the low murmur of voices inside the office, although the conversation sounded one-sided. Abruptly, the door swung open, and Trey Tottenger stomped out, red to his ears. A voice called after him, "I'd recommend basket weaving. You'd at least graduate with a skill." A pause. "Next!"

Kat sidled in. The only chair was positioned directly across the desk from the Professor. He was older than she'd expected, snow white hair in waves to his shirt collar, the hand that waved her in flecked with liver spots. But his eyes, when he looked up, were blue, bright, oddly intense.

"Major?" he barked as she slid into the chair.

"Uh, English."

"I see." He rapped the desktop with his pencil. "Let me guess. You needed a science credit and decided my course wouldn't be too much of a heavy lift."

She nodded, then quickly shook her head.

"Well, which is it?" he snapped. "Yes or no?"

She felt a hot flush rise. He was trying to fluster her; that pissed her off. "Yes, I need a science credit. But I really want to know more about the universe."

"Is that so you can write odes to the summer's full moon?" He waved his hand languidly. *'Art thou pale for weariness, of climbing heaven and gazing on the earth, wandering companionless, among the stars that have a different birth.'* He snorted. "You're wasting your time. Wordsworth did it better than you could ever hope."

"Shelley." Kat returned his stare with a bland look. "That's Shelley. Not Wordsworth."

The Professor grinned. "Speak truth to power, my dear. I stand corrected. Alright, for entry to my class and all the marbles, tell me what you think is the most significant advance humankind has made in space exploration in the last one-hundred years." He leaned back, closing his eyes, lacing his fingers across his paunch. "I'll warn you," he murmured, "your predecessor in that chair thought it might be warp drive. I hope you can do better."

Kat thought for a moment. "Voyager," she said finally.

He sounded bored. "I imagine you're referring to the television series. Or, lord help me, to that benighted movie with the aliens who couldn't spell? Vegan? Verger?"

"V-ger. No. The Voyager space probes."

He opened his eyes; she thought he almost looked surprised. "Explain."

"Because when we launched the probes we looked outward, not in. We said, hello, is anyone out there? We didn't just look up and wonder. We took the leap. We hoped." She stopped, embarrassed.

The Professor closed his eyes again. "Acceptable. Pick up your books in the bookstore. There will be two papers and a final. Do not be late for class. Next!"

A buzz, a click, and she was back waiting in the cold. The door opened. A muscular man in scrubs and a high fade stood inside the entry, a small bare foyer behind him. She noticed there was no reception desk, no chairs. They really didn't get many visitors. He motioned her in.

"Miss Dobrovolsky? I'm Frank, Professor Cervine's health care aide." He looked her over. "The Professor didn't say anyone was coming today. Is he expecting you?"

She gave him her most engaging smile. "He said come anytime, so here I am. I hope that's okay. It was kind of a long drive."

"Oh? Where are you coming from?"

"Boston. I was back in the area visiting and thought I'd drive over to see my old professor. I was a huge fan. Well, me and about a thousand other students. He's — was — just an incredible lecturer. Getting into one of his courses was cutthroat. I did his introductory course, and I was hooked. Not that I went into the sciences. No brain for numbers. But I've always loved astronomy. And he was one of my advisors on my senior thesis. Sorry," she stopped, blushing. "I'm babbling." Lie number two, well-buried. But it had done the trick. Frank's wary look faded to polite boredom.

"That's okay. He's feeling pretty good today, so you're in luck. Follow me, I'll take you to him." They headed down a long brightly lit corridor with tasteful bucolic reproductions on soothing pastel walls. At regular intervals on both sides, they passed numbered doors. At her Nana's facility, all the residents decorated the doors to their rooms. Photos of grandkids. Artwork. Political signs. Holiday wreaths. Not here. One door was like the next. Uniform. Regimented. Frank stopped outside Room A219, his hand on the knob. "What was your thesis on, if you don't mind me asking?"

"Uhm. Cultural acceptance and acclimation to scientific progression through mass media saturation. Yeah, it's a mouthful. I was an English major."

"The elevator version?"

"Basically, figuring out how often people need to read or hear about some scientific breakthrough before they actually believe it."

"And did you? Figure it out?"

"Not really. People are hard. They believe stupid things all the time for their own reasons. And once they do, it's hard to shift them."

"Everyone thinks they've got the inside track, huh?"

"That's right."

He didn't move to open the door. "So, you're a journalist?"

Her smile tightened. "Not quite. Science writer, slash editor. I translate what the science guys write into something actual people can understand. Those who can't do, write, I guess."

"Working on anything now?"

There was no point trying to get by him, she had to play. Lie number three coming up.

"A children's book. Introduction to the giants of astronomy. You know, Newton, Copernicus, Galileo."

"Professor Cervine?"

She shook her head. "He's big, but not quite in their league. I was hoping to run the list by him though, see if I missed anyone. And catch up on how he's doing, of course." Lie number four.

He took the hint. "Right. He tires easily, so I'll ask you to keep your visit short." He opened the door and stuck his head in. "Professor? Your guest is here. I'll be down the hall if you need me." He stood aside to let her in. She could feel Frank's eyes on her back for a long moment. Then, quietly, the door closed behind her.

The room was like any university professor's office: crammed bookcases, drifts of paper, professional journals stacked in corners, and a desk barely visible beneath the detritus. All typical, apart from the hospital bed near the window. Its occupant turned his head on the pillow to regard her, his eyes overlarge in a skull pared down to a few strands of white hair and skin thin as tissue paper, sallow, and wrinkled.

"Professor Cervine? Remember me? Kathy Dobrovolsky."

He raised a bony hand from the crisp white sheets, immediately dropped it, as though the effort was exhausting.

"Well, come in. Don't stand there gawking. Find your seat. I can't stand late arrivals. Disrupts my chain of thought. Disrupts the class. Hurry up." The tone was testy, but the voice was nearly as she remembered, giving the lie to the frail form.

She scurried over to the chair beside the bed, throwing her coat across the back, and sat down, setting her handbag at her feet. He stared hard at her. She stared back.

"Do I know you?"

"Yes, Professor. We spoke. Well, we texted. I was one of your students at university. You knew me as Kathy Dobs. Well, that's what you called me. I've come to say hello."

"Have you?" He looked away. She followed his gaze. Outside the windows, an aide pushed a wheelchair containing an elderly man bent nearly double in the seat. "I don't do outings, if that's what you had in mind."

"We don't need to, if you don't want. I brought you the last print copy of the British Astrophysics Journal. I thought you'd like it."

He turned back, looking peeved. "The last?"

She shrugged apologetically. "They're going online. Save the trees."

He made a noise between a snarl and a sneeze. "Continuous publication since the 1800s and now it's some mishmash on a computer screen. What depths will we plumb next? Lego models of the universe? Well? Give it to me."

She handed it over. "I was in Oxford looking at Sir Isaac Newton's papers. I was writing a piece for a magazine there. The editor said he knew you. I think he was one of your graduate students."

Frankly, she'd been surprised by the assignment. Out of the blue, the magazine had reached out to her, all expenses paid to the U.K., top dollar for an article any hack could have written. Who did that?

The Professor flipped open to the table of contents, running a finger down the titles. "I can't be expected to remember the names of all my students. And Newton was at Cambridge. Wrong place entirely."

"Yes, I know. But the Bodleian had a recent acquisition from a private library. An amateur astronomer. Contemporary of Newton's."

"May is still banging on about cosmic dust, I see," he grumbled, flicking the journal page with a finger that looked too fragile to take that kind of abuse. "I told him to move on, but he never listens. It's dirt! Get over it. What were you saying about Newton?"

"One of his contemporaries. It turns out, they exchanged several letters. That's what I was looking at in the Bodleian."

He flung the journal down on the bed and fixed her with a glare perfected during eons of oral exams and faculty meetings.

"In my experience, correspondence between such intellectually mismatched individuals as Sir Isaac Newton and some dilettante in knee pants is useful only as mulch. I see you hesitate. Let me guess, this unknown pen pal told our boy Newton he'd transmuted lead into gold."

She smiled. "There was some of that."

"Why am I not surprised."

"Not all of it. One of Newton's letters was interesting."

"Was it? You sound pleased with yourself." He scowled at her. "Don't be coy. It's boring."

"Newton wrote to this friend about an astronomical observation he'd made. He described it as, 'A most wonderous sight. Three nights standing.' Based on his notes, he was describing something near or possibly from the star Elnath, in the Taurus Constellation."

"I hadn't realized our English department was churning out qualified astronomers these days. Elnath? That's 100 light years away."

"131. He reported it in 1700."

"I know when Sir Isaac lived," he retorted. "I'm not senile. Yet." His fingers beat a tattoo on the sheet. "And so?"

"So?" she repeated blankly.

He clicked his tongue against his front teeth impatiently. "Does this particle, this mere mote of information carry some earth-shaking import? Elnath, as far as I am aware, would not be described as a wonderous sight. Giant star. Blue-white in color. Nothing to write home about, so to speak."

"True, but it made me curious. What did he see exactly? Who else saw it?" This part always excited her. She couldn't help it. "So, I started digging. Did you know that one hundred years before Newton, Copernicus studied the occultation of Aldebaran? Also, in the Taurus Constellation."

"Oooooh, I'm getting goose bumps. Two astronomers studied stars in the same constellation. Rewrite the textbooks!" He rolled his eyes.

She fished in her handbag, pulled out her phone, holding the screen up for him to see. "I found a note he made, marginalia, about the star Alcyone. He wrote, and I quote, *'Trinitas in tenebris. Mirabilis.'* 'Trinity from the darkness. Wonderous.' Trinity. Three. Just like Newton's three nights. And wonderous. Obviously, they saw something similar."

He sighed. "No, obviously you are in thrall to an illusion peculiar to our ignorant times, my dear. That there must be a causal connection between two completely unrelated events."

She ignored him. "I kept digging. I went back in history to observations by Chinese astronomers. Year 1054, the supernova in the Crab Nebula. Incidentally, also in Taurus."

"Let me guess," he sighed. "Three sightings or events or however you're mislabeling them."

She ignored that too. "I couldn't believe it. Three unique observations that can be traced back to some part of the Taurus Constellation. Professor," she leaned in, lowering her voice. "I think there's a pattern. I think this is contact."

He snorted. "Contact? I presume you mean some alien intelligence signaling to us from across the universe. Based on what? Three random observations? Do you have any concept of the distances you're describing? How vast? No. You were probably watching cat videos on your little phone when I covered that topic in class. I'll put it in terms you might understand. One light year is 5.88 trillion miles. Rounding up so even you may comprehend, six trillion is 6 with 12 zeros behind it. Alcyone is 370 light years away, the Crab Nebula is, let me see," he paused, but only for a second, "6,523 light years away. Multiply either number by a 6 with all those little zeroes and you'll realize you're talking complete nonsense."

She edged her chair closer to the bed. "But Professor, I've found others."

"Paleolithic cave drawings?" he scoffed. "Some daubing of stars on rocks."

"What about the WOW signal? August 15, 1977. A signal was detected by Ohio State University's Big Ear radio telescope for 72 seconds. It came from the Sagittarius constellation."

"Discredited. Never detected again. Or do you imagine your aliens are playing some intergalactic game of ring the doorbell and run away? Besides, you're mixing your constellations. Or are you simply throwing anything into the pot to prove your point?"

She sat back, silent.

"Have I stymied you?" he sneered. "Good. Next time, get your facts straight before you bother me with nonsense." He shifted in bed, closing his eyes. "I think I've had enough entertainment for today. Go away."

"Humor me. One more."

He opened his eyes to object but saw the mulish look on her face. "In 1945," she began, "a graduate student at our old university — who will remain nameless — observed a signal originating from Alpha Tauri, 65 light years away."

"Odd, I've never seen anything published. That would have been quite the coup," he said.

"It was rumored the War Department suppressed his paper in the interests of national security. They probably thought they had enough problems with a world war here on earth without worrying about extraterrestrials."

"You're citing rumors now! The true hallmark of a failed argument," he said. The contempt in his voice stung her.

"He was — is — a dedicated and brilliant astronomer. He believed in rigorous scientific observation."

"Sounds like a swot. Did your Bodleian friends tell you what a swot is?" he asked sweetly.

She leaned in, lowering her voice. "Also, he was a little anal about keeping stuff. I know, because I helped him pack it up. Books, notes, drafts. He squirreled everything away. In time, I imagine, he completely forgot he'd kept a draft. It happens. A lifetime of stuff piles up, retirement rolls around. Who wants to go through all that paper? Just box it up and shove it into the archives. Forget it. Practical obscurity."

The door opened. Frank stuck his head in. "You ready, Professor?"

Cervine who had been lying in bed, immobile, nearly levitated. "Get out! I'll tell you when I'm ready. Get! Out!"

Frank's head disappeared; Kathy sat back.

"Oh, don't look so worried," the Professor growled. "I haven't thrown you out. Yet." But the outburst seemed to have drained him. He lay back against his pillows, his breathing labored. He took a deep breath.

"This feels like explaining fission to a sleep-deprived toddler, but let me try," he said. "In terms of the Earth's development, all 4.5 billion years of it, our pathetic human civilization is but a blip. Less than the last half-second on the timeline. For an exceedingly small portion of that time, barely 60 years, we have actively looked for others of our kind, although I am at a loss to understand why. We don't get along with the neighbors we have. Regardless, we've listened for signs of intelligent life in the universe. And do you know what we've heard?"

"But..."

He held up a hand, forestalling her. "Nothing. We've heard nothing. Of course, techno transmissions may be exceedingly rare. Maybe none have crossed our path in the last 60 years. Maybe they only transmit to our part of the universe every 100 years or so." He chuckled. "The other equally valid possibility is there are no transmissions to receive."

"Carl Sagan said..." Kathy interrupted.

He groaned. "Dear Carl. Let me guess: 'The universe is a pretty big place. If it's just us, seems like an awful waste of space.' Spare me."

"We're finding earth-like planets every day. Based on dozens of factors, one researcher estimated an intelligent civilization would be at most 17,000 light years away. And that was in a peer-reviewed publication," she added quickly.

"Pie-eyed optimists. And how do you suggest we talk with them? We have no technology that can transmit to those distances. And what would be the point? Our message, optimally sent at the speed of light, reaches them;

they send one back. Do you really believe there will be anyone here to receive it? As a species, we'll be lucky to survive into the next century."

"But that's my point, Professor. They're not sending a message. They're coming here. Look at it: Crab Nebula, 6,523 light years away; Alcyone, 370 light years; Elnath, 131; Alpha Tauri, 65 light years. Every time, they're getting closer."

"Please listen to the voice of reason. I'm sure I covered this in one of my lectures, it was certainly an exam question. The Space Shuttle travels five miles a second. At that speed, optimistically, how long would it take a person — or an E.T., if you insist — to travel one light year?"

"37,200 years," she replied. "I got it right on the exam."

"I'm sure you did. And yet, you believe these intergalactic interlopers, these E.T.s, are traveling hundreds of light years within the span of our own written history. It is not possible. Do the math. It should be well within even your limited capabilities."

"But suppose they can travel faster than light?"

"Impossible!"

"They said men flying and the Higgs boson particle were impossible, too. How else would you explain the signals? They're leap-frogging across the universe."

"I've always envied the latitude writers have to wax poetic when they fail to understand basic science," he murmured. "I sincerely hope you're not thinking of writing about this wild theory of yours. You'll be finished, professionally. Unless you enjoy being lumped in with the crazies and conspiracy nuts."

He waggled a hand in the direction of the carafe on his nightstand. She jumped up to pour him a glass of water, waiting while he took a sip. As he handed the glass back, he held her gaze.

"Do you remember what I wrote on your thesis?" he asked. She looked blank for a moment, then her eyes widened. "I see you do. You always were a bright one. My final affirmation of all your hard work. Do not disappoint me now." He slid down in bed. "Trying to reason with you has been exhausting. Thank you for coming. Leave."

Frank was waiting for her in the hallway. "Good visit?"

She nodded. "So-so. I think I upset him."

"Believe it or not, he was in a good mood today. Get everything you need?"

"What?" She wished Frank would shut up so she could think. Her thesis, where had she packed it?

"Did you talk to him about the book?" He stopped beside the front entrance, watching her. "You said you needed to talk to him about your children's book."

"Oh. No. We got off on a tangent. That's okay."

"Yeah? Say, about your thesis. You said the Professor was one of your advisors. I'll bet he had some good comments. He always has a lot to say."

"You know him," she replied, going over in her head the boxes she'd stored in the attic at her parent's house. There wasn't much room in a studio apartment. The thesis had to be in there somewhere.

"So, like what?" He was waiting, all friendly curiosity. But his persistence made her wary.

"I'm not sure," she said slowly. "Something about science needing more scribes." Lie number five. She was getting good at this.

"That's harsh." He opened the door. "Have a safe trip back. Looks like the snow's holding off. But any day now, it's going to get here."

She nodded. It wasn't until she was back on the Interstate that she thought about Frank's questions. How had he known the Professor had asked about her thesis? She checked the rear-view mirror and sped up.

In his bed, the Professor waited. He could practically predict the next move. So when the phone on his bedside table rang, he let it ring itself out. In the quiet, he felt the sweet pull of sleep. The phone rang again, jarring him awake. This time he picked up.

"I'm sleeping," he snapped, then listened in silence. "No, I don't see any need for concern. A tissue of conjecture and twaddle. Yes, I told her that," he replied. "I have no idea if she'll listen to her favorite professor, as you so unctuously phrase it. I can tell you she's bluffing about my papers. I went through them all myself. As I'm sure you did." He listened again with a bored look. "Your threats are wasted on me. You harbor the mistaken belief I care what you do to me now. And tell that useless blob you call my aide not to disturb me." He hung up. The phone remained resolutely mute. Still, for a long time he kept watch on the driveway, alert for comings and goings. After a while, darkness obscured the distant tree line, then gathered itself up to fill the room. The stars appeared. Tomorrow maybe there'd be snow, but tonight the sky was clear and cold.

He looked up at the twinkling lights, seeking out the constellation Taurus, the bull. Catalogued by Ptolemy in the second century, known since the Bronze Age. In the Northern Hemisphere, the constellation passes through the sky from November to March but is most visible in January. That was a lift from one of his lectures. What had she called it? Leap frogging. Inelegant, but accurate. He preferred a skipping stone. The Crab Nebula, Alcyone, Elnath, Alpha Tauri. Closer and closer. And the last one, from his red dwarf, 8.72 light years away, the signal he'd detected when he'd nearly given up hope, just before his abrupt and unwilling retirement. In terms of the universe, 8.72 light years was practically next door. He hadn't bothered trying to publish this time. He was too old and tired to fight them now, but he wasn't going to let the knowledge die with him. When she'd asked him to be her senior thesis advisor, he'd agreed, already plotting. If the universe teaches you one thing, it is the long view. Signing off on her thesis, he'd written the signal coordinates for the red dwarf as though they were random scribbles. His way of telling her, when she finally put it all together, that she was right.

He'd counted on them discounting her. Wrong major. Wrong sex. Why did they always underestimate women? But she was bright, and she'd always been stubborn. He'd known she'd figure it out eventually. With his help, of course. All the breadcrumbs he'd strewn in her path. The draft of his so-long ago graduate paper, his notes on the red dwarf, left where she had to find them, packing up his office. The magazine assignment he'd finagled for her. Little nudges. Trusting to her curiosity to piece it all together. And with the internet, social media, she had resources he'd never dreamed of. This time they'd have trouble stuffing that genie back in the bottle. Let them try. Speak truth to power, indeed.

He recited it over and over like a mantra. Crab, Alcyone, Elnath, Alpha Tauri, 6,523, 370, 131, 65, 8.72 light years away. Getting closer. He almost wished he'd be around for it. In the dark, he chuckled. They'd run in circles screaming. He could just hear them. The stock market would have a seizure, if it didn't crash. The arrival of extraterrestrials would certainly take the shine off capitalism. Not to mention organized religion. Where do little green men fit in God's great plan? Do they get their own image of the Deity, their own Savior? Their own heaven? It would almost be worth it to hear how they worked aliens into Creation. Countdown: 6,523, 370, 131, 65, 8.72.

He smiled slyly at Taurus. "Any day now. Any day."

K.E. Redmond's story "Any Day Now" was originally published in Metaphorosis on Friday, 6 October 2023. See magazine.metaphorosis.com

About the author

K.E. Redmond writes about the extraordinary possibilities of our everyday world, that interstice shared by mystery and hard science.

Shortcut to Happily Ever After

Ben Wan

Dedicated to Dr. Larry Yip

"Wanna grab coffee sometime?" Daniel Woo looked across at the cute cashier with the big glasses for her reaction. Her name tag read 'STEPH'. As he watched her surprised expression form into a smile, he logged her name into his memory.

"You're awfully forward, aren't you?"

Daniel smiled back. "I just don't like wasting time."

Steph laughed. "Alright. Phone?" Daniel handed it over to her as she typed in her number. "When's your day off?" he asked.

"Tuesday."

"How 'bout next Tuesday then? Five o'clock? The place next door?"

Steph laughed. "*Wow*. You really don't waste time."

You have no idea, he thought, as he took his phone back, said good-bye, and walked out. To Steph, Daniel must have seemed incredibly confident. But had she met him months ago, she would've met a completely different man. A timid man. Because back then, he hadn't had *the watch*.

Outside, he unrolled his sleeve to reach it; his key to finding love, his shortcut to 'happily ever after', conveniently wrapped around his wrist.

He made it a habit now, when asking someone on a date, to set up a specific time and place. The women usually thought he just liked to plan. But really, it was so he'd know where to tell the watch to go. *Next Tuesday. 5PM. Place next door.* He finished with the settings, took a breath, and pushed in the dials on the watch.

In an instant, he was standing on the same street, but the cars and pedestrians had all changed around him. He still hadn't gotten used to jumping between the present and the future. It felt like skipping from chapter to chapter on a Blu-ray disc. Except he was actually *in* the movie.

He peeked into the window of the coffee shop. Sure enough, his future self and Steph were inside. *So she shows up to the first date*, he thought. *But how* well *does it go?*

He programmed the watch again and jumped forward an hour later, where he saw the two of them outside the shop. Together, they were laughing. He overheard himself set up the next date at a restaurant next week.

Daniel knew exactly where it was. He took a long walk over to it a few blocks away and programmed the watch again. This time, he watched himself and Steph walk out, nervous laughter from both of them. As they stopped by the street, there was a pause. He had to cringe just watching the awkwardness, along with the fact that for some reason, neither of them seemed to be as happy as on the previous date.

He hid, hearing his nervous future self ask, "So, uh, want a ride back?"

There was a pause and Steph awkwardly said, "Listen, Daniel...you seem like a great guy..."

He didn't need to hear more. He had heard it all before.

'We just don't seem like a fit.'

'I'm just not feeling the chemistry.'

'Maybe we could be friends.'

He watched his future self's expression change to disappointment. It was that same expression that made Daniel feel relieved. So it wouldn't work out. *No need to go on this date, then. Saved myself from getting my hopes up.*

His other self, after a minute, regained his composure and told her, "I understand. It was, uh, it was fun." As Steph walked off to her own Uber, Daniel turned away from his future disappointment and set the watch back to the present day.

Now, he was outside of the shop again, looking back through the window at Steph, who had just given out her number to him. A Steph who had no idea what he had just seen.

A few hours later, Steph got a sincere phone call from Daniel.

"I know this is gonna sound really weird," he said, "But I'm gonna have to cancel next Tuesday. It's not you, it's just...I realized I'm just not in a place to date right now."

"Oh," said Steph, who was more surprised by the sudden news than hurt. "Uhh, no problem. Thanks for not wasting time. Again."

"Of course."

"See you around the shop?"

"Sure," said Daniel. After hanging up, he sighed in relief. He always felt bad about doing this, but in the end, he knew he was dodging a bullet. Just like he had done with the others.

Steph was the third woman he had canceled on before even the first date. There were no hard feelings, especially given that none of these women had a chance to develop any attachment to him. It wasn't selfish either. He had spared all of *them* the same hurt too. The hurt he saw from simply looking into their futures. No more failed relationships. No more heartbreak. He would keep peeking into the future until he *knew* for certain that he had found a relationship that would last.

He set the phone down on his dining table. Only to jump.

There, standing in his living room, was a tall woman with a ponytail. She wore a long black coat of a snakeskin leather material. And she was pointing something that looked an awful lot like a gun at him.

"What have you been doing with that watch?!"

"What?!" Daniel put his hands up. *Oh fuck*, he thought.

He looked at the gun. It didn't look anything like the firearms he was familiar with. And then he saw it on her wrist...the same 'watch' he wore. Just in a different color.

He had wondered about the origin of the 'watch' when he found it. Now it was catching up to him.

The owner of the 'watch' was here. And she wasn't happy.

He stammered. "Okay, okay, I can explain..."

Six Months Ago...

The night Chloe left him wasn't the worst part. Sure, Daniel cried after it was all over. But it was just a couple hours until the mercy of sleep took him. Asleep, he could forget what happened. Asleep, he and Chloe would still be together...

No, the worst part of the breakup was the day after.

Because now he had an entire day to remember that she had walked out on him. He'd wake up and look across at her empty spot in bed, knowing he would never see her face there again. He had spent their entire relationship in this one bedroom apartment, yet now it felt even smaller.

It seemed like this was always something that happened to him. Ever since he was a child, he had wanted to live out the stories he grew up with, where the hero would always find love. Yet whenever he found someone special and got attached, she'd inevitably leave him. Chloe was just the latest in a series. Once again, he was left with unfulfilled dreams and fantasies. Trips they would never travel together. Movies he would never get to watch with her. Gifts he would never to give to her. The worst, of course, was the feeling of being chronically unwanted, that all he would find was rejection, heartbreak, and loneliness. And yet, there was always a part of him that hoped that he'd find someone who'd help him prove that wrong. Someone who would prove that he *was* wanted and could be loved.

Chloe had felt like that 'someone' at first, but something had been holding her back. She had admitted several times that she had trouble getting close to the guys she dated. He had hoped, or rather expected, that as he continued to show he cared, she'd see that he was different, and gradually be as intimate and vulnerable with him as he was with her.

Instead, all he did was drive her away. Maybe she was afraid he'd hurt her the same way that the other guys did. Yet the more he tried to forgive her, the more resentment he felt towards her for punishing him for the sins of her exes. *She could at least have punished me for my own sins,* he thought. *That at least would have been fair.*

The pain carried over from one day to the next.

He started burying himself at work in the morgue to distract himself. Suicides, unfortunately, spiked during the holidays. There was a common depression, triggered by a yearning to be with others and a realization, for many, that the yearning could never be fulfilled.

He looked around at the dead around him. He knew he should feel grateful to be the only one in the room breathing. But instead, he felt like he could relate to them, at least on the inside. Cold. Numb. Nothing left to care about.

1:30 came around. Daniel had heated up his lunch, a can of clam chowder that he usually packed because it was easy to microwave in the kitchen.

He took it back to his office, only for his boss to barge in.

"The cops have been asking about this John Doe for way too long. I need you to perform the autopsy *asap.*"

The John Doe was a man in his forties. Nothing unusual about his appearance. But there was an ID card that was unrecognizable from any state's driver's license, giving the name John Tempest.

To everyone, it seemed fake. The police were at a loss. The fingerprints matched no database. Neither did his DNA. Nor, strangely enough, did his teeth match any dental records.

The man was a complete ghost.

Daniel performed the autopsy, as requested. It seemed that the cause of death was a heart attack. No murder or suicide. Just his heart giving out. (In a way, he could relate.)

It was about halfway through the autopsy that he remembered the clam chowder sitting back at his office. Probably cold and likely spoiled by now.

He went back to his desk and tossed out his lunch. The *thud* as the bowl hit the bottom of the trash can felt satisfying, but it wasn't enough to quell the anger he felt.

Now he'd have to wait until dinner to eat. Which pissed him off further. Work was supposed to be his distraction. But now it had become such a distraction that he was skipping lunch. And skipping lunch would just remind him of Chloe and how she always packed lunch for him...and well, work wasn't such a distraction anymore now, was it?

Towards the end of his shift, he looked through the belongings that were found on 'John Tempest'. Perhaps he could help the police find a clue to the man's identity.

Among the belongings was a watch. It didn't match any brand that Daniel had been familiar with. Instead of a single dial to adjust the time and the date, there were multiple ones. There even seemed to be ones to adjust the month and the year, which made it even more unusual.

Daniel played with one of the dials absentmindedly. *It seems like a good watch,* he thought as he turned the hand back a few hours.

Lost in thought, he snapped the dial back in. That was when he felt *the jump*.

He was still in his office. But his surroundings felt... different.

Because the clam chowder was now back to sitting on his desk. Still warm, steam rising from it.

That was strange, he thought. How could that be back there? He hadn't had it out since lunch time, which was...

He looked at the dead man's watch. Sure enough, it had been set to lunch hour. *1:30PM.*

There was no way. Or was there?

His mind must be playing tricks on him. And yet, here was the soup, as it would have sat. But if he had really gone back, where was his past self? He snuck out into the hallway, towards the lab, took a peek in the window...

And *there he was.* Performing the autopsy on the dead body, forgetting all about his lunch back in the office.

He had traveled in time.

Which likely then explained John Tempest. Tempest. As in *Tempus*. As in *time*.

The man was a time traveler. A *dead* time traveler. He wouldn't have any record. Was he from the past? The future? A different world entirely?

Daniel didn't know. All he wanted to learn about now was the watch.

He turned the dial and adjusted it a few hours further back. Then a few hours forward. Each time, he kept adjusting, spying on his past self in the lab or office, and testing the watch further. *Shit, what time was it when I first started jumping around?* he wondered. He needed to go back to his present time. His *real* time. He remembered it being towards the end of his shift and estimated that it must have been around 5:30. He set the watch and jumped once again, finding himself back in his office at the end of the day. The clam chowder was gone and John Tempest's belongings were all on his desk. He had returned to the present. Daniel wasn't sure whether to sigh in relief or cheer in excitement. It *worked*.

What now? Anyone he reported this to would think he was crazy, until he demonstrated it. But then they'd surely take it away. Examine its functions. Use it for their own purposes. No, he had a unique opportunity here.

John Tempest, whoever he was, seemed to have used this watch for time travel. So far, Daniel could only move through time in the same spot. Which probably meant that if he wanted to go back in time to watch the Beatles debut on the Ed Sullivan Show, he'd have to physically *go* to the Ed Sullivan Theater in New York in the present before setting anything.

Tempest had wound up in this timeline where he died. He certainly wasn't using it anymore. So if Daniel took the watch...who would miss it?

Plus, who would even find out? The police might have a record of the watch's existence, but with other cases preoccupying them, they probably wouldn't notice if he kept it to himself. And considering that Tempest probably wasn't even from this time period, the police would never find any leads about him.

It was settled, then. He was going to keep it. But what would he do with it? It didn't take him long to think about it. He knew deep down what he wanted...

He was going to use it to find the love of his life.

At first, he was tempted to go back and undo the breakup with Chloe. But what exactly would he undo? Would he even be able to convince her to stay with him? If he couldn't, he'd just be opening up an old wound. He wanted to make himself feel *better*, not worse.

No, he'd only use the watch to take peeks into the future and come back, rather than change his past. And this time, the watch could help him know that he was moving on with the *right* person, rather than wasting any more time with the *wrong* person.

So Daniel started putting himself out there.

First, he met Ann at a party through his co-worker Simon. "You're not seeing anyone. She's not seeing anyone. I'll set you guys up," he told Daniel.

"Why don't you go for her?"

"Already tried," said Simon. "But she goes for nice guys."

Daniel shook his head. That was a backhanded compliment if he knew it. But he was intrigued.

Simon gestured him over. "Hey, Ann. Meet my buddy, Daniel."

Daniel looked over at a cute girl in a leather jacket. Okay, he wasn't hating this experience so far.

"Hey Daniel," said Ann.

"Alright, you two talk. I'm out."

Daniel watched Simon go. Ann said, "Well that wasn't an awkward introduction at all."

"Not at all," he agreed. "So how do you know Simon? Other than him trying to hit on you?"

She laughed. "Is that what he said he did?"

"Clearly he wasn't that successful."

"I'm friends with his roommate. We met that way, unfortunately."

Daniel nodded. He could tell that she was wondering what his connection was. "Well, I work with Simon," he said.

"With the dead people."

"Yep, with the dead people. Which kinda sucks, actually. Because I thought that meant I wouldn't have to deal with anyone annoying. But then I met him."

She laughed. Once they hit it off about classic literature, she gave him her number and he decided to take the watch for a spin.

The planning was simple. He'd make it a habit of scheduling each new date at the end of the previous one. As an observer, he'd bounce around and spy on how the date went. Then, he'd overhear his future self set up the next time and know exactly where and when to pop up.

After calling Ann to schedule a meeting at a local bookstore, he used the watch to jump to the first date. Then the second. The third. Then months of dating until the night he asked her to be his girlfriend.

Daniel had been tempted to stop peeking then, already satisfied with the future. But he didn't just want another relationship. He wanted *the* relationship. The last relationship he'd ever be in. He wanted to know the *whole* future. So he watched Cliff Notes of an entire relationship unfold. Their first time meeting the parents. Their first fight.

And then, after a year of dating, the breakup. Another girl out of the blue who would leave and break his heart.

And once again, he'd find himself alone in a one bedroom apartment that was starting to feel even smaller.

He wound the watch back to the day after the party when they first met. Then he called Ann, telling her that he'd have to cancel their date at the bookstore and that he just wasn't really in a good place to see anyone. Maybe he'd just see her at another of his friend's parties again and save her from Simon trying to shoot his shot a second time. She found his honesty refreshing and genuinely wished him luck.

There was a wave of relief in what he had done, not to mention pride. He hadn't wasted Ann's time and she hadn't wasted his. They could move on to the right people without baggage. He felt ready to use the watch again on the next girl he met.

That was Kristine.

They had matched online. Daniel wasn't really a fan of online dating and trying to make conversations on the apps.

But, as a change, Kristine had started the conversation first.

She seemed like the opposite of Ann. For one thing, she wasn't a book nerd at all. For another, she was less sarcastic and more direct in her interest. The day after they started talking, she was already messaging him, 'Hey, handsome', and before he could float the idea by her first, she was the one proposing, 'Wanna get drinks this week?'

Still, Daniel wanted to see what would happen. So once again he used the watch to skip forward.

A couple of dates in, he saw that he'd invited her to his place. They both seemed to like cooking and he had wanted to show off his pasta maker. Though for some reason, it wasn't in its usual place and he'd had to buy a new one. That was odd. He could have sworn that he always kept it in the same spot in the same cabinet.

He knew this relationship would last longer than the previous one once he saw that, two years in, he and Kristine were still together.

Then eventually, engaged.

But he just kept pushing and jumping forward. Would she marry him? He had to *know*. Even when the wedding was already planned, a date set, invites sent out...he felt that he needed the confirmation. He needed to see himself married before he'd go on that date.

So it was discouraging, but not at all surprising that, when he jumped forward, he saw Kristine call off the engagement.

He overheard himself from the other room, asking, "What did I do?"

Kristine replied, "I just feel like...you don't put in any effort with me anymore."

At that point, Daniel stopped listening. He couldn't stand the sound of his own future voice breaking and crying. And he couldn't stand to keep watching Kristine break his heart even further.

If he was feeling that from just witnessing everything, he could only imagine what it'd be like to *live* it. And it made him even more grateful. This watch from John Tempest was a gift that spared him from pain.

He didn't even want to hear the rest of the argument or wait until Kristine had left. He knew her well enough, at least from observing their relationship, that she wouldn't change her mind.

And he'd be alone, once again, in a studio apartment that was still feeling smaller.

Better to just go back in time and end it. He reset the watch so the sound of his crying in the background would stop.

A month later, he went into the shop and met Steph.

The Present

Daniel finished his story. The woman with the gun had settled in at his dining table, drinking coffee that he had brewed for her. She had put the weapon down too, though the barrel was still pointed in his general direction.

She sipped the coffee in silence, thinking over Daniel's story. He cleared his throat.

"So...you must have known John Tempest, then. Miss...?"

She set down the cup, staring down at it and seeming to ignore him until she finally answered.

"Call me the Overseer."

"Overseer...so what, is that a title or something? For, like, time travelers?"

"Something like that. We're the ones assigned to stop the time ripples."

"Time ripples?"

Then, as if on cue, the coffee cup disappeared from the table.

It wasn't a magic trick. But it felt like one. Almost as if something had just *edited* a jump cut from a movie into reality. Even stranger, the Overseer had looked satisfied, almost having expected it to happen.

Daniel sat up, alarmed. "What...What just happened? What the hell is this?"

"Like I said. Time ripple." She stood up. "Mr. Woo, I tracked you down because your apartment appears to be the center of a set of time ripples."

"What are those? Some kind of butterfly effect?"

"In a way. When time gets undone, your environment changes around you. Usually, you don't even notice the changes. They usually start with your living arrangements..."

Daniel thought it through. He'd been living in a studio apartment for the last six years...but had it always been a studio?

Hadn't he been in a *one bedroom* apartment at some point? Or had he just dreamed or imagined that? No, that couldn't be right. Was she causing him to remember new things or was she causing him to *think* he was remembering new things?

She continued. "Then, certain things go missing. It's probably happened to you before. You can't find something. You don't know where you put it. And if it's not where you last put it, you chalk it up to a bad memory. But it's not. It's actually the beginning of a time ripple."

Things go missing...like a pasta maker? he thought.

"Because for just a few moments in time, whatever's missing actually *stopped existing.* You get residual memories of something that's no longer there and the mind just rationalizes that it's lost or misplaced. Until you stop remembering that it actually existed at all."

Daniel looked alarmed. The Overseer noticed. "Don't worry. Sometimes, what's lost gets found. Sure, it's not where you remember it. But you're so happy you found it again, you don't really question how it got there. You chalk it up to bad memory or just being forgetful. But you didn't forget. Time just set itself right again. And it took an Overseer to bring it back."

Daniel thought of all the times he had found something that he had once lost and how it never seemed to be in the last place he remembered. Just how common were these time ripples?

"Your...dating adventures are responsible for the time ripples in this sector. To put it mildly, you undid things that shouldn't have been undone. And time is making us all pay the consequences. So here's what we'll do, kid. You're gonna return that to me. That's Overseer property."

She grabbed his wrist, undoing the clasp on the watch without letting him object. "Next, you're gonna fix the mess you created."

"How?"

"All those women you turned down. You have to go back and date them. In *real* time."

Daniel froze. That had to be a joke. "But... But I know the future. That'd just be a waste of time."

"Would it?"

"I spent like two years with one of them! I know how it ends!"

"Do you?"

"Can you stop asking me questions?!"

She shot him a glare. "Something that was supposed to happen never happened. That's the cause of this. To fix it, you have to *make* those events happen. Everyone you were supposed to date. You have to *date* them. That's the only way this works."

Daniel could sense the judgment in her tone. He tried to think of another way to get out of this. "I'd be wasting years of my life!" he argued.

"You'd be saving life as we know it. Sounds dramatic, I know, but I'm not wrong. If we don't stop the ripples, all of us are eventually gonna disappear. Like that coffee cup. Which you're gonna forget, by the way, after we're done with this conversation. So you can either do this and make it right or I have to do something drastic."

"Like what?"

She tapped on her gun. "Like go back to when you got the watch and erase you from this timeline." Daniel blinked, speechless. "Not up for that? Didn't think so," she said.

And with that, the Overseer set the dials on her own watch, then grabbed his hand.

Their surroundings snapped into place in an instant. They were back at his room as it had been months ago. "Here we are," she said.

Daniel looked outside. It had gone from day to night. Two dogs were in the middle of a barking match with each other while their owners were trying to restrain them. "So wait, where am *I*? Like, where's the old me?"

"You've set up a date with Ann and now you've gone forward in time to see if you two have a future. But instead of you coming back to cancel on her, we're just gonna branch off into a new timeline from here. One where you actually date Ann. You know, like a normal person."

The Overseer clicked her watch. The barking outside stopped. Daniel peeked out. The dogs and their owners were completely frozen.

"If it doesn't work with her, then we go onto Kristine. And then Steph. Until you experience everything you were supposed to experience. Text Ann to reconfirm you're still going out. Time will resume and the new timeline will begin."

"But I'm undoing what I actually lived through. Doesn't that create, like, another paradox? If I didn't live through turning down these women, how would I still exist to do this?"

"Doesn't work that way," said the Overseer. "As long as these *new* paradoxes fulfill what was supposed to happen, time will fix itself. You know how a string gets tangled and knotted?"

"Yeah?"

"There's always that grace period where you can still untangle it. Before it gets too much. That's where we're at, kid. Right before the point of no return. The point where we can still untangle the string."

The Overseer took his phone and pulled up Ann's number, then handed it back to him.

"So do it," she said. "Untangle it."

●

Daniel stood by the front door of the bookstore, waiting on his first date, his *real* first date, with Ann. It occurred to him that he might have watched this date before, but it wasn't actually him who had gone through it.

What if he said something stupid and he never got into a relationship with her in the first place? He remembered seeing his heartbroken self back on the couch, feeling the way he had felt after Chloe left. Yes, maybe he'd actually prefer to just screw it all up now. It'd be a quicker way to get to the next person. Finish the mission for the Overseer. Correct his mistake. Get out of this mess.

Then Ann walked in and the plan went out the window.

For Ann, it had just been a few days ago since she met Daniel, but for him, it had been *months*.

He forgot how much he had liked looking in her eyes at the party and the way she had made him feel the first time that he met her.

Their first date, time-wise, lasted about twelve hours.

But neither he nor Ann really felt time go by. She spent the night at his place, which was something he hadn't predicted, since he hadn't stuck around long enough to find out the first time he watched. Other than the embarrassment of not having a clean coffee cup for her in the morning (and feeling like it was weird that he had so few in the first place), it was the perfect first date.

After she left his place, he got to thinking. Yes, he knew the future. Yes, he had seen that in a year from now, it wouldn't work out. But...couldn't he just enjoy being around her for now? Couldn't he just enjoy not being lonely and broken up over Chloe again?

So he kept seeing her. A couple dates in and she was all he could think about. Whenever she texted, he'd always smile and text back as soon as he could. Eventually, she was *constantly* texting him. Maybe she was getting clingy, but since he liked her already, he didn't mind. He *wanted* to text her all day. It was refreshing to not have to fight for someone's attention, the way he always had to with Chloe.

A few months in, he asked her to be his girlfriend. A month after that, they took their first trip together. But as the relationship grew, so did the fear.

Because he knew the future. He knew this relationship was doomed. That she was going to hurt him in the end. He tried to brush it aside and convince himself he was too in love right now to care.

But that love was starting to deteriorate. Whenever they'd argue, even over something small like what type of onions to buy at the grocery store, it was another nail in the coffin. *Is this why she's gonna leave?* he thought.

And yet whenever she said something nice or gave him a surprise gift or comforted him when he had a bad day, he couldn't really believe her either, even though he wanted to. She'd say, "I love you," and he'd wonder, *Do you really? You won't in a couple of months.*

Soon their one-year anniversary was approaching and the anxiety was taking over him. Ann would be leaving any day now. She'd drop him just like Chloe had. He'd go back to crying himself to sleep, waking up next to an empty space in the bed, and sleepwalking from day to day.

He knew what he had to do. And he didn't like it.

When he came over to her place the next night, he told her that it was over. That he felt like he didn't see a future anymore with her. He said it very matter-of-fact. After all, he thought, she was on the same page "You've probably been feeling this too anyway," he said.

But when he looked in her eyes, all he saw was hurt and confusion. She stammered, "No, I...I haven't been feeling that way at all." Daniel stared back with the same confusion. "But I thought...I saw..."

"You saw what, Daniel?"

What could he possibly tell her? That he had time traveled? He'd sound insane. And yet somehow, in knowing how it was going to end, he had acted so differently that he had changed the outcome and the timeline itself. Worse, after all these months of hating Chloe, now he felt like he *was* Chloe. He felt a sense of *loathing* towards himself for putting someone through what he had experienced. Chloe had left him out of fear of getting hurt and ended up hurting him instead. And now he was about to do the same thing to a sweet girl he loved who didn't deserve it.

"Okay, look, I'm sorry, I didn't mean what I said. I've just been confused." He reached out for her hand. He had to fix this.

But she turned away. "You don't know what you want, Daniel. That's the problem."

"No, that's not true."

"It *is* true. You say you want to be with me, but half the time, your mind's somewhere else. Whatever I try, it's not enough. So maybe you're right. Maybe we should just end this."

"I'm sorry, I — I didn't mean for it to be like this."

"Just go." She kept herself turned away and waited. Daniel couldn't think of anything else to do but comply. She hadn't shown much emotion, but when he walked out, he could hear her crying on the other side of the door.

He wasn't anything special. Just part of a vicious cycle. Hearts were broken. Heartbroken people went off to break other hearts. And it would continue over and over and over again. He had to stop it. He gave Ann a couple days of space before calling her.

Except when he called, the voice of an old man picked up on the other end. "Johnson Residence."

No. Daniel immediately hung up. He searched for Ann on social media. All her accounts were gone. He had hoped that she had just blocked him, but why would she have changed her number?

Then he visited her apartment building to check the register. There was a different name in her unit. She couldn't have moved out in just *two days* just because of him. He hoped she did because the alternative was much worse. At work, he approached Simon to see if he was right. "Ann and I broke up."

"Ann?"

"Yeah. You know, my girlfriend. The one you introduced me to at a party..."

"You had a girlfriend?"

Daniel ran off. He needed answers. Sure enough, when he was alone, the Overseer appeared.

"I warned you," she said. "The world's population just dropped by 1 million and nobody noticed except you."

"But how do I still remember?"

"You're a time traveler. Your memories linger longer than others. But you'll still forget eventually. Like that coffee cup."

"What coffee cup?"

"Exactly. Or your pasta maker."

"What pasta — never mind. If I keep going with the plan, do these people come back?"

"It's still possible, but you can't waste any more time. You still have to date the other two women."

"Wait," said Daniel. But the Overseer had already taken his phone. "On to Kristine."

"How? I only met her because I never went out with Ann."

"Not a problem," said the Overseer.

"She might not even exist now!"

But the Overseer went into the dating apps and started randomly swiping on the women. After a few matches, she handed the phone over to him.

"That should do it. Scroll through. One of them's her." She said with confidence.

Daniel looked through his matches. Sure enough, Kristine's profile was in the queue.

"How did you — ?"

"Like I said, your relationships were events that *had* to happen. No matter what, Kristine would still end up matching with you on these apps."

Daniel set the phone down, shaking his head. "I just had a breakup."

"Sorry," said the Overseer. "But you don't have time. None of us do."

So Daniel reluctantly started talking to Kristine. This time, *he* started the conversation. He didn't remember exactly what he had said to her when they first talked, but he had the gist of it. He thought about the future with her he had seen. How they had almost gotten married, if he hadn't screwed it all up.

He remembered the words that she had told him. 'You don't put in any effort with me.' Maybe he would just do the opposite of what he'd seen. Maybe that would give him a different result. Put in effort.

In a way, he'd be making up for what he had just done to Ann.

So this time Daniel was the one to ask Kristine for drinks next week.

Soon enough, they were dating and he had her over for cooking dinner, so he could show off this new pasta maker he had bought, though he had no idea how to use it. (And he couldn't help shake the nagging feeling that he was *supposed* to know how to use it).

Kristine was already different from Ann. For one thing, she wasn't as quick to open up. In fact, for some time, it still felt as if he hardly knew her at all. He knew what she did for a living, of course. Her general interests. How many siblings she had. What she liked in bed.

Maybe he just needed to give it time. So he did everything he could to be a great boyfriend. He went all out on her birthday. Made sure to befriend all her friends. Gave her all his attention when she was with him.

So why was it that every time he did something nice for her, she'd always seem to run away? She'd thank him in the moment, sure, but then, she'd retreat into work and barely talk to him for a week. Naturally, this just made him push harder. He'd text her more to ask how her day went. He'd offer to cook for her more often. *Anything* to avoid being accused of not 'putting in the effort'.

Which was why it shocked him, four months into the relationship, when she said, "I don't think this is working for me."

No. No, this isn't right, he thought. *We aren't even close to the time that we broke up.*

Daniel wondered if maybe he had missed an initial breakup from his travels and the two of them would get together again after this.

But he knew that was just wishful thinking. It was the way she had said, 'I don't think this is working for me'. It was the same tone he had heard when she called off the wedding.

All he could muster in response was one word: "Why?" As in, why was this over, out of nowhere, *again*? Why couldn't he just make something work? Why was nothing he did good enough for her (or for Chloe for that matter)? *Why?*

And Kristine simply responded, "I just feel like you're too...clingy for me."

The first time, he hadn't made enough effort with Kristine. Now he had made *too* much. Maybe Kristine had just never really wanted him. Maybe she was destined to make an excuse to leave.

Maybe it wasn't even Kristine. Maybe it was just his luck in general with love. Maybe he'd always be disappointed and never find the right person.

And the Overseer returned again. This time, Daniel had nothing to share. He simply asked, "Those ripples still happening?" She nodded. Before she could elaborate, Daniel cut her off. He didn't care anymore. "Let's just get this over with."

There was one woman left: Steph.

"Lucky for you, she hasn't been rippled out of existence yet. I checked. You still have a shot at fixing this," said the Overseer. She looked like she was about to leave, but she stopped. Perhaps there was sympathy in her step. "Good luck." And with that, she was gone. It occurred to Daniel that if he pulled this off, he might never see the Overseer again.

With Ann and Kristine, he had tried to go against what he had seen. Now, what would his strategy be?

This time, there'd be no strategy. And maybe that, in itself, was a strategy. Maybe he just needed to act as if he *didn't* know the future. A part of him hoped that meant this would work out. Another part of him told him to stop being an idiot in getting his hopes up.

If the Overseer had been right about these relationships being destined to happen, then Steph would still be working at the shop now.

So he drove over and walked in. Sure enough, there she was at the cash register. He almost didn't recognize her at first without the big glasses. She must've been wearing contacts today. She wore her hair tied back and her outfit was different from what he remembered, but he figured he could have the same conversation. That was going to be the easy part.

As expected, she agreed to get coffee with him. Like before, he asked when she was off work. And like before, he scheduled it for her day off. So he arrived on that Tuesday. 5PM. The coffee shop next to the place that she worked at. And the two of them talked.

They talked for six *hours*, to the point that the place closed before they were done.

Daniel was surprised by Steph at first. It had been maybe even a year at this point since he had *actually* met her for the first time. She seemed *funnier* than he had remembered. Was she actually funnier? Or did he just *get* her humor better? And did he also find her more attractive now than before because of it?

"You know, it seems weird," she said, "But the other day when you came into the shop, I felt like I almost knew you from before."

Daniel laughed. "Really?"

"Yeah, I don't know. You just seemed so...familiar. Or I seemed familiar to you. Like did we go to school together or something?"

"I'm a SoCal boy and you're from the East Coast. I doubt it."

"I know, but still! I don't know, you just seemed like... someone I've already known for awhile. Like, you *knew* I'd say yes to coffee. Like you expected it."

Daniel just shrugged. She wasn't completely wrong. "Well I didn't know for sure. But I figured I didn't have anything to lose."

"See, a lot of people say that. But most of them don't actually act like it," she said, "What's your secret?"

He shrugged. "I'd say, learn not to expect anything."

"That's it? So you just expect to be disappointed and let yourself be surprised."

"No, expecting to be disappointed is different from not expecting anything. Because if you expect to be disappointed, you're still expecting. Which is the problem." Daniel hardly recognized what was coming out of his mouth. It felt like he was making shit up as he went along and it just happened to sound profound.

But Steph smiled and said, "I like that."

Hell, maybe it was *profound, then.* He continued, "I mean, it's basically what they say. Hope for the best, prepare for the worst..."

He'd have to put that mentality to the test soon. Because later that night, Steph agreed to go on a second date.

And in another life, it was the second date that was also their last date.

Daniel had figured that the outcome would be different from before. But whether that would be better or worse, he'd have to see.

He went into the date half excited and half feeling like a prisoner due for execution. About thirty minutes into it, she said. "I have something to confess."

Uh oh, he thought. A part of him wondered if this would be when she'd end it. Which would be really awkward, since the food hadn't even come yet.

What she actually said, however, was very different: "I just got out of a relationship like a month ago."

"Wow," he said. Then without thinking, "Me too."

"Really?! Oh my God, I totally thought I'd scare you off."

Daniel laughed. *On the contrary...*

Questions then swirled in his brain. "So that day I asked you out to coffee...what made you say 'yes' then? I mean you could've just said that you were still recovering from the last relationship. I would've gotten it..."

"Yeah, well, breakups suck. But there's no use punishing the next guy about it, is there?"

Jesus, where were you three relationships ago? Daniel thought as he took a second to collect his response. "No... no, definitely not."

He was starting to feel something for the first time. Was it comfort? No, that wasn't it. Maybe it was *desire,* but not in the sexual sense of desiring her (though he wasn't opposed to that either). It was almost a desire to open up. To share again. To just be vulnerable.

He continued talking, "You know, if I'm being frank, there's a part of me that almost didn't ask you out. Not because of you, I mean, but because I guess I was just getting jaded from the whole experience."

"Yeah, I get you. It's hard not to get hurt doing all this."

Daniel leaned forward with interest. "What helps you just put yourself out there then?"

Steph let out a breath and thought about it. "Knowing it's worse if I don't."

"And you're not afraid of getting hurt again?"

"Oh, all the time," she said, "But if I let that stop me, I'm never gonna find it, am I?"

"I guess you're right."

"How about you? What keeps you going?"

Daniel thought about how he should phrase it. Then said, "Same as you, I guess. Faith."

Steph raised a glass. "To faith, then."

They toasted and kept talking through the rest of their dinner, but Steph's attitude stuck out in his mind. Here he had been, using a stolen time traveler's watch to avoid getting hurt, while Steph had done the complete opposite. No time travel, no peeks or knowledge of how things would turn out. Just complete faith that at some point, someone was going to make all the heartache worth it.

He paid the bill, of course, and as they walked out, Daniel could feel his heart pounding.

Here it is. The moment she turns me down.

He had *really* started to like her already. He hoped things would turn out differently this time, but he felt an odd sense of calmness as he walked next to her.

He had seen this play out from the outside. The hesitation. The potential preamble on how he *seemed* like a great guy *but...*

But nothing. He had been wrong before. Maybe he'd be wrong again. He wouldn't know unless he went for it.

"So...want a ride back?" he asked. The same question he had heard himself ask in the other timeline. He noticed it came out differently from what he remembered. When he had heard himself say it originally, it felt very tentative, as if he weren't really sure if she would say yes. Here, it seemed casual. Indifferent. Almost as if he had asked her to pass the salt.

It wasn't that he needed her to say 'yes' anymore.

It was that he'd be fine if she said 'no'. That no matter what answer she gave him...he'd be okay.

He stopped, waiting for her answer. She smiled.

"A ride? Sure."

Somewhere, in a kitchen across town, a coffee cup and a pasta maker reappeared, as if they had been there all along.

A girl named Ann was back in her apartment, pouring over a book.

And Daniel was walking Steph back to his car for a ride home.

He smiled. For once, he had no idea what was going to happen next.

●

Ben Wan's story "Shortcut to Happily Ever After" was originally published in Metaphorosis on Friday, 7 April 2023. See magazine.metaphorosis.com

About the author

Ben Wan is a cancer survivor who's been making the most out of his second chance at life. Aside from writing, he's a former musician who's performed in Carnegie Hall, a first degree black belt in Kung Fu San Soo, and a coach for Become Sharp in helping introverted clients succeed with dating, confidence, and social skills. He's currently the co-host and "Man Who Knows Too Much About Batman" for the podcast *Superhero Stuff You Should Know*, where his cat Alfie makes cameo appearances.

www.benwanwriter.com, @SuperHousePod

An Aftertaste of Earth

Pauline Yates

The arrival of delegates from the Planetary Migration Program raised false hope in my district. Not only has the maximum age for entry to the off-world colony been lowered, we were given less than a week to prepare a concept to prove worth of passage. But with the demise of earth a certainty, hope is all I have left. This event is my last chance to secure a future for my family.

With my eligibility for potential passage verified, I enter the town hall and find my allocated table. I'm in the last row at the back, too far away to catch a roaming delegate's immediate attention, but at least I'm not near the entrance doors. As the delegates arrive to inspect the concepts on display, Desperates — those who have long lost any sense of community cohesion — accost the delegates with pleas for passage, or try to peddle stolen ideas. Security guards keep the most vocal Desperates in the foyer, but amongst the crowds that clog the aisles — those too old, too stubborn or too scared to leave — I recognise a Desperate seen lurking through our district. I check the name tag that's pinned to my pocket. I'm glad I used two pins. Ideas aren't the only thing Desperates steal.

As I arrange the boxes containing my entry on the table, despair creeps into my thoughts. If I'm unsuccessful today, will I end up behaving like a Desperate in order to keep my family alive? But to what end? Our district is supplemented with food packs but the last delivery never arrived. While evidence of theft points to Desperates, the decreasing amount in my allocated ration points to the limited food left on earth. My own tests reveal the poison in the atmosphere from the earthquake that split the mantle is far worse than reported, but what good is knowledge when there is no hope of survival? Better the people of my district embrace an us-against-them mentality with the Desperates than dwell on a slow death from starvation.

A blue-jacketed delegate enters my aisle. His robust frame is as alien as the planet I'm trying to get to. He stops at a table down two from mine, but when the presenter fumbles the mechanics of his concept, the delegate shakes his head and turns away. As he continues along the aisle, he's followed by the Desperate I'd spotted earlier. The Desperate's cunning expression puts me on edge but with a delegate so close, I've no time for caution. Opening one of the boxes, I lift out a pie and place it on the table, waving my hand over its top to make the aromas swirl through the air. Cinnamon. Ginger. Cloves. Nutmeg. Chemical replicates; fresh spices were lost long ago. The scent catches the delegate's attention. He ignores the next table and strides to mine.

His eyes feast on my offering. "Is that — ?"

"Pumpkin pie." Unlike the previous presenter, I smile.

The delegate raises an eyebrow. "Edible?"

I pick up a knife, slice through the rich custard and pastry, and place a piece of pie on a napkin. "My mother's recipe."

He picks up the pie and nibbles the baked custard, rolling the sweet desert over his tongue. Taking a larger bite, he pauses to contemplate before consuming the whole piece. When he's finished, he pats his lips with the napkin. "That's good pie." He places the napkin on the table. "As good as this is, our colony doesn't have the resources for pie. We need new ideas to help people assimilate to their alien environment."

I nod. "But without giving them the security of familiarity, their yearning for Earth will impede their acceptance of their new planet."

The delegate grimaces. "Variety in food is an unfortunate sacrifice for continuity."

I open the second box, lift out a white bowl filled with a porridge-like substance and place it next to the pie. "The colony's current food source?"

He peers into the bowl. "It's similar in appearance."

"And bland." I hold up a spoon. "Will you taste to confirm that's what this is?"

The delegate hesitates, but plucks the spoon from my fingers, scoops the porridge from the edge of the bowl and tastes it with the tip of his tongue. He nods in agreement.

Reaching into the breast pocket of my jacket, I pull out a glass vial. "I can make you think that staple food tastes like this pumpkin pie."

The delegate looks dubious but he doesn't walk away. Taking back the spoon, I add the clear liquid from the vial to the porridge on the spoon. One drop will suffice. I hand the spoon back to the delegate.

Eating the porridge, his eyes widen. "It tastes like pumpkin pie." He stares at the vial, then at the pie. But then he frowns. "This is not new. Flavours have been trialled." He shakes his head. "I'm sor —"

"It's not a flavour." I raise the vial to hold his interest. "This liquid will make that porridge taste like the food you crave, no matter what you choose."

The delegate eyes me like a Desperate but then nods at the bowl. "If you can turn that into a roast vegetable salad, you'll have my attention."

"I can." Dripping three drops of liquid onto the porridge in the bowl, I stir it through then hand the spoon to the delegate. He picks up the bowl and tastes the new offering. With raised eyebrows, he eats the entire serving of porridge.

When he finishes, his eyes snap to mine. "Explain."

Seeing the Desperate loitering behind him, I lower my voice. "I've developed a chemical that triggers the subliminal thought receptors in your brain to make you think you're eating whatever you desire. The pumpkin pie was an implant test. You chose the salad. You can choose anything."

The delegate's eyes narrow. "Anything?"

"Whatever you desire."

He places his hands behind his back. "Your credentials?"

"I was a research assistant for the Institute of Future Technologies, biochemistry division."

He stares at the vial and then reaches into his breast pocket and pulls out a metal ticket. "The transport leaves at fourteen hundred tomorrow." He swipes the ticket across a band on his wrist and then hands it to me. "Guard this. Only the bearer will be able to board."

I clutch the one ticket. "My family?"

"How many?"

"My wife. My child." My mother has already insisted she'll die an Earthling.

The delegate shakes his head. "Seats are limited."

"I won't leave them behind."

There's a long pause. He rubs his thumb over his lower lip. "The last time I enjoyed vegetables that good was two years ago."

I tuck three tickets next to the vial in my breast pocket. I leave the pie on the table. Hopefully, the aroma will distract the Desperate while I escape.

Pauline Yates's story "An Aftertaste of Earth" was originally published in Metaphorosis on Friday, 25 August 2017. See magazine.metaphorosis.com

About the author

Pauline Yates from Queensland, Australia is the award-winning author of *Memories Don't Lie*, a 2024 BookFest Award 3x first place winner in YA — Science Fiction, Sci-Fi — Action/Adventure, and Sci-fi — Genetic Engineering. She's an Aurealis Awards finalist and a 2x Australasian Shadows Awards shortlist recipient, and her AHWA Robert N Stephenson winning short story, "The Best Medicine" was chosen for translation in the *Mondi Incantati* series produced by Riflessi di Lunare (RiLL), Italy. Her fiction and poetry appear in numerous online publications, magazines, and podcasts and she darkens the pages of many anthologies with her vast collection of micro-fiction. Read more at paulineyates (dotcom)

Copyright

Title information

Ignition!

ISBN: 978-1-64076-292-3 (e-book)
ISBN: 978-1-64076-293-0 (paperback)
ISBN: 978-1-64076-294-7 (hardcover)

Copyright

All stories previously appeared in *Metaphorosis* magazine.

Works of fiction

Publisher

Metaphorosis
a magazine of speculative fiction

Metaphorosis Magazine is an imprint of
Metaphorosis Publishing
Neskowin, OR, USA

www.metaphorosis.com

"Metaphorosis" is a registered trademark.

Discounts available

Substantial discounts are available for educational institutions, including writing workshops. Discounts are also available for quantity purchases. For details, contact Metaphorosis at metaphorosis.com/about

Metaphorosis Publishing

Metaphorosis offers beautifully written science fiction and fantasy. Our imprints include:

Metaphorosis Magazine

Plant Based Press

Verdage

Vestige

Joyful Heave

You can also find us:
@metaphorosis.bsky.social (Bluesky)
@Metaphorosis@writing.exchange (Mastodon)
www.facebook.com/metaphorosis

Help keep Metaphorosis running at
Patreon.com/metaphorosis

See more about some of our books on the following pages.

Metaphorosis Magazine

Metaphorosis
a magazine of speculative fiction

Metaphorosis is an online speculative fiction magazine dedicated to quality writing. We publish an original story every week (2016-2023) or month (2024), along with author bios, interviews, and notes on story origins.

We also publish monthly print and e-book issues, as well as yearly Best of and Complete anthologies.

Come and see us online at magazine.Metaphorosis.com.

The Metaphorosis Library Collection

Plant Based Press

Vegan-friendly science fiction and fantasy, including anthologies of the year's best SFF stories, from 2016-2020.

Chambers of the Heart
speculative stories
by
B. Morris Allen

A heart that's a building, a dog that's a program, a woman sinking irretrievably — stories about love, loss, and movement.

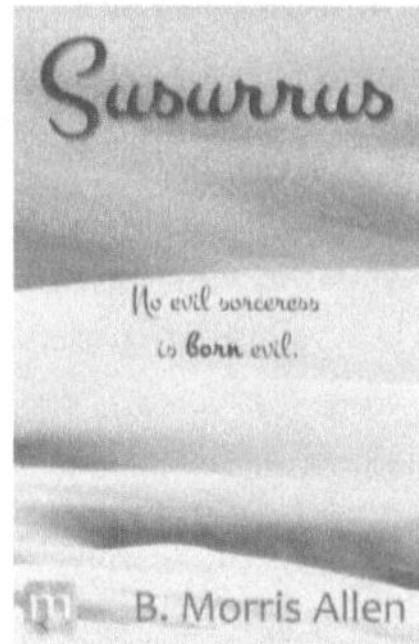

Susurrus

A darkly romantic story of magic, love, and suffering.

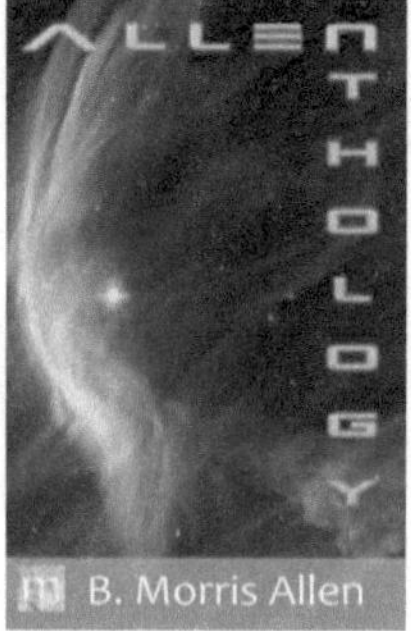

Allenthology: Volume I

Including three full collections of SFF stories.

Verdage

Science fiction and fantasy books for writers — full of great stories, often with an additional focus on the craft of speculative fiction writing.

Reading 5X5 x3

Changes

How do stories move from 'maybe' to published?

Here are 15 case studies of stories published in *Metaphorosis* magazine.

Reading 5X5 x2

Duets

How do authors' voices change when they collaborate?

A round-robin of five talented science fiction and fantasy authors collaborating with each other and writing solo.

Including stories by Evan Marcroft, David Gallay, J. Tynan Burke, L'Erin Ogle, and Douglas Anstruther.

Score

an SFF symphony

An anthology with an emotional score from the heights of joy to the depths of despair — but always with a little hope shining through.

Reading 5X5

Five stories, five times

See how different writers take on the same material.

Reading 5X5

Writers' Edition

Two extra stories, the story seed, and authors' notes on writing.

Vestige

Novelettes, novellas, and novels by Metaphorosis authors.

The Nocturnals
Mariah Montoya

Night is Dangerous. Day is deadly.
Where day and night last thirty years, humans move constantly stay ahead of the night and cruel Nocturnals that call it home. But a boy is lost out there.

Science fiction and fantasy anthologies with innovative and unusual themes.

Museum Piece
an unusual collection

A gallery of the strange and outrageous

Step right up and enter a world of wonder and oddities! These museums are not your typical tourist traps. From the Museum of Lost Dreams to the Museum of Fine Regrets, each exhibit will take you on a journey you won't soon forget.

www.ingramcontent.com/pod-product-compliance
Lightning Source LLC
Chambersburg PA
CBHW020336310726
48979CB00015B/2398/J
* 9 7 8 1 6 4 0 7 6 2 9 4 7 *